# NEBULA AWARDS SHOWCASE 2015

## ALSO AVAILABLE:

*Nebula Awards Showcase 2014*
   edited by Kij Johnson

*Nebula Awards Showcase 2013*
   edited by Catherine Asaro

*Nebula Awards Showcase 2012*
   edited by James Patrick Kelly and John Kessel

# NEBULA AWARDS SHOWCASE 2015

## STORIES, EXCERPTS, AND POEMS BY

Rachel Swirsky, Matthew Kressel, Sophia Samatar, Kenneth Schneyer,
Sylvia Spruck Wrigley, Aliette de Bodard, Christopher Barzak,
Alaya Dawn Johnson, Henry Lien, Sarah Pinsker, Ken Liu, Vylar Kaftan,
Ann Leckie, Robin Wayne Bailey, Nalo Hopkinson, Samuel R. Delany,
Terry A. Garey, Deborah P Kolodji, and Andrew Robert Sutton

## THE YEAR'S BEST SCIENCE FICTION AND FANTASY
Selected by the Science Fiction and Fantasy Writers of America

## EDITED BY
# GREG BEAR

an Imprint of Prometheus Books
Amherst, NY

Published 2015 by Pyr®, an imprint of Prometheus Books

Cover design by Jacqueline Nasso Cooke
Cover illustration © John Harris

Inquiries should be addressed to

Pyr
59 John Glenn Drive
Amherst, New York 14228
VOICE: 716–691–0133
FAX: 716–691–0137
WWW.PYRSF.COM

19 18 17 16 15    5 4 3 2 1

Library of Congress Cataloging-in-Publication Data Pending

Printed in the United States of America

*To my favorite professor,*
*and one of my very favorite human beings,*
*Elizabeth Chater*

# PERMISSIONS

# CONTENTS

# CONTENTS

## Nebula Award Winner: Best Novelette

## Nebula Award Nominees: Best Novelette

## Nebula Award Winner: Best Novella

## Nebula Award Winner: Best Novel

# CONTENTS

## 2013 Rhysling Award Winner: Best Long Poem

INTRODUCTION

# THE LONG, HOT SUMMER OF SCIENCE FICTION

## GREG BEAR

I was clueless. Enthusiastic, idealistic, and clueless. It was April of 1978, and I had been publishing some decent stories that had attracted gratifying attention, but no novels. Everything was potential. I was still doing illustrations of one sort or another, anything to make a little money . . .

I had established a track record with the *Los Angeles Times Calendar* section, publishing think pieces about the current run of blockbuster science-fiction films—*Star Wars* among them. I suggested to the *LA Times Book Review*—at that time a substantial pull-out section in the paper—that perhaps I should act as a stringer and cover the 1978 Nebula Awards ceremony being held in downtown San Francisco. The editor agreed, and I arrived at the hotels around Union Square full of energy and ideas, hoping to help spread the word about the ever-ascending marvel that was science fiction and fantasy.

I should have known that this was all too good to be true. At that time, there was an undercurrent of contempt that I did not feel at *Calendar*. A subeditor at the *Book Review* strongly advised me that if I didn't get pictures of people in Spock ears and wild costumes, my piece might not run—clearly implying that the subject was faintly risible. I tried to explain that this wasn't a costume event; professional writers were gathering to celebrate the achievements of their peers. This was serious (mostly); this was about literature.

"Ears, costumes," the subeditor insisted.

Of course, there were no Spock ears, and my relationship with the *Book Review* went south from there. I wrote up my piece, with subtle and wise criticisms of some of the more conservative publishing trends of the day, and the text was awkwardly trimmed (without my approval) in such a way that I ended up pissing off Judy-Lynn del Rey, probably the most powerful editor in the field. Maybe I would have irritated her anyway; we'll never know. (I later tried to make it up to her with an apologetic letter and another *Calendar* piece lauding the supremacy of Ballantine/Del Rey's marketing skills.)

I fled from the *Book Review* but continued my fruitful work with *Calendar* editor Irv Letofsky, a lovely and intelligent man. Getting into the movie studios to see previews of new features was fabulous. Irv published my film pieces through the 1980s, including examinations of *Close Encounters of the Third Kind*, *Alien*, *Superman*, and *Raiders of the Lost Ark*—as well as an *Omen/Exorcist 3* mashup. He rejected my piece on *Dune*. It was an interesting film and a good article, but Irv didn't think the movie would stay in theaters long. It didn't, but it's still a favorite—despite its flaws.

When not going to previews or running around Long Beach visiting bookstores and record shops, I was busy writing novels, which began to be published. In 1979, James Turner of Arkham House requested a short-story collection. Things were looking up!

The 1984 Nebula Awards ceremony was held at the *Queen Mary* Hotel in Long Beach, California. The event was in a wide, bright dining room—I don't remember where on the ship, but it was well decked out with white tablecloths. The food was okay, I recall.

The highlight for me was when toastmaster Gregory Benford arranged the list of presenters. My wife, Astrid, and her parents, Poul and Karen Anderson, were in the audience, along with my agent, Richard Curtis, and my own parents, Dale and Wilma Bear. Elizabeth "Bette" Chater—one of my favorite people and very favorite professors from my alma mater, San Diego State University—was also able to attend and was accompanied by her daughter Patty. What a setup! None better since.

As the awards moved along that evening, Poul Anderson and Gregory Benford switched off to hand me two Nebulas: one for *Hardfought* and one for *Blood Music*. Fellow Killer B David Brin picked up Best Novel for *Startide Rising*.

Richard Curtis approached Lou Aronica and ebulliently proclaimed, with reference to advances, "To the moon, Lou! To the *moon!*"

And so it all began.

To this day, I hate losing awards, and I feel guilty winning them. What is this "best" nonsense? I know far too much about modern literary judgments to put much stock in contemporary assessments.

But it is fun to win! And so congratulations to our winners and a sideways wink to the nominees. I've been there. Some of my best novels were never even nominated. What's that about? Award ceremonies are designed to make writers suffer, and then, on occasion, to feel overwhelming pride. So be it.

My other favorite Nebula moment was when I was elected SFWA president in 1988. Back then, it was the president's sole discretion as to who would be awarded the Grand Master Award. I chose Ray Bradbury. Trying to be a little coy, I called him at his office in Los Angeles and suggested that he needed to be in New York City on a certain date, in appropriate attire—an ice cream suit would do fine. He demurred at first, but I was still too coy to tell him straight out, so I said, "Ray, you will *really, really* want to be in New York on this night, at this location! And invite your friends and editors. This is *big*."

He finally got the point, arrived in New York, and was duly celebrated. The night before the Nebula event, a group of us, including Donn Albright, a collector, archivist, and dear friend of Ray's, took a limo down to the South Street Seaport. While we were waiting for our table, the Irish singer holding forth from the stage spotted Ray and dedicated a song to him. The dinner itself was jovial and lasted a couple of hours, with copious servings of wine. I'm not sure what Ray ate, but it wasn't fish—he was deathly allergic to seafood!

The next night at the banquet, Ray's first agent and early promoter, Julius "Julie" Schwartz, a famous "Silver Age" editor at DC Comics, handed Ray a magnificent hunk of Lucite with nebula and mineral specimens inside. In turn, Ray delivered a stirring speech, and a fine time was had by all. Shortly thereafter, Bantam Books released special Grand Master editions of Ray's paperbacks.

That was the most fun I had being president.

So here's my love and fond hopes to all who compete—and to all those fine authors who create amazing works year after year and keep running up the odds!

My wife, Astrid, is rightfully coeditor of this anthology, due in part to my medical emergency. She's done a marvelous job communicating with the authors, preparing the manuscript, and generally running the show. I'm the figurehead here. Love and thanks to this marvelous woman, my partner of many decades!

# ABOUT THE SCIENCE FICTION AND FANTASY WRITERS OF AMERICA

The Science Fiction and Fantasy Writers of America, Inc. (formerly known as the Science Fiction Writers of America; the original acronym "SFWA" was retained), includes among its members many active writers of science fiction and fantasy. According to the bylaws of the organization, its purpose "shall be to promote the furtherance of the writing of science fiction, fantasy, and related genres as a profession." SFWA informs writers on professional matters, protects their interests, and helps them in dealings with agents, editors, anthologists, and producers of nonprint media. It also strives to encourage public interest in and appreciation of science fiction and fantasy.

Anyone may become an active member of SFWA after the acceptance of and payment for one professionally published novel, one professionally produced dramatic script, or three professionally published pieces of short fiction. Only science fiction, fantasy, horror, or other prose fiction of a related genre, in English, shall be considered as qualifying for active membership. Beginning writers who do not yet qualify for active membership but have published qualifying professional work may join as associate members; other classes of membership include affiliate members (editors, agents, reviewers, and anthologists), estate members (representatives of the estates of active members who have died), and institutional members (high schools, colleges, universities, libraries, broadcasters, film producers, futurist groups, and individuals associated with such an institution).

Readers are invited to visit the SFWA website at www.sfwa.org.

# ABOUT THE NEBULA AWARDS

Shortly after the founding of SFWA in 1965, its first secretary-treasurer, Lloyd Biggle Jr., proposed that the organization periodically select and publish the year's best stories. This notion evolved into an elaborate balloting process, an annual awards banquet, and a series of Nebula anthologies.

Throughout every calendar year, members of SFWA read and recommend novels and stories for the Nebula Awards. The editor of the *Nebula Awards Report* (NAR) collects the recommendations and publishes them in the *SFWA Forum* and on the SFWA members' private web page. At the end of the year, the NAR editor tallies the endorsements, draws up a preliminary ballot containing ten or more recommendations, and sends it to all active SFWA members. Under the current rules, each work enjoys a one-year eligibility period from its date of publication in the United States. If a work fails to receive ten recommendations during the one-year interval, it is dropped from further Nebula Award consideration.

The *NAR* editor processes the results of the preliminary ballot and then compiles a final ballot listing the five most popular novels, novellas, novelettes, and short stories. For purposes of the award, a novel is determined to be 40,000 words or more; a novella is 17,500 to 39,999 words; a novelette is 7,500 to 17,499 words; and a short story is 7,499 words or fewer. Additionally, each year SFWA impanels a member jury, which is empowered to supplement the five nominees with a sixth choice in cases where it feels a worthy title was neglected by the membership at large. Thus, the appearance of more than five finalists in a category reflects two distinct processes: jury discretion and ties.

A complete set of Nebula rules can be found at www.sfwa.org/awards/rules.htm.

## RAY BRADBURY AWARD FOR OUTSTANDING DRAMATIC PRESENTATION

The Ray Bradbury Award for Outstanding Dramatic Presentation is not a Nebula Award, but it follows Nebula nomination, voting, and award rules and guidelines, and it is given each year at the annual awards banquet. Founded in 2009, it replaces the earlier Nebula Award for Best Script. It was named in honor of science fiction and fantasy author Ray Bradbury, whose work appeared frequently in movies and on television.

## ANDRE NORTON AWARD FOR YOUNG ADULT SCIENCE FICTION AND FANTASY

The Andre Norton Award for Young Adult Science Fiction and Fantasy is an annual award presented by SFWA to the author of the best young-adult or middle-grade science fiction or fantasy book published in the United States in the preceding year.

The Andre Norton Award is not a Nebula Award, but it follows Nebula nomination, voting, and award rules and guidelines. It was founded in 2005 to honor popular science fiction and fantasy author Andre Norton.

# 2013 NEBULA AWARDS
# FINAL BALLOT

## NOVEL

Winner: *Ancillary Justice* by Ann Leckie (Orbit US; Orbit UK)
Nominees:

*We Are All Completely Beside Ourselves* by Karen Joy Fowler (Marian Wood)
*The Ocean at the End of the Lane* by Neil Gaiman (William Morrow; Headline)
*Fire with Fire* by Charles E. Gannon (Baen)
*Hild* by Nicola Griffith (Farrar, Straus and Giroux)
*The Red: First Light* by Linda Nagata (Mythic Island)
*A Stranger in Olondria* by Sofia Samatar (Small Beer)
*The Golem and the Jinni* by Helene Wecker (Harper)

## NOVELLA

Winner: "The Weight of the Sunrise" by Vylar Kaftan (*Asimov's Science Fiction*, February 2013)
Nominees:

"Wakulla Springs" by Andy Duncan and Ellen Klages (*Tor.com*, October 2, 2013)
"Annabel Lee" by Nancy Kress (*New Under the Sun*, Arc Manor/Phoenix Pick)
"Burning Girls" by Veronica Schanoes (*Tor.com*, June 19, 2013)
"Trial of the Century" by Lawrence M. Schoen (lawrencemschoen.com, August 2013; *World Jumping*, Hadley Rille Books)
*Six-Gun Snow White* by Catherynne M. Valente (Subterranean)

## NOVELETTE

Winner: "The Waiting Stars" by Aliette de Bodard (*The Other Half of the Sky*, Candlemark & Gleam)
Nominees:
   "Paranormal Romance" by Christopher Barzak (*Lightspeed*, June 2013)
   "They Shall Salt the Earth with Seeds of Glass" by Alaya Dawn Johnson (*Asimov's Science Fiction*, January 2013)
   "Pearl Rehabilitative Colony for Ungrateful Daughters" by Henry Lien (*Asimov's Science Fiction*, December 2013)
   "The Litigation Master and the Monkey King" by Ken Liu (*Lightspeed*, August 2013)
   "In Joy, Knowing the Abyss Behind" by Sarah Pinsker (*Strange Horizons*, July 1, 2013, and July 8, 2013)

## SHORT STORY

Winner: "If You Were a Dinosaur, My Love" by Rachel Swirsky (*Apex Magazine*, March 2013)
Nominees:
   "The Sounds of Old Earth" by Matthew Kressel (*Lightspeed*, January 2013)
   "Selkie Stories Are for Losers" by Sofia Samatar (*Strange Horizons*, January 7, 2013)
   "Selected Program Notes from the Retrospective Exhibition of Theresa Rosenberg Latimer" by Kenneth Schneyer (*Clockwork Phoenix 4*, Mythic Delirium Books)
   "Alive, Alive Oh" by Sylvia Spruck Wrigley (*Lightspeed*, June 2013)

# RAY BRADBURY AWARD FOR OUTSTANDING DRAMIC PRESENTATION

Winner: *Gravity*, Alfonso Cuarón (director); Alfonso Cuarón and Jonás Cuarón (writers) (Warner Bros.)
Nominees:

*Doctor Who*: "The Day of the Doctor," Nick Hurran (director); Steven Moffat (writer) (BBC Wales)

*Europa Report*, Sebastián Cordero (director); Philip Gelatt (writer) (Start Motion Pictures)

*Her*, Spike Jonze (director); Spike Jonze (writer) (Warner Bros.)

*The Hunger Games: Catching Fire*, Francis Lawrence (director); Simon Beaufoy and Michael deBruyn (writers) (Lionsgate)

*Pacific Rim*, Guillermo del Toro (director); Travis Beacham and Guillermo del Toro (writers) (Warner Bros.)

# ANDRE NORTON AWARD FOR YOUNG ADULT SCIENCE FICTION AND FANTASY

Winner: *Sister Mine* by Nalo Hopkinson (Grand Central)
Nominees:

*The Coldest Girl in Coldtown* by Holly Black (Little, Brown; Indigo)

*When We Wake* by Karen Healey (Allen & Unwin; Little, Brown)

*The Summer Prince* by Alaya Dawn Johnson (Levine)

*Hero* by Alethea Kontis (Harcourt)

*September Girls* by Bennett Madison (Harper Teen)

*A Corner of White* by Jaclyn Moriarty (Levine)

## NEBULA AWARD WINNER
### BEST SHORT STORY

# "IF YOU WERE A DINOSAUR, MY LOVE"

## RACHEL SWIRSKY

*Rachel Swirsky has previously won a 2010 Nebula Award and has also been nominated for the Hugo Award and the World Fantasy Award. "If You Were a Dinosaur, My Love" was published in* Apex Magazine.

If you were a dinosaur, my love, then you would be a T-Rex. You'd be a small one, only five foot ten inches, the same height as human-you. You'd be fragile-boned and you'd walk with as delicate and polite a gait as you could manage on massive talons. Your eyes would gaze gently from beneath your bony brow ridge.

If you were a T-Rex, then I would become a zookeeper so that I could spend all my time with you. I'd bring you raw chickens and live goats. I'd watch the gore shining on your teeth. I'd make my bed on the floor of your cage, in the moist dirt, cushioned by leaves. When you couldn't sleep, I'd sing you lullabies.

If I sang you lullabies, I'd soon notice how quickly you picked up music. You'd harmonize with me, your rough, vibrating voice a strange counterpoint to mine. When you thought I was asleep, you'd cry unrequited love songs into the night.

If you sang unrequited love songs, I'd take you on tour. We'd go to Broadway. You'd stand onstage, talons digging into the floorboards. Audiences would weep at the melancholy beauty of your singing.

If audiences wept at the melancholy beauty of your singing, they'd rally to fund new research into reviving extinct species. Money would flood into scientific institutions. Biologists would reverse engineer chickens until they could discover how to give them jaws with teeth. Paleontologists would mine ancient fossils for traces of collagen. Geneticists would figure out how to build a dinosaur from nothing by discovering exactly what DNA sequences code everything about a creature, from the size of its pupils to what enables a brain to contemplate a sunset. They'd work until they'd built you a mate.

If they built you a mate, I'd stand as the best woman at your wedding. I'd watch awkwardly in green chiffon that made me look sallow as I listened to your vows. I'd be jealous, of course, and also sad, because I want to marry you. Still, I'd know that it was for the best that you marry another creature like yourself, one that shares your body and bone and genetic template. I'd stare at the two of you standing together by the altar and I'd love you even more than I do now. My soul would feel light because I'd know that you and I had made something new in the world and at the same time revived something very old. I would be borrowed, too, because I'd be borrowing your happiness. All I'd need would be something blue.

If all I needed was something blue, I'd run across the church, heels clicking on the marble, until I reached a vase by the front pew. I'd pull out a hydrangea the shade of the sky and press it against my heart and my heart would beat like a flower. I'd bloom. My happiness would become petals. Green chiffon would turn into leaves. My legs would be pale stems, my hair delicate pistils. From my throat, bees would drink exotic nectars. I would astonish everyone assembled, the biologists and the paleontologists and the geneticists, the reporters and the rubberneckers and the music aficionados, all those people who—deceived by the helix-and-fossil trappings of cloned dinosaurs—believed that they lived in a science fictional world when really they lived in a world of magic where anything was possible.

If we lived in a world of magic where anything was possible, then you would be a dinosaur, my love. You'd be a creature of courage and strength but also gentleness. Your claws and fangs would intimidate your foes effortlessly. Whereas you—fragile, lovely, human you—must rely on wits and charm.

A T-Rex, even a small one, would never have to stand against five blustering men soaked in gin and malice. A T-Rex would bare its fangs and they would cower. They'd hide beneath the tables instead of knocking them over. They'd grasp each other for comfort instead of seizing the pool cues with which they beat you, calling you a fag, a towel-head, a shemale, a sissy, a spic, every epithet they could think of, regardless of whether it had anything to do with you or not, shouting and shouting as you slid to the floor in the slick of your own blood.

If you were a dinosaur, my love, I'd teach you the scents of those men. I'd lead you to them quietly, oh so quietly. Still, they would see you. They'd run. Your nostrils would flare as you inhaled the night and then, with the suddenness of a predator, you'd strike. I'd watch as you decanted their lives—the flood of red; the spill of glistening, coiled things—and I'd laugh, laugh, laugh.

If I laughed, laughed, laughed, I'd eventually feel guilty. I'd promise never to do something like that again. I'd avert my eyes from the newspapers when they showed photographs of the men's tearful widows and fatherless children, just as they must avert their eyes from the newspapers that show my face. How reporters adore my face, the face of the paleontologist's fiancée with her half-planned wedding, bouquets of hydrangeas already ordered, green chiffon bridesmaid dresses already picked out. The paleontologist's fiancée who waits by the bedside of a man who will probably never wake.

If you were a dinosaur, my love, then nothing could break you, and if nothing could break you, then nothing could break me. I would bloom into the most beautiful flower. I would stretch joyfully toward the sun. I'd trust in your teeth and talons to keep you/me/us safe now and forever from the scratch of chalk on pool cues, and the scuff of the nurses' shoes in the hospital corridor, and the stuttering of my broken heart.

## NEBULA AWARD NOMINEE
### BEST SHORT STORY

# "THE SOUNDS OF OLD EARTH"

## MATTHEW KRESSEL

*This is Matthew Kressel's first nomination for a Nebula Award. "The Sounds of Old Earth" was first published in* Lightspeed.

Earth has grown quiet since everyone's shipped off to the new one. I walk New Paltz's empty streets with an ox-mask tight about my face. An acidic rain mists my body, and a thick fog obscures the vac-sealed storefronts. Last week they hauled the Pyramids of Giza to New Earth. The week before, Stonehenge. The week before that, Versailles and a good chunk of the Great Wall. But the minor landmarks are too expensive to move, the NEU says, and so New Paltz's Huguenot Street, seven centuries old, will remain here, to be sliced to pieces in a few months when the planetary lasers begin to cut the Earth apart.

I pump nano into my bloodstream to alleviate my creeping osteoarthritis and nod to a few fellow holdouts. We take our strolls through these dusty streets at ten every morning, our little act of rebellion against the mandatory evacuation orders. I wave hello to Marta, ninety-six, in her stylishly pink ox-mask. I shake hands with Dr. Wu, who performed the op to insert my cranial when I was a boy. I smile at Cordelia, one hundred and thirty three, as she trots by on her quad servo-legs. All of us have lived in New Paltz our entire lives and all of us plan to die here.

Someone laughs behind me, a sound I haven't heard in a long time. A group of teenage boys and girls ride ancient turbocycles over the cracked pavement toward me. They skid to a halt and their eager, flushed faces take me in. None wear ox-masks, which is against the law. I like them already.

"Hey shinhun!" a boy says. "Do you know where the frogs are?"

Before I can answer, an attractive girl with a techplant on her cheek blows a dreadlock of green hair from her eyes and says, "We heard some wankuzidi has an old house where he keeps a gose-load of frogs." A boy pops a wheelie and another takes a hit of braino from an orange inhaler. A third puffs a cigalectric and exhales fluorescent smoke.

"Behind my house I have a pond with a few frogs still alive," I say.

"Xin!" she exclaims. "How 'bout you ride with us? I'm Lin."

These kids are as high as orbitals, but it's not as if I have much left to lose. "Abner," I say.

And just like that I'm hanging on to her waist as we speed toward my house over broken roads no ground vehicle has used in decades. The wind in my face feels exhilarating.

"We're from Albany," Lin says, "We tried taking the old Interstate down, but after Juan got tossed when he hit a cheeda crack, we decided to go local. Took us yungyeh!"

The stascreen around my property makes my fifty acres of forest flicker like water in sunlight. It's a matter of pride that I keep it functioning at high efficiency; after all, I designed the damn technology. When we pass through the screen's charged threshold, I take off my ox-mask, and breathe deep. The kids smile when they smell the fertile earth, the decaying leaves.

"It don't smell like this in Albany," Lin says.

We park the cycles on the overgrown grass and I lead them into the woods behind my house. The kids stare up at the huge maples and birches and fall quiet.

"The frogs croak loudest at sunset and before it rains," I say. "That's when the males are trying to attract a mate." The kids giggle as they leap over branches. "If you really want to hear them, you should stay until it gets dark."

"You got anything to eat?" a boy says. "We haven't eaten since yesterday."

I search inside the house and return with some readimades, pretty much all you can buy on Earth these days, while the kids shudder and wobble as they inhale braino. The green-haired Lin wanders off to vomit in the trees.

"Is she going to be all right?" I ask a boy.

"Oh, Lin always pukes after her first hit. Want some?" He offers a red inhaler, but I decline.

We sit beside the pond, all of us squeezed on a log. Lin sits next to me, and I pop up the straw of the readimade for her. "You okay?" I say.

"Yeah, I always get all shunbeen when I deepen."

"It's probably none of my business," I say. "But shouldn't you kids be in school or something?"

"School closed four months ago," she says. "Not enough teachers."

"So what do you do all day?"

She wipes saliva from her cheek and shrugs. "I don't know. *This*."

Another boy goes off to puke in the woods.

"What about you?" she says. "You live here all by yourself?"

I nod.

"And what do *you* do all day? Hang out with the frogs?"

"Most of my time I just try to keep the stascreen working."

"That your job or something?"

"Used to be. I was a stascreen engineer for fifty-one years. I designed the nanofilters that keep ecosystems like this free of envirotoxins. But the NRDC laid me off four years back."

"Why? This place is xin!"

I smile wanly. "Because toxfiltering's a dead business now. People are only interested in making new life, not preserving the old."

She seems to take me in for the first time. "And how old is this place, Abner? These trees look cheeda ancient."

"I know that when my ancestor built this house four hundred years ago, the frog pond was already here."

She sighs. "Fucking NEU making you leave this place?"

"They're making everyone leave."

She throws a rock into the pond, and a dozen frogs squeak away in fright.

"Please," I say, gently touching her arm. "You'll scare them off."

"How long?" she says, giving me a tender look, and I'm not sure if she means the frogs or my eviction.

"Soon."

The kids grow hungry again. I had been saving some hard-to-find vegisteaks for my grandkids, but they haven't visited in ages. As I grill them on the deck the smoke rises through the trees, and the dipping sun sends girders of light through the branches.

The kids inhale more braino, howl with laughter, and Lin pukes again. And when they tire, I glimpse something desperate in their bloodshot eyes, something I've seen in the expressions of Cordelia and Dr. Wu and Marta and the other holdouts. Regret doesn't spare you just because you're young.

"You cycled all the way from Albany for this?" I ask Lin.

"Nothing but dust and skyscrapers there," she says. "No real trees. We heard this was xin. Do you have kids, Abner?"

The question catches me off-guard. "Yeah, a son and daughter. And two grandkids. You sort of remind me of my granddaughter, Rachael."

She pauses to consider this. "They come here lots?"

"Not anymore."

"Why not? I'd be here every day."

"They've moved." I point to the sky.

She frowns, and her body sags like an old tree. "We're moving too."

"New Earth?"

She harrumphs. "Nah, that's only for rich kids. We're going to Wal-Mart Toyota."

"Haven't heard of it."

"You wouldn't. It's like cheeda ancient, one of the first orbitals. But you gotta go where they send you, or else, you know?"

"I know," I say, staring at the upside-down trees reflected in the water.

Night creeps over the forest and the frogs begin their mating calls in earnest. The croaking rises to a din, and the kids pause and listen. The glorious stars emerge, and I'm not sure if it's my imagination, but the frogs seem to plead to them, over and over again, "Save us, save us, *save us*!"

We listen for a while, until the frogs tire. "It's late," I say. "It's a long way back to Albany. Why don't you kids stay? There are plenty of beds."

So we head inside. I set them up with fresh linen I haven't used in years, and during the night I hear fucking and shuffling and laughing as I pour myself tumbler after tumbler of rye whiskey until I pass out. Late in the night, I hear someone whimpering outside my door, and I rise groggily from bed. Lin sits in the hallway, her eyes as red as cinders as she looks up at me.

"I'm sorry," she says, wiping away tears. "I didn't know that was your bedroom."

"What are you doing?"

"Nothing," she says as she climbs to her feet.

"You okay?"

"I was just thinking. You don't know us, Abner, but you welcomed us into your home."

I shrug. "This place was made for guests."

She stares at the walls. "Must have been beautiful, when it was full of people."

I nod. "It was."

She stands there, and again she reminds me of my granddaughter who I never see. I want to hug her and tell her the future will be xin, that everything will work out, eventually. But I'm too drunk to lie. "It's late, Lin. Go to bed."

A tear rolls down her cheek. She nods and turns away. I close the door, feeling as if I've missed something important. It takes me forever to fall back asleep.

The next morning, the kids are gone. The house looks as if a tornado has blown through. But one bedroom has been tidied, and there's a note on the nightstand.

"The frogs are beautiful. You are beautiful. Thank you for a perfect day. —Lin."

I hold the note in my hand and stare out the window into the empty yard. I already miss their laughter.

Several months before I received the evac order, I visited New Earth for the first time. My son Josef played the guide and took me to the Ishibuto-Mori preserve, a dense rainforest on the northern hemisphere. Giant sequoias planted a few years ago had already grown hundreds of feet tall, carrion flowers had been gengineered to smell like cotton candy, and the rains came precisely at two p.m. every day.

Clear plexi walls kept us safe on a paved path that led us, like Dorothy to Oz, to John Muir Mall. It was a palatial marketplace where they seemed to have anticipated every human need. Food, clothing, jewelry, a pub, an immersion cinema, a spa. All was here, square in the middle of the rainforest. A holo-host welcomed us to the mall's courtyard and carefully explained, as if he were speaking to children, how Old Earth had become uninhabitable, how humanity's first home was ruined forever because Those Before had no appreciation for the natural world. But the Ishibuto-Mori Corporation, along with dozens of other companies, were hard at work ensuring that New Earth avoided this fate.

As my son and I ate oversized burgers in the courtyard of Pfizer's McDonald's, I noticed that no one looked up when Earth rose above the forest canopy. Before the next scheduled rain we left for home.

Josef's family lived in a spacious and many-windowed apartment on the ninety-seventh floor of a three-hundred-story tower. Luxury condos like these, Josef said, were popping up all over New Earth. My heart warmed when I saw my grandkids, Rachael and Pim. It had been several years since I'd seen them in person—they didn't visit Earth anymore. Today was Pim's twelfth birthday.

My grandson blew out his candles and we all shared papaya cake. On cues from my daughter-in-law, a shining mahogany andro poured coffee, brought out cookies, and cleared the dirty dishes. I felt like a princely CEO. On Earth natural grain was absurdly expensive and hard to come by, but on New Earth it seemed as plentiful as the scheduled rain.

"Pim's not the only one celebrating today," Josef said, in between sips of coffee. "Tell Grandpa the good news, Rach."

My granddaughter beamed and said, "I got a full scholarship to GE Sinopec!"

"GE Sinopec?" I said.

"An orbital university!"

"Oh, wa!" I said. "A full scholarship? That's xin!"

"As a reward," Josef said, "Esther and I have decided to buy Rach a small lobber. You'd be surprised at how affordable they've become."

"I can visit Mom and Dad on weekends," Rachael said, "and fly back to school on Sundays. And Grandpa, there's this low-fuel maneuver called a Hohmann Transfer that lets you fly over to Old Earth in a couple hours. Me and Leva are definitely headed there when they start dismantling it, to get a closer view."

"*Rachael*," Esther said with an admonishing tone. "Why don't you see if Grandpa wants more coffee?"

"He's got coffee. And isn't that what you bought the andro for?"

"Rachael, don't be rude!"

"But, Mom, his cup is full!"

"Rachael Kopperfeld!"

"Please!" I said. "Yes, yes, they're dismantling Old Earth. It's no gaise secret. Why does everyone avoid that subject around me?"

"Because every time we bring it up," Josef said, "you go on a rant about how they're tearing down your home."

I stared at my son. "It was once your home too, if you remember."

Josef frowned. "That was a long time ago, Dad." He waved his hand at his apartment. "*This* is my home now, and I'd like to have a nice birthday for Pim."

"Is the frog pond still there, Grandpa?" Pim asked.

"Yes! It's been a struggle to keep the pond free of toxins, but the frogs still croak away on summer nights. Do you remember when you used to put them in boxes to scare the hell out of Grandma Shosh?"

He giggled. "And Rach used make up silly names and marry them."

"They got so loud some nights," Rachael said, smiling, "that my ears would ring the next morning."

I shook my head and stared down at the plate of cookies. "Those poor creatures don't know that their ancient home will soon be destroyed."

"Not destroyed," Josef said. "Dismantled. There's a difference."

"Countless species will be killed. I don't know what you call that."

"Some death will occur," Rachael said. "But the Geoengineers are making heroic efforts to save every documented species."

"Heroic?" I said. "Rachael, the cradle of humanity is being left to rot."

"I love Earth too, Dad," Josef said. "But the air is poison. The soil is toxic. You spent your whole gaise life trying to clean it, and for what? So we could watch Mom die slowly from the Tox?" He paused and took a deep breath. "I want a better life for my kids, and your Earth can't give that."

I put down my cup. "Since when did it become *my* Earth? Once, it was *ours*."

Esther loudly sipped her coffee, a sign she was not amused by the conversation.

"Grandpa," Rachael said, "it's not just the toxins, it's the overpopulation. We used up all the matter in the asteroid and Kuiper belts to make New Earth. We need Old Earth's mantle to build more colonies. And besides, it's natural."

"*Natural?*" I said as my belly grew hot.

"Yes." Rachael sat up straight and looked at her mother, as if she had been preparing this for weeks. "In living creatures, new cells are born from old ones, then the old cells die. But life continues. Your body's cells have replicated themselves dozens of times. Old Earth isn't ending, Grandpa, it's rejuvenating. The old cell is giving birth to a new one. And when the old cell dies, its contents are broken up and recycled. That's the course of life. The body of Old Earth will be gone, but its essence lives on."

I stared at my family, all of them willing to throw away the priceless Earth as if it were an obsolete piece of technology, and disagreed.

Three days after Lin's visit, I set my car down in central Albany. In a foggy rain, I wander past empty skyscrapers, drifts of windblown debris, and vac-sealed buildings, kicking up clouds of gray dust. On Livingston Avenue I meet a holdout who introduces herself as Helen. A sickly looking kitten walks at her heel.

"Not many kids left," Helen says, her voice muffled by a scratched ox-mask, "Green hair, techplant on her cheek, neh? Yeah, that's Lin Bar-Martin. Yeoung's kid. Hangs out with a bunch of liumangs. If I recall, her father Yeoung worked in nanotesting."

"A scientist?" I ask.

"Ha! No, they tested nano *on* him."

"Oh. Where do they live?"

"Nowhere."

"What do you mean? She's homeless?"

"As if. No, plenty of places to live here. She's gone."

"Gone where?"

"To Wal-Mart Toyota. An orbital."

"You mean, for good?"

"Where've you been, baichi? No one comes back to Earth."

"What about her friends?" I hate myself that I can't remember their names. "Are they still around?"

"Haven't seen a kid in days. The whole north side of the city shipped off to Wal-Mart Toyota. Heard the place is dreadful. They abandoned it mid-construction because they found better ways to build colonies using nano."

"But the kids were at my house three days ago!"

"And they left two days ago. A fleet of ships took 'em away like it was a parade."

And then I know why the kids cycled all the way down to New Paltz over dangerous roads, and I know the look in Lin's eyes when she was crying outside my door that night, the feeling that I'd missed something. That was Lin's last day on Earth. The kids wanted to see a piece of ancient Earth before they left it forever.

"Thank you," I say to Helen.

I pet the sick kitten, then I leave her empty city. By the time I arrive home, it's getting dark. There's a strange car in the driveway, and a young woman sits on my porch. For a moment, I think it's Lin. But then I recognize my granddaughter's dark hair.

"Hi, Grandpa."

"Rach, what are you doing here?"

"I came to say hi."

I hug her hello. "You came all the way here just to say 'hi'? Why didn't you call? I could have prepared dinner."

"It was kind of a last-minute thing."

"It's great to see you! You look good, Rach." The wicker chair creaks as I sit beside her. "How's school?"

"It's tough, but otherwise xin." We stare at the overgrown grass as a wind whispers through the trees. "The grounds look really healthy."

"I try."

"I remember when I used to sit on your lap and you'd tell me the silliest stories."

"I'd say come on over, but I think you're too big for that now."

She smiles, but it quickly fades. "Grandpa, the NEU can spot a flea from orbit. There's nowhere to hide."

"I don't plan to hide. I plan to stay right here."

"They'll force you out."

Beyond the trees, a troublesome spot on my stascreen wavers. "Maybe I won't give them the chance."

"Grandpa . . ." She puts a warm hand on mine. "You and I disagree on a lot of things. Promise me that when the time comes, you won't do anything stupid."

"Rachael . . ."

"Promise me."

When I look at her I see the child she once was, the girl who married frogs and danced in fields of sunflowers. "I'm sorry," I say. "But this isn't your Earth. You don't understand."

"Maybe I understand more than you." She leaps to her feet. "Neh, I have to go."

"Already? You just got here."

"I have an exam in the morning."

She hugs me, squeezes a little too hard. "Goodbye, Grandpa. I love you."

And in seconds her lobber is flying up into the sky. I watch it recede until it's just another star. Out back the frogs croak louder than I've ever heard them.

I sit on the wet grass under the stars, hugging a bottle of rye. Yesterday, another hurricane blew through the area, a product of Earth's new gravitational partner. A decade ago they would have burnt the storms away with their orbital lasers, but Earth just isn't worth it anymore. They didn't even bother to give the hurricane a name.

The storm washed away the dust, and the moon and New Earth lay hidden below the horizon. And in the dark, how beautiful is the sky! The stars are so bright they cast shadows, their points are so clear I feel I could pluck them like apples from the sky. Jupiter rises slowly in the east, bright as an angel. And the Milky Way swaths gloriously across the heavens. If I could leap into the sky, I'd fall into it forever.

"Ashey," I say to my cranial, "Play 'Grandkids Visit, Summer '98.'"

A holo projects over my eyes. Little Rach sits on my knee, giggling. Birds chirp in the summer sun. The smell of roses. A soft breeze on my cheeks, all under the warm comfort of well-functioning stascreen. "Can we sit under the sunflowers again?" a five-year-old Rach asks a much younger me.

Sunlight trickles through fans of yellow petals as I follow her into my field of sunflowers. She sits on the ground beneath their giant blooms and says, "I want to live in your house, with you, Grandpa. I never want to go home."

I watch her draw a house in the dirt with a stick. "Like this one," she says. "Ashey, play 'Shoshanna's 60th Birthday.'"

Years earlier, Shosh opens the ancient oak door of our house. Everyone yells, "Surprise!" As my wife throws her hands to her mouth and shrieks, she drops a glass bowl. It shatters, and everyone chuckles nervously. A tear of happiness rolls down her sallow cheek. Even this far back she's already showing signs of the Tox.

I excelled at removing the worst pollutants from environments, but with all my knowledge I still couldn't protect my wife's body from them.

"You devil," she whispers to me, embarrassed. "I thought you had forgotten."

"Never," I say.

"Damn. That bowl was expensive."

"I'll make it up to you."

"Oh, yeah?"

I lean in to kiss her, and I feel the press of her soft lips even after the recording ends.

"Ashey, play 'Josef's first steps.'"

Our same house, decades earlier. Shosh, younger, healthier, Tox unmanifest. Little Josef bravely climbs to his feet, takes two teetering strides, then falls. Shosh leaps to publish the holo on the net for all to admire. She struts pridefully over to me and smiles. "Kid learns fast. He's already better at walking than you are."

My ancient self giggles.

"Ashey, pause playback."

Google-Wang Colony spins into view far above. I'd recognize the corporate colors from a billion miles away. I take another quaff of rye, then lay back on the wet grass. Cold moisture soaks into my back. Bank of Zhong Guo Colony winks distantly across the sky, and even though it's hundreds of miles up I think I can hear it tearing roughly across the Cosmos. I sit here, watching the stars, until New Earth rises, spoiling the glorious night.

I approach my house, plasteel container in one hand, rye in the other. I pour the liquid in the plasteel container into the foyer, and the hydrocarbon smell burns my nostrils.

With a small lighter I set flame to a soaked rag. I toss it into the house. For a moment, the rag burns like a candle, guttering in a bedroom. Shadows dance across my ancient walls like memories. A pang of dread hits me. Is this really what I want?

But it's too late. The foyer erupts in flame, and I leap back. In seconds the fire roars louder than the frogs ever have. The heat singes my face as the house burns.

And just like that, I destroy the home that my fifteenth generation great-grandmother built four hundred and seventeen years ago.

With the stascreen shut down, the fire corkscrews freely into the sky. A column of smoke arcs away for miles, lit by the light of New Earth. Once, this would have aroused a hundred suppressor-bots into action. Now, what is another fire when all will soon be ash?

My ancient house burns to the ground. It takes a while. So I sit beside the pond. The frogs are quiet, perhaps watching the flames with me. I think of Rachael, and the promise I made to her. And I think of Lin.

At dawn, when the police arrive, the only thing left of the house is a pile of cinders. The air is foul with soot as armed men read me the evac order. They bind me in plasticuffs and escort me off my property. They seat me inside a small craft, and the young man across from me, in bulky police regalia, offers me anti-nausea nano for the trip to space. I was hoping to glimpse my property one last time as we lift off, but there are no windows. This is a prison ship.

I paid a hefty fine and was ordered to take "reintegration" classes, then I was set free. The process seemed rote, and I suspect I'm one of thousands. Josef rented me an apartment in his condo for an absurd price, and he and Esther have been inviting me over nightly for dinner as if nothing at all has happened. Rachael calls from time to time to see how I'm fitting in.

When I'm not skipping the reintegration classes or finding excuses not to join Josef and Esther for dinner, I spend my time watching as the Earth gets sliced open like a piece of fruit, as geometric chunks are carved out of its pulpy flesh ten thousand kilometers at a time.

This evening my telescope and datafeeds focus on the Earth's northern hemisphere.

"It's time," Ashey warns. By piggybacking illegally onto satellite proxies,

I have real-time access to the Geoengineers' datanet. On my holoscreen a green light flashes twice, the signal from the Foreman. In Pan Mandarin, translated on my screen, the Foreman says, "EDHL-22, begin the first longitudinal cut at your discretion."

A full minute's pause. Then a blinding flash. A molten orange circle of light moves south along the seventieth longitude line for minutes, and even from this distance it's so bright it leaves spots in my vision. The cutting pauses as the laser's gyroscopes realign. Then it slices across the fortieth latitude line, just under an emptied New York City.

The laser traces out a great rectangle over the course of an hour. Then the grav-beams tug the huge section out. Like ice cream, the molten core drips toward Earth's center. By technology I don't pretend to understand, the layered walls of Earth don't collapse into the new space, but stay fixed. And the white-hot core, from what I've read, is being artificially cooled, eleven-point-five degrees per day.

I wonder if any of the holdouts, like Cordelia or Marta or Dr. Wu or Helen and her kitten, escaped the mandatory evacs. As they slowly floated into the sky, would they think they were flying up to meet God?

Over several hours, lasers break the chunk into hundreds of pieces.

"That one," Ashey says, highlighting a point in my vision.

The land that was my home is shunted up to Trump-Dominguez Colony. It will be used, the datanet says, as a counter mass so the colony can maintain its highly sought-after earth-forward views. Four and a half billion years, of algae and antelope, of brontosauri and bison, of woolly mammoths and glaciers, of trees and earthworms and amphibious frogs just to become a paperweight so the rich can wake up to their plastic earth.

That night, I dream of frogs screaming.

Years pass. Old Earth is gone, every last piece used up.

Today, I sit next to Josef, Esther, and Pim in an amphitheater of thousands. Rachael is graduating from GE Sinopec with a B.S. in Applied Biology. We sit through an endless procession of names. Pim and I converse a bit. His voice has deepened, and he looks more like a man these days. He's polite, and humors me, but I sense universes between us. I know this world isn't mine anymore.

After the ceremony, we eat dinner at an expensive restaurant, and the low-g does horrors to my stomach. Rachael, in her graduation gown, has been staring at me the entire meal. "Grandpa," she says, "will you come with me for a ride after dinner? I'd like to show you something."

Her mother smiles.

"I've had too much to eat. I'm a little tired. Maybe next time?"

Josef glares at me. "*Dad*," he says like he's scolding a child, because that's what I've become to all of them.

I sigh. "What did you want to show me?"

We head outside to Rachael's lobber, a frighteningly small vessel, and I climb into the passenger seat as eagerly as a man to the gallows. I was never good with zero-g. I try to hide my shakes as we leap off GE Sinopec and dive down to New Earth.

"For my graduation thesis we had to recreate an Old Earth ecosystem," she says, "as part of the bioprojects to save as much life as we can." I examine her face in the reflected light of the planet. She is beautiful, my granddaughter. From under her rolled up sleeve I see the glint of a techplant, expressly forbidden by her father. I smile.

"So I chose your backyard," she says.

"Excuse me?"

"Specifically, the lake behind your house, with all the frogs."

The lobber dips over a deciduous forest, and we descend tens of miles. My stomach feels like I left it back at the university.

"I didn't tell you," she says, "because I knew how you were always going on about New Earth." She holds her breath, and when I say nothing, she says, "And also because I really wasn't sure if it was going to work."

"What was going to work?" I say. We swoop over fields of swaying grass, muddy swamps and dense forests.

"Let me show you."

We set down in a field beside a thick wood. There are deep depressions in the mud, a sign of many previous landings. The sun hangs low on the horizon, and its orange light spills through the trees. She leads me into the woods, down a winding path, pausing to make sure I'm still with her, to warn me of a treacherous branch or root. The air here smells of mulch and earth and abundant life.

She smiles, and suddenly it's like she's a toddler again, leading me into a field of sunflowers.

And then I hear them.

Frogs. Thousands of them, croaking away with strange voices. We approach a small lake, not too different from the one that was once in my backyard.

"I came by your house when I knew you were away." She looks apologetically at me. "And I collected, um . . . *specimens*. They're not the same frogs, of course," she says. "They have genes better suited to this particular environment. But they're direct genetic descendants. Essentially, these are your frogs' great-grandchildren."

The sound of their croaking rekindles memories of a thousand summer nights.

I did it for you, Grandpa. I remember sitting beside your lake on summer evenings, listening to the frogs. Those times, when we were all together, are some of the happiest I remember. I wanted to bring a little of that here, to New Earth, for you. Now that I've got the population stabilized—and a passing grade." She laughs. "I could finally show you."

I am flabbergasted. "I don't know what to say."

"Say yes." She waves her hand and a long document arrives in my vision.

"What's this?"

"A deed," she says. "I used a few connections at school, and I got a little financial help from Mom and Dad. Well, *a lot* of help. But I bought this land. And now I've transferred the deed to you. These fifteen hectares are yours, Grandpa. It's my gift."

I'm stunned. "Rach, it's beautiful." I reach to hug her.

She whispers in my ear as she squeezes me, like she used to on summer nights on my porch so long ago, "I thought perhaps you could build a house here."

The frogs croak. Their sound is different, a little strange. And the trees are arrayed a bit too neatly. This isn't my Earth. It never will be. But I think of green-haired Lin and her friends, and Pim, and Josef and Esther, and Rachael, all coming to visit.

"Yes," I say. "A big house, with plenty of room for guests."

# "SELKIE STORIES ARE FOR LOSERS"

## SOPHIA SAMATAR

*Sofia Samatar has won the British Fantasy Award, the Crawford Award, and the John W. Campbell Award, and has been nominated for the Hugo, the Nebula, the World Fantasy Award, the British Science Fiction Association Award, and the Rhysling Award. "Selkie Stories Are for Losers" appeared in* **Strange Horizons.**

I hate selkie stories. They're always about how you went up to the attic to look for a book, and you found a disgusting old coat and brought it downstairs between finger and thumb and said "What's this?," and you never saw your mom again.

I work at a restaurant called Le Pacha. I got the job after my mom left, to help with the bills. On my first night at work I got yelled at twice by the head server, burnt my fingers on a hot dish, spilled lentil-parsley soup all over my apron, and left my keys in the kitchen.

I didn't realize at first I'd forgotten my keys. I stood in the parking lot, breathing slowly and letting the oil-smell lift away from my hair, and when all the other cars had started up and driven away I put my hand in my jacket pocket. Then I knew.

I ran back to the restaurant and banged on the door. Of course no one came. I smelled cigarette smoke an instant before I heard the voice.

"Hey."

I turned, and Mona was standing there, smoke rising white from between her fingers. "I left my keys inside," I said.

Mona is the only other server at Le Pacha who's a girl. She's related to everybody at the restaurant except me. The owner, who goes by "Uncle Tad," is really her uncle, her mom's brother. "Don't talk to him unless you have to," Mona advised me. "He's a creeper." That was after she'd sighed and dropped her cigarette and crushed it out with her shoe and stepped into my clasped hands so I could boost her up to the window, after she'd wriggled through into the kitchen and opened the door for me. She said, "Madame," in a dry voice, and bowed. At least, I think she said "Madame." She might have said "My lady." I don't remember that night too well, because we drank a lot of wine. Mona said that as long as we were breaking and entering we might as well steal something, and she lined up all the bottles of red wine that had already been opened. I shone the light from my phone on her while she took out the special rubber corks and poured some of each bottle into a plastic pitcher. She called it "The House Wine." I was surprised she was being so nice to me, since she'd hardly spoken to me while we were working. Later she told me she hates everybody the first time she meets them. I called home, but Dad didn't pick up; he was probably in the basement. I left him a message and turned off my phone.

"Do you know what this guy said to me tonight?" Mona asked. "He wanted beef couscous and he said, 'I'll have the beef conscious.'"

Mona's mom doesn't work at Le Pacha, but sometimes she comes in around three o'clock and sits in Mona's section and cries. Then Mona jams on her orange baseball cap and goes out through the back and smokes a cigarette, and I take over her section. Mona's mom won't order anything from me. She's got Mona's eyes, or Mona's got hers: huge, angry eyes with lashes that curl up at the ends. She shakes her head and says: "Nothing! Nothing!" Finally Uncle Tad comes over, and Mona's mom hugs and kisses him, sobbing in Arabic.

After work Mona says, "Got the keys?"

We get in my car and I drive us through town to the Bone Zone, a giant cemetery on a hill. I pull into the empty parking lot and Mona rolls a joint.

There's only one lamp, burning high and cold in the middle of the lot. Mona pushes her shoes off and puts her feet up on the dashboard and cries. She warned me about that the night we met: I said something stupid to her like "You're so funny" and she said, "Actually I cry a lot. That's something you should know." I was so happy she thought I should know things about her, I didn't care. I still don't care, but it's true that Mona cries a lot. She cries because she's scared her mom will take her away to Egypt, where the family used to live, and where Mona has never been. "What would I do there? I don't even speak Arabic." She wipes her mascara on her sleeve, and I tell her to look at the lamp outside and pretend that its glassy brightness is a bonfire, and that she and I are personally throwing every selkie story ever written onto it and watching them burn up.

"You and your selkie stories," she says. I tell her they're not my selkie stories, not ever, and I'll never tell one, which is true, I never will, and I don't tell her how I went up to the attic that day or that what I was looking for was a book I used to read when I was little, *Beauty and the Beast*, which is a really decent story about an animal who gets turned into a human and stays that way, the way it's supposed to be. I don't tell Mona that Beauty's black hair coiled to the edge of the page, or that the Beast had yellow horns and a smoking jacket, or that instead of finding the book I found the coat, and my mom put it on and went out the kitchen door and started up her car.

One selkie story tells about a man from Mýrdalur. He was on the cliffs one day and heard people singing and dancing inside a cave, and he noticed a bunch of skins piled on the rocks. He took one of the skins home and locked it in a chest, and when he went back a girl was sitting there alone, crying. She was naked, and he gave her some clothes and took her home. They got married and had kids. You know how this goes. One day the man changed his clothes and forgot to take the key to the chest out of his pocket, and when his wife washed the clothes, she found it.

"You're not going to Egypt," I tell Mona. "We're going to Colorado. Remember?"

That's our big dream, to go to Colorado. It's where Mona was born. She lived there until she was four. She still remembers the rocks and the pines and the cold, cold air. She says the clouds of Colorado are bright, like pieces of mirror. In Colorado, Mona's parents got divorced, and Mona's mom tried to kill herself for the first time. She tried it once here, too. She put her head in the oven, resting on a pillow. Mona was in seventh grade.

Selkies go back to the sea in a flash, like they've never been away. That's one of the ways they're different from human beings. Once, my dad tried to go back somewhere: he was in the army, stationed in Germany, and he went to Norway to look up the town my great-grandmother came from. He actually found the place, and even an old farm with the same name as us. In the town, he went into a restaurant and ordered lutefisk, a disgusting fish thing my grandmother makes. The cook came out of the kitchen and looked at him like he was nuts. She said they only eat lutefisk at Christmas.

There went Dad's plan of bringing back the original flavor of lutefisk. Now all he's got from Norway is my great-grandmother's Bible. There's also the diary she wrote on the farm up north, but we can't read it. There's only four English words in the whole book: *My God awful day*.

You might suspect my dad picked my mom up in Norway, where they have seals. He didn't, though. He met her at the pool.

As for Mom, she never talked about her relatives. I asked her once if she had any, and she said they were "no kind of people." At the time I thought she meant they were druggies or murderers, maybe in prison somewhere. Now I wish that was true.

One of the stories I don't tell Mona comes from *A Dictionary of British Folklore in the English Language*. In that story, it's the selkie's little girl who points out where the skin is hidden. She doesn't know what's going to happen, of course, she just knows her mother is looking for a skin, and she remembers her dad taking one out from under the bed and stroking it. The little girl's mother drags out the skin and says: "Fareweel, peerie buddo!" She doesn't think about how the little girl is going to miss her, or how if she's been breathing air all this time she can surely keep it up a little longer. She just throws on the skin and jumps into the sea.

After Mom left, I waited for my dad to get home from work. He didn't say anything when I told him about the coat. He stood in the light of the clock on the stove and rubbed his fingers together softly, almost like he was snapping but with no sound. Then he sat down at the kitchen table and lit a cigarette. I'd never seen him smoke in the house before. *Mom's gonna lose it*, I thought, and then I realized that no, my mom wasn't going to lose anything. We were the losers. Me and Dad.

He still waits up for me, so just before midnight I pull out of the parking lot. I'm hoping to get home early enough that he doesn't grumble, but late enough that he doesn't want to come up from the basement, where he takes apart old T.V.s, and talk to me about college. I've told him I'm not going to college. I'm going to Colorado, a landlocked state. Only twenty out of fifty states are completely landlocked, which means they don't touch the Great Lakes or the sea. Mona turns on the light and tries to put on eyeliner in the mirror, and I swerve to make her mess up. She turns out the light and hits me. All the windows are down to air out the car, and Mona's hair blows wild around her face. *Peerie buddo*, the book says, is "a term of endearment." "Peerie buddo," I say to Mona. She's got the hiccups. She can't stop laughing.

I've never kissed Mona. I've thought about it a lot, but I keep deciding it's not time. It's not that I think she'd freak out or anything. It's not even that I'm afraid she wouldn't kiss me back. It's worse: I'm afraid she'd kiss me back, but not mean it.

Probably one of the biggest losers to fall in love with a selkie was the man who carried her skin around in his knapsack. He was so scared she'd find it that he took the skin with him everywhere, when he went fishing, when he went drinking in the town. Then one day he had a wonderful catch of fish. There were so many that he couldn't drag them all home in his net. He emptied his knapsack and filled it with fish, and he put the skin over his shoulder, and on his way up the road to his house, he dropped it.

"Gray in front and gray in back, 'tis the very thing I lack." That's what the man's wife said, when she found the skin. The man ran to catch her, he even kissed her even though she was already a seal, but she squirmed off down the road and flopped into the water. The man stood knee-deep in the chilly waves, stinking of fish, and cried. In selkie stories, kissing never solves anything. No transformation happens because of a kiss. No one loves you just because you love them. What kind of fairy tale is that?

"She wouldn't wake up," Mona says. "I pulled her out of the oven onto the floor, and I turned off the gas and opened the windows. It's not that I was smart, I wasn't thinking at all. I called Uncle Tad and the police and I still wasn't thinking."

I don't believe she wasn't smart. She even tried to give her mom CPR, but her mom didn't wake up until later, in the hospital. They had to reach in and drag her out of death, she was so closed up in it. Death is skin-tight, Mona says. Gray in front and gray in back.

Dear Mona: When I look at you, my skin hurts.

I pull into her driveway to drop her off. The house is dark, the darkest house on her street, because Mona's mom doesn't like the porch light on. She says it shines in around the blinds and keeps her awake. Mona's mom has a beautiful bedroom upstairs, with lots of old photographs in gilt frames, but she sleeps on the living-room couch beside the aquarium. Looking at the fish helps her to sleep, although she also says this country has no real fish. That's what Mona calls one of her mom's "refrains."

Mona gets out, yanking the little piece of my heart that stays with her wherever she goes. She stands outside the car and leans in through the open door. I can hardly see her, but I can smell the lemon-scented stuff she puts on her hair, mixed up with the smells of sweat and weed. Mona smells like a forest, not the sea. "Oh my God," she says, "I forgot to tell you, tonight, you know table six? That big horde of Uncle Tad's friends?"

"Yeah."

"So they wanted the soup with the food, and I forgot, and you know what the old guy says to me? The little guy at the head of the table?"

"What?"

"He goes, *Vous êtes bête, mademoiselle!*"

She says it in a rough, growly voice, and laughs. I can tell it's French, but that's all. "What does it mean?"

"*You're an idiot, miss!*"

She ducks her head, stifling giggles. "He called you an idiot?"

"Yeah, *bête*, it's like *beast*."

She lifts her head, then shakes it. A light from someone else's porch bounces off her nose. She puts on a fake Norwegian accent and says: "*My God awful day.*"

I nod. "Awful day." And because we say it all the time, because it's the kind of silly, ordinary thing you could call one of our "refrains," or maybe because of the weed I've smoked, a whole bunch of days seem pressed together inside this moment, more than you could count. There's the time we all went out for New Year's Eve, and Uncle Tad drove me, and when he stopped and I opened the door he told me to close it, and I said "I will when I'm on the other side," and when I told Mona we laughed so hard we had to run away and hide in the bathroom. There's the day some people we know from school came in and we served them wine even though they were under age and Mona got nervous and spilled it all over the tablecloth, and the day her nice cousin came to visit and made us cheese-and-mint sandwiches in the microwave and got yelled at for wasting food. And the day of the party for Mona's mom's birthday, when Uncle Tad played music and made us all dance, and Mona's mom's eyes went jewelly with tears, and afterward Mona told me: "I should just run away. I'm the only thing keeping her here." My God, awful days. All the best days of my life.

"Bye," Mona whispers. I watch her until she disappears into the house.

My mom used to swim every morning at the YWCA. When I was little she took me along. I didn't like swimming. I'd sit in a chair with a book while she went up and down, up and down, a dim streak in the water. When I read *Mrs. Frisby and the Rats of NIMH*, it seemed like Mom was a lab rat doing tasks, the way she kept touching one side of the pool and then the other. At last she climbed out and pulled off her bathing cap. In the locker room she hung up her suit, a thin gray rag dripping on the floor. Most people put the hook of their padlock through the straps of their suit, so the suits could hang outside the lockers without getting stolen, but my mom never did that. She just tied her suit loosely onto the lock. "No one's going to steal that stretchy old thing," she said. And no one did.

That should have been the end of the story, but it wasn't. My dad says Mom was an elemental, a sort of stranger, not of our kind. It wasn't my fault she left, it was because she couldn't learn to breathe on land. That's the worst story I've ever heard. I'll never tell Mona, not ever, not even when we're leaving for Colorado with everything we need in the back of my car, and I meet her at the grocery store the way we've already planned, and she runs out smiling under her orange baseball cap. I won't tell her how dangerous attics are, or how some people can't start over, or how I still see my mom in shop windows with her long hair the same silver-gray as her coat, or how once when my little cousins came to visit we went to the zoo and the seals recognized me, they both stood up in the water and talked in a foreign language. I won't tell her. I'm too scared. I won't even tell her what she needs to know: that we've got to be tougher than our moms, that we've got to have different stories, that she'd better not change her mind and drop me in Colorado because I won't understand, I'll hate her forever and burn her stuff and stay up all night screaming at the woods, because it's stupid not to be able to breathe, who ever heard of somebody breathing in one place but not another, and we're not like that, Mona and me, and selkie stories are only for losers stuck on the wrong side of magic—people who drop things, who tell all, who leave keys around, who let go.

## NEBULA AWARD NOMINEE
### BEST SHORT STORY

# "SELECTED PROGRAM NOTES FROM THE RETROSPECTIVE EXHIBITION OF THERESA ROSENBERG LATIMER"

## KENNETH SCHNEYER

*This is Kenneth Schneyer's first Nebula nomination. "Selected Program Notes from the Retrospective Exhibition of Theresa Rosenberg Latimer" was also a finalist for the Theodore Sturgeon Memorial Award. It was published in* Clockwork Phoenix 4.

1. *Three Women* (1978)
   Oil on canvas, 30 x 40"
   Detroit Institute of Art, Detroit, Michigan

Latimer painted *Three Women* while still a student at the Rhode Island School of Design. It is the earliest completed painting that displays the hyperrealism characterizing the first period of her work.

Three young women sit close together on a park bench in autumn. Two hold hands, while the third has her hand on the knee of the center figure. Their expressions are serious, almost stern, as if they resent the artist's presumption in portraying them.

At this stage of her career, Latimer was still experimenting with issues of compositional balance. The brightness of the orange trees offsets the dour colors of the models' clothes; the tilt of the models' heads and the orientation of their legs impel the viewer to look at the trees rather than at them. It as if the viewer is being pushed away from people and towards nature.

None of these models appears in any of Latimer's later work. Presumably they were fellow RISD students. Latimer herself appears in early works of others who were at RISD at the time, including A. C. Stahl and J. J. Kramer.

*Discussion questions*:

a. Use the magnifying lens provided to examine the hairs on the models' arms, the loose fibers in their sweaters, and the veins in the leaves. Many details in a Latimer painting are not visible to those who view the work at ordinary distances. Why do you think she inserted such typically invisible minutiae? What effect do they have on your experience of the painting?

19. *Self-Portrait with Surrogates* (1984)

Oil on canvas, 51 x 77-1/4"

Rhode Island School of Design Museum, Providence, Rhode Island

The first of Latimer's paintings to draw critical attention, *Self-Portrait with Surrogates* portrays the notorious child abuse and murder case of the Wilson family, which dominated the Rhode Island news media at the time. Seven-year-old Lisa Wilson, clad only in underwear and displaying both old scars and fresh cuts, is being beaten with an electrical extension cord wielded by her father, while her mother holds her in place. None of the figures displays any emotion; it is as if they are spectators at the event.

The details, again in the hyperrealist style, closely match those of the Wilson case. The family home is accurately depicted, and the scars on Lisa Wilson's body correspond with photographs in the court file.

*Discussion questions*:

a. The composition and live-action flavor of this work resemble 18th- and 19th-century patriotic or polemical depictions of battles and famous events; David's *The Death of Socrates* (1787) (Fig. 5) is a clear influence. Why does Latimer employ such devices in a portrayal of domestic violence? Does it alter your perception of what you are "really" seeing?

b. Some biographers associate the painting's title with the emotional and physical abuse Latimer herself experienced as a child. Is there anything in the picture itself to show that this is really a "self portrait?"

c. Does the fact that Latimer's parents were living when she painted this work alter the way you perceive it?

34. *Magda #4* (1989)
     Oil on poplar wood, 30 x 21"
     Private collection

Sometimes called "Devotion" by critics, this nude is the earliest extant work featuring Magda Ridley Meszaros (1963–2023), Latimer's favorite model and later her wife. The lushness of the flesh and the rosiness of the skin are reminiscent of Renoir's paintings of Aline Charigot (*See, e.g., The Large Bathers* (1887) (Fig. 8)). Latimer maintains microscopic hyperrealism even as she employs radiating brushstrokes which emanate from the model, as if Meszaros is the source of reality itself.

*Discussion questions*:

a. The materials and dimensions of this painting duplicate those of Da Vinci's *La Gioconda* (c. 1503–1519) (Fig. 17). Is this merely a compositional joke or homage by Latimer? How does it change the way you see the painting?

b. Most biographers agree that Latimer and Meszaros were already lovers by the time this work was completed. Is this apparent from the composition or technique? From the pose of the model? As you proceed through the exhibit, note similarities and differences between this and other portrayals of Meszaros over the next 34 years.

48. *Conjuring* (1993)
     Acrylic on masonite, 48 x 96"
     Private collection

Her largest composition and only known landscape, *Conjuring* appeared during a fallow period in Latimer's work. In 1992 and 1993 she completed only three paintings.

The scene is an overcast day in a valley in northern New Hampshire. Although it is summer, the foliage on the hills contains much grey and purple, conveying a wintery feel. While Latimer renders exacting details in rocks, trees, even blades of grass, in this work she also employs a forced monotony in the brushwork; the shape of every stroke is practically identical to every other.

In the precise center of the composition, wearing baggy khaki clothing, Magda Ridley Meszaros walks along an empty dirt road, recognizable only under a magnifying lens. She does not appear to be aware of the artist.

*Discussion questions*:

a. The aforementioned slack period in Latimer's work coincided with several crises in her life: her only interval of estrangement from Magda Meszaros, precipitated by parental opposition to their relationship; the death by drug overdose of her close friend, the singer Pamela Enoch (1965–1993); and Latimer's own life-threatening illness. Her hyperrealist period ends with this painting. Can we see these life crises in this composition? Is there any hint of Latimer's coming change in style?

49. *Performance* (1994)
Acrylic on canvas, 32 x 41"
National Portrait Gallery, Washington, DC

Generally regarded as one of the outstanding memorial portraits of the 20th century, *Performance* is also the first painting of Latimer's "highlight" period, which occupied the rest of her career.

Latimer was fascinated by the restoration of the Sistine Chapel ceiling (1980–1994), which sharply enhanced the clarity and brightness of Michelangelo's colors. Although some still doubt whether the restoration reflected the artist's intentions, Latimer was most interested in the side-by-side contrast between the pre- and post-restoration appearance of the frescoes (*See* "before" and "after" pictures of *The Creation of Adam* (figs. 11 and 12)). In one of her diaries, she wrote:

*They stripped away the hurts and filth of five centuries and released the purity within. It's like looking at one of the Platonic forms—beneath the battered, mundane person, the person we see in everyday life, is the true person—the soul, maybe, or the heart. Of course it looks less "real" to us—we're so used to the violence and degradation imposed on us by the world that we're unprepared for ourselves without it.*

*How did I miss this before? Maybe I wasn't ready, til now, to understand it. But after what happened, what's still happening, this is the perfect tool, maybe the only tool.*

After 1994, nearly all of Latimer's paintings feature one or more "highlight figures," people in a painting whose coloration has the clarity and brightness of the restored Sistine Chapel frescoes, as contrasted with the duller, more commonplace tones of everything else in the composition. They seem out-of-place and fantastical, even cartoonish, and yet Latimer employed the same level of microscopic detail in her "highlight figures" as to their surroundings.

The first critics who saw *Performance* misunderstood Latimer's introduction of "highlight" figures, because the painting is set on the stage of the Providence Performing Arts Center, and the central figure is the artist's recently-deceased friend, the singer Pamela Enoch. Because she appears on the stage as if she were performing a concert, Enoch's heightened colors were taken at the time to represent the effect of theatrical spotlights. Arthur Mallory's review called the lighting "sentimental in an otherwise naturalistic work," noting that true spotlights would have enhanced the colors of the surrounding stage as well.

Magda Meszaros is visible in the front row, the only member of the audience. She has turned in her seat to face the artist. Meszaros is not portrayed as a "highlight" figure, but in the same comparatively muted tones as the theatre.

*Discussion questions*:

a. As you view the many "highlight" figures in the remaining paintings in this exhibit, consider whether these figures seem more or less "real" to you than those painted in ordinary colors. Why?

b. Critics and biographers have puzzled over Latimer's words, *"what happened, what's still happening,"* which seem to refer to the event or events that inspired or impelled her to adopt the "highlight" style. But what events were they, and how did they lead to this change?

c. Not until 2025 did Latimer paint Magda Ridley Meszaros as a "highlight" figure. Usually she appears in ordinary tones, as here. Why is this so?

d. Why does Meszaros wear a puzzled expression?


59. *Critique* (1997)
    Acrylic on canvas, 44 x 67"
    Davison Art Center
    Wesleyan University, Middletown, Connecticut

Latimer painted this piece to commemorate the addition of her *Self-Portrait with Surrogates* (#19) to the permanent collection of the RISD Museum. The setting is the Contemporary Artists gallery of the Museum;

*Self-Portrait with Surrogates* hangs at the center of the composition, with adjacent works also visible, notably *Intelligentsia* (1986) by her friend and classmate J. J. Kramer.

In the foreground is the child Lisa Wilson (the subject of *Self-Portrait with Surrogates*) painted as a "highlight" figure. The young girl is presented as if she were a critical viewer of *Self-Portrait with Surrogates*; she is turned three-quarters toward the artist, but her left hand is raised toward the painting in a dismissive gesture. Her face is wry and full of humor; she appears to like the artist, even if she does not think much of the painting.

*Discussion questions*:

a. How do you interpret Lisa Wilson's apparent attitude towards Latimer's earlier painting? Is Latimer ridiculing her own work?

b. Why is Lisa Wilson portrayed as younger than she was in *Self-Portrait with Surrogates*? Why without visible evidence of abuse? What is the significance of the party dress she wears?

60. Excerpt from *The Silent Voices* (1997)
    Video recording, 23 min.
    By permission of WGBH Television and the Public Broadcasting Service.

While working on *Critique*, Latimer was one of the subjects of Elijah Baptista's video documentary concerning contemporary artists, *The Silent Voices*. In the excerpt shown here, she stands in the Contemporary Artists Gallery, making preliminary drawings. Oddly, she is not sketching the gallery or the paintings on the wall, but detailing the face of Lisa Wilson herself. Although there are no photographs or prior sketches evident (apart from *Self-Portrait with Surrogates*), the drawing is precise, showing the same wry expression that will appear in the finished work.

*Discussion questions*:

a. Now that you see Latimer's manner of speaking and moving, are you surprised? Does she seem like the sort of person who would produce this sort of work?

b. At the end of the excerpt, Baptista asks Latimer why she needed to come to the Museum in order to sketch a study of Wilson's face. Latimer's answer is,

"You have to paint what you see, not what you think you're supposed to see." This admonition is a commonplace among visual artists. What does it mean when uttered by someone who paints with such obvious imagination?

72. *Grace* (2001)
    Acrylic on canvas, 20 x 60"
    Massachusetts Museum of Contemporary Art, North Adams,
        Massachusetts

One of several pieces recounting Latimer's difficult relationship with her parents, *Grace* portrays a Thanksgiving dinner in their home. Her father, Mason Latimer (1930–2008), poses as if saying grace before the meal, but both he and his wife Sheila Rosenberg (1935–2014) are staring scornfully at Theresa Rosenberg Latimer and Magda Ridley Meszaros, who sit at the opposite end of the table, looking down at their plates.

Standing behind the artist and Meszaros, apparently observed by no one, is Pamela Enoch (the subject of *Performance*, #49), the only "highlight" figure in the composition. Smiling, she holds her palms above the heads of her two friends as if in benediction.

*Discussion questions*:

a. Critics have noted references in this painting to both Rockwell's *Freedom From Want* (1943) (Fig. 18) and Dali's *Sacrament of the Last Supper* (1955) (Fig. 19). What is the point of quoting two such wildly disparate pieces together? Is this a parody?

b. Pamela Enoch appears in many of Latimer's works after 1994, always as a "highlight" figure in her mid-twenties, dressed for a performance. Why repeat the same person so often, and why always in the same clothes? Is Enoch a symbolic figure?

91. *The Mourners* (2008)
    Acrylic on canvas, 20 x 30"
    American Labor Museum, Haledon, New Jersey

The setting is a parking lot in Pawtucket, Rhode Island that stands on the location of the 1908 Alger's Mill fire, in which 34 workers were killed. Two distinct groups of "highlight" figures appear. Near the center stand the

Alger brothers, the Mill owners whose negligence was generally blamed for the deaths, although none were ever prosecuted. They bow their heads and clasp their hands before them. Standing in a circle around them are 25 victims of the fire, their own sorrowful gazes fixed on the Alger brothers. All are dressed as they would have been in the late 19th or early 20th centuries.

Here, as elsewhere, Latimer has been praised for the quality of her research. Although historians have authenticated the faces of most of the fire victims, many of the relevant photographs have taken years or even decades to find.

*Discussion questions*:

a. Most of the figures in this painting are younger than they were at the time of the 1908 fire. Tara Aquino, in her assiduous tally of Latimer's subjects (2038), has calculated that 84% of the "highlight" figures are in their 20s and 30s, and the rest are mostly children. By contrast, Latimer's non-highlighted figures show an ordinary spread of ages. Why does Latimer make this age distinction between "highlight" and "ordinary" figures? Why not portray people as they were at the time of the relevant events?

b. One of the striking things about this painting is that the victims appear to be mourning for those who were responsible for their deaths. What is Latimer's message here?

c. Young Lisa Wilson, a recurring figure in Latimer's work, is visible at the far right of the composition, gesturing towards the group of mourning figures. Why include a contemporary figure in an otherwise period group? Is there a connection between this painting and the others in which she appears?


117. *Self-Portrait with Family* (2015)
　　　Acrylic on canvas, 36 x 45"
　　　Private collection

The setting is Latimer's own bedroom, recognizable from the furniture and memorabilia. Latimer at her then-current age of 56 crouches in the bed in a nightgown, her face hidden in her hands as if in fear, sorrow or pain. Standing by the side of the bed, glowering down at their daughter in reproach or rage, are her parents Mason Latimer and Sheila Rosenberg. They are "highlight" figures.

Kneeling on the bed with Latimer is Magda Meszaros. Both are painted in muted colors, as contrasted with the highlighted parents. Meszaros is in a protective posture, one hand on Latimer's curved back and the other gesturing as to repel an invader.

*Discussion questions:*

a. Why does the artist paint her parents as they appeared in their twenties, before her own birth?

b. Why are neither Meszaros's fierce gaze nor her guardian hand directed at the figures of the parents (the only other people in the composition), but at a point beyond the right border of the picture?

c. This work was composed in the year following Sheila Rosenberg's death from brain cancer, which was also the year in which Latimer and Meszaros finally married. How many uses of the word "family" are implied by the title?

131. *To Interfere, for Good, in Human Matters* (2018)
   Acrylic on canvas, 30 x 60"
   F. Cooley Memorial Art Gallery, Reed College, Portland, Oregon

The scene is a crowded street in downtown Providence. A homeless woman with a young child sits on the doorstep of what may be a church; they are malnourished, shabbily dressed, and the woman holds out her hand as if asking for alms. The dozens of others on the street around her are a mix of both "highlight" figures and characters painted in muted colors (as are the beggar woman and her child). The composition pushes the eye of the viewer back and forth between the different groups in a sort of tennis match: from a "highlight" figure one is drawn to a muted figure, then to another "highlight" figure, then to another muted figure, back and forth until one has scrutinized every figure in the picture.

This oscillation forces the viewer to see the contrast between these two groups. Superficially, the muted figures wear everyday clothes contemporary to 2018, while the "highlight" figures are clad in varying styles from the previous 150 years. More significant, however, are their differing reactions to the homeless pair. The muted figures bypass the seated beggars, or approach them while looking elsewhere; a few are watching them from the corners of their eyes. The "highlight" figures, on the other hand, all stand motionless, each facing the mother and child, each with a look of pity or compassion on her or his face. Some reach out their hands as if to touch the pair, but none actually reach them.

*Discussion questions*:

a. As in other Latimer paintings, critics have observed references to other works, notably Courbet's *Real Allegory of the Artist's Studio* (1855) (Fig. 40) and Bosch's *Garden of Earthly Delights* (c. 1504) (Fig 41). Again, why does Latimer quote from two such different pieces?

b. Athena Ptolemaios (2025) has suggested that there is a racial or cultural message here. The muted figures are turning away from one of their own, while the "highlight" figures reach out to the stranger. Are we being shown than it is easier to feel compassion for those who are far away, or different?

c. While her technique here earned much praise, Latimer has been criticized for the blatantness of the message. Thomas Taney (2030) was particularly scornful of Latimer's unexplained use of a passage from Dickens's *A Christmas Carol* (1843) as the title of the piece. Do you agree with Taney?

146. *Almost* (2022)
Oil on poplar wood, 30 x 21"
Private collection

*Almost* is the last portrait Latimer made of Magda Ridley Meszaros during the latter's lifetime. It is an unsentimental portrayal, detailing the damage done by both breast cancer and chemotherapy with all the hyperrealist accuracy at Latimer's command. From her favorite chair, Meszaros gazes quietly at the artist. One detects neither fear, defiance, nor even acceptance, only the affection of one life partner for another.

Standing on either side of Meszaros are four "highlight" figures: Pamela Enoch and three other women who have not been identified. They are looking not at Meszaros but at the artist, their arms held wide.

*Discussion questions*:

a. The subject, size and materials of *Almost* are identical to those of *Magda #4* (#34), so that it is natural to compare them. Whereas the brushwork in *Magda #4* pointed to Meszaros herself, in *Almost* the strokes radiate from the "highlight" figures; even the strokes with which Meszaros is painted come from them. What other differences do you see between the two works? What similarities?

b. Why are the "highlight" figures smiling?

155. *Comfort* (2025)
    Acrylic on canvas, 11 x 8-1/2"
    Private collection

The last known completed work of Theresa Rosenberg Latimer is *Comfort*, found among her personal effects after her death by medication overdose at the age of 66.

It is a quadruple portrait, somewhat reminiscent of her *Three Women* (#1). The setting is the exterior of Latimer's home, although the focus is so tight that only certain abnormalities in the brickwork allow us to identify it. The four figures are Pamela Enoch dressed for a performance, Lisa Wilson in her party dress, Magda Meszaros as a young model, and Latimer herself at 30, the beginning of her most productive period. Latimer stands slightly in the foreground, one step ahead of the others; Enoch and Wilson are to her left, Meszaros to her right, as if they are ready to catch her if she falls.

All four women are "highlight" figures, bright and clear with strong definitions and confident lines. They are more radiant than the "highlight" figures of Latimer's earlier works; light pours from them, and they drown out the color of the bricks behind them. Enoch's, Wilson's and Meszaros's faces are fixed on Latimer, who is smiling broadly, with flushed cheeks and eyes full of hope.

*Discussion questions*:

a. The title *Comfort* was suggested by Paula Tarso, executrix of Latimer's artistic estate; we do not know what Latimer herself planned to call it. Do you think the name fits?

# "ALIVE, ALIVE OH"

## SYLVIA SPRUCK WRIGLEY

*This is Sylvia Spruck Wrigley's first Nebula nomination. "Alive, Alive Oh" appeared in* Lightspeed.

The waves crash onto the blood-red shore, sounding just like the surf on Earth: a dark rumbling full of power. It's been seventeen years since we left.

Owen and I got married at the register office in Cardiff. We took a flat near the University, a tiny bedsit. I felt very cosmopolitan, living in the capital city, and only a little bit homesick for Swansea. Then Owen came home one night and asked me what I thought about going into space. I laughed because I thought he must be joking, but he wasn't: They'd offered him a position in a new terraforming colony on G851.5.32 and of course he wanted to go. I was frightened, but it's not the kind of opportunity you can say no to, is it? And it was only for ten years; afterward we could come back to a full pension. Fame and fortune, he said. I did like the thought of telling my friends. *Oooh, hello Emma, how have you been? Yes, it has been quite some time, hasn't it? You've moved to Mumbles Road, have you? That's nice. We moved to an exoplanet eighteen light-years away. Oh well, we're back now, of course . . .*

That was back when I thought we'd return to Wales one day.

The water here is nothing like the salty sea of home. It's acidic and eats into the flesh. I shouldn't even be this close to the shore, in case the spray splashes across and burns me. Everything about G851.5.32 is toxic; I've been here so long, even *I* am.

Megan was born after we'd been here five years. My best friend Jeanine (my *only* friend) was present for the birth. Owen started off holding my hand, but he couldn't stand to see me in such pain. In the end, he paced outside until Jeanine went out to tell him that it was all over, that he was the father of a baby girl.

"She looks so fragile," he said. "I'm afraid to touch her in case she breaks." It's true: Megan was a tiny little thing, ice-blue eyes peering at everything, curious.

I worried about her growing up in the colony dome; it was such a sterile environment. "Children need to get muddy," I said. "They need to be able to explore and get out from under everyone's feet and just burn up energy."

"She'll be running down the sandbars of Swansea Bay before long," he promised, tickling under her chin. She stared back at him with a serious face.

When she was a baby, I sang Suo Gân to her, the Welsh lullaby. As she got older, I made her laugh with songs about a world she'd never seen: "Oranges and Lemons," "The Bishop of Bangor's Jig," "Sweet Molly Malone." I told her stories about day-to-day life in Swansea: the covered market, the sandy beach of the bay, Blackpill Lido, the rain. These were as fantastical to her as gold spun from straw.

Once Megan could walk, Owen had protective goggles made for her small face and we took to taking long strolls outside, around the edges of the dome. We went as far as the craggy coastline, where the dark waves crashed against red silt. She sang "Molly Malone" while I told her about making sandcastles and the mewling cries of the seagulls. She gazed at everything with curious eyes.

"Didn't you get dirty, Mummy?" The colony has very strict rules about sterile conditions. The idea of playing in the sand was as alien to Megan as life in space would be to my school friends. She grew up with constant warnings, having to wear three layers of protective clothing just to open a window. That afternoon, she clutched her favourite toy—a stuffed octopus I made from scraps of synthetic fabric—in one hand and held my hand tightly with the other. She was four years old and she had never been free. I did what I could, kept telling her the stories she loved, tried to explain what a child's life should be like. It wasn't the same. She knew it wasn't.

"Yes," I told her, "we got very dirty. And then we'd go home and our mummies would make us wash and we'd be clean again." Megan looked dubious.

"It was a different type of dirty, child," I admitted eventually. "Dirt on Earth doesn't hurt. In fact, sometimes pregnant women even eat soil." She laughed at me, the idea so ludicrous, she couldn't imagine it. When we returned to the dome, we left all our outerwear in the entry bay, where it would be collected and sterilised. The commanders weren't very pleased with me taking Megan out of the base for walks, but once I found out they weren't letting us return to Earth, I didn't much care what they thought.

Owen and I were in the third wave of researchers to come to the colony; there were a few thousand of us at the peak. It was a long trip: five months' travel and then ten years on the base and another five months home. Still, it seemed reasonable until a few years after Megan was born. The first return mission to California was a disaster. The initial researchers—including my friend Jeanine Davies—were so excited about going home. Jeanine stayed up all night in anticipation. She told me she was going to gorge herself on fresh fruit and vegetables and then go outside and enjoy the feel of the wind against her face. We made plans to meet in Cardiff once Owen's time was finished. Her only regret was that she wouldn't see Megan for a few years. She was full of energy, the picture of health. She was going home.

When the capsule delivered them to the space centre in the California desert, the occupants became violently ill. It took a while to get the news. Jeanine was dead. All of them, dead. They carried some unknown bacteria in their gut, which went malignant once they arrived in Earth's atmosphere. Not just the homecomers, everyone: The bacteria spread with a virulence that hadn't been seen since the plague. So G851.5.32 was put under quarantine and all further trips to Mother Earth cancelled with no clue as to when we could return.

"It's autumn on the Gower right now," I told Megan. "We'd be picking blackberries if we were home. The skies are grey and rain falls from the sky. The wind is crisp and the roads full of puddles."

"Did you really go outside without goggles or anything?" Megan had never felt the air against her bare skin. We walked along the high end of the beach, safely away from the acid water. She begged me to tell her more about "the past," as she called it: Wales was an unobtainable world that only existed in stories. I stopped correcting her after a few years went by. There seemed no point.

"Just an umbrella and sturdy shoes. Mind, we got flu and colds that lasted all winter long as well. You're lucky in that respect."

Illness is not common here on our sterilised colony and the medical centre is quick to treat any symptoms. They've spent thousands of hours trying to find the bacterium that killed our homecomers, but it appears to be inactive here, mutating to a malicious killer only in the Earth's atmosphere. And they can't just send people to Earth to die, even if the scientists on the ground were willing to risk themselves trying to do the research. They isolated the plague in California by cordoning off the entire desert, leaving the carriers to die alone.

"The sea was always cold, but by October it would be freezing. We would walk along the beach on the way home from school. We dared each other to run in and brave it. The water was so cold it felt as if it burned." Sometimes it took a couple of sips of vodka to get the nerve. The cold would make your heart stop.

I wish I had a bottle of vodka now. The sun's low in the sky. If I squint, I can almost pretend it's a brilliant Swansea sunset, rays reflecting off the low clouds to turn the landscape red. I can almost pretend I'm at Oystermouth Road, standing at the long stretch of beach, Jacquelyn daring me to take my togs off and run into the waves.

Megan had the same enthusiastic curiosity about the world as her father the scientist. The dome was stifling to a young girl's spirit. We explored the local area, but I didn't dare go very far. Megan complained bitterly when it was time to return. It came to a head when she was caught sneaking out in the middle of the night, without authorisation, without the proper gear. Owen was furious, but I couldn't blame her for rebelling against the rules and regulations.

"How can we learn more if we lock ourselves away?" she complained. "When I grow up, I'm going to live outdoors and I'm going to see the entire planet. I'm going to study the Homecoming Plague until I find a solution and we can travel again."

"If you do, I'll be on the first ship home. I'll take you to the pier for ice cream."

Ice cream was one of the few traditional treats that Megan recognized. She never had food except from a container: synthesised vitamins and American processed meat. "You could really just go someplace and get food? You didn't have a canteen?"

"No. Well, we had restaurants, where we could meet up and have a meal together. It was a social thing. It was a choice." She was bemused by the concept of choice. Our food is doled out in scoops. If you don't go to the canteen, you don't eat.

By her twelfth birthday, food was tightly restricted. We lived on carbohydrate dishes that tasted of cotton, with the tinned goods tightly rationed. Two unmanned ships had successfully reached us with supplies since the quarantine began. Many others failed. We had no idea when the next might come. I fought off the hunger pangs by telling Megan about my favourite dinners when I was her age.

"The beaches of the Gower are full of treasure," I told her. "We'd go to the beach after school and fish for our supper. Mum would peel a couple of potatoes and fry our catch in butter and that would be dinner." Mostly Mum heated up frozen dinners from Tesco, but I didn't like to tell Megan that. Besides, when Mum was sober, she was a pretty good cook. She would always have a go at preparing anything we brought home. "I didn't have the patience for fishing. My line was always getting tangled up and I hated touching the lugworms. But you could collect all kinds of shellfish at the changing of the tides. Nan used to take us out in the middle of the night with a thermos of whisky and coffee. We'd collect what we could find: oysters, mussels, even crabs."

Megan's mouth fell open and she stared at the distant beach disbelievingly. "So they were just there waiting for you to take them? Did you eat them?"

"We steamed them and then we ate them with just a squeeze of lemon juice. Lemons grow on trees, but we bought our fruit from the market."

"How does steaming work?" It was hard for her to imagine the world I took for granted. Megan never had raw food so she didn't understand about cooking. The closest she came to seafood was the tinned salmon they served on New Year's Day.

"You have to steam them to force the shells open so you can get to the meat inside." Megan looked disappointed. She relished the idea of a movable feast, food simply there for the taking. Our dependence within the colony was so constant; the concept of fending for yourself was a favourite source of wonder for her.

I liked to indulge her. "Sometimes you could catch them with the shells open. I caught buckets of razor clams at the estuary. Find a hole in the sand, that's where they've dug themselves into. You just drop a bit of salt into the hole and then reach in and drag the clams straight out of their shells. They're plump and meaty. If you were hungry enough, I guess you could simply eat them on the spot. In the old days, they had special knives to pry the shells open and eat them alive."

"How would you know they weren't poisonous?"

"There's not much from the sea that will kill you, not if it's fresh."

Not in the Celtic Sea, anyway. I stare out at the poisonous waves of G851.5.32, a mystery to me. Who knows what beasts lurk within its softly glowing swells. The scent is sharp and chemical rather than the briny breeze of Swansea Bay. Everything here is toxic.

"What does it taste like? Food you find on your own, I mean." By the time Megan was thirteen, I'd given up all hope of returning home. We were "self-sufficient" and a perfect test bed for the colonies of the future, with sterilised capsules transferring data back to Earth. All wonderful research, except that I'd never signed up for this, never wanted to spend a lifetime in space, never would have started a family if I'd known the antiseptic life in the colony was all she'd ever see. Megan's curiosity became insatiable as she begged for details of a "normal" life, of what she'd missed. I told her about wine and thunderstorms and aeroplanes and guitars. I taught her church hymns and Bonnie Tyler songs and rugby chants. Megan continued to sneak out of the dome, "taking liberties with her safety" it said on the reports. Colony security wasn't designed to hold in rebellious teenagers; she didn't find it difficult. I never said anything. How could she grow up in this barren collection of plastic buildings? She needed to explore.

Owen grew distressed. "You are making her homesick for a world she's never known," he told me. I didn't care. I wanted her to know, to understand where she had come from. So I kept telling her the stories, answering her questions. I never noticed how often we returned to the subject of food.

"Shellfish tastes better than anything else in the universe," I told her. "Especially if you caught it yourself. The fresh air seasons it, we say. But it's because you put the effort in, you made the food happen."

"But specifically, what is it like? What do cockles and mussels taste of?"

I didn't know how to answer that. She had never eaten anything that wasn't full of preservatives and salt. "They taste like the sea. They taste slick and primordial. They taste of brine and dark blue depths. It's an Earth flavour. I can't explain." She glared at me and stomped out of the room. She wanted facts, not metaphors. She wanted to know and I wasn't helping. She wanted to go home and taste them for herself.

The silt of the shore is soft and powdery, nothing like the golden sand of Swansea Bay. When I press my fingers into it, the edges of my gloves begin to singe against the damp soil underneath. Everything about this planet is poison. It was never meant for families.

The day Megan told me she had a stomach ache, I didn't think too much about it. "Have you finished your school work?" I asked her. She had daily one-on-one tutorials, taught by some the best scientists of our time, not that an education was any use up here. Still, we stuck to the routines, pretended there was a future.

"I don't feel well at all," she said. Those were her last coherent words. She collapsed before I made it across the room to feel her forehead. I carried her to the med station myself, her long legs dragging along the polished hallways. Megan's eyes opened as I screamed for the nurse to help me. She twisted and began to vomit blood as they pulled her onto the bed and wheeled her into the back rooms. Within a few hours, she was dead.

Owen found refuge in process. He told me they thought she might have the same bacteria that stopped us returning to Earth, that she might be the key to finding the cure. I turned away as he stuttered platitudes, that maybe they would solve the quarantine, that maybe her death wouldn't be in vain. I couldn't stand to hear him try to make sense of the tragedy. He stayed at the medical station, signing consent forms, overseeing the process as they cut her open and examined her insides.

I went home and sat in her room, touching her things. I bunched her favourite dress in my fists, hoping to banish the last sight of her, flesh pale as marble, splattered with blood, blue eyes colder than any ice. I collapsed onto her bunk. Once the tears slowed, I ran my fingers over her stuffed octopus like a blind woman, touching the ragged cloth and glassy eyes as if it might hold some of her essence.

The sharp edges of something under her pillow stopped me. I opened my eyes and moved the pillow to see a pair of stolen protective gloves, singed away at the tips, and half a dozen blood-red shells. Two of them were cracked and pried open; the insides sparkled like mother of pearl, wiped clean. Licked clean.

Owen told me that Megan's death was not preventable. It was an unknown illness, he said, there was nothing that we could have done. He cried as he told me that she'd ingested some sort of parasites. They had rampaged through her flesh, feasting on her organs. He promised me that it was quick, as if I didn't already know that, as if that was a consolation. I took the shells she'd hidden under her pillow and said nothing.

I press my bare toes into the powdery silt of the barren shore of G851.5.32. It stings, a million pins and needles pricking my flesh. When I was a girl, we would dare each other to dash into the frigid waves of the sea, the water so cold that it burned.

I wonder if it will feel the same, in this alien sea so far from home. I clench the broken shells in my fists and run forward into the breaking waves.

I think it will feel just the same.

# "THE WAITING STARS"

## ALIETTE de BODARD

*Aliette de Bodard has won a Nebula Award, a Locus Award, a British Science Fiction Association Award, and Writers of the Future. "The Waiting Stars" was first published in* The Other Half of the Sky.

The derelict ship ward was in an isolated section of Outsider space, one of the numerous spots left blank on interstellar maps, no more or no less tantalising than its neighbouring quadrants. To most people, it would be just that: a boring part of a long journey to be avoided—skipped over by Mind-ships as they cut through deep space, passed around at low speeds by Outsider ships while their passengers slept in their hibernation cradles.

Only if anyone got closer would they see the hulking masses of ships: the glint of starlight on metal, the sharp, pristine beauty of their hulls, even though they all lay quiescent and crippled, forever unable to move—living corpses kept as a reminder of how far they had fallen; the Outsiders' brash statement of their military might, a reminder that their weapons held the means to fell any Mind-ships they chose to hound.

On the sensors of *The Cinnabar Mansions*, the ships all appeared small and diminished, like toy models or avatars—things Lan Nhen could have held in the palm of her hand and just as easily crushed. As the sensors' line of sight moved—catching ship after ship in their field of view, wreck after wreck, in-distinct masses of burnt and twisted metal, of ripped-out engines, of shattered life pods and crushed shuttles—Lan Nhen felt as if an icy fist were squeezing her heart into shards. To think of the Minds within—dead or crippled, forever unable to move . . .

"She's not there," she said, as more and more ships appeared on the screen in front of her, a mass of corpses that all threatened to overwhelm her with sorrow and grief and anger.

"Be patient, child," *The Cinnabar Mansions* said. The Mind's voice was amused, as it always was—after all, she'd lived for five centuries, and would outlive Lan Nhen and Lan Nhen's own children by so many years that the pronoun "child" seemed small and inappropriate to express the vast gulf of generations between them. "We already knew it was going to take time."

"She was supposed to be on the outskirts of the wards," Lan Nhen said, biting her lip. She had to be, or the rescue mission was going to be infinitely more complicated. "According to Cuc . . ."

"Your cousin knows what she's talking about," *The Cinnabar Mansions* said.

"I guess." Lan Nhen wished Cuc was there with them, and not sleeping in her cabin as peacefully as a baby—but *The Cinnabar Mansions* had pointed out Cuc needed to be rested for what lay ahead; and Lan Nhen had given in, vastly outranked. Still, Cuc was reliable, for narrow definitions of the term—as long as anything didn't involve social skills, or deft negotiation. For technical information, though, she didn't have an equal within the family; and her network of contacts extended deep within Outsider space. That was how they'd found out about the ward in the first place . . .

"There." The sensors beeped, and the view on the screen pulled into enhanced mode on a ship on the edge of the yard, which seemed even smaller than the hulking masses of her companions. *The Turtle's Citadel* had been from the newer generation of ships, its body more compact and more agile than its predecessors: designed for flight and manoeuvres rather than for transport, more elegant and refined than anything to come out of the Imperial Workshops—unlike the other ships, its prow and hull were decorated, painted with numerous designs from old legends and myths, all the way to the Dai Viet of Old Earth. A single gunshot marred the outside of its hull—a burn mark that had transfixed the painted citadel through one of its towers, going all the way into the heartroom and crippling the Mind that animated the ship.

"That's her," Lan Nhen said. "I would know her anywhere."

*The Cinnabar Mansions* had the grace not to say anything, though of course she could have matched the design to her vast databases in an eyeblink. "It's time, then. Shall I extrude a pod?"

Lan Nhen found that her hands had gone slippery with sweat, all of a sudden; and her heart was beating a frantic rhythm within her chest, like temple gongs gone mad. "I guess it's time, yes." By any standards, what they were planning was madness. To infiltrate Outsider space, no matter how isolated—to repair a ship, no matter how lightly damaged . . .

Lan Nhen watched *The Turtle's Citadel* for a while—watched the curve of the hull, the graceful tilt of the engines, away from the living quarters; the burn mark through the hull like a gunshot through a human chest. On the prow was a smaller painting, all but invisible unless one had good eyes: a single sprig of apricot flowers, signifying the New Year's good luck—calligraphied on the ship more than thirty years ago by Lan Nhen's own mother, a parting gift to her great-aunt before the ship left for her last, doomed mission.

Of course, Lan Nhen already knew every detail of that shape by heart, every single bend of the corridors within, every little nook and cranny available outside—from the blueprints, and even before that, before the rescue plan had even been the seed of a thought in her mind—when she'd stood before her ancestral altar, watching the rotating holo of a ship who was also her great-aunt, and wondering how a Mind could ever be brought down, or given up for lost.

Now she was older; old enough to have seen enough things to freeze her blood; old enough to plot her own foolishness, and drag her cousin and her great-great-aunt into it.

Older, certainly. Wiser, perhaps; if they were blessed enough to survive.

There were tales, at the Institution, of what they were—and, in any case, one only had to look at them, at their squatter, darker shapes, at the way their eyes crinkled when they laughed. There were other clues, too: the memories that made Catherine wake up breathless and disoriented, staring at the white walls of the dormitory until the pulsing, writhing images of something she couldn't quite identify had gone, and the breath of dozens of her dorm-mates had lulled her back to sleep. The craving for odd food like fish sauce and fermented meat.

The dim, distant feeling of not fitting in, of being compressed on all sides by a society that made little sense to her.

It should have, though. She'd been taken as a child, like all her schoolmates—saved from the squalor and danger among the savages and brought forward into the light of civilisation—of white sterile rooms and bland food, of awkward embraces that always felt too informal. Rescued, Matron always said, her entire face transfigured, the bones of her cheeks made sharply visible through the pallor of her skin. Made safe.

Catherine had asked what she was safe from. They all did, in the beginning—all the girls in the Institution, Johanna and Catherine being the most vehement amongst them.

That was until Matron showed them the vid.

They all sat at their tables, watching the screen in the centre of the amphitheatre—silent, for once, not jostling or joking among themselves. Even Johanna, who was always first with a biting remark, had said nothing—had sat, transfixed, watching it.

The first picture was a woman who looked like them—smaller and darker-skinned than the Galactics—except that her belly protruded in front of her, huge and swollen like a tumour from some disaster movie. There was a man next to her, his unfocused eyes suggesting that he was checking something on the network through his implants—until the woman grimaced, putting a hand to her belly and calling out to him. His eyes focused in a heartbeat, and fear replaced the blank expression on his face.

There was a split second before the language overlays kicked in—a moment, frozen in time, when the words, the sounds of the syllables put together, sounded achingly familiar to Catherine, like a memory of the childhood she never could quite manage to piece together—there was a brief flash, of New Year's Eve firecrackers going off in a confined space, of her fear that they would burn her, damage her body's ability to heal . . . And then the moment was gone like a popped bubble, because the vid changed in the most horrific manner.

The camera was wobbling, rushing along a pulsing corridor—they could all hear the heavy breath of the woman, the whimpering sounds she made like an animal in pain; the soft, encouraging patter of the physician's words to her.

"She's coming," the woman whispered, over and over, and the physician nodded—keeping one hand on her shoulder, squeezing it so hard his own knuckles had turned the colour of a muddy moon.

"You have to be strong," he said. "Hanh, please. Be strong for me. It's all for the good of the Empire, may it live ten thousand years. Be strong."

The vid cut away, then—and it was wobbling more and more crazily, its field of view showing erratic bits of a cramped room with scrolling letters on the wall, the host of other attendants with similar expressions of fear on their faces; the woman, lying on a flat surface, crying out in pain—blood splattering out of her with every thrust of her hips—the camera moving, shifting between her legs, the physician's hands reaching into the darker opening—easing out a sleek, glinting shape, even as the woman screamed again—and blood, more blood running out, rivers of blood she couldn't possibly have in her body, even as the *thing* within her pulled free, and it became all too clear that, though it had the bare shape of a baby with an oversized head, it had too many cables and sharp angles to be human . . .

Then a quiet fade-to-black, and the same woman being cleaned up by the physician—the thing—the baby being nowhere to be seen. She stared up at the camera; but her gaze was unfocused, and drool was pearling at the corner of her lips, even as her hands spasmed uncontrollably.

Fade to black again; and the lights came up again, on a room that seemed to have grown infinitely colder . . .

"This," Matron said in the growing silence, "is how the Dai Viet birth Minds for their spaceships: by incubating them within the wombs of their women. This is the fate that would have been reserved for all of you. For each of you within this room." Her gaze raked them all; stopping longer than usual on Catherine and Johanna, the known troublemakers in the class. "This is why we had to take you away, so that you wouldn't become brood mares for abominations."

"We," of course, meant the Board—the religious nuts, as Johanna liked to call them, a redemptionist church with a fortune to throw around, financing the children's rescues and their education—and who thought every life from humans to insects was sacred (they'd all wondered, of course, where they fitted into the scheme).

After the class had dispersed like a flock of sparrows, Johanna held court in the yard, her eyes bright and feverish. "They faked it. They had to. They came up with some stupid explanation on how to keep us cooped here. I mean, why would anyone still use natural births and not artificial wombs?"

Catherine, still seeing the splatters of blood on the floor, shivered. "Matron said that they wouldn't. That they thought the birth created a special bond between the Mind and its mother—but that they had to be there, to be awake during the birth."

"Rubbish." Johanna shook her head. "As if that's even remotely plausible. I'm telling you, it has to be fake."

"It looked real." Catherine remembered the woman's screams; the wet sound as the Mind wriggled free from her womb; the fear in the face of all the physicians. "Artificial vids aren't this . . . messy." They'd seen the artificial vids; slick, smooth things where the actors were tall and muscular, the actresses pretty and graceful, with only a thin veneer of artificially generated defects to make the entire thing believable. They'd learnt to tell them apart from the rest; because it was a survival skill in the Institution, to sort out the lies from the truth.

"I bet they can fake that, too," Johanna said. "They can fake everything if they feel like it." But her face belied her words; even she had been shocked. Even she didn't believe they would have gone that far.

"I don't think it's a lie," Catherine said, finally. "Not this time."

And she didn't need to look at the other girls' faces to know that they believed the same thing as her—even Johanna, for all her belligerence—and to feel in her gut that this changed everything.

Cuc came online when the shuttle pod launched from *The Cinnabar Mansions*— in the heart-wrenching moment when the gravity of the ship fell away from Lan Nhen, and the cozy darkness of the pod's cradle was replaced with the distant forms of the derelict ships. "Hey, cousin. Missed me?" Cuc asked.

"As much as I missed a raging fire." Lan Nhen checked her equipment a last time—the pod was basic and functional, with barely enough space for her to squeeze into the cockpit, and she'd had to stash her various cables and terminals into the nooks and crannies of a structure that hadn't been meant for more than emergency evacuation. She could have asked *The Cinnabar Mansions* for a regular transport shuttle, but the pod was smaller and more controllable; and it stood more chances of evading the derelict ward's defences.

"Hahaha," Cuc said, though she didn't sound amused. "The family found out what we were doing, by the way."

"And?" It would have devastated Lan Nhen, a few years ago; now she didn't much care. She *knew* she was doing the right thing. No filial daughter would let a member of the family rust away in a foreign cemetery—if she couldn't rescue her great-aunt, she'd at least bring the body back, for a proper funeral.

"They think we're following one of Great-great-aunt's crazy plans."

"Ha," Lan Nhen snorted. Her hands were dancing on the controls, plotting a trajectory that would get her to *The Turtle's Citadel* while leaving her the maximum thrust reserve in case of unexpected manoeuvres.

"I'm not the one coming up with crazy plans," *The Cinnabar Mansions* pointed out on the comms channel, distractedly. "I leave that to the young. Hang on—" she dropped out of sight. "I have incoming drones, child."

Of course. It was unlikely the Outsiders would leave their precious war trophies unprotected. "Where?"

A translucent overlay gradually fell over her field of vision through the pod's windshield; and points lit up all over its surface—a host of fast-moving, small crafts with contextual arrows showing basic kinematics information as well as projected trajectory cones. Lan Nhen repressed a curse. "That many? They really like their wrecked spaceships, don't they."

It wasn't a question, and neither Cuc nor *The Cinnabar Mansions* bothered to answer. "They're defence drones patrolling the perimeter. We'll walk you through," Cuc said. "Give me just a few moments to link up with Great-great-aunt's systems . . ."

Lan Nhen could imagine her cousin, lying half-prone on her bed in the lower decks of *The Cinnabar Mansions*, her face furrowed in that half-puzzled, half-focused expression that was typical of her thought processes—she'd remain that way for entire minutes, or as long as it took to find a solution. On her windshield, the squad of drones was spreading—coming straight at her from all directions, a dazzling ballet of movement meant to overwhelm her. And they would, if she didn't move fast enough.

Her fingers hovered over the pod's controls, before she made her decision and launched into a barrel manoeuvre away from the nearest incoming cluster. "Cousin, how about hurrying up?"

There was no answer from Cuc. Demons take her, this wasn't the moment to overthink the problem! Lan Nhen banked, sharply, narrowly avoiding a squad of drones, who bypassed her—and then turned around, much quicker than she'd anticipated. Ancestors, they moved fast, much too fast for ion-thrust motors. Cuc was going to have to rethink her trajectory. "Cousin, did you see this?"

"I saw." Cuc's voice was distant. "Already taken into account. Given the size of the craft, it was likely they were going to use helicoidal thrusters on those."

"This is all fascinating—" Lan Nhen wove her way through two more waves of drones, cursing wildly as shots made the pod rock around her—as long as her speed held, she'd be fine . . . She'd be fine. . . . "—but you'll have noticed I don't really much care about technology, especially not now!"

A thin thread of red appeared on her screen—a trajectory that wove and banked like a frightened fish's trail—all the way to *The Turtle's Citadel* and its clusters of pod-cradles. It looked as though it was headed straight into the heart of the cloud of drones, though that wasn't the most worrying aspect of it. "Cousin," Lan Nhen said. "I can't possibly do this—" The margin of error was null—if she slipped in one of the curves, she'd never regain the kinematics necessary to take the next.

"Only way." Cuc's voice was emotionless. "I'll update as we go, if Great-great-aunt sees an opening. But for the moment . . ."

Lan Nhen closed her eyes, for a brief moment—turned them towards Heaven, though Heaven was all around her—and whispered a prayer to her ancestors, begging them to watch over her. Then she turned her gaze to the screen, and launched into flight—her hands flying and shifting over the controls, automatically adjusting the pod's path—dancing into the heart of the drones' swarm—into them, away from them, weaving an erratic path across the section of space that separated her from *The Turtle's Citadel*. Her eyes, all the while, remained on the overlay—her fingers speeding across the controls, matching the slightest deviation of her course to the set trajectory—inflecting curves a fraction of a second before the error on her course became perceptible.

"Almost there," Cuc said—with a hint of encouragement in her voice. "Come on, cousin, you can do it—"

Ahead of her, a few measures away, was *The Turtle's Citadel*: its pod cradles had shrivelled from long atrophy, but the hangar for docking the external shuttles and pods remained, its entrance a thin line of grey across the metallic surface of the ship's lower half.

"It's closed," Lan Nhen said, breathing hard—she was coming fast, much too fast, scattering drones out of her way like scared mice, and if the hangar wasn't opened . . . "Cousin!"

Cuc's voice seemed to come from very far away; distant and muted somehow on the comms system. "We've discussed this. Normally, the ship went into emergency standby when it was hit, and it should open—"

"But what if it doesn't?" Lan Nhen asked—the ship was looming over her, spreading to cover her entire windshield, close enough so she could count the pod cradles, could see their pockmarked surfaces—could imagine how much of a messy impact she'd make, if her own pod crashed on an unyielding surface.

Cuc didn't answer. She didn't need to; they both knew what would happen if that turned out to be true. Ancestors, watch over me, Lan Nhen thought, over and over, as the hangar doors rushed towards her, still closed—ancestors watch over me . . .

She was close enough to see the fine layers of engravings on the doors when they opened—the expanse of metal flowing away from the centre, to reveal a gaping hole just large enough to let a small craft through. Her own pod squeezed into the available space: darkness fell over her cockpit as the doors flowed shut, and the pod skidded to a halt, jerking her body like a disarticulated doll.

It was a while before she could stop shaking for long enough to unstrap herself from the pod; and to take her first, tentative steps on the ship.

The small lamp in her suit lit nothing but a vast, roiling mass of shadows: the hangar was huge enough to hold much larger ships. Thirty years ago, it had no doubt been full, but the Outsiders must have removed them all as they dragged the wreck out there.

"I'm in," she whispered; and set out through the darkness, to find the heartroom and the Mind that was her great-aunt.

"I'm sorry," Jason said to Catherine. "Your first choice of posting was declined by the Board."

Catherine sat very straight in her chair, trying to ignore how uncomfortable she felt in her suit—it gaped too large over her chest, flared too much at her hips, and she'd had to hastily readjust the trouser-legs after she and Johanna discovered the seamstress had got the length wrong. "I see," she said, because there was nothing else she could say, really.

Jason looked at his desk, his gaze boring into the metal as if he could summon an assignment out of nothing—she knew he meant well, that he had probably volunteered to tell her this himself, instead of leaving it for some stranger who wouldn't care a jot for her—but in that moment, she didn't want to be reminded that he worked for the Board for the Protection of Dai Viet Refugees; that he'd had a hand, no matter how small, in denying her wishes for the future.

At length Jason said, slowly, carefully—reciting a speech he'd no doubt given a dozen times that day, "The government puts the greatest care into choosing postings for the refugees. It was felt that that putting you onboard a space station would be—unproductive."

Unproductive. Catherine kept smiling; kept her mask plastered on, even though it hurt to turn the corners of her mouth upwards, to crinkle her eyes as if she were pleased. "I see," she said, again, knowing anything else was useless. "Thanks, Jason."

Jason coloured. "I tried arguing your case, but . . ."

"I know," Catherine said. He was a clerk; that was all; a young civil servant at the bottom of the Board's hierarchy, and he couldn't possibly get her what she wanted, even if he'd been willing to favour her. And it hadn't been such a surprise, anyway. After Mary and Olivia and Johanna . . .

"Look," Jason said. "Let's see each other tonight, right? I'll take you some-place you can forget all about this."

"You know it's not that simple," Catherine said. As if a restaurant, or a wild waterfall ride, or whatever delight Jason had in mind could make her forget this.

"No, but I can't do anything about the Board." Jason's voice was firm. "I can, however, make sure that you have a good time tonight."

Catherine forced a smile she didn't feel. "I'll keep it in mind. Thanks."

As she exited the building, passing under the wide arches, the sun sparkled on the glass windows—and for a brief moment she wasn't herself—she was staring at starlight reflected in a glass panel, watching an older woman running hands on a wall and smiling at her with gut-wrenching sadness . . . She blinked, and the moment was gone; though the sense of sadness, of unease remained, as if she were missing something essential.

Johanna was waiting for her on the steps, her arms crossed in front of her, and a gaze that looked as though it would bore holes into the lawn.

"What did they tell you?"

Catherine shrugged, wondering how a simple gesture could cost so much. "The same they told you, I'd imagine. Unproductive."

They'd all applied to the same postings—all asked for something related to space, whether it was one of the observatories, a space station; or, in Johanna's case, outright asking to board a slow-ship as crew. They'd all been denied, for variations of the same reason.

"What did you get?" Johanna asked. Her own rumpled slip of paper had already been recycled at the nearest terminal; she was heading north, to Steele, where she'd join an archaeological dig.

Catherine shrugged, with a casualness she didn't feel. They'd always felt at ease under the stars—had always yearned to take to space, felt the same craving to be closer to their home planets—to hang, weightless and without ties, in a place where they wouldn't be weighed, wouldn't be judged for falling short of values that ultimately didn't belong to them. "I got newswriter."

"At least you're not moving very far," Johanna said, a tad resentfully.

"No." The offices of the network company were a mere two streets away from the Institution.

"I bet Jason had a hand in your posting," Johanna said.

"He didn't say anything about that—"

"Of course he wouldn't." Johanna snorted, gently. She didn't much care for Jason; but she knew how much his company meant to Catherine—how much more it would come to mean, if the weight of an entire continent separated Catherine and her. "Jason broadcasts his failures because they bother him; you'll hardly ever hear him talk of his successes. He'd feel too much like boasting." Her face changed, softened. "He cares for you, you know—truly. You have the best luck in the world."

"I know," Catherine said—thinking of the touch of his lips on hers; of his arms, holding her close until she felt whole, fulfilled. "I know."

The best luck in the world—she and Jason and her new flat, and her old haunts, not far away from the Institution—though she wasn't sure, really, if that last was a blessing—if she wanted to remember the years Matron had spent hammering proper behaviour into them: the deprivations whenever they spoke anything less than perfect Galactic, the hours spent cleaning the dormitory's toilets for expressing mild revulsion at the food; or the night they'd spent shut outside, naked, in the growing cold, because they couldn't remember which Galactic president had colonised Longevity Station—how Matron had found them all huddled against each other, in an effort to keep warm and awake, and had sent them to Discipline for a further five hours, scolding them for behaving like wild animals.

Catherine dug her nails into the palms of her hands—letting the pain anchor her back to the present; to where she sat on the steps of the Board's central offices, away from the Institution and all it meant to them.

"We're free," she said, at last. "That's all that matters."

"We'll never be free." Johanna's tone was dark, intense. "Your records have a mark that says 'Institution.' And even if it didn't—do you honestly believe we would blend right in?"

There was no one quite like them on Prime, where Dai Viet were unwelcome; not with those eyes, not with that skin colour—not with that demeanour, which even years of Institution hadn't been enough to erase.

"Do you ever wonder . . ." Johanna's voice trailed off into silence, as if she were contemplating something too large to put into words.

"Wonder what?" Catherine asked.

Johanna bit her lip. "Do you ever wonder what it would have been like, with our parents? Our real parents."

The parents they couldn't remember. They'd done the maths, too—no children at the Institution could remember anything before coming there. Matron had said it was because they were really young when they were taken away—that it had been for the best. Johanna, of course, had blamed something more sinister, some fix-up done by the Institution to its wards to keep them docile.

Catherine thought, for a moment, of a life among the Dai Viet—an idyllic image of a harmonious family like in the holo-movies—a mirage that dashed itself to pieces against the inescapable reality of the birth vid. "They'd have used us like brood mares," Catherine said. "You saw—"

"I know what I saw," Johanna snapped. "But maybe . . ." Her face was pale. "Maybe it wouldn't have been so bad, in return for the rest."

For being loved; for being made worthy; for fitting in, being able to stare at the stars without wondering which was their home—without dreaming of when they might go back to their families.

Catherine rubbed her belly, thinking of the vid—and the *thing* crawling out of the woman's belly, all metal edges and shining crystal, coated in the blood of its mother—and, for a moment she felt as though she were the woman—floating above her body, detached from her cloak of flesh, watching herself give birth in pain. And then the sensation ended, but she was still feeling spread out, larger than she ought to have been—looking at herself from a distance and watching her own life pass her by, petty and meaningless, and utterly bounded from end to end.

Maybe Johanna was right. Maybe it wouldn't have been so bad, after all.

The ship was smaller than Lan Nhen had expected—she'd been going by her experience with *The Cinnabar Mansions*, which was an older generation, but *The Turtle's Citadel* was much smaller for the same functionalities.

Lan Nhen went up from the hangar to the living quarters, her equipment slung over her shoulders. She'd expected a sophisticated defence system like the drones, but there was nothing. Just the familiar slimy feeling of a quickened ship on the walls, a sign that the Mind that it hosted was still alive—albeit barely. The walls were bare, instead of the elaborate decoration Lan Nhen was used to from *The Cinnabar Mansions*—no scrolling calligraphy, no flowing paintings of starscapes or flowers; no ambient sound of zither or anything to enliven the silence.

She didn't have much time to waste—Cuc had said they had two hours between the moment the perimeter defences kicked in, and the moment more hefty safeguards were manually activated—but she couldn't help herself: she looked into one of the living quarters. It was empty as well, its walls scored with gunfire. The only colour in the room was a few splatters of dried blood on a chair, a reminder of the tragedy of the ship's fall—the execution of its occupants, the dragging of its wreck to the derelict ward—dried blood, and a single holo of a woman on a table, a beloved mother or grandmother: a bare, abandoned picture with no offerings or incense, all that remained from a wrecked ancestral altar. Lan Nhen spat on the ground, to ward off evil ghosts, and went back to the corridors.

She truly felt as though she were within a mausoleum—like that one time her elder sister had dared her and Cuc to spend the night within the family's ancestral shrine, and they'd barely slept—not because of monsters or anything, but because of the vast silence that permeated the whole place amidst the smell of incense and funeral offerings, reminding them that they, too, were mortal.

That Minds, too, could die—that rescues were useless—no, she couldn't afford to think like that. She had Cuc with her, and together they would . . .

She hadn't heard Cuc for a while.

She stopped, when she realised—that it wasn't only the silence on the ship, but also the deathly quiet of her own comms system. Since—since she'd entered *The Turtle's Citadel*—that was the last time she'd heard her cousin, calmly pointing out about emergency standby and hangar doors and how everything was going to work out, in the end . . .

She checked her comms. There appeared to be nothing wrong; but whichever frequency she selected, she could hear nothing but static. At last, she managed to find one slot that seemed less crowded than others. "Cousin? Can you hear me?"

Noise on the line. "Very—badly." Cuc's voice was barely recognisable. "There—is—something—interference—"

"I know," Lan Nhen said. "Every channel is filled with noise."

Cuc didn't answer for a while; and when she did, her voice seemed to have become more distant—a problem had her interest again. "Not—noise. They're broadcasting—data. Need—to . . ." And then the comms cut. Lan Nhen tried all frequencies, trying to find one that would be less noisy; but there was nothing. She bit down a curse—she had no doubt Cuc would find a way around whatever blockage the Outsiders had put on the ship, but this was downright bizarre. Why broadcast data? Cutting down the comms of prospective attackers somehow didn't seem significant enough—at least not compared to defence drones or similar mechanisms.

She walked through the corridors, following the spiral path to the heart-room—nothing but the static in her ears, a throbbing song that erased every coherent thought from her mind—at least it was better than the silence, than that feeling of moving underwater in an abandoned city—that feeling that she was too late, that her great-aunt was already dead and past recovery, that all she could do here was kill her once and for all, end her misery . . .

She thought, incongruously, of a vid she'd seen, which showed her great-grandmother ensconced in the heartroom—in the first few years of *The Turtle's Citadel*'s life, those crucial moments of childhood when the ship's mother remained onboard to guide the Mind to adulthood. Great-grandmother was telling stories to the ship—and *The Turtle's Citadel* was struggling to mimic the spoken words in scrolling texts on her walls, laughing delightedly whenever she succeeded—all sweet and young, unaware of what her existence would come to, in the end.

Unlike the rest of the ship, the heartroom was crowded—packed with Outsider equipment that crawled over the Mind's resting place in the centre, covering her from end to end until Lan Nhen could barely see the glint of metal underneath. She gave the entire contraption a wide berth—the spikes and protrusions from the original ship poked at odd angles, glistening with a dark liquid she couldn't quite identify—and the Outsider equipment piled atop the Mind, a mass of cables and unfamiliar machines, looked as though it was going to take a while to sort out.

There were screens all around, showing dozens of graphs and diagrams, shifting as they tracked variables that Lan Nhen couldn't guess at—vital signs, it looked like, though she wouldn't have been able to tell what.

Lan Nhen bowed in the direction of the Mind, from younger to elder—perfunctorily, since she was unsure whether the Mind could see her at all. There was no acknowledgement, either verbal or otherwise.

Her great-aunt was in there. She had to be.

"Cousin." Cuc's voice was back in her ears—crisp and clear and uncommonly worried.

"How come I can hear you?" Lan Nhen asked. "Because I'm in the heartroom?"

Cuc snorted. "Hardly. The heartroom is where all the data is streaming from. I've merely found a way to filter the transmissions on both ends. Fascinating problem . . ."

"Is this really the moment?" Lan Nhen asked. "I need you to walk me through the reanimation—"

"No you don't," Cuc said. "First you need to hear what I have to say."

The call came during the night: a man in the uniform of the Board asked for Catherine George—as if he couldn't tell that it was her, that she was standing dishevelled and pale in front of her screen at three in the morning. "Yes, it's me," Catherine said. She fought off the weight of nightmares—more and more, she was waking in the night with memories of blood splattered across her entire body; of stars collapsing while she watched, powerless—of a crunch, and a moment where she hung alone in darkness, knowing that she had been struck a death blow—

The man's voice was quiet, emotionless. There had been an accident in Steele; a regrettable occurrence that hadn't been meant to happen, and the Board would have liked to extend its condolences to her—they apologised for calling so late, but they thought she should know . . .

"I see," Catherine said. She kept herself uncomfortably straight—aware of the last time she'd faced the Board—when Jason had told her her desire for space would have been unproductive. When they'd told Johanna . . .

Johanna.

After a while, the man's words slid past her like water on glass—hollow reassurances, empty condolences, whereas she stood as if her heart had been torn away from her, fighting a desire to weep, to retch—she wanted to turn back time, to go back to the previous week and the sprigs of apricot flowers Jason had given her with a shy smile—to breathe in the sharp, tangy flavour of the lemon cake he'd baked for her, see again the carefully blank expression on his face as he waited to see if she'd like it—she wanted to be held tight in his arms and told that it was fine, that everything was going to be fine, that Johanna was going to be fine.

"We're calling her other friends," the man was saying, "but since you were close to each other . . ."

"I see," Catherine said—of course he didn't understand the irony, that it was the answer she'd given the Board—Jason—the last time.

The man cut off the communication; and she was left alone, standing in her living room and fighting back the feeling that threatened to overwhelm her—a not-entirely unfamiliar sensation of dislocation in her belly, the awareness that she didn't belong here among the Galactics; that she wasn't there by choice, and couldn't leave; that her own life should have been larger, more fulfilling than this slow death by inches, writing copy for feeds without any acknowledgement of her contributions—that Johanna's life should have been larger . . .

Her screen was still blinking—an earlier message from the Board that she hadn't seen? But why—

Her hands, fumbling away in the darkness, made the command to retrieve the message—the screen faded briefly to black while the message was decompressed, and then she was staring at Johanna's face.

For a moment—a timeless, painful moment—Catherine thought with relief that it had been a mistake, that Johanna was alive after all; and then she realised how foolish she'd been—that it wasn't a call, but merely a message from beyond the grave.

Johanna's face was pale, so pale Catherine wanted to hug her, to tell her the old lie that things were going to be fine—but she'd never get to say those words now, not ever.

"I'm sorry, Catherine," she said. Her voice was shaking; and the circles under her eyes took up half of her face, turning her into some pale nightmare from horror movies—a ghost, a restless soul, a ghoul hungry for human flesh. "I can't do this, not anymore. The Institution was fine; but it's got worse. I wake up at night, and feel sick—as if everything good has been leeched from the world—as if the food had no taste, as if I drifted like a ghost through my days, as if my entire life held no meaning or truth. Whatever they did to our memories in the Institution—it's breaking down now. It's tearing me apart. I'm sorry, but I can't take any more of this. I—" she looked away from the camera for a brief moment, and then back at Catherine. "I have to go."

"No," Catherine whispered, but she couldn't change it. She couldn't do anything.

"You were always the strongest of us," Johanna said. "Please remember this. Please. Catherine." And then the camera cut, and silence spread through the room, heavy and unbearable, and Catherine felt like weeping, though she had no tears left.

"Catherine?" Jason called in a sleepy voice from the bedroom. "It's too early to check your work inbox . . ."

Work. Love. Meaningless, Johanna had said. Catherine walked to the huge window pane, and stared at the city spread out below her—the mighty Prime, centre of the Galactic Federation, its buildings shrouded in light, its streets crisscrossed by floaters; with the bulky shape of the Parliament at the centre, a proud statement that the Galactic Federation still controlled most of their home galaxy.

Too many lights to see the stars; but she could still guess; could still feel their pull—could still remember that one of them was her home.

A lie, Johanna had said. A construction to keep us here.

"Catherine?" Jason stood behind her, one hand wrapped around her shoulder—awkwardly tender as always, like that day when he'd offered to share a flat, standing balanced on one foot and not looking at her.

"Johanna is dead. She killed herself."

She felt rather than saw him freeze—and, after a while, he said in a changed voice, "I'm so sorry. I know how much she meant . . ." His voice trailed off, and he too, fell silent, watching the city underneath.

There was a feeling—the same feeling she'd had when waking up as a child, a diffuse sense that something was not quite right with the world; that the shadows held men watching, waiting for the best time to snatch her; that she was not wholly back in her body—that Jason's hand on her shoulder was just the touch of a ghost, that even his love wasn't enough to keep her safe. That the world was fracturing around her, time and time again—she breathed in, hoping to dispel the sensation. Surely it was nothing more than grief, than fatigue—but the sensation wouldn't go away, leaving her on the verge of nausea.

"You should have killed us," Catherine said. "It would have been kinder."

"Killed you?" Jason sounded genuinely shocked.

"When you took us from our parents."

Jason was silent for a while. Then: "We don't kill. What do you think we are, monsters from the fairytales, killing and burning everyone who looks different? Of course we're not like that." Jason no longer sounded uncertain or awkward; it was as if she'd touched some wellspring, scratched some skin to find only primal reflexes underneath.

"You erased our memories." She didn't make any effort to keep the bitterness from her voice.

"We had to." Jason shook his head. "They'd have killed you, otherwise. You know this."

"How can I trust you?" Look at Johanna, she wanted to say. Look at me. How can you say it was all worth it?

"Catherine . . ." Jason's voice was weary. "We've been over this before. You've seen the vids from the early days. We didn't set out to steal your childhood, or anyone's childhood. But when you were left—intact . . . accidents happened. Carelessness. Like Johanna."

"Like Johanna." Her voice was shaking now; but he didn't move, didn't do anything to comfort her or hold her close. She turned at last, to stare into his face; and saw him transfixed by light, by faith, his gaze turned away from her and every pore of his being permeated by the utter conviction that he was right, that they were all right and that a stolen childhood was a small price to pay to be a Galactic.

"Anything would do." Jason's voice was slow, quiet—explaining life to a child, a script they'd gone over and over in their years together, always coming back to the same enormous, inexcusable choice that had been made for them. "Scissors, knives, broken bottles. You sliced your veins, hanged yourselves, pumped yourselves full of drugs . . . We had to . . . we had to block your memories, to make you blank slates."

"Had to." She was shaking now; and still he didn't see. Still she couldn't make him see.

"I swear to you, Catherine. It was the only way."

And she knew, she'd always known he was telling the truth—not because he was right, but because he genuinely could not envision any other future for them.

"I see," she said. The nausea, the sense of dislocation, wouldn't leave her—disgust for him, for this life that trapped her, for everything she'd turned into or been turned into. "I see."

"Do you think I like it?" His voice was bitter. "Do you think it makes me sleep better at night? Every day I hate that choice, even though I wasn't the one who made it. Every day I wonder if there was something else the Board could have done, some other solution that wouldn't have robbed you of everything you were."

"Not everything," Catherine said—slowly, carefully. "We still look Dai Viet."

Jason grimaced, looking ill at ease. "That's your *body*, Catherine. Of course they weren't going to steal that."

Of course; and suddenly, seeing how uneasy he was, it occurred to Catherine that they could have changed that, too, just as easily as they'd tampered with her memories; made her skin clearer, her eyes less distinctive; could have helped her fit into Galactic society. But they hadn't. Holding the strings to the last, Johanna would have said. "You draw the line at my body, but stealing my memories is fine?"

Jason sighed; he turned towards the window, looking at the streets. "No, it's not, and I'm sorry. But how else were we supposed to keep you alive?"

"Perhaps we didn't want to be alive."

"Don't say that, please." His voice had changed, had become fearful, protective. "Catherine. Everyone deserves to live. You especially."

Perhaps I don't, she thought, but he was holding her close to him, not letting her go—her anchor to the flat—to the living room, to life. "You're not Johanna," he said. "You know that."

The strongest of us, Johanna had said. She didn't feel strong; just frail and adrift. "No," she said, at last. "Of course I'm not."

"Come on," Jason said. "Let me make you a tisane. We'll talk in the kitchen—you look as though you need it."

"No." And she looked up—sought out his lips in the darkness, drinking in his breath and his warmth to fill the emptiness within her. "That's not what I need."

"Are you sure?" Jason looked uncertain—sweet and innocent and naïve, everything that had drawn her to him. "You're not in a state to—"

"Ssh," she said, and laid a hand on his lips, where she'd kissed him. "Ssh."

Later, after they'd made love, she lay her head in the hollow of his arm, listening to the slow beat of his heart like a lifeline; and wondered how long she'd be able to keep the emptiness at bay.

"It goes to Prime," Cuc said. "All the data is beamed to Prime, and it's coming from almost every ship in the ward."

"I don't understand," Lan Nhen said. She'd plugged her own equipment into the ship, carefully shifting the terminals she couldn't make sense of— hadn't dared to go closer to the centre, where Outsider technology had crawled all over her great-aunt's resting place, obscuring the Mind and the mass of connectors that linked her to the ship.

On one of the screens, a screensaver had launched: night on a planet Lan Nhen couldn't recognise—an Outsider one, with their sleek floaters and their swarms of helper bots, their wide, impersonal streets planted with trees that were too tall and too perfect to be anything but the product of years of breeding.

"She's not here," Cuc said.

"I—" Lan Nhen was about to say she didn't understand, and then the true import of Cuc's words hit her. "Not here? She's alive, Cuc. I can see the ship; I can hear her all around me . . ."

"Yes, yes," Cuc said, a tad impatiently. "But that's . . . the equivalent of unconscious processes, like breathing in your sleep."

"She's dreaming?"

"No," Cuc said. A pause, then, very carefully: "I think she's on Prime, Cousin. The data that's being broadcast—it looks like Mind thought-processes, compressed with a high rate and all mixed together. There's probably something on the other end that decompresses the data and sends it to . . . Arg, I don't know! Wherever they think is appropriate."

Lan Nhen bit back another admission of ignorance, and fell back on the commonplace. "On Prime." The enormity of the thing; that you could take a Mind—a beloved ship with a family of her own—that you could put her to sleep and cause her to wake up somewhere else, on an unfamiliar planet and an alien culture—that you could just transplant her like a flower or a tree . . . "She's on Prime."

"In a terminal or as the power source for something," Cuc said, darkly.

"Why would they bother?" Lan Nhen asked. "It's a lot of power expenditure just to get an extra computer."

"Do I look as though I have insight into Outsiders?" Lan Nhen could imagine Cuc throwing her hands up in the air, in that oft-practised gesture. "I'm just telling you what I have, Cousin."

Outsiders—the Galactic Federation of United Planets—were barely comprehensible in any case. They were the descendants of an Exodus fleet that had hit an isolated galaxy: left to themselves and isolated for decades, they had turned on each other in huge ethnic cleansings before emerging from their home planets as relentless competitors for resources and inhabitable planets.

"Fine. Fine." Lan Nhen breathed in, slowly; tried to focus on the problem at hand. "Can you walk me through cutting the radio broadcast?"

Cuc snorted. "I'd fix the ship, first, if I were you."

Lan Nhen knelt by the equipment, and stared at a cable that had curled around one of the ship's spines. "Fine, let's start with what we came for. Can you see?"

Silence; and then a life-sized holo of Cuc hovered in front of her—even though the avatar was little more than broad strokes, great-great-aunt had still managed to render it in enough details to make it unmistakably Cuc. "Cute," Lan Nhen said.

"Hahaha," Cuc said. "No bandwidth for trivialities—gotta save for detail on your end." She raised a hand, pointed to one of the outermost screens on the edge of the room. "Disconnect this one first."

It was slow, and painful. Cuc pointed; and Lan Nhen checked before disconnecting and moving. Twice, she jammed her fingers very close to a cable, and felt electricity crackle near her—entirely too close for comfort.

They moved from the outskirts of the room to the centre—tackling the huge mound of equipment last. Cuc's first attempts resulted in a cable coming loose with an ominous sound; they waited, but nothing happened. "We might have fried something," Lan Nhen said.

"Too bad. There's no time for being cautious, as you well know. There's . . . maybe half an hour left before the other defences go live." Cuc moved again, pointed to another squat terminal. "This goes off."

When they were finished, Lan Nhen stepped back, to look at their handiwork.

The heartroom was back to its former glory: instead of Outsider equipment, the familiar protrusions and sharp organic needles of the Mind's resting place; and they could see the Mind herself—resting snug in her cradle, wrapped around the controls of the ship—her myriad arms each seizing one rack of connectors; her huge head glinting in the light—a vague globe shape covered with glistening cables and veins. The burn mark from the Outsider attack was clearly visible, a dark, elongated shape on the edge of her head that had bruised a couple of veins—it had hit one of the connectors as well, burnt it right down to the colour of ink.

Lan Nhen let out a breath she hadn't been aware of holding. "It scrambled the connector."

"And scarred her, but didn't kill her," Cuc said. "Just like you said."

"Yes, but—" But it was one thing to run simulations of the attack over and over, always getting the same prognosis; and quite another to see that the simulations held true, and that the damage was repairable.

"There should be another connector rack in your bag," Cuc said. "I'll walk you through slotting it in."

After she was done, Lan Nhen took a step back; and stared at her great-aunt—feeling, in some odd way, as though she were violating the Mind's privacy. A Mind's heartroom was their stronghold, a place where they could twist reality as they wished, and appear as they wished to. To see her great-aunt like this, without any kind of appearance change or pretence, was . . . more disturbing than she'd thought.

"And now?" she asked Cuc.

Even without details, Lan Nhen knew her cousin was smiling. "Now we pray to our ancestors that cutting the broadcast is going to be enough to get her back."

Another night on Prime, and Catherine wakes up breathless, in the grip of another nightmare—images of red lights, and scrolling texts, and a feeling of growing cold in her bones, a cold so deep she cannot believe she will ever feel warm no matter how many layers she's put on.

Johanna is not there; beside her, Jason sleeps, snoring softly; and she's suddenly seized by nausea, remembering what he said to her—how casually he spoke of blocking her memories, of giving a home to her after stealing her original one from her. She waits for it to pass; waits to settle into her old life as usual. But it doesn't.

Instead, she rises, walks towards the window, and stands watching Prime—the clean wide streets, the perfect trees, the ballet of floaters at night—

the myriad dances that make up the society that constrains her from dawn to dusk and beyond—she wonders what Johanna would say, but of course Johanna won't ever say anything anymore. Johanna has gone ahead, into the dark.

The feeling of nausea in her belly will not go away: instead it spreads, until her body feels like a cage—at first, she thinks the sensation is in her belly, but it moves upwards, until her limbs, too, feel too heavy and too small—until it's an effort to move any part of her. She raises her hands, struggling against a feeling of moving appendages that don't belong to her—and traces the contours of her face, looking for familiar shapes, for anything that will anchor her to reality. The heaviness spreads, compresses her chest until she can hardly breathe—cracks her ribs and pins her legs to the ground. Her head spins, as if she were about to faint; but the mercy of blackness does not come to her.

"Catherine," she whispers. "My name is Catherine."

Another name, unbidden, rises to her lips. *Mi Chau.* A name she gave to herself in the Viet language—in the split instant before the lasers took her apart, before she sank into darkness: Mi Chau, the princess who unwittingly betrayed her father and her people, and whose blood became the pearls at the bottom of the sea. She tastes it on her tongue, and it's the only thing that seems to belong to her anymore.

She remembers that first time—waking up on Prime in a strange body, struggling to breathe, struggling to make sense of being so small, so far away from the stars that had guided her through space—remembers walking like a ghost through the corridors of the Institution, until the knowledge of what the Galactics had done broke her, and she cut her veins in a bathroom, watching blood lazily pool at her feet and thinking only of escape. She remembers the second time she woke up; the second, oblivious life as Catherine.

Johanna. Johanna didn't survive her second life; and even now is starting her third, somewhere in the bowels of the Institution—a dark-skinned child indistinguishable from other dark-skinned children, with no memories of anything beyond a confused jumble . . .

Outside, the lights haven't dimmed, but there are stars—brash and alien, hovering above Prime, in configurations that look *wrong*; and she remembers, suddenly, how they lay around her, how they showed her the way from planet to planet—how the cold of the deep spaces seized her just as she entered them to travel faster, just like it's holding her now, seizing her bones—remembers how much larger, how much wider she ought to be . . .

There are stars everywhere; and superimposed on them, the faces of two Dai Viet women, calling her over and over. Calling her back, into the body that belonged to her all along; into the arms of her family.

"Come on, come on," the women whisper, and their voices are stronger than any other noise; than Jason's breath in the bedroom; than the motors of the floaters or the vague smell of garlic from the kitchen. "Come on, great-aunt!"

She is more than this body; more than this constrained life—her thoughts spread out, encompassing hangars and living quarters; and the liquid weight of pods held in their cradles—she remembers family reunions, entire generations of children putting their hands on her corridors, remembers the touch of their skin on her metal walls; the sound of their laughter as they raced each other; the quiet chatter of their mothers in the heartroom, keeping her company as the New Year began; and the touch of a brush on her outer hull, drawing the shape of an apricot flower, for good luck . . .

"Catherine?" Jason calls behind her.

She turns, through sheer effort of will; finding, somehow, the strength to maintain her consciousness in a small and crammed body alongside her other, vaster one. He's standing with one hand on the doorjamb, staring at her—his face pale, leeched of colours in the starlight.

"I remember," she whispers.

His hands stretch, beseeching. "Catherine, please. Don't leave."

He means well, she knows. All the things that he hid from her, he hid out of love; to keep her alive and happy, to hold her close in spite of all that should have separated them; and even now, the thought of his love is a barb in her heart, a last lingering regret, slight and pitiful against the flood of her memories—but not wholly insignificant.

Where she goes, she'll never be alone—not in the way she was with Jason, feeling that nothing else but her mattered in the entire world. She'll have a family; a gaggle of children and aunts and uncles waiting on her, but nothing like the sweet, unspoiled privacy where Jason and she could share anything and everything. She won't have another lover like him—naïve and frank and so terribly sure of what he wants and what he's ready to do to get it. Dai Viet society has no place for people like Jason—who do not know their place, who do not know how to be humble, how to accept failure or how to bow down to expediency.

Where she goes, she'll never be alone; and yet she'll be so terribly lonely.

"Please," Jason says.

"I'm sorry," she says. "I'll come back—" a promise made to him; to Johanna, who cannot hear or recognise her anymore. Her entire being spreads out, thins like water thrown on the fire—and, in that last moment, she finds herself reaching out for him, trying to touch him one last time, to catch one last glimpse of his face, even as a heart she didn't know she had breaks.

"Catherine."

He whispers her name, weeping, over and over; and it's that name, that lie that still clings to her with its bittersweet memories, that she takes with her as her entire being unfolds—as she flies away, towards the waiting stars.

NEBULA AWARD NOMINEE
BEST NOVELETTE

# "PARANORMAL ROMANCE"

## CHRISTOPHER BARZAK

*Christopher Barzak's fiction has previously been nominated for three Nebulas and two James Tiptree, Jr. Awards and has won the Shirley Jackson Award, the Spectrum Award, and the Crawford Award. "Paranormal Romance" appeared in* Lightspeed.

This is a story about a witch. Not the kind you're thinking of either. She didn't have a long nose with a wart on it. She didn't have green skin or long black hair. She didn't wear a pointed hat or a cape, and she didn't have a cat, a spider, a rat, or any of those animals that are usually hanging around witches. She didn't live in a ramshackle house, a gingerbread house, a Victorian house, or a cave. And she didn't have any sisters. This witch wasn't the kind you read about in fairytales and in plays by Shakespeare. This witch lived in a red brick bungalow that had been turned into an upstairs/downstairs apartment house on an old industrial street that had lost all of its industry in Cleveland, Ohio. The apartment house had two other people living in it: a young gay couple who were terribly in love with one another. The couple had a dog, an incredibly happy-faced Eskimo they'd named Snowman, but the witch never spoke to it, even though she could. She didn't like dogs, but she did like the gay couple. She tried not to hold their pet against them.

The witch—her name was Sheila—specialized in love magic. She didn't like curses. Curses were all about hate and—occasionally—vengeance, and Sheila had long ago decided that she'd spend her time productively, rather than wasting energy on dealing with perceived injustices located in her—or someone else's—past. Years ago, when she was in college, she had dabbled in curses, but they were mainly favors the girls in her dorm asked of her, usually after a boyfriend dumped them, cheated on them, used them as a means for money and mobility, or some other power or shame thing. A curse always sounded nice to them. Fast and dirty justice. Sheila sometimes helped them, but soon she grew tired of the knocks on her door in the middle of the night, grew annoyed after opening the door to find a teary-eyed girl just back from a frat party with blood boiling so hard that the skin on her face seemed to roil. Eventually Sheila started closing the door on their tear-stained faces, and after a while the girls stopped bothering her for curses. Instead, they started coming to her for love charms.

The gay couple who lived in the downstairs rooms of the apartment house were named Trent and Gary. They'd been together for nearly two years, but had only lived together for the past ten months. Their love was still fresh. Sheila could smell it whenever she stopped in to visit them on weekends, when Trent and Gary could be found on the back deck, barbequing and drinking glasses of red wine. They could make ordinary things like cooking out feel magical because of the sheer completeness they exuded, like a fine sparking mist, when they were near each other. That was pure early love, in Sheila's assessment, and she sipped at it from the edges.

Trent was the manager of a small software company and Gary worked at an environmental nonprofit. They'd met in college ten years ago, but had circled around each other at the time. They'd shared a Venn diagram of friends, but naturally some of them didn't like each other. Their mutual friends spent a lot of time telling Trent about how much they hated Gary's friends, or telling Gary about how much they hated Trent's. Because of this, for years, Trent and Gary had kept a safe distance from each other, assuming that they would also hate each other. Which was probably a good thing, they said now, nodding in accord on the back deck of the red brick bungalow, where Trent turned shish kabobs on the grill and Gary poured Sheila another glass of wine.

"Why was it probably a good thing you assumed you'd hate each other?" Sheila asked.

"Because," Gary said as he spilled wine into Sheila's glass, "we were so young and stupid back then."

"Also kind of bitchy," Trent added over his shoulder.

"We would have hurt each other," said Gary, "before we knew what we had to lose."

Sheila blushed at this open display of emotion and Gary laughed. "Look at you!" he said, pointing a finger and turning to look over his shoulder at Trent. "Trent," he said, "Look. We've embarrassed Sheila."

Trent laughed, too, and Sheila rolled her eyes. "I'm not embarrassed, you jerks," she said. "I know what love is. People pay me to help them find it or make it. It's just that, with you two—I don't know—there's something special about your love."

Trent turned a kabob with his tongs and said, "Maybe it's because we didn't need you to make it happen."

It was quite possible that Trent's theory had some kind of truth to it, but whatever the reason, Sheila didn't care. She just wanted to sit with them and drink wine and watch the lightning bugs blink in the backyard on a mid-summer evening in Cleveland.

It was a good night. The shish kabobs were spiced with dill and lemon. The wine was a middlebrow Syrah. Trent and Gary always provided good thirty-somethings conversation. Listening to the two of them, Sheila felt like she understood much of what she would have gleaned from reading a newspaper or an intelligent magazine. For the past three months, she'd simply begun to rely on them to relay the goings-on of the world to her, and to supply her with these evenings where, for a small moment in time, she could feel normal.

In the center of the deck several scraps of wood burned in a fire pit, throwing shadows and orange light over their faces as smoke climbed into the darkening sky. Trent swirled his glass of wine before taking the last sip, then stood and slid the back door open so he could go inside to retrieve a fresh bottle.

"That sounds terrible," Sheila was saying as Trent left. Gary had been complaining about natural gas companies coming into Ohio to frack for gas deposits beneath the shale, and how his nonprofit was about to hold a forum on the dangers of the process. But before Sheila could say another word, her cell phone rang. "One second," she said, holding up a finger as she looked at the screen. "It's my mom. I've got to take this."

Sheila pressed the answer button. "Hey, Mom," she said. "What's up?"

"Where are you?" her mother asked, blunt as a bludgeoning weapon as usual.

"I'm having a glass of wine with the boys," Sheila said. Right then, Trent returned, twisting the cork out of the new bottle as he attempted to slide the back door shut with his foot. Sheila furrowed her brows and shook her head at him. "Is there something you need, Mom?" she asked.

Before her mother could answer, though, and before Trent could slide the door shut, the dog Sheila disliked in the way that she disliked all dogs—without any particular hatred for the individual, just the species—darted out the open door and raced past Sheila's legs, down the deck steps, into the bushes at the bottom of the backyard.

"Hey!" Gary said, rising from his chair, nearly spilling his wine. He looked out at the dog, a white furry thing with an impossibly red tongue hanging out of its permanently smiling face, and then placed his glass on the deck railing before heading down the stairs. "Snowman!" he called. "Get back here!"

"Oh, Christ," Trent said, one foot still held against the sliding door he hadn't shut in time. "That dog is going to be the death of me."

"What's going on over there?" Sheila's mother asked. Her voice was loud and drawn out, as if she were speaking to someone hard of hearing.

"Dog escaped," said Sheila. "Hold on a second, Mom."

Sheila held the phone against her chest and said, "Guys, I've got to go. Gary, I hope your forum goes well. Snowman, stop being so bad!" Then she edged through the door Trent still held open, crossed through their kitchen and living room to the front foyer they shared, and took the steps up to her second floor apartment.

"Sorry about that," she said when she sat down at her kitchen table.

"Why do you continue living there, Sheila?" her mother said. Sheila could hear steam hissing off her mother's voice, flat as an iron. "Why," her mother said, "do you continue to live with this illusion of having a full life, my daughter?"

"Ma," Sheila said. "What are you talking about now?"

"*The boys*," said her mother. "You're always with *the boys*. But those boys like each other, Sheila, not you. You should find other boys. Boys who like girls. When are you going to grow up, make your own life? Don't you want children?"

"I have a life," said Sheila, evenly, as she might speak to a demanding child.

"And I don't want children." She could have also told her mother that she was open to girls who liked girls, and had even had a fling or two that had never developed into anything substantial; looking around the kitchen, however, Sheila realized she'd unfortunately forgotten to bring her wine with her, which she would have needed to have that conversation.

"Well, you should want something," her mother said. "I'm worried about you. You don't know how much I worry about you."

Sheila knew how much her mother worried about her. Her mother had been telling her how much she worried about her for years now. Probably from before Sheila was even conceived, her mother was worrying about her. But it was when Sheila turned fifteen that she'd started to make sure Sheila knew just how much. Sheila was now thirty-seven, and the verbal reminders of worry that had started when she'd begun dating had never stopped, even after she took a break from it. So far, it had been a six-year break.

Sheila didn't miss dating, really. Besides, being alone—being a single woman—was the one witchlike quality she possessed, and it was probably the best of the stereotypical witch features to have if she had to have one.

"Ma," Sheila said.

But before she could tell her mother that she didn't have time to play games, her mother said, "I've met someone."

Sheila blinked. "You've met someone?" she said. Was her mother now, at the age of fifty-eight, going to surprise Sheila and find love with someone after being divorced for the past eighteen years?

"Yes," her mother said. "A man. I'd like you to meet him."

"Ma," Sheila said. "I'm speechless. Of course I'll meet him. If he's someone important to you, I'd love to meet him."

"Thank you, lovey," her mother said, and Sheila knew that she'd made her mother happy. "I think you'll like him."

"I'm sure I'll like him, Mom, but I'm just happy if you like him." What Sheila didn't say was how, at that moment, it felt like a huge weight was being lifted from her.

"Well, no," her mother said. "You have to like him, too. As much as I'm glad you trust my judgment in men, it's you who will be going on the date with him."

"*Ma*," Sheila said, and the weight resumed its old position across her shoulders.

Her mother made a guttural noise, though, a sound that meant she was not going to listen to anything Sheila said after the guttural noise reached completion.

"He'll pick you up at seven o'clock tomorrow. Be ready to go to dinner. Don't bring up witch stuff. No talking shop on a date. His name is Lyle."

"Lyle?" Sheila said, as if the name seemed completely made-up—a fantasy novel sort of name, one of those books with a cover that features castle spires and portentous red moons covered in strands of cloud. One of those novels where people are called things like Roland, Aristial, Leandor, Jandari, or . . . Lyle.

"Lyle," said her mother. Then the phone went dead. Sheila looked down at it for a while as if it were a gun that had accidentally gone off, leaving a bullet lodged in her stomach.

The bullet sat in Sheila's stomach and festered for the rest of that night, and the feeling was not unfamiliar. Sheila's mother had a habit of mugging her with unwanted surprises. Furniture that didn't go with Sheila's décor. Clothes that didn't fit her. Blind dates with men named Lyle.

Her mother was a mugger. Always had been. So why was she still surprised whenever it happened, as if this were a sudden, unexpected event? By the next morning, Sheila had come up with several jokes about her mother the mugger that she would tell to the two clients who had appointments with her that afternoon.

"Mugger fucker," Sheila mumbled as she brushed her hair in the bathroom mirror. "Mugger Goose. Holy Mugger of God. Mugger may I?"

Her first client was a regular named Mary, who was forty-three, had three children, and was married to a husband she'd fallen out of love with four years ago. Mary came every other month for a reboot of the spell that helped her love her husband a little longer. She'd tried counseling, she'd tried herbal remedies, she'd even tried Zumba (both individually and with several girlfriends as a group), but nothing seemed to work, and in desperation she'd found Sheila through a friend of a friend of a former client who Sheila had helped rekindle a relationship gone sour years ago, back when Sheila had first started to make her living by witching instead of working at the drugstore that had hired her while she was in college.

The knock came at exactly ten in the morning. Mary was never late and never early. Her sessions always lasted for exactly thirty minutes. Sheila was willing to go beyond that, but Mary said she felt that Sheila's power faded a little more with every second past the thirty-minute mark. She still paid Sheila three hundred dollars for each session, and walked away a happy—or at least a happier—woman. She'd go home and, for five to six weeks, she'd love her husband. Sheila couldn't work a permanent fix for Mary, because Mary had fallen so out of love with her husband that no spell could sustain it forever. Their relationship was an old, used-up car in constant need of repairs. Sheila was the mechanic.

When Sheila opened the door, Mary pushed in, already complaining loudly about her husband, Ted. Sheila had never met him, though she did have a lock of his hair in an envelope that stayed in her living room curio cabinet. Except on appointment days with Mary; on those days, Sheila would bring the hair out for the renewal ritual.

"I don't know if I want the spell again," Mary said. She hadn't even looked at Sheila yet. She just sat down heavily on the living room couch and sighed. "I don't know if I want to fix things any longer."

"What else would you do?" Sheila asked, closing the door before coming over to sit in the chair across from Mary. "Divorce? Start over? You know you could do that, right?"

Mary clutched a small black beaded purse in her lap. She was a beautiful woman, long limbed, peach-skinned, with dark hair that fell to the small of her back like a curtain. She exercised, ate healthy, and didn't drink too much alcohol—even when alcohol sounded like a good idea. She wore upper middle class clothes that weren't particularly major designer labels but weren't from a mall store, either.

"I don't know," Mary said, pushing a piece of her layered black hair away from her face. Sheila noticed that Mary had gotten a nose piercing in the time between their last appointment and this one. A tiny diamond stud glinted in the sunlight coming through the living room windows. "The children . . ." said Mary. Sheila nodded, and stood, then went to her curio cabinet and took out the envelope with the hank of Ted's hair in it.

Sheila opened the envelope and placed the lock of hair on the coffee table between them. It was a thick brown curl that Mary had cut from Ted's mop one night while he was asleep. When Mary had come to Sheila for help four years ago, Sheila had said, "I'll need you to bring me something of his. Something you love about him. Otherwise, I'll have nothing to work with." Mary had said she didn't love him anymore, so how could she bring Sheila anything? "Surely you must love *something* about him," Sheila said, and Mary had nodded, her mouth a firm line, and said that, yes, she did love Ted's hair. It was beautiful. Thick and curly. She loved to run her fingers through it, even after she'd stopped loving Ted.

Now Mary looked down at the lock of curled hair as if it were a dead mouse Sheila had set out in front of her. "You know the drill," Sheila said, and together the two pinched an end of the hair and lifted it into the air above the coffee table.

Sheila closed her eyes and tried to feel Mary's love come through the coil of hair. Like an electrical current, a slight hum flowed through it, but it was weaker than ever and Sheila worried that she wouldn't be able to help Mary once this slight affection for Ted's hair eventually disappeared. She took the lingering love in through her fingers anyway, whipped it like cream, semiconsciously chanting an incantation—or more like noises that helped her focus on the energy in the feeling than anything of significance—and after she'd turned Mary's weak affection into a fluffy meringue-like substance, Sheila pushed it back through the hair, slowly but surely, until Mary was filled with a large, aerated love.

When Sheila opened her eyes, she noticed Mary's face had lifted a little. The firm line of her mouth had softened and curled up at the edges, as if she wanted to smile but was perhaps just a little shy. "Thank you, Sheila," said Mary, blinking sweetly on the couch. This was when Sheila went soft, too. Whenever a client like Mary, hardened by a deficiency of love, took on a shade of her former self—a youthful self who loved and was loved, who trusted in love to see her through—Sheila had to fight to hold back tears. Not because seeing the return of love made her happy—no, the pressure behind her eyes was more a force of sadness, because the person in front of her was under an illusion, and no illusion, thought Sheila, was pleasant. They were more like the narcotics those with chronic pain took to ease their days. This returned love would only be brief and temporary.

At the door, Mary took out three hundred-dollar bills. "Worth every penny," she said, folding them into Sheila's palm, meeting Sheila's eyes and holding her stare.

When Sheila closed the door behind her, she turned and looked at the face of her cell phone. Thirty minutes had passed. On the dot.

Her next client was new: a good-looking young man who was a bit too earnest for only being a twenty-three year old recent college graduate. His name was Ben, and he had just acquired a decent job in an advertising company. He'd gotten a mortgage, purchased a house, and was ready to fill it with someone else and him together, the kids, the dogs, the cats: the works. Sheila could see all of this as he sat in front of her and told her that he wanted to find love. That was simple, really. No need to drum up love where love already fizzed and popped. He just needed someone to really see him. Someone who wanted the same things. He wasn't the completely bland sort of guy that no one would notice, but he wasn't emitting a strong signal either. Sheila did a quick invocation that would enhance Ben's desire so that it would beam like a lighthouse toward ships looking for harbor.

She charged him a hundred dollars and told him that if he didn't get engaged within a year, she'd give him his money back. Ben thanked her, and after she saw him out of the house, it was time for Sheila to sit in her living room and stare at the television, where the vague outline of her body was reflected in the blank screen.

Lyle would be coming to pick her up in several hours. *Lyle, Lyle.* She said his name a few times, but it was no good. She still couldn't believe a man named Lyle was coming for her.

Sheila had tried to make the thing that made her different the most normal aspect of her life. Hence her business: Paranormal Romance. She had business cards and left them on the bulletin boards of grocery store entryways, in the fishbowls full of cards that sat on the register counters of some restaurants, and on the bars of every lowdown drink-your-blues-away kind of joint in the city of

Cleveland, where people sometimes, while crying into a beer, would notice the card propped against the napkin holder in front of them and think about Sheila possibly being the solution to their loneliness, as the cards declared.

She had made herself as non-paranormal as possible, while at the same time living completely out in the open about being a witch, probably because of what her father had once told her, years ago, when she was just a little girl and even Sheila hadn't known she had magic in her fingertips. "If I had to be some creepy weirdo like the vampires and werewolves or whatever the hell else is out there these days," her father had said while watching a news report about the increasing appearance of paranormal creatures, "then I suppose a witch would be the way to go."

*The way to go.* That's what he'd said. As though there was a choice about being cursed or born with magic flowing through you. Vampire, werewolf. *Whatever the hell else.* The memory stuck with Sheila because of the way her father had talked as if it were one of those "If you had to" games.

*If you had to lose a sense, which one?*

*If you had to live on a deserted island with only one book, which one?*

It was only later, after Sheila felt magic welling up in her as a teenager, that she realized how upset he was when she accidentally revealed her abilities—a tactless spell she'd cast to bring him and her mother closer. Unfortunately, her father had noticed Sheila's fingers weaving through the air as she attempted to surreptitiously cast the spell while her parents were watching television one evening. Her mother stuck by Sheila, but he filed for divorce and disappeared from their lives altogether.

Thus her business, *Paranormal Romance*, was born. She would make it work for her, Sheila decided in her late twenties. She would use this magic in a way that someone with good legs, flexibility, and balance might become a dancer or a yoga instructor.

This desire for normality also explained why Sheila wanted to kill her mother after she opened the door that evening to find a man dressed in a black leather jacket, tight blue jeans, a black V-neck shirt, and work boots, sporting a scraggly goatee, whose first words were, "Wow, you don't look like a witch. That's interesting."

"Probably the least interesting thing about me," said Sheila. She tried to restrain herself, but couldn't refrain from arching her eyebrows as a cat might raise its back.

"I'm Lyle. Nice to meet you," the somewhat ruggedly good-looking Lyle said.

"Charmed," Sheila said, trying to sound like she meant it.

"No," said Lyle, "that's what you're supposed to do to me, right?" He winked. Sheila's smile felt frail, as if it might begin to splinter.

"How do you know I'm a witch," Sheila asked, "when my mother specifically told me not to bring it up?"

"Don't know why she told you that," said Lyle. "First thing she mentioned to me was that's what you are."

"Great," said Sheila. "And I know nothing about you to make it even, and here we are, standing in my doorway like we're new neighbors instead of going somewhere."

Lyle nodded his head in the direction of the staircase and said, "I got us a reservation at a great steakhouse downtown."

Sheila smiled. It was a lip-only smile—no teeth—but she followed Lyle down the steps of her apartment to the front porch, where she found Gary dragging Snowman up the steps by his collar. The dog had its ridiculous grin plastered on as usual, but started to yap in the direction of Lyle as soon as he noticed him. Gary himself was grimacing with frustration. "What's the matter?" Sheila asked.

"This guy," said Gary. "When he ran off last night, he really ran off. Someone on the neighborhood Facebook group messaged me to say she had him penned in her back yard. Three blocks from here. You're a bad dog, Snowman. A bad dog, you hear?"

Snowman was barking like crazy now, twisting around Gary's legs. He looked up at Lyle and for the first time in Sheila's experience, the dog did not look like it was smiling, but was baring its teeth.

"Woof!" said Lyle, and Snowman began to whimper.

"Well, it's a good thing she was able to corral him," Sheila said, even as she attempted to telepathically communicate with Gary: *Did this guy just* woof? "I've never gotten along with dogs, so he'd have probably run away from me if I were the one to find him."

"Oh, really?" Lyle raised his brows, as if Sheila had suddenly taken off a mask and revealed herself to be an alien with tentacles wriggling, Medusa-like, out of her head. "You don't like dogs?"

"And dogs," Sheila said, "don't like me."

"I can't believe that," said Lyle, shaking his head and wincing.

Sheila shrugged and said, "That's just the way things are, I guess."

"Who *are* you again?" Gary asked, looking at Lyle with narrowed eyes, as if he'd put Lyle under a microscope.

Sheila apologized for not introducing them. "This is my date," she said, trying to signal to Gary that it was also the last date by rolling her eyes as she turned away from Lyle.

"A *date?*" Gary said, clapping one hand over his mouth as he said it. "Sheila is going on a *date?*"

"That's right," said Lyle. He nodded curtly. "And we should probably get started. Come on," he said, pointing toward his car parked against the curb. Sheila inwardly groaned when she saw that it was one of those muscle cars macho guys collect, like they're still little boys with Matchbox vehicles. "Let's go get some grub," Lyle said, patting his stomach.

"*Grub?*" Gary whispered as Lyle and Sheila went past him, and Sheila could only look over her shoulder with a *Help Me!* look painfully stretched across her face.

The steakhouse Lyle took her to was one of those places where people crack peanuts open, dislodge the nut, and discard the shells on the floor. The lighting was dim, but the room was permeated with the glow from a variety of neon beer signs that hung on every wall like a collection in an art gallery. Lyle said it was his favorite place to dine.

*He said it like that too*, Sheila could already hear herself saying later as she recounted the evening to Trent and Gary. *He said, "It's my favorite place to dine." Can you believe it? What was my mother thinking?*

"Oh, really," Sheila said. The server had just brought her a vodka martini with a slice of lemon dangling over the rim. Sheila looked up at her briefly to say thank you, and noticed immediately that the server—a young woman with long mahogany hair and caramel-colored skin—was a witch. The employee tag on the server's shirt said her name was Corrine; she winked as Sheila grasped after her words. "Thank you," Sheila managed to say without making the moment of recognition awkward. She took a sip, licked her lips, then turned back to Lyle as the server walked away, and said, "What were you saying?"

"'This is my favorite place to dine,' I said. I come here a couple of times a week," said Lyle. "Best steaks in town."

Sheila said, "I don't eat meat."

To which Lyle's face dropped like a hot air balloon that had lost all of its hot air. "Your mother didn't tell me that," said Lyle.

"No," said Sheila, "but for some reason she *did* tell you that I'm a witch, even after she forbade me from speaking of it. Clearly the woman can't be trusted."

"Clearly," Lyle agreed, which actually scored him a tiny little point for the first time that evening. There it was in Sheila's mind's eye, a little scoreboard. *Lyle: 1. Sheila: Anxious.*

He apologized profusely, in a rough-around-the-edges way that seemed to be who he was down to his core. He wasn't really Sheila's type, not that Sheila had a specific type, but he wasn't the sort of guy she'd ever gone out on a date with before, either. Her mother would have known that too. Sheila's mother had always wanted to know what was going on, back when Sheila actually dated. When Myspace and Facebook came around, and her mother began commenting on photos Sheila had posted from some of her date nights with statements like, "He's a hottie!" and "Now that's a keeper!" Sheila had had to block her mother. And only weeks later she discovered that on her mother's own social networking walls, her mother was publicly bemoaning the fact that her daughter had blocked her.

But really, her mother would have known that Lyle wasn't her sort of guy. "So what gives?" she finally asked, after Lyle had finished a tall beer and she'd gotten close to the bottom of her martini. "How do you know my mother? Why would she think we'd make a good pair?"

"I'm her butcher."

Sheila almost spat out the vodka swirling in her mouth, but managed to swallow before saying, "Her butcher? Really? I didn't know my mother *had* a butcher."

"She comes to the West Side Market every Saturday," said Lyle. "I work at Doreen's Meats. Your mother always buys her meat for the week there. As for why would she think we'd make a good pair? I don't know." Lyle shrugged and held his palms up in the air. "I guess maybe she thought we'd get along because of what we have in common."

Sheila snorted, then raised her hand to signal Corrine back over. "I'd like another martini," she said, and smiled in the way some people do when they need to smother an uncivil reaction: lips firmly held together. She turned back to Lyle, who was cracking another peanut shell between his thick, hairy fingers, and said, "So what do we have in common, besides my mother?"

"I'm a werewolf," said Lyle. Then he flicked the peanut off his thumb and snatched it out of the air, midflight, in his mouth.

Sheila watched as Lyle crunched the peanut, and noticed only after he'd swallowed and smiled across the table at her that he had a particularly large set of canines. "You're kidding," said Sheila. "Ha ha, very funny. You might as well start telling witch jokes at this point."

"Not kidding," said Lyle. Corrine stopped at their table, halting the conversation as she placed another tall beer in front of Lyle, another martini in front of Sheila, and asked what they'd like to order.

"I think we're just here to drink tonight," said Lyle, not taking his eyes off Sheila.

Sheila nodded vigorously at Corrine, though, agreeing. And after she left, Sheila said, "Well, this is a new achievement for my mother. Set her daughter up with a werewolf."

"What? You don't like werewolves?" Lyle asked. One corner of his mouth lifted into a 1970s drug dealer grin.

Sheila blinked a lot for a while, took another sip of her martini, then shrugged. "It's not something I've ever thought about, you know," she said. "I mean, werewolves aren't generally on my radar. I get a lot of people who come around with minor psychic powers, and they're attracted to me because they can sense I'm something out of the ordinary but can't quite place *what* exactly, and of course I know a decent amount of witches—we can spot each other on the street without knowing one another, really—but werewolves are generally outside of my experience. Especially my dating experience."

"From what I understand, your dating experience has been pretty nonexistent in general."

Sheila decided it was time to take yet another drink. After swallowing a large gulp of vodka, she said, "My mother has a big mouth for someone who hasn't gotten back in the saddle since my father left her nearly two decades ago. And you can tell her I said that next time she comes in to stock up on meat."

Lyle laughed. It was a full, throaty laugh that made heads turn in the steakhouse. When he realized this, he reined himself in, but Sheila could see that the laugh—the sheer volume of it when he'd let himself go—was beyond ordinary. It bordered on the wild. She could imagine him as a wolf in that moment, howling at a blood red moon.

"So what is it? Once a month you get hairy and run around the city killing people?" Sheila asked.

Lyle leaned back on his side of the booth and said, "Are you serious?"

"Well, I don't know," said Sheila. "I hear it's quite difficult to control bloodlust in times like that."

"I make arrangements for those times," said Lyle.

"Arrangements, huh," said Sheila. "What sort of arrangements?"

"I rent an underground garage, have it filled with plenty of raw steaks, and get locked in for the night."

"That's responsible of you," said Sheila.

"What about you?" Lyle asked. "Any inclinations to doing evil? Casting hexes?"

"No bloodlust for witches," said Sheila, "and I gave up the vicious cycle of curse drama in college. Not worth it. That shit comes back on you sevenfold."

Lyle snickered. He ran his thumb and forefinger over his scraggly goatee, then took another drink of beer. "Looks like we're a pair," he said, "just like your mother imagined."

"Why?" Sheila asked. "Because you put yourself in a werewolf kennel on full moon nights and I don't dabble in wreaking havoc in other people's lives?"

Lyle nodded, his lips rising into a grin that revealed his pointy, slightly yellowed canines.

"I hardly think that constitutes being a pair," said Sheila. "We certainly have that in common, but it's a bit like saying we should start dating because we're both single and living in Cleveland."

"Why *are* you so single?" Lyle asked. His nostrils flared several times. *Oh my God, he is totally sniffing me!* "I need to use the ladies' room," she said.

In the restroom, Sheila leaned against the counter and stared at herself in the mirror. She was wearing a short black dress and had hung her favorite opal earrings on her earlobes. They glowed in the strange orange neon beer-sign light of the restroom. She shouldn't have answered when he knocked. She should have kept things in order. Weekend BBQs with Trent and Gary, even with the obnoxious Snowman running between their legs and wanting to jump on her and lick her. Working a few hours a day with clients, helping them to love or be loved, to find love. Evening runs in the park. Grocery shopping on Wednesdays. That's what she wanted, not a werewolf butcher/lover her mother had found in the West Side Market.

The last time Sheila dated someone had been slightly less than under-whelming. He'd been an utterly normal man named Paul who worked at the Federal Reserve Bank of Cleveland downtown, and he talked endlessly of bank capitalization and exchange-traded funds. Sheila had tried to love him, but it was as if all the bank talk was more powerful than any spell she might cast on herself, and so she'd had to add Paul to her long list of previous candidates for love.

There had been Jim, a guy who owned a car dealership in Lakewood, but he always came off as a salesman, and Sheila wasn't the consumer type. There had been Alexis, a law student at Case Western, but despite her girlish good looks and intelligence, Alexis had worried about Sheila's under-the-table Paranormal Romance business—concerned that she was possibly defrauding the govern-ment of taxable income. There had been Mark, the CPA (say no more). There had been Lola, the karaoke DJ (say no more). And there had been a string of potentials before that, too, once Sheila began sorting through the memories of her twenties, a long line of cute young men and women whose faces faded a little more each day. She had tried—she had tried so hard—hoping one of them would take the weight of her existence and toss it into the air like a beach ball. The love line went back and back and back, so far back, but none of those boys or girls had been able to do this. None of them.

Except Trent and Gary, of course. Not that they were romance for Sheila. But they did love her. They cared about her. They didn't make her feel like she had to be anyone but who she wanted to be, even if who Sheila wanted to be wasn't entirely who Sheila was.

Sheila washed her hands under the faucet and dried them with the air dryer, appreciating the whir of the fan drowning out the voice in her head. She would walk out on Lyle, she decided. She'd go home and call her mother and tell her, "Never again," then hang up on her. She would sit in front of the blank television screen, watching her shadowy reflection held within it, and maybe she would let herself cry, just a little bit, for being a love witch who couldn't make love happen for herself.

"Are you okay?" a voice said over the whir of the hand dryer. Sheila blinked and turned. Behind her, Corrine the server was coming out of a stall. She came to stand beside Sheila at the sinks and quickly washed her hands.

"You're a witch," Sheila said stupidly, and realized at that moment that two martinis were too many for her.

Corrine laughed, but nodded and said, "Yes. I am. So are you." Corrine reached for the paper towel to dry her hands, since Sheila was spellbound in front of the electric dryer. "What kind?" she asked Sheila as she wiped her hands.

"Love," said Sheila.

"Love?" said Corrine, raising her thin eyebrows. "That's pretty fancy."

"It's okay," said Sheila.

"Just okay?" said Corrine. "I don't know. Sounds nice to be able to do something like that with it. Me? I can't do much but weird things."

"What do you mean?" Sheila asked.

"You know," said Corrine. "Odds and ends. Nothing so defined as love. Bad end of the magic stick, maybe. I can smell fear on people, or danger. And I can open doors. But that's about it."

"Open doors?" said Sheila.

"Yeah," said Corrine. "Doors. I guess it does make a kind of sense when I think about it long enough. I smell danger coming, I can get out of just about anywhere if I want to. Open a door. Any old door. It might look like it leads into a broom closet or an office, but I can make it open onto other places I've been, or have at least seen in a picture."

"Wow," said Sheila. "You should totally be a cat burglar."

Corrine laughed. Sheila laughed with her. "Sorry," she said. "I don't know why I said that."

"It's okay," Corrine said. "It was funny. I think you said it because it was funny."

"I guess I better get back out there," said Sheila.

"Date?" said Corrine.

"Blind date," Sheila answered. "Bad date. Last date."

Corrine frowned in sympathy. "I knew it wasn't going well."

"How?" Sheila asked.

"I could smell it on you. Not quite fear, but anxiety and frustration. I figured that's why you asked for the second martini. That guy comes in a lot. He seems okay, but yeah, I couldn't imagine why you were here with him."

Sheila looked down at her hands, which were twitching a little, as if her fingers had minds of their own. They were twitching in Corrine's direction, like they wanted to go to her. Sheila laughed. Her poor fingers. All of that love magic stored up inside them and nowhere to go.

"You need help?" Corrine asked suddenly. She had just taken off her name badge and was now fluffing her hair in the mirror.

"Help?" said Sheila.

Corrine looked over and said, "If you want out, we can just go. You don't even have to say goodbye to him. My shift's over. A friend of mine will be closing out your table. We can leave by the bathroom door."

Sheila laughed. Her fingers twitched again. She took one hand and clamped it over the other.

"What are you afraid of?" Corrine asked. Her eyes had started to narrow. "I'm getting a sense that you're afraid of me now."

"You?" Sheila said. "No, no, not you."

"Well, you're giving off the vibe," said Corrine. She dropped her name badge into her purse and took out a tube of lipstick, applied some to her lips so that they were a shade of dark ruby. When she was done, she slipped the tube into her purse and turned to Sheila. "What's wrong with your hands?" she asked.

Sheila was still fidgeting. "I think," she said. "I think they like you."

Corrine threw her head back and laughed. "Like?" she said, grinning. "That's sweet of them. You can tell your hands I like them too."

Sheila said, "I'm so sorry. This is embarrassing. I'm usually not such a weirdo." For a moment, Sheila heard her father's voice come through—*Creepy weirdoes. Whatever the hell else is out there*—and she shivered.

"You're not weird," said Corrine. "Just flustered. It happens."

*It happens.* Sheila blinked and blinked again. Actually, it didn't happen. Not for her. Her fingers only twitched like this when she was working magic for other people. Anytime she had tried to work magic for herself, they were still and cold, as if she had bad circulation. "No," Sheila said. "It doesn't usually happen. Not for me. This is strange."

"Listen," said Corrine. "You seem interesting. I'm off shift and you have a bad blind date happening. I'm about to leave by that door and go somewhere I know that has good music and way better food than this place. And it's friendly to people like you and me. What do you say?"

Sheila thought of her plans for the rest of the evening in a blinding flash.

Awkward moment before she ditched Lyle.

Awkward and angry moment on the phone while she told her mother off.

The vague reflection of her body held in the screen of the television as she allowed herself to cry a little.

Then she looked up at Corrine, who was pulling on a zippered hoody, and said, "I say yes."

"Yes?" Corrine said, smiling.

"Yes," said Sheila. "Yes, let's go there, wherever it is you're going."

Corrine held her hand out, and Sheila looked down at her own hands again, clamped together as if in prayer, holding each other back from the world. "You can let one of them go," Corrine said, grinning. "Otherwise, I can't take you with me."

Sheila laughed nervously and nodded. She released her hands from one another and cautiously put one into the palm of Corrine's hand, where it settled in smoothly and turned warm in an instant. "This way," Corrine said, and put her other hand on the bathroom doorknob, twisted, then opened it.

For a moment, Sheila could see nothing but a bright light fill the space of the doorway—no Lyle or the sounds of rock and roll music spilled in from the dining area—and she worried that she'd made a mistake, not being able to see where she was going with this woman who was a complete stranger. Then

Corrine looked back at her and said, "Don't be afraid," and Sheila heard the sound of jazz music suddenly float toward her, a soft saxophone, a piano melody, though the doorway was still filled with white light she couldn't see through.

"I'm not," said Sheila suddenly, and was surprised to realize that she truly wasn't.

Corrine winked at her the way she had done at the table, as if they shared a secret, which, of course, they did. Then she tugged on Sheila's hand and they stepped through the white light into somewhere different.

NEBULA AWARD NOMINEE
BEST NOVELETTE

# "THEY SHALL SALT THE EARTH WITH SEEDS OF GLASS"

## ALAYA DAWN JOHNSON

*Alaya Dawn Johnson's YA SF novel,* The Summer Prince, *was on the long list for the National Book Award for Young People's Literature. This is her first Nebula nomination. "They Shall Salt the Earth with Seeds of Glass" appeared in* Asimov's Science Fiction.

It's noon, the middle of wheat harvest, and Tris is standing on the edge of the field while Bill and Harris and I drive three ancient combine threshers across the grain. It's dangerous to stand so close and Tris knows it. Tris knows better than to get in the way during harvest, too. Not a good idea if she wants to survive the winter. Fifteen days ago a cluster bomb dropped on the east field, so no combines there. No harvest. Just a feast for the crows.

Tris wrote the signs (with pictures for the ones who don't read) warning the kids to stay off the grass, stay out of the fields, don't pick up the bright-colored glass jewels. So I raise my hand, wave my straw hat in the sun—it's hot as hell out here, we could use a break, no problem—and the deafening noise of eighty-year-old engines forced unwillingly into service chokes, gasps, falls silent.

Bill stands and cups his hands over his mouth. "Something wrong with Meshach, Libby?"

I shake my head, realize he can't see, and holler, "The old man's doing fine. It's just hot. Give me ten?"

Harris, closer to me, takes a long drink from his bottle and climbs off Abednego. I don't mind his silence. This is the sort of sticky day that makes it hard to move, let alone bring in a harvest, and this sun is hot enough to burn darker skin than his.

It's enough to burn Tris, standing without a hat and wearing a skinny strappy dress of faded red that stands out against the wheat's dusty gold. I hop off Meshach, check to make sure he's not leaking oil, and head over to my sister. I'm a little worried. Tris wouldn't be here if it wasn't important. Another cluster bomb? But I haven't heard the whining drone of any reapers. The sky is clear. But even though I'm too far to read her expression, I can tell Tris is worried. That way she has of balancing on one leg, a red stork in a wheat marsh. I hurry as I get closer, though my overalls stick to the slick sweat on my thighs and I have to hitch them up like a skirt to move quickly.

"Is it Dad?" I ask, when I'm close.

She frowns and shakes her head. "Told me this morning he's going fishing again."

"And you let him?"

She shrugs. "What do you want me to do, take away his cane? He's old, Libs. A few toxic fish won't kill him any faster."

"They might," I grumble, but this is an old argument, one I'm not winning, and besides that's not why Tris is here.

"So what is it?"

She smiles, but it shakes at the edges. She's scared and I wonder if that makes her look old or just reminds me of our age. Dad is eighty, but I'm forty-two and we had a funeral for an eight-year-old last week. Every night since I was ten I've gone to sleep thinking I might not wake up the next morning. I don't know how you get to forty-two doing that.

Tris is thirty-eight, but she looks twenty-five—at least, when she isn't scanning the skies for reapers, or walking behind a tiny coffin in a funeral procession.

"Walk with me," she says, her voice low, as though Harris can hear us from under that magnolia tree twenty feet away. I sigh and roll my eyes and mutter under my breath, but she's my baby sister and she knows I'll follow her anywhere. We climb to the top of the hill, so I can see the muddy creek that irrigates the little postage stamp of our corn field, and the big hill just north of town, with its wood tower and reassuring white flag. Yolanda usually takes the morning shift, spending her hours watching the sky for that subtle disturbance, too smooth for a bird, too fast for a cloud. Reapers. If she rings the bell, some of us might get to cover in time.

Sometimes I don't like to look at the sky, so I sprawl belly-down on the ground, drink half of the warm water from my bottle and offer the rest to Tris. She finishes it and grimaces.

"Don't know how you stand it," she says. "Aren't you hot?"

"You won't complain when you're eating cornbread tonight."

"You made some?"

"Who does everything around here, bookworm?" I nudge her in the ribs and she laughs reluctantly and smiles at me with our smile. I remember learning to comb her hair after Mom got sick; the careful part I would make while she squirmed and hollered at me, the two hair balls I would twist and fasten to each side of her head. I would make the bottom of her hair immaculate: brushed and gelled and fastened into glossy, thick homogeneity. But on top it would sprout like a bunch of curly kale, straight up and out and olive-oil shiny. She would parade around the house in this flouncy slip she thought was a dress and pose for photos with her hand on her hip. I'm in a few of those pictures, usually in overalls or a smock. I look awkward and drab as an old sock next to her, but maybe it doesn't matter, because we have the same slightly bucked front teeth, the same fat cheeks, the same wide eyes going wider. We have a nice smile, Tris and I.

Tris doesn't wear afro-puffs any more. She keeps her hair in a bun and I keep mine short.

"Libs, oh Libs, things aren't so bad, are they?"

I look up at Tris, startled. She's sitting in the grass with her hands beneath her thighs and tears are dripping off the tip of her nose. I was lulled by her laugh—we don't often talk about the shit we can't control. Our lives, for instance.

I think about the field that we're going to leave for crows so no one gets blown up for touching one of a thousand beautiful multi-colored jewels. I think about funerals and Dad killing himself faster just so he can eat catfish with bellies full of white phosphorus.

"It's not that great, Tris."

"You think it's shit."

"No, not *shit*—"

"Close. You think it's close."

I sigh. "Some days. Tris. I have to get back to Meshach in a minute. What is going on?"

"I'm pregnant," she says.

I make myself meet her eyes, and see she's scared; almost as scared as I am.

"How do you know?"

"I suspected for a while. Yolanda finally got some test kits last night from a river trader."

Yolanda has done her best as the town midwife since she was drafted into service five years ago, when a glassman raid killed our last one. I'm surprised Tris managed to get a test at all.

"What are you going to do? Will you . . ." I can't even bring myself to say "keep it." But could Yolanda help her do anything else?

She reaches out, hugs me, buries her head in my shirt and sobs like a baby. Her muffled words sound like "Christ" and "Jesus" and "God," which ought to be funny since Tris is a capital-A atheist, but it isn't.

"No," she's saying, "Christ, no. I have to . . . someone has to . . . I need an abortion, Libby."

Relief like the first snow melt, like surviving another winter. Not someone else to worry about, to love, to feed.

But an abortion? There hasn't been a real doctor in this town since I was twelve.

Bill's mom used to be a registered nurse before the occupation, and she took care of everyone in town as best she could until glassman robots raided her house and called in reapers to bomb it five years ago. Bill left town after that. We never thought we'd see him again, but then two planting seasons ago, there he was with this green giant, a forty-year-old Deere combine—Shadrach, he called it, because it would make the third with our two older, smaller machines. He brought engine parts with him, too, and oil and enough seed for a poppy field. He had a bullet scar in his forearm and three strange, triangular burns on the back of his neck. You could see them because he'd been shaved bald and his hair was only starting to grow back, a patchy gray peach-fuzz.

He'd been in prison, that much was obvious. Whether the glassmen let him go or he escaped, he never said and we never asked. We harvested twice as much wheat from the field that season, and the money from the poppy paid for a new generator. If the bell on lookout hill rang more often than normal, if surveillance drones whirred through the grass and the water more than they used to, well, who was to say what the glassmen were doing? Killing us, that's all we knew, and Bill was one of our own.

So I ask Bill if his mother left anything behind that might help us—like a pill, or instructions for a procedure. He frowns.

"Aren't you a little old, Libby?" he says, and I tell him to fuck off. He puts a hand on my shoulder—conciliatory, regretful—and looks over to where Tris is trudging back home. "You saw what the reapers did to my Mom's house. I couldn't even find all of her *teeth*."

I'm not often on that side of town, but I can picture the ruin exactly. There's still a crater on Mill Street. I shuffle backward, contrite. "God, Bill. I'm sorry. I wasn't thinking."

He shrugs. "Sorry, Libs. Ask Yolanda, if you got to do something like that." I don't like the way he frowns at me; I can hear his judgment even when all he does is turn and climb back inside Shadrach.

"Fucking hot out here," I say, and walk back over to Meshach. I wish Bill wasn't so goddamn judgmental. I wish Tris hadn't messed up with whichever of her men provided the sperm donation. I wish we hadn't lost the east field to another cluster bomb.

But I can wish or I can drive, and the old man's engine coughs loud enough to drown even my thoughts.

Tris pukes right after dinner. That was some of my best cornbread, but I don't say anything. I just clean it up.

"How far along are you?" I ask. I feel like vomit entitles me to this much.

She pinches her lips together and I hope she isn't about to do it again. Instead, she stands up and walks out of the kitchen. I think that's her answer, but she returns a moment later with a box about the size of my hand. It's got a hole on one side and a dial like a gas gauge on the other. The gauge is marked with large glassman writing and regular letters in tiny print: "Fetal Progression," it reads, then on the far left "Not Pregnant," running through "Nine Months" on the far right. I can't imagine what the point of that last would be, but Tris's dial is still barely on the left hand side, settled neatly between three and four. A little late for morning sickness, but maybe it's terror as much as the baby that makes her queasy.

"There's a note on the side. It says 'All pregnant women will receive free rehabilitative healthcare in regional facilities.'" She says the last like she's spent a long day memorizing tiny print.

"Glassmen won't do abortions, Tris."

No one knows what they really look like. They only interact with us through their remote-controlled robots. Maybe they're made of glass themselves—they give us pregnancy kits, but won't bother with burn dressings. Dad says the glassmen are alien scientists studying our behavior, like a human would smash an anthill to see how they scatter. Reverend Beale always points to the pipeline a hundred miles west of us. They're just men stealing our resources, he says, like the white man stole the Africans', though even he can't say what those resources might be. It's a pipeline from nowhere, to nothing, as far as any of us know.

Tris leans against the exposed brick of our kitchen wall. "All fetuses are to be carried to full term," she whispers, and I turn the box over and see her words printed in plain English, in larger type than anything else on the box. Only one woman in our town ever took the glassmen up on their offer. I don't know how it went for her; she never came home.

"Three months!" I say, though I don't mean to.

Tris rubs her knuckles beneath her eyes, though she isn't crying. She looks fierce, daring me to ask her how the hell she waited this long. But I don't, because I know. Wishful thinking is a powerful curse, almost as bad as storytelling.

I don't go to church much these days, not after our old pastor died and Beale moved into town to take his place. Reverend Beale likes his fire and brimstone, week after week of too much punishment and too little brotherhood. I felt exhausted listening to him rant in that high collar, sweat pouring down his temples. But he's popular, and I wait on an old bench outside the red brick church for the congregation to let out. Main Street is quiet except for the faint echoes of the reverend's sonorous preaching. Mostly I hear the cicadas, the water lapping against a few old fishing boats and the long stretch of rotting pier. There used to be dozens of sailboats here, gleaming creations of white fiberglass and heavy canvas sails with names like "Bay Princess" and "Prospero's Dream." I know because Dad has pictures. Main Street was longer then, a stretch of brightly painted Tudors and Victorians with little shops and restaurants on the bottom floors and rooms above. A lot of those old buildings are boarded up now, and those that aren't look as patched-over and jury-rigged as our thresher combines. The church has held up the best of any of the town's buildings. Time has hardly worn its stately red brick and shingled steeples. It used to be Methodist, I think, but we don't have enough people to be overly concerned about denominations these days. I've heard of some towns where they make everyone go Baptist, or Lutheran, but we're lucky that no one's thought to do anything like that here. Though I'm sure Beale would try if he could get away with it. Maybe Tris was right to leave the whole thing behind. Now she sits the children while their parents go to church.

The sun tips past its zenith when the doors finally open and my neighbors walk out of the church in twos and threes. Beale shakes parishioners' hands as they leave, mopping his face with a handkerchief. His smile looks more like a grimace to me; three years in town and he still looks uncomfortable anywhere but behind a pulpit. Men like him think the glassmen are right to require "full gestation." Men like him think Tris is a damned sinner, just because she has a few men and won't settle down with one. He hates the glassmen as much as the rest of us, but his views help them just the same.

Bill comes out with Pam. The bones in her neck stand out like twigs, but she looks a hell of a lot better than the last time I saw her, at Georgia's funeral. Pam fainted when we laid her daughter in the earth, and Bill had to take her home before the ceremony ended. Pam is Bill's cousin, and Georgia was her only child—blown to bits after riding her bicycle over a hidden jewel in the fields outside town. To my surprise, Bill gives me a tired smile before walking Pam down the street.

Bill and I used to dig clams from the mud at low tide in the summers. We were in our twenties and my mother had just died of a cancer the glassmen could have cured if they gave a damn. Sometimes we would build fires of cedar and pine and whatever other tinder lay around and roast the clams right there by the water. We talked about anything in the world other than glassmen and dead friends while the moon arced above. We planned the cornfield eating those clams, and plotted all the ways we might get the threshers for the job. The cow dairy, the chicken coop, the extra garden plots—we schemed and dreamt of ways to help our town hurt a little less each winter. Bill had a girlfriend then, though she vanished not long after; we never did more than touch.

That was a long time ago, but I remember the taste of cedar ash and sea salt as I look at the back of him. I never once thought those moments would last forever, and yet here I am, regretful and old.

Yolanda is one of the last to leave, stately and elegant with her braided white hair and black church hat with netting. I catch up with her as she heads down the steps.

"Can we talk?" I ask.

Her shoulders slump a little when I ask, but she bids the reverend farewell and walks with me until we are out of earshot.

"Tris needs an abortion," I say.

Yolanda nods up and down like a sea bird, while she takes deep breaths. She became our midwife because she'd helped Bill's mother with some births, but I don't think she wants the job. There's just no one else.

"Libby, the glassmen don't like abortions."

"If the glassmen are paying us enough attention to notice, we have bigger problems."

"I don't have the proper equipment for a procedure. Even if I did, I couldn't."

"Don't tell me you agree with Beale."

She draws herself up and glares at me. "I don't know *how*, Libby! Do you want me to kill Tris to get rid of her baby? They say the midwife in Toddville can do them if it's early enough. How far along is she?"

I see the needle in my mind, far too close to the center line for comfort. "Three and a half months," I say.

She looks away, but she puts her arm around my shoulders. "I understand why she would, I do. But it's too late. We'll all help her."

*Raise the child*, she means. I know Yolanda is making sense, but I don't want to hear her. I don't want to think about Tris carrying a child she doesn't want to term. I don't want to think about that test kit needle pointing inexorably at *too fucking late*. So I thank Yolanda and head off in the other direction, down the cracked tarmac as familiar as a scar, to Pam's house. She lives in a small cottage Victorian with peeling gray paint that used to be blue. Sure enough, Bill sits in an old rocking chair on the porch, thumbing through a book. I loved to see him like that in our clam-digging days, just sitting and listening. I would dream of him after he disappeared.

"Libs?" he says. He leans forward.

"Help her, Bill. You've been outside, you know people. Help her find a doctor, someone who can do this after three months."

He sighs and the book thumps on the floor. "I'll see."

Three days later, Bill comes over after dinner.

"There's rumors of something closer to Annapolis," he says. "I couldn't find out more than that. None of my . . . I mean, I only know some dudes, Libby. And whoever runs this place only talks to women."

"Your mother didn't know?" Tris asks, braver than me.

Bill rubs the back of his head. "If she did, she sure didn't tell me."

"You've got to have more than that," she says. "Does this place even have a name? How near Annapolis? What do you want us to do, sail into the city and ask the nearest glassman which way to the abortion clinic?"

"What do I want you to do? Maybe I want you to count your goddamn blessings and not risk your life to murder a child. It's a *sin*, Tris, not like you'd care about that, but I'd've thought Libby would."

"God I know," I say, "but I've never had much use for sin. Now why don't you get your nose out of our business?"

"You invited me in, Libby."

"For *help*—"

He shakes his head. "If you could see what Pam's going through right now . . ."

Bill has dealt with as much grief as any of us. I can understand why he's moralizing in our kitchen, but that doesn't mean I have to tolerate it.

But Tris doesn't even give me time. She stands and shakes a wooden spatula under his nose. Bill's a big man, but he flinches. "So I should have this baby just so I can watch it get blown up later, is that it? Don't put Pam's grief on me, Bill. I'm sorrier than I can say about Georgia. I taught that girl to read! And I can't. I just can't."

Bill breathes ragged. His dark hands twist his muddy flannel shirt, his grip so tight his veins are stark against sun-baked skin. Tris is still holding that spatula.

Bill turns his head abruptly, stalks back to the kitchen door with a "Fuck," and he wipes his eyes. Tris leans against the sink.

"Esther," he says quietly, his back to us. "The name of a person, the name of a place, I don't know. But you ask for that, my buddy says you should find what you're after."

I follow him outside, barefoot and confused that I'd bother when he's so clearly had enough of us. I call his name, then start jogging and catch his elbow. He turns around.

"What, Libby?"

He's so angry. His hair didn't grow in very long or thick after he came back. He looks like someone mashed him up, stretched him out and then did a hasty job of putting him back together. Maybe I look like that, too.

"Thanks," I say. We don't touch.

"Don't die, Libs."

The air is thick with crickets chirping and fireflies glowing and the swampy, seaweed-and-salt air from the Chesapeake. He turns to walk away. I don't stop him.

We take Dad's boat. There's not enough gas left to visit Bishop's Head, the mouth of our estuary, let alone Annapolis. So we bring oars, along with enough supplies to keep the old dinghy low in the water.

"I hope we don't hit a storm," Tris says, squinting at the clear, indigo sky as though thunderheads might be hiding behind the stars.

"We're all right for now. Feel the air? Humidity's dropped at least 20 percent."

Tris has the right oar and I have the left. I don't want to use the gas unless we absolutely have to, and I'm hoping the low-tech approach will make us less noticeable to any patrolling glassmen. It's tough work, even in the relatively cool night air, and I check the stars to make sure we're heading in more or less the right direction. None of the towns on our estuary keep lights on at night. I only know when we pass Toddville because of the old lighthouse silhouetted against the stars. I lost sight of our home within five minutes of setting out, and God how a part of me wanted to turn the dinghy right around and go back. The rest of the world isn't safe. Home isn't either, but it's familiar.

Dad gave us a nautical chart of the Chesapeake Bay, with markers for towns long destroyed, lighthouses long abandoned, by people long dead. He marked our town and told us to get back safe. We promised him we would and we hugged like we might never see each other again.

"What if we hit a jewel?" Tris asks. In the dark, I can't tell if it's fear or exertion that aspirates her words. I've had that thought myself, but what can we do? The glassmen make sure their cluster bombs spread gifts everywhere.

"They don't detonate that well in water," I offer.

A shift in the dark; Tris rests her oar in the boat and stretches her arms. "Well enough to kill you slowly."

I'm not as tired, but I take the break. "We've got a gun. It ought to do the trick, if it comes to that."

"Promise?"

"To what? Mercy kill you?"

"Sure."

"Aren't you being a little melodramatic?"

"And we're just out here to do a little night fishing."

I laugh, though my belly aches like she's punched me. "Christ, Tris." I lean back in the boat, the canvas of our food sack rough and comforting on my slick skin, like Mom's gloves when she first taught me to plant seeds.

"Libs?"

"Yeah?"

"You really don't care who the father is?"

I snort. "If it were important, I'm sure you would have told me."

I look up at the sky: there's the Milky Way, the North Star, Orion's belt. I remember when I was six, before the occupation. There was so much light on the bay you could hardly see the moon.

"Reckon we'll get to Ohio, Jim?" Tris asks in a fake Southern drawl.

I grin. "Reckon we might. If'n we can figure out just how you got yerself pregnant, Huck."

Tris leans over the side of the boat, and a spray of brackish water hits my open mouth. I shriek and dump two handfuls on her head and she splutters and grabs me from behind so I can't do more than wiggle in her embrace.

"Promise," she says, breathing hard, still laughing.

The bay tastes like home to me, like everything I've ever loved. "Christ, Tris," I say, and I guess that's enough.

We round Bishop's Head at dawn. Tris is nearly asleep on her oar, though she hasn't complained. I'm worried about her, and it's dangerous to travel during the day until we can be sure the water is clear. We pull into Hopkins Cove, an Edenic horseshoe of brown sand and forest. It doesn't look like a human foot has touched this place since the invasion, which reassures me. Drones don't do much exploring. They care about people.

Tris falls asleep as soon as we pull the boat onto the sand. I wonder if I should feed her more—does she need extra for the baby? Then I wonder if that's irrational, since we're going all this way to kill it. But for now, at least, the fetus is part of her, which means we have to take it into consideration. I think about Bill with his big, dumb eyes and patchy bald head telling me that it's a *sin*, as though that has anything to do with your sister crying like her insides have been torn out.

I eat some cornbread and a peach, though I'm not hungry. I sit on the shore with my feet in the water and watch for other boats or drones or reapers overhead. I don't see anything but seagulls and ospreys and minnows that tickle my toes.

"Ain't nothing here, Libs," I say, in my mother's best imitation of *her* mother's voice. I never knew my grandmother, but Mom said she looked just like Tris, so I loved her on principle. She and Tris even share a name: Leatrice. I told Mom that I'd name my daughter Tamar, after her. I'd always sort of planned to, but when my monthlies stopped a year ago, I figured it was just as well. *Stupid Bill, and his stupid patchy hair*, I think.

I dream of giant combines made from black chrome and crystal, with head-lights of wide, unblinking eyes. I take them to the fields, but something is wrong with the thresher. There's bonemeal dust on the wheat berries.

"Now, Libby," Bill says, but I can't hear the rest of what he's saying because the earth starts shaking and—

I scramble to my feet, kicking up sand with the dream still in my eyes. There's lights in the afternoon sky and this awful thunder, like a thousand lightning bolts are striking the earth at once.

"Oh, Christ," I say. A murder of reapers swarm to the north, and even with the sun in the sky their bombs light the ground beneath like hellfire. It's easier to see reapers from far away, because they paint their underbellies light blue to blend with the sky.

Tris stands beside me and grips my wrist. "That's not . . . it has to be Tod-dville, right? Or Cedar Creek? They're not far enough away for home, right?"

I don't say anything. I don't know. I can only look.

Bill's hair is patchy because the glassmen arrested him and they tortured him. Bill asked his outside contacts if they knew anything about a place to get an illegal abortion. Bill brought back a hundred thousand dollars' worth of farm equipment and scars from wounds that would have killed someone without access to a doctor. But what kind of prisoner has access to a real doctor? Why did the glassmen arrest him? What if his contacts are exactly the type of men the glassmen like to bomb with their reapers? What if Bill is?

But I know it isn't that simple. No one knows why the glassmen bomb us. No one *really* knows the reason for the whole damn mess, their reapers and their drones and their arcane rules you're shot for not following.

"Should we go back?"

She says it like she's declared war on a cardinal direction, like she really will get on that boat and walk into a reaper wasteland and salvage what's left of our lives and have that baby.

I squeeze her hand. "It's too close," I say. "Toddville, I think you're right. Let's get going, though. Probably not safe here."

She nods. She doesn't look me in the eye. We paddle through the choppy water until sun sets. And then, without saying anything, we ship the oars and I turn on the engine.

Three nights later, we see lights on the shore. It's a glassmen military installation. Dad marked it on the map, but still I'm surprised by its size, its brightness, the brazen way it sits on the coastline, as though daring to attract attention.

"I'd never thought a building could be so . . ."

"Angry?" Tris says.

"Violent."

"It's like a giant middle finger up the ass of the Chesapeake."

I laugh despite myself. "You're ridiculous."

We're whispering, though we're on the far side of the bay and the water is smooth and quiet. After that reaper drone attack, I'm remembering more than I like of my childhood terror of the glassmen. Dad and Mom had to talk to security drones a few times after the occupation, and I remember the oddly modulated voices, distinctly male, and the bright unblinking eyes behind the glass masks of their robot heads. I don't know anyone who has met a real glassman, instead of one of their remote robots. It's a retaliatory offense to harm a drone because the connection between the drone and the glassman on the other side of the world (or up in some space station) is so tight that sudden violence can cause brain damage. I wonder how they can square *potential brain damage* with *dead children*, but I guess I'm not a glassman.

So we row carefully, but fast as we can, hoping to distance our little fishing boat from the towering building complex. Its lights pulse so brightly they leave spots behind my eyes.

And then, above us, we hear the chopping whirr of blades cutting the air, the whine of unmanned machinery readying for deployment. I look up and shade my eyes: a reaper.

Tris drops her oar. It slides straight into the bay, but neither of us bother to catch it. If we don't get away now, a lost oar won't matter anyway. She lunges into our supply bag, brings out a bag of apples. The noise of the reaper is close, almost deafening. I can't hear what she yells at me before she jumps into the bay. I hesitate in the boat, afraid to leave our supplies and afraid to be blown to pieces by a reaper. I look back up and see a panel slide open on its bright blue belly. The panel reveals dark glass; behind it, a single, unblinking eye.

I jump into the water, but my foot catches on the remaining oar. The boat rocks behind me, but panic won't let me think—I tug and tug until the boat capsizes and suddenly ten pounds of supplies are falling on my head, dragging me deeper into the dark water. I try to kick out, but my leg is tangled with the drawstring of a canvas bag, and I can't make myself focus enough to get it loose. All I can think of is that big glass eye waiting to kill me. My chest burns and my ears fill to bursting with pressure. I'd always thought I would die in fire, but water isn't much better. I don't even know if Tris made it, or if the eye caught her, too.

I try to look up, but I'm too deep; it's too dark to even know which way that is. *God*, I think, *save her. Let her get back home.* It's rude to demand things of God, but I figure dying ought to excuse the presumption.

Something tickles my back. I gasp and the water flows in, drowning my lungs, flooding out what air I had left. But the thing in the water with me has a light on its head and strange, shiny legs and it's using them to get under my arms and drag me up until we reach the surface and I cough and retch and *breathe, thank you God.* The thing takes me to shore, where Tris is waiting to hug me and kiss my forehead like I'm the little sister.

"Jesus," she says, and I wonder if God really does take kindly to demands until I turn my head and understand: my savior is a drone.

***

"I will feed you," the glassman says. He looks like a spider with an oversized glassman head: eight chrome legs and two glass eyes. "The pregnant one should eat. Her daughter is growing."

I wonder if some glassman technology is translating his words into English. If in his language, whatever it is, *the pregnant one* is a kind of respectful address. Or maybe they taught him to speak to us that way.

I'm too busy appreciating the bounty of air in my lungs to notice the other thing he said.

"Daughter?" Tris says.

The glassman nods. "Yes. I have been equipped with a body-safe sonic scanning device. Your baby has not been harmed by your ordeal. I am here to help and reassure you."

Tris looks at me, carefully. I sit up. "You said something about food?"

"Yes!" It's hard to tell, his voice is so strange, but he sounds happy. As though rescuing two women threatened by one of his reaper fellows is the best piece of luck he's had all day. "I will be back," he says, and scuttles away, into the forest.

Tris hands me one of her rescued apples. "What the hell?" Her voice is low, but I'm afraid the glassman can hear us anyway.

"A trap?" I whisper, barely vocalizing into her left ear.

She shakes her head. "He seems awfully . . ."

"Eager?"

"Young."

The glassman comes back a minute later, walking on six legs and holding two boxes in the others. His robot must be a new model; the others I've seen look more human. "I have meals! A nearby convoy has provided them for you," he says, and places the boxes carefully in front of us. "The one with a red ribbon is for the pregnant one. It has nutrients."

Tris's hands shake as she opens it. The food doesn't look dangerous, though it resembles the strange pictures in Tris's old magazines more than the stuff I make at home. A perfectly rectangular steak, peas, corn mash. Mine is the same, except I have regular corn. We eat silently, while the glassman gives every impression of smiling upon us benevolently.

"Good news," he pipes, when I'm nearly done forcing the bland food down my raw throat. "I have been authorized to escort you both to a safe hospital facility."

"Hospital?" Tris asks, in a way that makes me sit up and put my arm around her.

"Yes," the glassman says. "To ensure the safe delivery of your daughter."

The next morning, the glassman takes us to an old highway a mile from the water's edge. A convoy waits for us, four armored tanks and two platform trucks. One of the platform beds is filled with mechanical supplies, including two dozen glass-and-chrome heads. The faces are blank, the heads unattached to any robot body, but the effect makes me nauseous. Tris digs her nails into my forearm. The other platform bed is mostly empty except for a few boxes and one man tied to the guardrails. He lies prone on the floor and doesn't move when we climb in after our glassman. At first I'm afraid that he's dead, but then he twitches and groans before falling silent again.

"Who is he?" Tris asks.

"Non-state actor," our glassman says, and pulls up the grate behind us.

"What?"

The convoy engines whirr to life—quiet compared to the three old men, but the noise shocks me after our days of silence on the bay.

The glassman swivels his head, his wide unblinking eyes fully focused on my sister. I'm afraid she's set him off and they'll tie us to the railings like that poor man. Instead, he clicks his two front legs together for no reason that I can see except maybe it gives him something to do.

"Terrorist," he says, quietly.

Tris looks at me and I widen my eyes: *don't you dare say another word*. She nods.

"The convoy will be moving now. You should sit for your safety."

He clacks away before we can respond. He hooks his hind legs through the side rail opposite us and settles down, looking like nothing so much as a contented cat.

The armored tanks get into formation around us and then we lurch forward, rattling over the broken road. Tris makes it for half an hour before she pukes over the side.

For two days, Tris and I barely speak. The other man in our truck wakes up about once every ten hours, just in time for one of the two-legged glassmen from the armored tanks to clomp over and give us all some food and water. The man gets less than we do, though none of it is very good. He eats in such perfect silence that I wonder if the glassmen have cut out his tongue. As soon as he finishes, one of the tank glassmen presses a glowing metal bar to the back of his neck. The mark it leaves is a perfect triangle, raw and red like a fresh burn. The prisoner doesn't struggle when the giant articulated metal hand grips his shoulders, he only stares, and soon after he slumps against the railing. I have lots of time to wonder about those marks; hour after slow hour with a rattling truck bruising my tailbone and regrets settling into my joints like dried tears. Sometimes Tris massages knots from my neck, and sometimes they come right back while I knead hers. I can't see any way to escape, so I try not to think about it. But there's no helping the sick, desperate knowledge that every hour we're closer to locking Tris in a hospital for six months so the glassmen can force her to have a baby.

During the third wake-up and feeding of the bound man, our glassman shakes out his legs and clacks over to the edge of the truck bed. The robots who drive the tanks are at least eight feet tall, with oversized arms and legs equipped with artillery rifles. They would be terrifying even if we weren't completely at their mercy. The two glassmen stare at each other, eerily silent and still.

The bound man, I'd guess Indian from his thick straight hair and dark skin, strains as far forward as he can. He nods at us.

"They're talking," he says. His words are slow and painstakingly formed. We crawl closer to hear him better. "In their real bodies."

I look back up, wondering how he knows. They're so still, but then glassmen are always uncanny.

Tris leans forward, so her lips are at my ear. "Their eyes," she whispers.

Glassman robot eyes never blink. But their pupils dilate and contract just like ours do. Only now both robots' eyes are pupil-blasted black despite the glaring noon sun. Talking in their real bodies? That must mean they've stopped paying us any attention.

"Could we leave?" I whisper. No one has tied us up. I think our glassman is under the impression he's doing us a favor.

Tris buries her face in the back of my short nappy hair and wraps her arms around me. I know it's a ploy, but it comforts me all the same. "The rest of the convoy."

Even as I nod, the two glassmen step away from each other, and our convoy is soon enough on its way. This time, though, the prisoner gets to pass his time awake and silent. No one tells us to move away from him.

"I have convinced the field soldier to allow me to watch the operative," our glassman says proudly.

"That's very nice," Tris says. She's hardly touched her food.

"I am glad you appreciate my efforts! It is my job to assess mission parameter achievables. Would you mind if I asked you questions?"

I frown at him and quickly look away. Tris, unfortunately, has decided she'd rather play with fire than her food.

"Of course," she says.

We spend the next few hours subjected to a tireless onslaught of questions. Things like, "How would you rate our society-building efforts in the Tidewater Region?" and "What issue would you most like to see addressed in the upcoming Societal Health Meeting?" and "Are you mostly satisfied or somewhat dissatisfied with the cleanliness of the estuary?"

"The fish are toxic," I say to this last question. My first honest answer. It seems to startle him. At least, that's how I interpret the way he clicks his front two legs together.

Tris pinches my arm, but I ignore her.

"Well," says the glassman. "That is potentially true. We have been monitoring the unusually high levels of radiation and heavy metal toxicity. But you can rest assured that we are addressing the problem and its potential harmful side-effects on Beneficial Societal Development."

"Like dying of mercury poisoning?" Tris pinches me again, but she smiles for the first time in days.

"I do not recommend it for the pregnant one! I have been serving you both nutritious foods well within the regulatory limits."

I have no idea what those regulatory limits might be, but I don't ask.

"In any case," he says. "Aside from that issue, the estuary is very clean."

"Thank you," Tris says, before I can respond.

"You're very welcome. We are here to help you."

"How far away is the hospital?" she asks.

I feel like a giant broom has swept the air from the convoy, like our glassman has tossed me back into the bay to drown. I knew Tris was desperate; I didn't realize how much.

"Oh," he says, and his pupils go very wide. I could kiss the prisoner for telling us what that means: no one's at home.

The man now leans toward us, noticing the same thing. "You pregnant?" he asks Tris.

She nods.

He whistles through a gap between his front teeth. "Some rotten luck," he says. "I never seen a baby leave one of their clinics. Fuck knows what they do to them."

"And the mothers?" I ask.

He doesn't answer, just lowers his eyes and looks sidelong at our dormant glassman. "Depends," he whispers, "on who they think you are."

That's all we have time for; the glassman's eyes contract again and his head tilts like a bird's. "There is a rehabilitative facility in the military installation to which we are bound. Twenty-three hours ETA."

"A prison?" Tris asks.

"A hospital," the glassman says firmly.

When we reach the pipeline, I know we're close. The truck bounces over fewer potholes and cracks; we even meet a convoy heading in the other direction. The pipeline is a perfect clear tube about sixteen feet high. It looks empty to me, a giant hollow tube that distorts the landscape on the other side like warped glass. It doesn't run near the bay, and no one from home knows enough to plot it on a map. Maybe this is the reason the glassmen are here. I wonder what could be so valuable in that hollow tube that Tris has to give birth in a cage, that little Georgia has to die, that a cluster bomb has to destroy half our wheat crop. What's so valuable that looks like nothing at all?

The man spends long hours staring out the railing of the truck, as though he's never seen anything more beautiful or more terrifying. Sometimes he talks to us, small nothings, pointing out a crane overhead or a derelict road with a speed limit sign—55 *miles per hour,* it says, *radar enforced.*

At first our glassman noses around these conversations, but he decides they're innocuous enough. He tells the man to "refrain from exerting a corrupting influence," and resumes his perch on the other side of the truck bed. The prisoner's name is Simon, he tells us, and he's on watch. For what, I wonder, but know well enough not to ask.

"What's in it?" I say instead, pointing to the towering pipeline.

"I heard it's a wormhole." He rests his chin on his hands, a gesture that draws careful, casual attention to the fact that his left hand has loosened the knots. He catches my eye for a blink and then looks away. My breath catches— Is he trying to escape? Do we dare?

"A wormhole? Like, in space?" Tris says, oblivious. Or maybe not. Looking at her, I realize she might just be a better actor.

I don't know what Tris means, but Simon nods. "A passage through space, that's what I heard."

"That is incorrect!"

The three of us snap our heads around, startled to see the glassman so close. His eyes whirr with excitement. "The Designated Area Project is not what you refer to as a wormhole, which are in fact impractical as transportation devices."

Simon shivers and looks down at his feet. My lips feel swollen with regret— what if he thinks we're corrupted? What if he notices Simon's left hand? But Tris raises her chin, stubborn and defiant at the worst possible time—I guess the threat of that glassman hospital is making her too crazy to feel anything as reasonable as fear.

"Then what is it?" she asks, so plainly that Simon's mouth opens, just a little.

Our glassman stutters forward on his delicate metallic legs. "I am not authorized to tell you," he says, clipped.

"Why not? It's the whole goddamned reason all your glassman reapers and drones and robots are swarming all over the place, isn't it? We don't even get to know what the hell it's all for?"

"Societal redevelopment is one of our highest mission priorities," he says, a little desperately.

I lean forward and grab Tris's hand as she takes a sharp, angry breath. "Honey," I say, "Tris, *please.*"

She pulls away from me, hard as a slap, but she stops talking. The glassman says nothing; just quietly urges us a few yards away from Simon. No more corruption on his watch.

Night falls, revealing artificial lights gleaming on the horizon. Our glassman doesn't sleep. Not even in his own place, I suppose, because whenever I check with a question his eyes stay the same and he answers without hesitation. Maybe they have drugs to keep themselves awake for a week at a time. Maybe he's not human. I don't ask—I'm still a little afraid he might shoot me for saying the wrong thing, and more afraid that he'll start talking about Ideal Societal Redevelopment.

At the first hint of dawn, Simon coughs and leans back against the railing, catching my eye. Tris is dozing on my shoulder, drool slowly soaking my shirt. Simon flexes his hands, now free. He can't speak, but our glassman isn't looking at him. He points to the floor of the truckbed, then lays himself out with his hands over his head. There's something urgent in his face. Something knowledgeable. To the glassmen he's a terrorist, but what does that make him to us? I shake Tris awake.

"Libs?"

"Glassman," I say, "I have a question about societal redevelopment deliverables."

Tris sits straight up.

"I would be pleased to hear it!" the glassman says.

"I would like to know what you plan to do with my sister's baby."

"Oh," the glassman says. The movement of his pupils is hardly discernible in this low light, but I've been looking. I grab Tris by her shoulder and we scramble over to Simon.

"Duck!" he says. Tris goes down before I do, so only I can see the explosion light up the front of the convoy. Sparks and embers fly through the air like a starfall. The pipeline glows pink and purple and orange. Even the strafe of bullets seems beautiful until it blows out the tires of our truck. We crash and tumble. Tris holds onto me, because I've forgotten how to hold onto myself.

The glassmen are frozen. Some have tumbled from the overturned trucks, their glass and metal arms halfway to their guns. Their eyes don't move, not even when three men in muddy camouflage lob sticky black balls into the heart of the burning convoy.

Tris hauls me to my feet. Simon shouts something at one of the other men, who turns out to be a woman.

"What the hell was that?" I ask.

"EMP," Simon says. "Knocks them out for a minute or two. We have to haul ass."

The woman gives Simon a hard stare. "They're clean?"

"They were prisoners, too," he says.

The woman—light skinned, close-cropped hair—hoists an extra gun, unconvinced. Tris straightens up. "I'm pregnant," she says. "And ain't nothing going to convince me to stay here."

"Fair enough," the woman says, and hands Tris a gun. "We have ninety seconds. Just enough time to detonate."

Our glassman lies on his back, legs curled in the air. One of those sticky black balls has lodged a foot away from his blank glass face. It's a retaliatory offense to harm a drone. I remember what they say about brain damage when the glassmen are connected. Is he connected? Will this hurt him? I don't like the kid, but he's so young. Not unredeemable. He saved my life.

I don't know why I do it, but while Tris and the others are distracted, I use a broken piece of the guard rail to knock off the black ball. I watch it roll under the truck, yards away. I don't want to hurt him; I just want my sister and me safe and away.

"Libs!" It's Tris, looking too much like a terrorist with her big black gun. Dad taught us both to use them, but the difference between us is I wish that I didn't know how, and Tris is glad.

I run to catch up. A man idles a pickup ten yards down the road from the convoy.

"They're coming back on," he says.

"Detonating!" The woman's voice is a bird-call, a swoop from high to low. She presses a sequence of buttons on a remote and suddenly the light ahead is fiercer than the sun and it smells like gasoline and woodsmoke and tar. I've seen plenty enough bomb wreckage in my life; I feel like when it's *ours* it should look different. Better. It doesn't.

Tris pulls me into the back of the pickup and we're bouncing away before we can even shut the back door. We turn off the highway and drive down a long dirt road through the woods. I watch the back of the woman's head through the rear window. She has four triangular scars at the base of her neck, the same as Bill's.

Something breaks out of the underbrush on the side of the road. Something that moves unnaturally fast, even on the six legs he has left. Something that calls out, in that stupid, naive, inhuman voice:

"Stop the vehicle! Pregnant one, do not worry, I will—"

"Fuck!" Tris's terror cuts off the last of the speech. The car swerves, tossing me against the door. I must not have latched it properly, because next thing I know I'm tumbling to the dirt with a thud that jars my teeth. The glassman scrambles on top of me without any regard for the pricking pain of his long, metallic limbs.

"Kill that thing!" It's a man, I'm not sure who. I can't look, pinioned as I am.

"Pregnant one, step down from the terrorist vehicle and I will lead you to safety. There is a Reaper Support Flyer on its way."

He grips me between two metallic arms and hauls me up with surprising strength. The woman and Simon have guns trained on the glassman, but they hesitate—if they shoot him, they have to shoot me. Tris has her gun up as well, but she's shaking so hard she can't even get her finger on the trigger.

"Let go of me," I say to him. He presses his legs more firmly into my side.

"I will save the pregnant one," he repeats, as though to reassure both of us. He's young, but he's still a glassman. He knows enough to use me as a human shield.

Tris lowers the gun to her side. She slides from the truck bed and walks forward.

"Don't you dare, Tris!" I yell, but she just shakes her head. My sister, giving herself to a glassman? What would Dad say? I can't even free a hand to wipe my eyes. I hate this boy behind the glass face. I hate him because he's too young and ignorant to even understand what he's doing wrong. Evil is good to a glassman. Wrong is right. The pregnant one has to be saved.

I pray to God, then. I say, *God, please let her not be a fool. Please let her escape.*

And I guess God heard, because when she's just a couple of feet away she looks straight at me and smiles like she's about to cry. "I'm sorry, Libs," she whispers. "I love you. I just can't let him take me again."

"Pregnant one! Please drop your weapon and we will—"

And then she raises her gun and shoots.

My arm hurts. Goddamn it hurts, like there's some small, toothy animal burrowing inside. I groan and feel my sister's hands, cool on my forehead.

"They know the doctor," she says. "That Esther that Bill told us about, remember? She's a regular doctor, too, not just abortions. You'll be fine."

I squint up at her. The sun has moved since she shot me; I can hardly see her face for the light behind it. But even at the edges I can see her grief. Her tears drip on my hairline and down my forehead.

"I don't care," I say, with some effort. "I wanted you to do it."

"I was so afraid, Libs."

"I know."

"We'll get home now, won't we?"

"Sure," I say. *If it's there.*

The terrorists take us to a town fifty miles from Annapolis. Even though it's close to the city, the glassmen mostly leave it alone. It's far enough out from the pipeline, and there's not much here, otherwise: just a postage stamp of a barley field, thirty or so houses and one of those large, old, whitewashed barn-door churches. At night, the town is ghost empty.

Tris helps me down from the truck. Even that's an effort. My head feels half-filled with syrup. Simon and the others say their goodbyes and head out quickly. It's too dangerous for fighters to stay this close to the city. Depending on how much the glassmen know about Tris and me, it isn't safe for us either. But between a baby and a bullet, we don't have much choice.

Alone, now, we read the church's name above the door: *Esther Zion Congregation Church, Methodist.*

Tris and I look at each other. "Oh, Christ," she says. "Did Bill lie, Libby? Is he really so hung up on that sin bullshit that he sent me all the way out here, to a *church* . . ."

I lean against her and wonder how he ever survived to come back to us. It feels like a gift, now, with my life half bled out along the road behind. "Bill wouldn't lie, Tris. Maybe he got it wrong. But he wouldn't lie."

The pews are old but well-kept. The prayer books look like someone's been using them. The only person inside is a white lady, sweeping the altar.

"Simon and Sybil sent you," she says, not a question. Sybil—we never even asked the woman's name.

"My sister," we both say, and then, improbably, laugh.

A month later, Tris and I round Bishop's Head and face north. At the mouth of our estuary, we aren't close enough to see Toddville, let alone our home, but we can't see any drones either. The weather is chillier this time around, the water harder to navigate with the small boat. Tris looks healthy and happy; older and younger. No one will mistake her for twenty-five again, but there's nothing wrong with wisdom.

The doctor fixed up my arm and found us an old, leaky rowboat when it was clear we were determined to go back. Tris has had to do most of the work; her arms are starting to look like they belong to someone who doesn't spend all her time reading. I think about the harvest and hope the bombs didn't reap the grain before we could. If anyone could manage those fields without me, Bill can. We won't starve this winter, assuming reapers didn't destroy everything. Libby ships the oars and lets us float, staring at the deep gray sky and its reflection on the water that seems to stretch endlessly before us.

"Bill will have brought the harvest in just fine," I say.

"You love him, don't you?"

I think about his short, patchy hair. That giant green monster he brought back like a dowry. "He's good with the old engines. Better than me."

"I think he loves you. Maybe one of you could get around to doing something about it?"

"Maybe so."

Tris and I sit like that for a long time. The boat drifts toward shore, and neither of us stop it. A fish jumps in the water to my left; a heron circles overhead.

"Dad's probably out fishing," she says, maneuvering us around. "We might catch him on the way in."

"That'll be a surprise! Though he won't be happy about his boat."

"He might let it slide. Libby?"

"Yes?"

"I'm sorry—"

"You aren't sorry if you'd do it again," I say. "And I'm not sorry if I'd let you." She holds my gaze. "Do you know how much I love you?"

We have the same smile, my sister and I. It's a nice smile, even when it's scared and a little sad.

# "PEARL REHABILITATIVE COLONY FOR UNGRATEFUL DAUGHTERS"

## HENRY LIEN

*This is Henry Lien's first nomination for a Nebula. "Pearl Rehabilitative Colony for Ungrateful Daughters" appeared in* Asimov's Science Fiction.

I am called familial name Jiang, personal name Suki, although I prefer to be referred to as Her Grace, Radiant Goddess Princess Suki, and I think that this is the stupidest essay ever assigned and I think that Pearl Rehabilitative Colony for Ungrateful Daughters is the stupidest place under Heaven.

You wish us to write this essay about what we have done and learned during our sentence here at Pearl Colony. You have "Wicked Girls Return as Good" carved over the entrance gate. You think that girls can be humiliated into excellence. You think that we can be shamed into preparing for the examination for Pearl Opera Academy next year by making us say that we are lazy and ungrateful. Think whatever you want. I do not have any "acts of undutiful disrespect of my Honorable Parents" to confess in this essay because my parents were stupid to send me here. Piss me off to death!

Even if they had wanted a boy. Even if I was adopted. If they did not want me, they could have just thrown me away with the kitchen trash instead of sending me here to be tortured to death.

I want to go home.

Except my stupid, stupid parents are there.

I miss my cat. I fear no one has been tinting her fur while I have been gone.

Most of all, I miss my hair. Aiyah, I think I am going to cry again. My beautiful hair. My legendary hair. And all you nuns were so mean to me when you cut it off.

"You are not going to cut my hair," I say to the nuns.

"Mistress Suki. Your parents have sent you here so that we can save you from your own undutiful nature. You shall learn to obey so that you can learn to excel. And we shall cut your hair."

Half of the girls have gone through the line and all submitted to having their hair amputated by the nuns without fighting back.

I say to the nuns, "I have my hair massaged and dressed twice each month at the most high-grade beauty sanctuary in all of Tsukoshita Bay by a former first assistant to the second personal lady-in-waiting of the Empress Dowager." And they think I am going to permit them to touch my hair? Make me die of laughing! "You are just a bunch of ugly, talentless nuns who hide here because you could not survive in the real world."

"Aiyah!" they cry. "How dare you say such things to your elders, you wicked, ungrateful girl?"

"Is that not the sort of thing that wicked, ungrateful girls say?"

"Aiyah!" they all gasp. "You shall learn your place, wicked one!"

All of the girls are looking away from me. Except one girl. What is she staring at?

As the nuns come at me, I prepare to enter combat position and I dig the inner edges of my skates in. The surface of the pearl under my skates feels a little too grippy. They think that the pearl here at Pearl Colony is high-grade pearl, but it is just common road-grade pearl, as sufficient for skating on as any other street or handrail or rooftop in the city of Pearl, but really unacceptable for fighting on. The entire miserable campus of Pearl Colony is made out of this cheap road-grade pearl. Why do they even bother? They might as well just make buildings out of cut rocks and tree slices like primitives used to before they discovered the pearl, or like out in Fallen-Behind places like the Shin mainland.

The four nuns prepare to encircle me. However, they are not Academy-level practitioners of Wu-Liu. Since no other form of Kung-Fu is performed on bladed skates, any weakness in either skating training or combat training leaves you full of weaknesses in the combined art form of Wu-Liu. I can see just from how the nuns shift their weight that none of them received equal training in both skating and combat.

They skate in a circle around me, tighter and tighter, hoping to rein me in like a frightened animal. The wrong technique, as this leaves their wall of defense no stronger at any point than one person deep.

I prepare to skate with full force into one of the nuns, and enter into position to perform the two-palm lightning butterfly block chop. As she sees me charging her, the old turd crouches down into position to perform the incredibly stupid five-point fire chicken move and I am laughing so hard, I almost lose hold of my position. Make me die of laughing! I change the energy flow of the nun's ridiculous pecking hand and use the fulcrum of her elbow to send her hand slapping against her own shoulder.

I break out of the circle and cartwheel into a double-toe flying jump. I land onto a curved, ornamental retaining wall made out of the pearl and skate along its top away from the nuns.

Behind me, the four nuns leap onto the wall one after another. They skate in pursuit on the top of the undulating wall behind me in a line, rising and falling with the rhythms of the wall like a New Year's dragon. A slow, ugly New Year's dragon. Do they really think they can ever catch me?

But then, behind them, I see someone. She is skating hard. From the way that she balances on one skate and pushes behind with the other skate, I can tell that this girl has received proper Wu-Liu training and that she is not without talent.

It is the girl who was staring at me in the line for the hair amputations, with the long, straight hair like a waterfall and the stinking expression on her face. As she catches up with the train of nuns, she extends her arms straight out. She knows the lightning lotus forward flip! This girl has received some serious Wu-Liu training. I see her cantilever and flip on the axis formed by her own arms and sail over the entire train of nuns to land in front of them.

As she closes the distance between us, she begins to do one lily pad forward flip after another, building her momentum and gathering her center of Chi. Pump, flip, glide. When her center of Chi is fully gathered, she unleashes it into a seven-fingered somersault flip. She catapults over my head and lands in front of me.

I reach out and grab her long length of waterfall hair as she lands. Wah! Her hair is silky and beautiful. It is hard to get a grip on it, as it feels like it was dressed with whale placenta extract. This girl must come from money.

The girl's fist shoots out and twists itself into my hair. Aiyah, she is going to crease it! In the distance, I see the four nuns skating in a line towards me, like some evil, brown sea serpent. The one in the lead has a sword drawn.

"Why are you doing this to me?" I cry at the girl with the waterfall hair. "Who are you?"

The girl does not answer.

"They are going to cut your hair, too!" I scream at her. "Why are you helping them?"

"Because you talk too much," says the girl with the waterfall hair.

We continue to wrench each other's beautiful hair, neither of us releasing our grip. Aiyah, I am crying thinking about all that beautiful hair being creased but it is as if she does not even care! Then, when it is clear that neither of us will gain the advantage over the other, the girl pushes me as far away as my grip on her hair will allow. With her hair stretched between us, she does a strange sort of twisting single-toe flip that I have never seen before and *uses the blade of her own skate to cut through her own hair*. It makes a sickening sound as it cuts through, half creak and half crunch, as if I had just skated over somebody's arm. She twists free of my grip. I am holding her length of beautiful hair that must have taken ten years to grow and thousands of taels to dress, and I am so shocked and sickened by her mutilation of herself that I drop my defense.

In that moment, she whips me in a half circle by my hair and sends me sliding into the four nuns. They grab my limbs and, with one ringing swing of the sword, amputate my beautiful, legendary hair.

Aiyah, why me? Why me? Why me? I want to die.

But first, I must have my revenge on this evil, evil girl.

I learn that the evil girl who helped the nuns to amputate my beautiful hair is called familial name Liang, personal name Doi. Her father is Chairman of

New Dei-Tsei Pearlworks Company. They live in a compound at the top of Dowager's Peak.

It turns out that Doi Liang was in fact Baby Swan Doi. Of course! When she was ten years old, Baby Swan Doi became the youngest person ever to win first place at the Season of Glimmers Pageant of Lanterns Wu-Liu Invitational. Her short routine, "The Dragon and the Swan" became a sensation because of the interplay between the train of taiko drummers on skates thundering after her and her little fluttering swan moves to evade the dragon. But people say she ran into some "trouble" and disappeared from view and no one has heard anything about her in the last four years.

Doi Liang's parents probably sent her to Pearl Colony to clean her up and stage a comeback so that they can make sure she passes this year's examination to get into Pearl Opera Academy to properly complete her Wu-Liu training.

I suppose that some people might think that she is a little bit more beautiful than I am, but her mouth is too wide and her complexion has exactly zero radiance. Also, she is always looking down at the ground, so you cannot even tell if her eyelids are monolid or duolid.

By the end of the day when they amputated my hair, I have gotten all 24 girls enrolled at Pearl Colony to make vows of sisterhood with me to take down that Doi Liang and get her kicked out of Pearl Colony at all costs. No one likes a traitor.

If Doi Liang gets kicked out of Pearl Colony, there is no way that Pearl Opera Academy will ever accept her. Not with an expulsion on her record. She will never perform legitimate Wu-Liu again. She will never get cast in a role again, except in some variety show production called "Has-Beens of Wu-Liu" or "Nobodies on Skates" or else some topless skating chorus in a saloon in Cleanside.

But the question is how can we get her kicked out of Pearl Colony? Normally, girls get kicked out for smoking sinkweed or violating curfew or getting caught with boys in their rooms, but this one is so uptight, she probably wipes her ass with lace scarves.

On the first day of class, we are presented with the perfect way to get that Doi Liang kicked out. When we assemble on the training court on the first day, we are all devastated to see that our Wu-Liu instructor is Sensei Madame Tong. She is an instructor at Pearl Opera Academy. However, she also wrote that ghastly parenting guide "How to Raise Dutiful, Successful Children the Traditional Imperial Way" that has been giving our parents stupid ideas. Piss me off to death. How am I going to survive three months under her rule?

However, the lesson system and grading plan that Sensei Madame Tong sets forth for us that first day give us the perfect path to get that Doi Liang kicked out of Pearl Colony.

"Wicked, ungrateful daughters," says Sensei Madame Tong. She would be beautiful if she did not purse her lips so much.

"Question: What is the greatest cause of all evil in this world? Answer: Undutiful children.

"Question: What is the greatest joy that a person can have in this life? Answer: To show respect to one's esteemed parents.

"As we start our first day of lessons at Pearl Rehabilitative Colony for Ungrateful Daughters, let us remember the story of young Mei-Ching the Dutiful, who, when her parents were too old and weak to work, chopped all the trees on the mountain where they lived to give them firewood, then cut off her own head to make soup to feed her parents.

"You shall be subject to a Motivation at the end of each of the three months of this term. The Motivation is an examination to make you all perform your best and place as high in the rankings as you can. You shall be ranked from first place to last place based on your performance during the Motivation.

"Your final rankings after all three Motivations shall be taken into consideration when you take the entrance examination for Pearl Opera Academy next year. Further, after each Motivation, the girl ranked in last place shall be expelled, as reminder to all of what happens to lazy, ungrateful girls with no virtue or excellence."

All of us girls start whispering in excitement to each other, and then we all look at that Doi Liang. We will seize every opportunity when Sensei Madame Tong is not looking to sabotage her and take her down and get her kicked out of Pearl Colony.

On that first day, Sensei Madame Tong starts us with three hours of basic tan-toe kicking and drills. No toilet breaks.

At the end of the three hours, she allows us to rest for five minutes. We can choose to either rest or rush back to the dormitory compound to try to use the two toilets there.

Then she has us immediately start with six hours of jumping drills. At the end of the first three hours, we are allowed a five-minute break but instead of allowing us to rest, she makes us kneel directly on the hard pearl, with our skates on, and listen to the nuns recite poems from the twilight of the Zhang Dynasty of the empire of Shin. They mumble on and on about how the empire was brought down not by the floods following the Great Leap of Shin, but as Heaven's punishment for all the ungrateful children in the empire.

Several girls pull muscles during the last three hours of jumping drills. One girl even slips on a triple jump and falls, cutting her leg with her own skate. We all rush to help her, but Sensei Madame Tong does not permit us. She says the girl has dishonored her parents and wasted their money by failing in front of her Colony mates and she should be made to feel the full force of her shame so that her parents get their money's value.

At the end of the last hour of jumping drills, Sensei Madame Tong has the Shinian servant girls skate out with our dinner, a bowl of wakame miso soup with a scoop of rice dropped in it. She announces that only girls who are able to successfully do a combination triple scissor kick quadruple spin will be allowed to eat. And we each get only one try.

Only a few girls manage to do the combination triple scissor kick quadruple spin on the first try. I am one of them. Two of the others who succeed are sisters, Chiriko and Yoneko, whom I already knew because their parents are friends with my parents. I think it was their parents who gave my parents a copy of Sensei Madame Tong's book, though, and gave them the idea to send me to Pearl Colony. Piss me off to death. But then they were among the first to agree to help me get Doi Liang kicked out so then we became very close friends again.

Also, another girl named Lin-En did the combination move successfully. Her father is a high-ranking bureaucrat in the Tariff Blockade Ministry. Sweet girl. She seems to want to become friends with me very much. She is not talentless, which is a good thing, since no one is going to give her a role based on her face.

And also that girl Doi Liang. She also did the combination on the first try.

Sensei Madame Tong makes the five of us eat our bowls of soup in front of the other girls, who are denied any dinner. When we have finished, Sensei Madame Tong orders the Shinian servant girls to take the uneaten nineteen bowls of soup and empty them into the ocean. Then we are sent to bathe and go to sleep.

We thought that that miserable first day was just Sensei Madame Tong's way of scaring us, but no. That first day was just the beginning of a month of terrible days.

At the end of each day, Sensei Madame Tong tallies the points of all the girls made during the jumps for the day. She continually adjusts our rankings based on our performance and posts them outside the principal skating court.

The top five rankings never change day to day. I am ranked first, of course, and Chiriko and Yoneko are ranked third and fourth, and then sweet Lin-En is ranked fifth.

That Doi Liang also ranks pretty well. Too well.

At the end of the first month, we face the First Motivation. Sensei Madame Tong reveals the full depth of her evil by making us take a twelve-hour Motivation. For the first eight hours, we do endless competitions testing kicking, jumping, spins, free hand combat, footwork routines, short weapons combat, and long weapons combat. For the last four hours, we are tested on combining these skills with lyrical skating and carving figures into the pearl with our skates.

At the end of the First Motivation, the results are no surprise. In the top five positions, I am first, Chiriko and Yoneko are third and fourth, and sweet Lin-En is fifth.

And that Doi Liang is ranked second.

The pretty, fair-skinned girl with the big eyes is ranked last. As we watch her pack up her belongings and leave the colony in failure and shame, my heart is filled with a thousand strains of sorrow and tears roll down my face because it is not that Doi Liang that is getting kicked out.

I cannot just stand aside and do nothing about this. I have to do something. We all have to do something.

At the beginning of the second month at Pearl Colony, Sensei Madame Tong tells the remaining girls that we will spend the next month preparing for the Second Motivation, the Imperial Tea-Service test.

The Imperial Tea-Service test requires you to take a little teacup filled with hot tea. You are required to skate a circuit atop the perimeter wall encircling the campus of Pearl Colony without spilling the cup of tea. Everyone is ranked by how quickly they complete the circuit. However, if you come back without at least half a cupful of tea left, you fail.

When Sensei Madame Tong has finished explaining the rules, all the girls look at me, and then we all look at that Doi Liang.

This will be easy. When the Second Motivation is given, we will all attack Doi Liang when Sensei Madame Tong is not looking and knock the tea out of her cup, causing her to fail the Motivation.

The second month turns out to be far more difficult than the first month. We train for fourteen hours each day. We have not only to practice all the moves that we trained during the first month. We must also learn the architecture of the perimeter wall that we will be skating on during the Second Motivation. We must learn how to navigate the towers, turrets, and minarets that break the wall, and how to use adjoining rooftops and balconies to avoid the obstacles and overtake each other, since the wall is only one skater wide. And we must learn to keep our cups in such perfect balance during all of these leaps that we do not spill the tea in them.

On the day of the Second Motivation, we are all lifted up in joyful anticipation of the opportunity to take out that Doi Liang. We take our cups of tea and form a pack at the starting line.

Sensei Madame Tong counts down. "San. Ni. I. Let fly!"

We all burst and flip or cartwheel onto the perimeter wall and set off. Because the perimeter wall is only wide enough for one skater at a time, we all must follow along in a line. However, you can sprint when you skate past the rooftop of an adjacent building and do a diagonal three-point skid-step to pass somebody.

Doi Liang keeps trying to pass the skater in front of her and move to the front of the line. However, we anticipate her moves and we work in unison against her like a school of fish.

When we skate to a point that is blocked from Sensei Madame Tong's view by the natural geography of the campus, we all let loose with our combat moves at Doi Liang, trying to make her spill her cup of tea.

She is taken by surprise at the assault from ten sides. She performs quite well considering all those arms and skate blades coming at her.

She quickly changes to the Pulling Hands technique, grabbing the girls' limbs as they come at her, using the forward motion of their moves against them, and turning sideways to let them fly past her. The girl is not talentless, I must say that.

But she is no match for so many girls. She is blocking off four girls who have stopped curbing their kicks and appear to be aiming open blades at her. If they are going to be using illegal moves on Doi Liang, I cannot stop them.

Then, as Doi Liang passes the rooftop of the dormitory, little Lin-En skates up from the left side and slaps Doi Liang's cup of tea. Good girl! It flies up in the air. Lin-En ends up skating right through the cloud of tea droplets, which stain all over her uniform robes. But at least we have succeeded in our mission. For Doi Liang snatches her teacup as it tumbles in the air and it is completely empty.

As we skate into view of the Sensei Madame Tong again, I see that not only have I made Doi Liang come in last place, I am going to come in first place.

See. Do not underestimate Her Grace, Radiant Goddess Princess Suki. No one will shame me. No one will deny me. As I streak down the finish line in first place, I sing out triumphantly,

"No dutiful daughter am I!

"No father or mother ruled by!

"Behold me, for I am the Radiant Goddess!

"I fly up and rip down the sky!"

I finish first, Doi Liang is right behind me but with an empty teacup, then Yoneko, then Chiriko, then Lin-En.

I am glad to see that sweet Lin-En managed to place in the top few places again. For some reason, I am cheering for that girl. I skate over to her and say, "Keep skating like that and when we get to Pearl Opera Academy, I will start a sisterhood and you can be my first lady in waiting." From the look of happiness on her face, you would think that I just gave her a gift of the moon. Sweet, open-hearted girl.

When all the girls have crossed the finish line, it turns out that everyone finished with their cups at least half full except for Doi Liang. I figure that

that means that she places 23rd, dead last in this Motivation and she will be expelled! I am overcome with joy.

"What happened when the rise of the hill obscured all of you from my view?" asks Sensei Madame Tong. "Mistress Lin-En. Why is your uniform covered with tea?"

Lin-En cries, "Doi Liang fell in front of me and spilled her tea on me."

Sensei Madame Tong's neck and face fill with color. "Do not lie to me, worthless, shameful girl! Doi Liang has not fallen once during these weeks of training."

Lin-En begins to stutter and protest, but Sensei Madame Tong turns instead to Doi Liang.

"Mistress Doi. Did you fall and spill your tea?"

Doi Liang is silent, then finally answers in her low, hoarse voice, "No."

"Did Mistress Lin-En slap your teacup out of your hand?"

Doi Liang does not look at Sensei Madame Tong. She does not look at Lin-En.

She looks straight at me.

She says, "Yes."

"Mistress Lin-En," says Sensei Madame Tong. "Go pack your things. You are expelled."

Brave Yoneko skates to the front of the group and protests. "You cannot do that to her! You have no right to just disbelieve her!"

I have never seen an adult turn so furious. "You are expelled, too, Mistress Yoneko! For disrespect to a Sensei. Now get out of here!"

That night, after Lin-En and Yoneko are escorted out by the evil nuns, we also learn that Sensei Madame Tong calculated the rankings in a different way from how I thought. After expelling Lin-En and Yoneko, 21 girls were left. Thus, Doi Liang's finishing last means that she finished in 21st place. However, that combined with her second place ranking in First Motivation means that she averages out to between eleventh and twelfth place overall. Not last place. And not expelled. Instead, the tall girl with the beauty mark on her chin averages in last place and is expelled.

Piss me off to death. The girls all want to make Doi Liang pay for what she did to Lin-En and Yoneko and they want to enjoy watching her pay.

But I know it was not Lin-En and Yoneko that she was trying to hurt. It was me. And she succeeded.

Poor Lin-En. We were becoming friends. And she slapped Doi Liang's teacup to get revenge *for me*. Now she is going to pay with her career. There is no way that she is going to get into Pearl Opera Academy with an expulsion on her record, especially for cheating and lying to a Sensei. Such a waste of talent. And what is she going to do with her life now? The world is not a kind place for homely girls. I should know. It is people like me that make it so. Ah, poor Lin-En!

And poor Yoneko! She was only speaking up for Lin-En, as I should have. But did not. And now her career is ruined, too. And she comes from an important, public family. Oh, how they will punish her for the shame she has brought on their public face.

If I accomplish nothing else in this life, I will at least see that that Doi Liang is destroyed.

For the next two weeks, I look for opportunities to sabotage Doi Liang without breaking any rules myself, but there is no opportunity since there are no tests until the Final Motivation at the end of the month. For the entire time, we only practice pairs Wu-Liu.

We are surprised at how long this training lasts. We all hate it. It is very difficult work because you have to be careful not to strike or kick your partner with your skate blades, while learning to use her as a second pair of arms and legs, while taking on an opponent. None of us is feeling very confident about how we would test in pairs work right now.

Except for me, of course. I am equally trained in single and pairs combat. I am skilled in all twelve of the zodiacal pairs moves, in either head or rear position.

The only small beacon of joy during this time is that that Doi Liang is doing horribly! She tore a cord in one arm defending herself during the Imperial Tea-Service examination and has had it in a sling ever since. Watching her have to work so hard during training to reroute her Chi around the injury and watching her Wu-Liu suffer terribly for it fills my heart with peace.

Sensei Madame Tong is furious at our lack of progress in pairs work. After two weeks of nothing but pairs drills for twelve hours each day, she gathers us on the training court for a speech.

"Worthless Girls of Pearl Rehabilitative Colony. Your performance in pairs Wu-Liu has been disgraceful. If I were you, I would beg my parents for permission to commit ritual suicide out of shame for how I have disgraced my ancestors with my laziness and lack of excellence. You are all of you selfish, conceited girls. None of you has learned anything about the virtue of teamwork.

"There is going to be a change to the Grading system. For the rest of the term, you shall work only in pairs. For the Final Motivation, each pair shall receive one grade so that every girl's grade shall be tied to her partner's.

"You are all allowed to choose your own pairs partner. Choose wisely."

There is much chittering among the girls at this. You can imagine all the drama and possibility for wounded feelings this will create.

"One exception to the right to choose. It is clear from the Second Motivation that none of you shall choose Mistress Doi Liang as a partner. Yet, she needs a partner, so Mistress Doi Liang has the right to choose anyone she wants as her partner."

All eyes turn to Doi Liang.

Doi Liang looks at Sensei Madame Tong.

Then Doi Liang turns her head and looks straight at me.

No, no, no.

No, oh, no, no, oh, no, oh, no, oh, why, oh, why, oh, why me?

Why me, why me, why always, always me?

Aiyah! I want to die.

Doi Liang raises her one good arm, points a finger at me, and says, "Her. I choose her."


That night, I write a letter to my father and my mother.

"Esteemed and Honorable Parents,

"I know you think I am a worthless daughter, but how could you send me to such a stupid, stupid place? Why did you not just tie me in a bag and throw me into the ocean when I was born? I know you wanted to, because I was not born a boy. Tell me the truth. I was adopted, was I not. I always knew it. That is why you never loved me, no matter how gentle and sweet a daughter I was.

But even if you never loved me, you did not have to send me to a stupid place like Pearl Colony to be horribly tortured to death like an animal. I hate it here, but not as much as I hate you. I hate you, I hate you, I hate you.

"Your Worthless, Unloved, Female, Adopted Daughter, Suki."


How am I going to survive this term at Pearl Colony? My first place ranking combines with that Doi Liang's eleventh place ranking so that it averages out to somewhere around sixth place. The evil nuns keep saying that the brutal training at Pearl Colony prepares all girls for the examination to get into Pearl Opera Academy but everyone knows that no one but the top two or three finishers here ever get into the Academy.

And with her stupid crippled arm, how are we ever going to complete the Final Motivation successfully? It was fun to watch her struggle during training to compensate for the injury and try to perform the moves with only three fourths of her limb strength. We all loved watching her fall and splatter flat on the pearl again and again as she tried so hard to reposition her center of Chi to balance out the injury. We all laughed so hard and it was beautiful, but now it is not funny any more. Piss me off to death.

Also, this girl is dangerous and insane. And she hates me for no reason. I am afraid that it might be more important to Doi Liang to see me get kicked out and to ruin my career than for her to save her own career. What would it matter to her? She will never again be as famous as she was when she was Baby Swan Doi. She was already used up at ten years of age.

We train the twelve zodiacal animal pairs moves. For moves where one skater plays the head and one skater plays the rear of the animal, there is always a silent struggle between that Doi Liang and me about who will play the head, but she always yields.

The side to side pairs moves are easier with her, but I hate having to hold her cold, rough hand and we keep having to modify the moves to accommodate her stupid injury.

Two days before the Final Motivation, Sensei Madame Tong announces that she is going to have us fight against actual Pearl Opera Academy students at our Final Motivation. Aiyah, we are so unready for this.

On the last day before Final Motivation, Doi Liang and I are training in the

Swinging Monkey routine together. During the entire final week, she has said nothing to me. Not one word.

As we practice racing along the perimeter wall of Pearl Colony, I finally grow tired of her silence.

"Why do you not ever talk," I say. "What is wrong with you?"

She says nothing.

I say what I suspect is going to be a sore spot, to try to provoke a reaction from her. "Everyone knows why you disappeared for four years after you got famous as Baby Swan Doi." Actually, I am still working on learning exactly what the trouble was that she got into that made her have to hide from public view all those years but I figure that it is worth a try. "You and your parents think you were so clean in covering it up, but everybody knows. I cannot believe you do not realize that. We all talk about it and we all think it is just disgusting."

No reaction. "But what does it matter now? You are much too old and used up to perform 'The Dragon and the Swan' ever again. You will never be limber enough again to do that little swan move where you grab your skate behind you and spin like a blossom. Which was a vulgar little gimmick anyway."

Still no reaction. Piss me off to death. I have to be more creative. "I know about your brother."

She does not look at me.

"I know what you are thinking," I say, making it up as I go. "Your mother had a difficult pregnancy with twins. And you know that if they had had to choose one twin to sacrifice to save the other, you would not be here, would you. See, there is nothing about you that I cannot see." I shoot this arrow into the air to see where it will land.

She still says nothing. She still does not look at me. However, I can tell that she is not looking at me only through great self control. I can see these things.

"Well," I say, "do not think that you have some special right to act so tragic just because of that. My parents wanted a boy. And I think that I was adopted. But you do not see me going around feeling sorry for myself about it."

Aiyah, just thinking about it makes me start to cry. It is so unfair. Why me? When all I have ever wanted was for them to treat me like a human being, not some worthless embarrassment.

As we skate towards the central minaret in the middle of the perimeter wall, we begin swinging each other in half-moon sweeps and passing the fulcrum of our collective Chi back and forth between us. I hate having her evil Chi in my body, even for a moment. As we approach the minaret, we press our bodies together. We launch our bodies off into the space to one side of the minaret. We whip in orbit around each other like a pair of thrown nunchaku, but we wobble because of her stupid injured arm throwing us off. The centripetal force is barely enough to arc us around the minaret and land us on the other side.

As we land, Doi Liang says, "Do not be stupid. It cannot be both."

I am so surprised to hear her speak that I say nothing.

She continues in that low, hoarse voice, "If your parents wanted a boy, why would they have adopted a girl? They are certainly rich enough to adopt a boy if they wanted. Either they wanted a boy, or you are adopted. It cannot be both."

I am stunned by her outrageous presumption. How dare she bring up my private family matters.

That evening, I keep thinking about that Doi Liang's words. "If your parents wanted a boy, why would they have adopted a girl? Do not be stupid. It cannot be both."

My face grows hot again thinking about her daring to talk about my private family matters.

But I cannot stop thinking about her words. "It cannot be both." If my parents were rich enough to adopt a boy . . . either they wanted a boy and I am not adopted, or they did not want a boy, and they adopted me.

Who is this girl to be trying to twist my mind. So arrogant! So unfeeling!

Yet, somehow, I am not as angry about it now as I was this afternoon.

It must be because I am exhausted from the week's training.

When the Final Motivation begins, we see that there are eight students from Pearl Opera Academy. Three pairs of girls and a pair of boys. Each pair representing a different difficulty level. We get to choose which difficulty level we want to attempt, and the boys are the highest difficulty because they are boys. And third year boys!

Most of the girls choose to fight against other girls. We all trained with the assumption that the pair we would have to defeat are girls, and all the girls have been training in moves that are focused for girl to girl combat.

Then, one brave pair of girls chooses to fight the Academy boys. So stupid of them. They find themselves unable to use their all-girl pairs moves to knock the boys off their skates and make them fall down. They make the mistake of flinging themselves directly at the boys. I watch them get knocked down by the boys before even completing one circuit of the perimeter wall of Pearl Colony. Stupid girls, why did they not lead the boys off of the campus and into narrow streets in the city? Combat on an open plane does not take advantage of girls' flexibility over boys. Sensei Madame Tong never said that we must limit the combat route to the campus.

Another pair of girls goes next and they choose to fight the pair of second year girls. After them, it will be our turn to skate. We still have not been able to eliminate the wobble in our combined center of Chi to compensate for her arm, especially when we are passing the Chi between us. And even if we could, how can I know whether she will go insane again just to take me down?

"You are better than they are," I say to her. "You want to win this. More than you want to take me down."

She says nothing.

But I see that I have struck a Chi point. I press all the way in. "You have people you want to say something to with this. So do I. If we win this, I will not have helped you and you will not have helped me. I will have advanced myself. You will have advanced yourself. It will just have happened at the same time. That is all."

She turns to look at me.

"Deal?" I ask her.

She says nothing. She looks at the boys. They are lazing about as if none of this cost them the least effort.

"What do I get out of it?" she says.

"What do you mean what do you get out of it? You get to win! You get to hold on to your chance to get into Pearl Opera Academy! You get to not lose face! You get to not shame your parents."

She says in that weird, low voice, "What makes you think I do not want to shame my parents?"

Oh, no, not now, she is going insane again. "What do you want, you crazy girl! Tell me what you want!"

"If we win," she says slowly, "then you have to keep your mouth shut for a whole day."

"What do you mean keep my mouth shut? What a stupid thing to say. Are you insane?"

"And if you break the promise, I get to grab and crease your hair every time you speak."

"Fine! Whatever! Just do not mess this up."

She makes me write down and sign the promise and rolls the scroll into her skate. She is so weird. "So do we have a deal?" I ask.

"Deal," she says.

It is our turn. Sensei Madame Tong asks what difficulty level we choose. Without looking at each other, Doi Liang and I both point to the boys.

We join the pair of Academy boys and take our position behind them on the top of the perimeter wall.

They crouch in position to burst away from us.

We assume the position to chase after them and prepare to unleash a Warring Sisters move at their backs like the other girls did.

Sensei Madame Tong lifts the trumpet of whale bone to her lips.

The clarion call sounds.

The boys bound away from us along the perimeter wall in a flurry of powerful lunges.

Instead of chasing after them, we turn the other way and hop over to a parallel aqueduct leading out of the campus of Pearl Colony and skate as hard as we can into the city of Pearl.

We hear the cries of surprise behind us. We see the boys half a li away from us realize our sabotage. They scrape to a stop, do one-footed backflip half-turns, and come pumping towards us. Sensei Madame Tong and the remaining girls also skate in a flock to follow us and see what will happen.

The aqueduct we are skating on opens onto an elegant waterfront garden district and twists toward a half-moon bridge arching over a sculpted, false canal. We ride the aqueduct as it slopes down, approaching the bridge, then leap off in a powerful combination single-toe double-heel spin onto the bridge and into the little tea pavilion there.

The boys bear down hard towards us. As the aqueduct slopes down, they both fling themselves into a triple axel scuttling scissor blossom spin, aiming their skate blades at us.

Before they reach us, we do a double-toe roundhouse and spring off at an angle. The boys speed after us as we lead them into a forest of close, tall alleys, deep in a fashionable residential district.

We skate down the alleys, whipping to the left and the right into side-alleys to try to lose the boys and double-back on them, but they keep up with us.

We lead them into a long straight lane of slender townhouses leading towards the waterfront. We see the glimmer of light on the water of Aroma Bay in front of us at the end of the lane.

Ah, but our center of Chi still wobbles! Piss me off to death. She is trying, but we cannot stabilize the Chi.

The boys pump hard towards us and crouch down, forming the Charging Ox position. When they have gathered their Chi, they spring at us.

When we hear their skates leave the pearl, Doi Liang and I entwine our arms together so that we join into a position with no arms and four legs. She winces as I grab her crippled arm, sending a wave rocking through our Chi, but we hold on to it. At the last possible moment, we get it right and execute the Leaping Rabbit pairs move and leap up out of their way.

The boys attempt to reposition and aim up towards us but they are unable to lock onto us as our trajectory wobbles. The unstable Chi is helping us! Like the Drunken Hen move, our random lurches are as unpredictable to our foes as to us.

As the boys slide under us towards the bay, they struggle to untangle from the Charging Ox position, but in this narrow residential lane, they cannot burst apart out of the position as they are trained to do and they used too much force in too small a space.

As they slide towards the bay, Doi Liang and I change in mid-air from the Leaping Rabbit position to the Charging Ram position. We curl our arms to form the ram's horns and channel the rest of the Chi from our downward trajectory to batter into the boys.

Our impact, the remaining Chi from the boys' Charging Ox move, and the boys' own weight combine. The momentum is too much for them to stop in time. We send them crashing through a grove of false cherry blossoms planted by the water. They go flying off the edge of the boardwalk in an explosion of pink petals straight into Aroma Bay, ending in two splashes so far away that they look like little plumes of dolphin spray.

As soon as we see that we have defeated the boys, Doi Liang and I untangle our limbs and push each other away as fast as we can.

Sensei Madame Tong and all the other girls catch up with us. They gaze in stun at the third year Academy boys in the sea, swimming back towards us. The girls look at each other and then bow to us. Doi Liang bows back to them as if they were honoring her. Her! Make me die of laughing!

Then that Doi Liang bows to Sensei Madame Tong, reaches into her skate, and gives her the scroll that I signed! Sensei Madame Tong reads the scroll and says, "Good."

She bows to Sensei Madame Tong again and says, "I have waited three months for a day of quiet."

If she thinks I am going to let her talk about me like that in front of everyone, she is even stupider than I thought! I skate up to her. "Do not think that they were bowing to you! Your stupid crippled arm almost lost us—Ai!" Doi Liang's hand shoots out at my head, grabs a fistful of hair, and squeezes! Aiyah, she has creased it! Three months of sleeping with a rolled cloth under my neck to allow the hair to grow back straight, and she has ruined it!

I start to do the double-bladed mantis chop move on Doi Liang's arm but Sensei Madame Tong shoots me an iron stare. She is taking that Doi Liang's side! Piss me off to death!

Doi Liang releases my hair. It is still only at the level of my chin, so I cannot see how badly she injured it, but I toss it side to side and can feel from how it swings that that passage of hair is permanently creased and ruined.

"You stupid, ugly, low-grade—Ai!" Doi Liang's fist is suddenly in my hair again, squeezing and crushing! "Do not do that, you crazy dog fart, you are going to—Ai!" Her other fist shoots into my hair! Her crippled arm is still strong enough to bend my hair. "Let go, you evil, insane—Ai!" Both her fists tighten and twist in my hair!

Out of the border of my vision, I see the two Academy boys climb out of the water onto the boardwalk. Oh, no, I cannot let them see me like this!

"Not in front of boys! Let me go, you stupid, stupid—Ai!" Doi Liang's hands perform the ten-spoked churning maw move right in my hair!

The boys come and join everyone to watch.

I think I am going to faint.

When she finally releases my hair, my hands reach up, afraid to discover how terrible the injury is.

My hair is so creased and crooked and matted and frizzed that it feels like I am wearing a giant bird's nest on my head.

I think I am going to vomit.

Then the boys laugh and applaud.

Why me, why me, why always, always me! I want to die!

I receive my Certificate of Successful Penitence from Pearl Colony. The victory against the boys finished us in first place. But I feel no victory.

For that Doi Liang and I are not done.

We are not equal.

We are not even.

We are tied.

So now, you ask us all to write this stupid essay to our parents about what we have learned during our sentence here at Pearl Colony.

Well, I will tell you what I learned here.

Nothing.

Not one stupid, stinking thing.

You tell me that I am a wicked girl, but you just hate me because I am more determined to be myself than you were ever strong enough to be.

You cannot shame me. You cannot deny me. For I am Her Grace, Radiant Goddess Princess Suki. I will take the entrance examination for Pearl Opera Academy and I will prevail.

Next year at Pearl Opera Academy, I will have skated out of here and forgotten you, and you will still be nuns, ugly, talentless nuns.

Next year at Pearl Opera Academy, I will battle this evil girl again and I will prevail.

Next year at Pearl Opera Academy, I will win the lead role in the Drift Season Pageant and in Beautymarch, and I will be crowned Super Princess of Wu-Liu.

Next year at Pearl Opera Academy, I will make my stupid parents so sorry that they ever sent me away and they will beg me to forgive them but I will not care because I will have already forgotten who they are, as everyone under Heaven will have forgotten them, as the nobodies that they are, while my name will live forever in glory.

Next year at Pearl Opera Academy, I will be a Legend.

## NEBULA AWARD NOMINEE
### BEST NOVELETTE

# "IN JOY, KNOWING THE ABYSS BEHIND"

## SARAH PINSKER

*This is Sarah Pinsker's first Nebula nomination. "In Joy, Knowing the Abyss Behind" won a Theodore Sturgeon Memorial Award and appeared in* **Strange Horizons.**

"Don't leave."

The first time he said it, it sounded like a command. The tone was so unlike George, Millie nearly dropped her hairbrush. They were in their bedroom, in their home of sixty-six years. Outside the French doors, fresh snow settled on top of old snow. The lights in George's sprawling treehouse made it stand out against the otherwise unbroken white. George sat in the chair at the telephone desk. He was in the middle of changing his socks, one leg crossed over the other, when he dropped the new sock to the floor and coughed once. Millie glanced in the mirror on her vanity, caught him staring at her.

"Don't leave," he said again.

She turned around to face him.

The third time it arrived as a question, a note of confusion lurking in the space between his words. "Don't leave, please?"

He seemed to struggle with the next sentence, his last. "I'm sorry."

"What are you talking about, old man?" she asked, but he was already someplace else. He opened his mouth as if to say more, but no words came out.

She had always been calm in the family's minor medical crises, but this time the words *this is it* blazed across her brain and crowded everything else out. She took deep breaths and tried to remember what she should do. She crossed to his chair, put her hand on his chest, felt the rise and fall. That was good. She didn't think she could get him to the floor, much less perform chest compressions. She stooped to put the clean sock on his bare foot, then reached across him to pick up the phone and dial for an ambulance. Should those actions have been the other way around? Possibly. *This is it.*

"I'll be right back," she told him before leaving the room to unlock the front door. He was still in the same place when she returned, collapsed slightly to the right in the chair. His left eye looked panicked, his right eye oddly calm. She dragged the chair from her vanity over and sat down facing him. Behind him the snow continued to fall.

"I wonder if this will be the storm that proves too heavy for that poor old sycamore," she said, taking her husband's hand in hers and looking out at the treehouse. "I think this is going to be a big one."

It had snowed the day they met. Chicago, Marshall Field's, December 1944. He had held the door for her as they both exited onto State Street.

"Ladies first," said the young man in the Army overcoat, gesturing with the fat notebook in his free hand. He was shorter than her by a few inches, and she was not terribly tall; if he hadn't been wearing the uniform she would have mistaken him for a boy.

"Thank you," she said, giving him a smile over her shoulder. She didn't see the patch of ice beyond the vestibule. Her left foot slipped out from under her, then her right. He caught her before she landed, losing his own footing in the process. The pages of his notebook fluttered to the ground around them as he broke her fall with his body. They both scrambled to their feet, red-faced and breathless.

"Thank you again," she said.

He brushed snow off his backside and bent to grab several loose pieces of paper from the pavement. She picked at one that had plastered itself to her leg.

He pointed at it. "It likes you. You should probably keep it."

She peeled the page from her nylon and examined it. Even as the ink blurred and ran she could tell it had been a skillful sketch of the grand staircase and the Tiffany dome at the library. The soaked paper tore in two in her hands.

"It's ruined!"

"It's okay, I have more." He held out the others. She saw the Field Museum, the Buckingham Fountain, the building they had just left, all bleeding away.

She put her hand to her mouth. "Your drawings are ruined, and you've torn your coat, too."

He shrugged, touching the ragged edges at his elbow. "Don't worry about it. These were just for fun. Practice. I'm an architect. George Gordon. You don't have to memorize it. Everybody'll know it someday."

"Millicent Berg. Nice to meet you. And I'm sorry about your drawings, even if they were only for fun. Can I make it up to you?"

He scratched his head in a pantomime of contemplation. "I'd ask you to have lunch with me, but I've already eaten. You might let me draw another for you over coffee, I suppose."

Millie glanced up at the clock jutting out from the building. She shook her head. "I'm afraid I'm already late to meet a friend."

"Another time?" he persisted, rubbing his elbow in an obvious fashion. In another man she might have found it rude, but there was something about him that she liked. Too bad.

"Sorry. I'm only visiting Chicago until Tuesday. I go to college in Baltimore," she said.

His grin chased everything ordinary from his face. "You may not get out of this so easily, then. I'm stationed in Maryland. Fort Meade."

Out of such coincidences, lives were built.


The emergency workers tore two buttons off of George's pajama top. Millie, who had dressed while she waited for them to arrive, slipped the buttons into the pocket of her cardigan. The EMTs checked George's pulse and vital signs. They talked to each other but not to her. She hovered behind them as they worked.

"Will he be okay?" she asked. Nobody answered her, and after a moment she wondered if she had asked out loud. She glanced at herself in the mirror. The old woman who had stolen her reflection several years ago stared back at her. They nodded to each other in greeting.

When one of the paramedics finally spoke to Millie, it was to tell her they didn't want her to ride in the ambulance with George.

"There isn't room," said the young one, the girl.

What she meant, thought Millie, was that they didn't want to have to worry about her, too. She was spared the trouble of arguing when Raymond and his boyfriend Mark arrived.

"Don't worry, Grandma," Ray said. "We can ride behind them."

Mark helped her into the passenger seat of their Toyota. They were good boys. They took her to the salon, took her and George to dinner and to plays and concerts. Of all of the children and grandchildren, she was glad that Ray was the one who lived nearby. He was the one she trusted most to actually listen to her if she said something.

Mark dropped Millie and Ray at the emergency bay. After filling out insurance paperwork, they sat in a waiting room until a tired-eyed woman in scrubs appeared. An ischemic stroke, the doctor said, on the left side of George's brain. They had stabilized him. She could see him if she liked. Millie wondered about the phrasing. Did anyone ever say no, thank you very much, I've waited all day, but on second thought, I wouldn't like to see him? After so many hours in one position she struggled to get to her feet. Raymond offered his arm, and she leaned on him all the way down the hallway to Intensive Care.

The right side of George's face sagged, the eye tugging downward at the outside corner. His right hand lay limp on his hip. His left hand busied itself, roaming the white sheets in sweeping motions.

"He's awake, but not really responding to anyone," the doctor told her. What was the doctor's name? DeSoto, like the mouse dentist in the book she had read to the grandchildren. She could remember that. "The stroke was on the left side, so we're looking at right side hemiparesis, possibly hemiplegia. He probably will need therapy to regain speech, and that may be a long way off. For now, we'd like to see if he acknowledges you in any way."

Millie approached with delicate steps. The man in the bed looked like George with all of the Georgeness scooped out.

"Hello, old man," she whispered, just for him. A little louder she said, "Hi, George. It's me, Millie." That felt oddly formal, like an introduction. She didn't want to touch the dead hand, and reached instead for the roving one, his left.

He brushed her away with a force she hadn't expected and then resumed his interrupted motions. Millie fought back tears. He hadn't meant it, couldn't mean it, but the insult still bruised her.

"Believe it or not, that's a positive sign, Mrs. Gordon. That's the first time he's responded to stimulus."

Ray rested a hand on her shoulder. "He probably didn't know it was you, Grandma. He wasn't pushing you away."

Millie looked at the doctor. "Doctor Gordon," she said.

"No, I'm Dr. DeSoto." The young woman glanced at Ray.

"And I'm Dr. Gordon," Millie said. "Just so you know."

She lowered herself into the chair by the bedside, then looked up at the doctor and her grandson. They both knew everything, and knew nothing.

"He's drawing," said Millie. "All that motion. He's trying to draw. He's left-handed."

In their first months of courtship, she had once asked him to show her his designs.

"They're just buildings," he said. "Nothing special."

She couldn't believe that anything he did might be less than special. As far as she was concerned, everything about him was clever and funny and attentive and romantic. He had called her father to ask permission to see her, and replaced the ruined picture of the Tiffany dome with one of her college's stately main hall. He brought her handmade bouquets of paper roses, since it was still winter. Her friends buzzed about the fact that she had found an older man, a qualified architect, twenty-four to her twenty. They all dated Hopkins boys, rich and bland.

"Bring me some of your blueprints," she begged him one night in her dormitory's well-policed lounge. "I know it can't be the ones you work on for the Army, but maybe something from when you were in school? I want to see what you do."

"Really, they'll bore you," he said, but he looked pleased. The next time he visited, he had a leather portfolio tucked under one arm. He spread the diagrams on the table in the visiting room.

"Is this a skyscraper?" Millie traced the outlines.

He grinned his charming grin, with a touch of sheepishness built in. "Yes—but that one isn't being built or anything. Not yet, anyway."

"I can tell it's going to be beautiful. The doorways, the decorative touches. It's lovelier than the Chrysler Building!"

He leaned over to kiss her, though a sharp cough from the dormitory matron interrupted his course. "The Chrysler Building was what inspired me to do this, you know," he said, pushing his drawings slightly to the side to sit on the corner of the table, facing her. The enthusiasm in his eyes lit his whole face. "That and the Empire State Building. We lived in New York back then, and I would slip out of school to watch them going up. Nine, ten years old, and I knew right then that I was going to make things that people would want to see."

He pointed to other drawings in the portfolio: towers, mansions, a stadium. Millie was amazed at his vision.

"When do you get to start making these?"

"As soon as the Army's done with me."

"I'll bet they don't have you designing anything as beautiful as this. Just barracks and bases."

"There are some interesting projects. Hypothetical stuff, with the engineers."

"Hypothetical?"

"Made up. Like out of the pulps. Barracks for soldiers who are ten feet tall, prisons built into the side of mountains, guard houses underwater. I know it's all ridiculous stuff, kid stuff, but it's fun to imagine. The engineers tell me what is and isn't possible. I draw, and then they take my sketches away or tell me things to change. Mill, I thought my skyscrapers would be the future, but they're showing me all kinds of futures I hardly know how to think about."

When he proposed to her a month later, she said yes. She loved the sweet touches, but also the dreamer architect. She wanted to be part of the future he envisioned.

A nurse brought a piece of butcher's paper into George's hospital room, and Dr. DeSoto put a fat marker in his hand. Millie sat in the chair by his bedside. Their son Charlie, Charles now, brought in a second chair to sit next to her.

Jane was due on a flight that evening. The room was getting crowded, but Millie didn't know whom she could ask to leave. She contemplated stepping out, excusing herself to go to the bathroom or the vending machine and not coming back. No, she would never get away with it. Charlie had become a hoverer, attending to needs she didn't have, fetching her tea and a pillow for her chair and antibacterial sanitizers that turned her skin to paper.

The odor of the marker cut through the hospital smells. Why was it only the acrid scents that came on so forcefully? Charlie had brought two huge bouquets, but Millie couldn't smell the flowers at all. Then again, it was winter, and these bouquets must have come from a supermarket or the hospital gift shop; they were probably scentless. She thought for a moment of the paper flowers that George used to make for her during the months that nothing bloomed.

George's good eye opened. He didn't seem to focus on anything in particular, but he began to draw again. Quick, sure strokes.

"The marker's going to bleed through the paper!" Charlie half-rose from his chair.

"Let it," said Millie. "White sheets are boring anyway."

"Wait until the hospital bills you for them," her son said under his breath. He had perfected that stage mutter at the age of five. She ignored it, as she always had.

Millie had seen enough of George's blueprints over the years to know that this was an unusual one. He started from the center, instead of the perimeter. The sweeping motions he had made without the pen in his hand now transformed into curved walls. Thick walls, judging from the way he returned to them over and over. Shapes she had never seen him draw in any of his professional work.

He labored for an hour. Dr. DeSoto excused herself, saying she would be back.

"Should we stop him?" Charlie asked at one point. "He's exhausting himself."

"He's almost finished, I think," said Millie. His hand was slowing down, making finer adjustments now. The thickness of the marker obscured the delicacy of his sketching. What was going on in his head?

Someone echoed that thought, and she looked up to see that the doctor had returned. Dr. DeSoto gently took the marker from George's hand, which trembled now. She held up the drawing.

"What did he draw?" Millie strained, but was unable to see well enough at that distance. The doctor brought it closer.

Charlie was the one to say it out loud. "I think it's some kind of prison."

Examining the sketch up close, she knew he was right. Thick concentric walls, ramps that suggested someplace far underground. No windows, no doors, except to and from the central guard tower. This was a place nobody was meant to leave.

In the early years, when he and the other junior architects were first throwing their hats into the partnership ring, George often stayed out for a drink after work or a late night in the office. They attended dinner parties and groundbreakings. Millie loved the meetings with new clients and their wives. She liked to watch George sell them on his vision for their buildings as if his ideas were their own.

"When I make partner, I'll build us our dream house," he said. In the meantime, they moved out to the county. He did his best to balance work and new fatherhood, though it was clear that fatherhood was tipping the balance. He started the tree house when Charlie was still an infant, making preliminary drawings with the baby asleep in the crook of his right arm. Millie would wake up to find the two of them in George's office. "We couldn't sleep, so we thought we'd get some work done," he would say. The early years were all sketches and crumpled paper, false starts and fresh ones.

"They're too young to ask for a tree house," Millie said once, after Jane was born. "How do you know they want one?"

"Look at that tree," George said, pointing to the enormous sycamore in their yard. Its leaves blazed gold and orange in the soft October sun. "How could they not?"

He started the actual construction when Jane was a year old and Charlie was three, working through the weekends and summer evenings. Millie didn't help with the tree house. Instead, she lingered in the garden, seeding and weeding and nurturing her flowers. She had only recently discovered the joys of gardening, but already it was becoming a passion for her. More than that, it was a chance for them all to be together, even if they were involved in different projects. She dug to a soundtrack of hammer and saw. A slight note of sawdust drifted in the air beneath the heady aroma of her roses and peonies. She liked listening to George explain to Charlie what he was doing, and loved the ways in which he involved Charlie, starting a nail and then inviting the boy to finish it. "You're some builder, kid. Look at that workmanship." If Millie could have bottled a moment, it might have been one of these.

As the children grew older, George allowed them to assert their own personalities on the design.

"I want a giraffe," said four-year-old Charlie, and so George tore out the conventional ladder and constructed a wooden giraffe with stairs built into the neck. When Jane wanted a Rapunzel tower, George built a platform accessible only by a thick flaxen braid. Long after the structure was completed, if one of them asked for a new element he found a way to incorporate it.

"Someday they'll stump you," said Millie.

"They haven't yet," her husband replied. He was right; they never did. The project that she had envisioned as a simple Our Gang style fort began to assert itself in contrast with her manicured flowerbeds. Over the years he created a pirate ship deck, a Pippi Longstocking wing, a Swiss Family Robinson addition, byzantine passages and secret compartments, and a crow's nest high in the branches. He wired it with thousands of lights, which switched on by timer every evening and danced like fireflies in all seasons.

He didn't let the sycamore limit his vision. He strayed yards from the tree in some directions, like an invasive vine. The tree was merely a guide; Millie suspected that if the tree were hit by lightning, George's structural supports would hold it in place. Some additions were more aesthetically pleasing than others, and some looked better in one season or another, but George didn't care about the aesthetics of the project; he seemed happiest when the whole thing was overrun with children, theirs and others, which was most of the time. The only thing he ever refused them was a rocket. "Spaceships aren't made of wood," he said, with more seriousness than Millie thought the topic was due. "It wouldn't make any sense."

Jane arrived from Seattle, buzzing into the room with the manic exhaustion of air travel. Hugs all around. Millie marveled, as always, at the fact that two such quiet people had created two such loud ones. Five of the six grandchildren were loud too, everyone but Raymond. Maybe silence was a recessive trait.

Charlie and Jane spent ten minutes arguing over who would stay the night and who would take Millie home. Millie wasn't sure if she was the prize or the punishment. In the end, Jane said she wanted to spend some time alone with her father, since she had only just gotten there, and Charlie said that he and Millie could both use some proper sleep in proper beds, and it was all decided. Millie considered arguing that she wanted to stay at the hospital as well, to make the point that she had a say in the matter. Truth be told, she did want to leave. Too much time in a hospital wasn't good for anyone, even a visitor.

She took George's sketch with her, folding it across her lap for the ride home. Charlie was a good driver, but everything felt too fast. The car was some strange rental, full of glowing buttons and gauges, like the cockpit of an airplane.

"We're going to have to make some plans," said George, no, Charlie. How strange that her son was now older than her husband when she pictured him in her mind. She knew he was Charlie. George never took his eyes off the road, but Charlie stared at her now, waiting for her response to his statement. What kind of response did he expect? She fought the urge to say "duuuuh," as the great-grandchildren did.

"Look where you're going, Charles." Millie pointed at the windshield. Charlie shifted his eyes to the road, but continued throwing glances her way.

"You've done a great job of staying independent, but if he needs rehab you won't be able to take care of him."

"I know," said Millie.

"And I'm not sure it's wise for you to stay in that big house all by yourself."

"Raymond checks on me."

"He's a good boy. I'm glad he lives so close to you. Still, he can't be expected to take on all the responsibility."

"I'll be fine," said Millie.

"You have to consider—"

"I'll consider."

"You're eighty-eight years old. The fact that the two of you have been able to live on your own for this long is a minor miracle."

"I'll consider," she said with finality.

They drove the rest of the way in silence. The snow that had fallen the day before had compacted. Charlie left her in the car with the engine running while he shoveled and de-iced the walk. Even from a distance she saw his exertion. How strange to watch her son grow old. Did he consider himself old? If he was old, what did that make her? Red faced and sweaty, he helped her up the salted steps.

Later, alone in her bedroom, Millie reached into the pocket of her cardigan and pulled out the two buttons from George's pajama top. She wondered what had happened to his pajamas now that he was in a hospital gown. These would be easy enough to sew back on for him, if they would only give her back the shirt. George was forever losing buttons, busting them off outgrown pants or catching his shirt on the edge of his drafting table. This time it wasn't his fault, of course.

She went through the motions: brushed her teeth, changed into her night-gown, walked her brush through her hair. No need to look in the mirror; she knew she was a mess. Instead, she looked out at the illuminated treehouse. What would happen if George wasn't around to change the lights? She couldn't bear the thought of it going dark for a single night.

Maybe Charlie was right, and they should consider moving someplace easier to maintain. If George passed, maybe it would be better to be elsewhere than to live with the memories that suffused each corner of this house. She couldn't think of a time when she had spent a night in the bed alone. No, that wasn't true. How had she forgotten? There had been a whole month in 1951, the year everything changed.

George had only ever taken one trip without Millie, in the fall of 1951. A letter had arrived from the army asking him to fly to New Mexico.

"You don't have to go," she said. "You're not a soldier anymore. They don't even tell you in the letter what they want you to go for. Just 'project maintenance.'"

"I suppose I'll find out. Maybe one of those theoretical designs actually got built. Maybe I'll fly into George Gordon Airport." He swooped Jane into his arms and then up into the air. "Maybe they want to give your Daddy a medal! Valor in the face of bureaucracy!" Jane giggled.

He was gone two weeks, then three weeks, then four. They picked him up at Friendship on the afternoon of Jane's third birthday. Up until the moment she loaded the children into the Packard, Millie kept expecting the telephone to ring and George's tired voice to say he had been delayed yet again and would she get by for another week. She attacked the ingredients for Jane's birthday cake, the batter fleeing up the sides of the bowl. Don't ring, she willed the telephone.

But no, he was already there when she drove up, his suit rumpled and his shoulders sagging. He looked every bit as exhausted as he had sounded. She had been prepared to let him know the stress his absence had caused her, but instead she kissed his stubbled cheek. The kids leaned in to hug or possibly strangle him from the back seat.

"Sit down, both of you," he said, slapping their hands from his neck.

"Do you have presents for us?" Charlie reached over the seatback for the blueprint tube George was holding between his knees.

"Don't touch that! Sorry, kid. No presents."

Millie saw Jane building up a wail, and tried to head it off. "I have a lovely dinner planned for tonight. All of Jane's favorites, and steak for you."

"Jane's favorites?"

"Yes, she got to pick for her birthday dinner, of course. Like a big girl."

He scratched at two days' growth of beard.

"Janie's birthday dinner. Of course," he repeated. "Janie, how would you like to pick your own present out tomorrow? Big girls do that."

The tantrum dissipated. In the backseat, Charlie began to run down a list of toys he thought Jane might like, all of which were actually toys he would like better. Millie glanced over at George, who was pinching the bridge of his nose between his fingers. She hoped to get a chance to ask him what was wrong, but when they got home he disappeared into his office. She busied herself making dinner. He snapped at the children twice for fidgeting over the meal; after losing patience a third time, he excused himself before they could sing to Jane.

That night, Millie rolled over in the bed to find George wasn't there. She checked his office, the kitchen, the children's rooms, the den, before finally noticing the unlatched patio door. The air and grass were already laced with frost. She wore a flannel robe, but wished she had put on shoes. George's sobs traveled down from the treehouse and across the lawn.

She climbed the giraffe's-neck ladder, crossed the bridge of the pirate ship. The first fallen leaves made some of the steps slippery. George cried like a child in the crow's nest above her. She wasn't sure which frightened her more, his strange mood earlier in the day or his tears now. Maybe he'd rather she climbed down, slipped back into bed, and pretended she had heard nothing.

Her foot crunched a leaf as she took her first step backward.

"Don't leave," he said.

She stopped. "George, what's the matter?"

"Don't leave, please," he said. "I had no idea. I had no choice."

She wanted him to continue. It wouldn't take much to keep him from speaking. One wrong word, one wrong step. She stood still, trying to figure out how close he was from the ragged sound of his breath.

"They said the scenarios were hypothetical."

She waited.

"They were real, Mill. Defenseless, harmless things. Their ship was destroyed. They've been in there four years, and the Army wants me to design a newer, better place, to make sure they're stuck 'for the indefinite future.' I should have said no and gotten right back on the plane. 'For the security of the country,' the lieutenant said. He said to think of you, and Charlie, and Jane. I had to, you see?"

She didn't see. She waited for him to say more. She asked questions in her mind: who were 'they' and why were they stuck and why couldn't they go back and where couldn't they go back to? Why did he call them things? Was it better to know or not to know? She decided he would tell if he wanted to tell. Minutes passed. Shivering, she climbed four wooden rungs bolted to the trunk. An ungraceful shimmy brought her into the crow's nest. George, in his striped pajamas, sat in the corner, his knees to his chest like a child.

She wanted to go to him, to hold him as he had always held her, to tell him to put it behind him. Instead, she kissed him on the top of his head and leaned out over the edge. She had never been all the way to the top of the tree house before. From this solid perch she could see the delicate curves of her dormant gardens. Then past that, over the rooftops, past the lamplit neighborhood, out to the dark farmland beyond. She didn't know what time it was, but the faintest glimmer of dawn colored the place where the earth met the sky.

Even at this height she trusted his workmanship. The platform was steady, the railing secure.

She sat down beside him. "You're a good man, and a good husband, and a good father," she said. "Whatever you did, I'm sure you had to do it."

After a moment, he put his arm around her. She knew that whatever he had allowed to surface he now had buried. Who would have imagined that such an intimate moment would become the line between before and after? Maybe she should have asked more, pushed more, given more comfort. How had it taken sixty years to come back around to the things he had spoken of that night? That night, she had no idea what he was talking about. She had let it go, let him carry it alone.

Millie dialed Raymond first thing when she woke up. Mark answered the phone, half-asleep, and she realized she had no idea what day of the week it was. If it was a weekend she was calling far too early. Mark put Ray on.

"I think I lost a day at the hospital," she said by way of apology.

"It's okay, Grandma. What's up?"

She took a deep breath. "I was wondering if you would do me a favor if you're planning on coming . . . no, actually, that part doesn't matter. Regardless of whether you're coming to the hospital today, I was wondering if you would stop by the house and help me look for something."

"No problem. What and where?"

"I'm not sure exactly what, and I'm guessing at the where. There may be nothing. I'm just curious, and I can't go up there myself."

"Up there?" he asked.

"The top of the tree house."

When Charlie woke, Millie insisted that he leave for the hospital without her. "Raymond is on his way," she said. "He'll take me."

"Why are you dragging him over here?" Charlie poured coffee into a mug for her, then rummaged in the cupboard until he found a travel cup for himself. He took the milk from the fridge, sniffed it, and then splashed some into her coffee and some into his own.

"He's going to help find some paperwork I misplaced." Before Charlie offered his own assistance, she added, "I had asked him to put it in a safe place for me, so it makes sense for him to be the one to figure out where he put it."

He clapped the lid onto his cup and gave her a smile of sympathy. "Like his uncle, huh? Do you remember all the stuff I never saw again that I had put away for safekeeping? I still expect you to call someday to say you found my Brooks Robinson rookie card."

She kissed him goodbye and managed to push him out the door. Poor Raymond didn't deserve to be lumped in with Charlie on this one. Nobody lost things like Charlie.

When Ray arrived, she explained what she wanted him to search for, or rather the fact that she had no idea what he was searching for, but he would know it if he found it. She made him put on one of George's hats and a pair of gloves before sending him out to the tree house.

Once he had stepped outside, Millie set about her own search. She made her way down the hallway and pushed open the door to the office. The air in the room was cold and stale; though Millie would be sitting at the drafting table in a few weeks to plan her spring gardens, neither she nor George had much use for the room in the winter. As in their bedroom next door, the windows faced the backyard. She watched Raymond's progress through the snow before turning to the task at hand. She didn't know if George had kept anything here that might explain his actions, but it was worth looking.

She started with the file cabinets: not hers with the house bills and contracts and warranties and receipts, but the wood-faced one he had built for himself. The drawer slid open easily. The plans inside were neatly labeled, arranged alphabetically. What might she find here? "S" for "secret." "P" for "prison." Unlikely.

The phone rang. Once, twice. Why had they never put a telephone in the office? Three times, four. The bedroom was closer than the kitchen, but she wasn't yet ready to sit at the desk where George had been. Five rings, six, seven. The ringing paused, then began again. She wasn't sure she wanted to speak to anybody who wanted to reach her that badly.

She lifted the phone from its cradle.

"He had another stroke, Ma. They don't know if he's going to wake up." Jane was crying. Millie tried to comfort her, feeling absurd in doing so. How could she explain that she had already begun mourning George as she had picked the buttons of his pajama top off the floor?

"Hang on, Janie," Millie said. "We'll be there as soon as we can. I have to wait for Raymond to come back inside."

She hung up and leaned against the doorframe. From the kitchen doorway, she saw into the den. George's childhood desk stood in a dark corner beside the stairs; he had brought it back to the house after his mother's death in 1969. Funny, the things that become background, beneath notice. She hadn't given that desk a second thought in years.

The writing surface swung upward on protesting hinges, revealing layers of children's hidden treasures: a princess doll from some Disney movie or another, a metal car, a comic book, some foreign coins, the joke wrappers from several pieces of Bazooka gum. Beneath three generations of lost toys, she discovered something else: a piece of plywood. It took her some effort to pry loose the false bottom.

Inside, she found a small leather-bound notebook of the type George had carried when they first met. George had signed and dated the inside of the front cover, 1931. Each page was filled with diagrams. Castles, skyscrapers, scaled city maps, all done in a more fanciful version of George's trained hand. Everything he had put away of himself, bound into one sketchbook.

In retrospect, Millie was able to look back on that single trip and the confession in the upper branches of the sycamore as a turning point. They climbed down as the sun rose, dressed the children, drove downtown to run some errands, went to Hutzler's for an early lunch and a belated birthday present for Jane. Life seemed back to normal. Millie put George's upset out of her mind over shrimp salad on cheese toast. Later there were other conversations, bigger battles. It was easy enough to say in hindsight that George had become different overnight, but by the time she noticed, the changes had already taken root. By the time she noticed, the architect was gone.

The man who replaced him was similar in most ways, but without any hint of boyishness. The only remnant of the child who had sketched skyscrapers was in his work on the treehouse; he still mustered enthusiasm when planning something with Charlie and Jane. He ceased to bring designs home from the office at all.

"Work can stay at work," he said.

She was baffled that someone who still poured so much of himself into a project for his children had stopped putting anything into his occupation. She watched as he was passed over for promotion after promotion, never progressing beyond junior partner at any of the firms he worked for.

"They wanted me to work overtime," he'd say after leaving another job. Or, "They wanted me to travel."

"So travel! The kids are old enough that I can manage for a few days on my own."

He just shook his head. It was as if he knew every trick for self-promotion and then set about sabotaging himself. Millie didn't complain. When money was tight, when Jane needed braces or when a storm blew the roof off the garage, Millie found work. She tried not to resent the change. Whatever it was the other architects had that drove them to create no longer seemed to be a part of George. He designed bland suburban houses, and later strip malls and office parks. The high-rises and mansions and museums went to other, more ambitious draftsmen.

"Show me your designs," she begged him. "The projects you want to work on."

"They're only buildings," he said, shrugging. This time it was true.

"A new subdivision?" She tried to ask in a way that sounded excited.

"Yes. A whole neighborhood, but just three different house designs."

"Are you designing all of them?"

"No, I'm in charge of the four bedroom, but I have to work with another fellow so that they look like they came from the same brain."

"You're very talented, you know." She said this as often as possible without sounding trite. "I wish you would get a chance to make all those things you used to talk about."

He laughed and turned away from the drafting table. "You're sweet to say so, but it's not art. It's just my job. I make what they want me to make."

When the wives of the firm's partners mentioned their husbands' latest endeavors, she smiled and volunteered nothing. If he didn't want to be an artist, he didn't have to be, but she couldn't understand how he took pride in his draftsmanship and dismissed it at the same time. Try as she might, she was unable to put her finger on what exactly he had lost. How could she complain about a man who helped with the dishes every night, who read to the children, who taught them to measure twice and cut once? She tried to encourage him, but he turned everything around.

"Why don't you get another degree?" he asked one day, after the children had both started high school. "You've always wanted to learn more about your plants."

She did it, half hoping to motivate him again as well. She had a master's degree and a doctorate in botany by the time she realized she would never goad him into competing with her. He let her take over his office and his drafting table when she needed them for her garden designs. He corrected others when they assumed he was the doctor in the family, and spoke of her accomplishments, but never said a word about his own. When she tried to brag to others about his work, he responded with self-deprecation. She hated herself for wishing him to be anything other than what he had become, and worked on loving him for the person that he was. He was a match that refused to ignite; she felt selfish for wanting him to burn brightly.

Over time, it ceased to matter as much. Her career bloomed, and she learned not to press him about his. The children grew up and left and came back and left and had children of their own. In retirement she found him to be much easier company. She enjoyed watching his comfortable way with the grandchildren and great-grandchildren, and loved it when he began to design new tree house additions for the new generations.

She wasn't sure if it was fair to judge anyone by the man he had been in his twenties. The person you marry is not the same person you grow old with. She was sure he could say the same thing about her. She was sorry it had taken her so long to learn that, to stop pushing him, but that was probably the way of it.

Raymond drove her to the hospital, then returned to the house. "I'm onto something," he said, kissing her on the forehead and dashing out again. Millie watched reruns from the straight-backed chair beside George's bed. Jane and Charlie took turns beside her, occasionally slipping out to talk in the hallway. She thought she heard Charlie say "retirement community" at least twice.

She let the TV distract her. Every man on television seemed to be an architect. Every sitcom and every movie, from the Brady Bunch on, seemed to feature some young man with blueprints and skyscraper dreams. Why was that? It was artsy but manly, she supposed. Sensitive without being soft. A perfect occupation for a man with a creative side who also wanted to support his family, at least until the day he decided he didn't want to do it anymore. That didn't seem to happen on television.

Raymond arrived back late in the evening, the glow of success evident in his face. It only took him a moment to convince his mother and uncle to go grab some dinner before the cafeteria closed.

"I think I found what you were looking for, Grandma." It was amazing how much he looked like a young George when he smiled. Taller, thankfully for him, and with a strange lop-sided haircut, but with the same rakish confidence that she had so admired. She returned the smile. She hadn't really thought there would be anything to find, but it had been worth a shot.

"There are a bunch of compartments all over the tree house, but most of them are still filled with toys and baseball cards and stuff. Anyway, I remembered that one time my cousin Joseph was chasing me 'cause he wanted my Steve Austin action figure. I didn't know where to put it that he wouldn't find it. I was almost to the top when I realized that the metal struts that support the crow's nest are hollow, if you have something to pry them open with. I had my pocket knife with me. The first one I opened had something wedged in it, so I stashed Steve Austin in the second one until Joseph went home. Never thought to look at what was in that first one until now."

With a flourish, he produced a blueprint tube from behind his back. "I opened it to make sure there was something in it—there is—but I didn't look at what's inside."

She tried to keep her voice from quavering. She hoped the others would stay away from the room a little longer. "Shall we?"

Ray slid the rolled paper out, laying the drawing across George's legs.

"George, we're looking at the blueprints you hid." She thought it was only fair to explain what was going on.

This was the same prison he had drawn on the butcher paper. Done on proper drafting paper, and more detailed, but still with an unfinished quality. He wouldn't have been allowed to bring the actual plans home; he must have sketched it again later. Her eye roved the paper, trying to understand the nuances of the horrible place. She had seen enough of George's plans that they rose from the paper as fully formed buildings in her mind.

"It's the same," she said, but as she said it, she caught the flaw that she had missed in the cruder drawing. She looked closer, but there was no mistaking it. In this all-seeing prison, a small blind spot. To her knowledge, George had never made an error on a blueprint. Had he done the same thing on the original? Had anyone else noticed, in the engineering or the construction? She had no way of knowing if this sketch was true to the thing that had been built, or if he had changed the design in retrospect. She could still only guess at what to say to ease his mind.

Millie leaned over to kiss George's stubbled cheek. She whispered in his ear. "Maybe you did it, old man. Maybe you gave them a chance."

Jane spent the drive home updating her mother on her own work and the escapades of various children and grandchildren. Millie lost track, but appreciated the diversion. When they got to the house, her daughter headed straight for the kitchen.

"Tea?" Jane was already picking up the kettle.

"Tea would be wonderful," Millie agreed, before excusing herself to the bedroom.

She crossed the room in the dark and opened the French doors, letting the winter air inside. She had never tired of this view, not in any season. Tonight, the light of the full moon reflected off the snow and disappeared in Raymond's footprints. The naked branches of the sycamore were long white fingers outlined in light; they performed benedictions over the empty platforms of the tree house.

Millie stepped through the doorway and onto the patio. The drifts were nearly up to her knees. She took two more steps, toward the tree. The cold made her eyes water.

She wished she could go back to that night in 1951, ask George what he had done and how she might share his burden. She was too late for so much. She allowed herself to grieve it all for a moment: her husband, their life together, the things they had shared and the things they had held back. It surrounded her like the cold, filling up the space expelled by her breath, until she fixed her eyes again on the treehouse. Everything missing from the body in the hospital was still here. The Georgeness.

"Oh," she whispered, as the day hit her.

"I won't leave," she said to the tree. Raymond would help her, maybe, or she would hire someone who would. The lights continued to dance after she had made her way back inside. They danced behind her eyelids when she closed her eyes.

Millie remembered the dream house that George used to promise her, back when this was a passing-through place, not their home. She was suddenly glad he had never gotten the chance to build it, that he had instead devoted himself to countless iterations of one mad project. Even the best plans get revised.

In the morning, there were pamphlets for a retirement village on the kitchen table.

Jane looked apologetic. "Charlie says we should talk about your options."

"I know my options," Millie said, setting a mug down on one of the smiling silver-haired faces.

She refused to let Jane help with the briefcase she carried with her to the hospital. When they got to George's room, she sent Charlie and Jane to get breakfast.

"I'd like some time with my husband," she said.

Then they were alone again, alone except for the noisy machines by the bedside and the ticking clock and the television and the nurses' station outside the door. None of that was hard to tune out.

"We're going to draw again, old man."

She opened the briefcase and pulled out a drawing board, a piece of paper, and a handful of pencils. She managed to angle a chair so that she was leaning half on the bed. George's hand closed around the pencil when she placed it against his palm. All the phantom energy of two days previous was gone. Her movement now led his, both of her hands clasped around his left.

He was the draftsman, but she knew plants. They started with the roots. She guided him through the shape of the tree, through the shape of his penance. Through every branch they both knew by heart, through every platform she had seen from her vantage point in the garden. The firehouse pole, the puppet theater, the Rapunzel tower. The crow's nest, which had kept his secret. Finally, around the treehouse, they started on her plans for the spring's gardens. All that mattered was his hand pressed in hers: long enough to feel like always, long enough to feel like everything trapped had been set free.

NEBULA AWARD NOMINEE

**BEST NOVELETTE**

# "THE LITIGATION MASTER AND THE MONKEY KING"

## KEN LIU

*Ken Liu has won a Nebula Award, a World Fantasy Award, and two Hugos. "The Litigation Master and the Monkey King" appeared in Lightspeed.*

The tiny cottage at the edge of Sanli Village—away from the villagers' noisy houses and busy clan shrines and next to the cool pond filled with lily pads, pink lotus flowers, and playful carp—would have made an ideal romantic summer hideaway for some dissolute poet and his silk-robed mistress from nearby bustling Yangzhou.

Indeed, having such a country lodge was the fashion among the literati in the lower Yangtze region in this second decade of the glorious reign of the Qianlong Emperor. Everyone agreed—as they visited each other in their vacation homes and sipped tea—that he was the best Emperor of the Qing Dynasty: so wise, so vigorous, and so solicitous of his subjects! And as the Qing Dynasty, founded by Manchu sages, was without a doubt the best dynasty ever to rule China, the scholars competed to compose poems that best showed their gratitude for having the luck to bear witness to this golden age, gift of the greatest Emperor who ever lived.

Alas, any scholar interested in *this* cottage must be disappointed for it was decrepit. The bamboo grove around it was wild and unkempt; the wooden walls crooked, rotting, and full of holes; the thatching over the roof uneven, with older layers peeking out through holes in the newer layers—not unlike the owner and sole inhabitant of the cottage, actually. Tian Haoli was in his fifties but looked ten years older. He was gaunt, sallow, his queue as thin as a pig's tail, and his breath often smelled of the cheapest rice wine and even cheaper tea. An accident in youth lamed his right leg, but he preferred to shuffle slowly rather than using a cane. His robe was patched all over, though his under-robe still showed through innumerable holes.

Unlike most in the village, Tian knew how to read and write, but as far as anyone knew, he never passed any level of the Imperial Examinations. From time to time, he would write a letter for some family or read an official notice in the teahouse in exchange for half a chicken or a bowl of dumplings.

But that was not how he really made his living.

The morning began like any other. As the sun rose lazily, the fog hanging over the pond dissipated like dissolving ink. Bit by bit, the pink lotus blossoms, the jade-green bamboo stalks, and the golden-yellow cottage roof emerged from the fog.

*Knock, knock.*

Tian stirred but did not wake up. The Monkey King was hosting a banquet, and Tian was going to eat his fill.

Ever since Tian was a little boy, he has been obsessed with the exploits of the Monkey King, the trickster demon who had seventy-two transformations and defeated hundreds of monsters, who had shaken the throne of the Jade Emperor with a troop of monkeys.

And Monkey liked good food and loved good wine, a must in a good host.

*Knock, Knock.*

Tian ignored the knocking. He was about to bite into a piece of drunken chicken dipped in four different exquisite sauces—

*You going to answer that?* Monkey said.

As Tian grew older, Monkey would visit him in his dreams, or, if he was awake, speak to him in his head. While others prayed to the Goddess of Mercy or the Buddha, Tian enjoyed conversing with Monkey, who he felt was a demon after his own heart.

*Whatever it is, it can wait*, said Tian.

*I think you have a client*, said Monkey.

*Knock-knock-knock—*

The insistent knocking whisked away Tian's chicken and abruptly ended his dream. His stomach growled, and he cursed as he rubbed his eyes.

"Just a moment!" Tian fumbled out of bed and struggled to put on his robe, muttering to himself all the while. "Why can't they wait till I've woken up properly and pissed and eaten? These unlettered fools are getting more and more unreasonable . . . I must demand a whole chicken this time . . . It was such a nice dream . . ."

*I'll save some plum wine for you*, said Monkey.

*You better.*

Tian opened the door. Li Xiaoyi, a woman so timid that she apologized even when some rambunctious child ran into *her*, stood there in a dark green dress, her hair pinned up in the manner prescribed for widows. Her fist was lifted and almost smashed into Tian's nose.

"Aiya!" Tian said. "You owe me the best drunk chicken in Yangzhou!" But Li's expression, a combination of desperation and fright, altered his tone. "Come on in."

He closed the door behind the woman and poured a cup of tea for her.

Men and women came to Tian as a last resort, for he helped them when they had nowhere else to turn, when they ran into trouble with the law.

The Qianlong Emperor might be all-wise and all-seeing, but he still needed the thousands of yamen courts to actually govern. Presided over by a magistrate, a judge-administrator who held the power of life and death over the local citizens in his charge, a yamen court was a mysterious, opaque place full of terror for the average man and woman.

Who knew the secrets of the Great Qing Code? Who understood how to plead and prove and defend and argue? When the magistrate spent his evenings at parties hosted by the local gentry, who could predict how a case brought by the poor against the rich would fare? Who could intuit the right clerk to bribe to avoid torture? Who could fathom the correct excuse to give to procure a prison visit?

No, one did not go near the yamen courts unless one had no other choice. When you sought justice, you gambled everything.

And you needed the help of a man like Tian Haoli.

Calmed by the warmth of the tea, Li Xiaoyi told Tian her story in halting sentences.

She had been struggling to feed herself and her two daughters on the produce from a tiny plot of land. To survive a bad harvest, she had mortgaged her land to Jie, a wealthy, distant cousin of her dead husband, who promised that she could redeem her land at any time, interest free. As Li could not read, she had gratefully inked her thumbprint to the contract her cousin handed her.

"He said it was just to make it official for the tax collector," Li said.

*Ah, a familiar story*, said the Monkey King.

Tian sighed and nodded.

"I paid him back at the beginning of this year, but yesterday, Jie came to my door with two bailiffs from the yamen. He said that my daughters and I had to leave our house immediately because we had not been making the payments on the loan. I was shocked, but he took out the contract and said that I had promised to pay him back double the amount loaned in one year or else the land would become his forever. 'It's all here in black characters on white paper,' he said, and waved the contract in my face. The bailiffs said that if I don't leave by tomorrow, they'll arrest me and sell me and my daughters to a blue house to satisfy the debt." She clenched her fists. "I don't know what to do!"

Tian refilled her teacup and said, "We'll have to go to court and defeat him."

*You sure about this?* said the Monkey King. *You haven't even seen the contract. You worry about the banquets, and I'll worry about the law.*

"How?" Li asked. "Maybe the contract does say what he said."

"I'm sure it does. But don't worry, I'll think of something."

To those who came to Tian for help, he was a *songshi*, a litigation master. But to the yamen magistrate and the local gentry, to the men who wielded money and power, Tian was a *songgun*, a "litigating hooligan."

The scholars who sipped tea and the merchants who caressed their silver taels despised Tian for daring to help the illiterate peasants draft complaints, devise legal strategies, and prepare for testimony and interrogation. After all, according to Confucius, neighbors should not sue neighbors. A conflict was nothing more than a misunderstanding that needed to be harmonized by a learned Confucian gentleman. But men like Tian Haoli dared to make the crafty peasants think that they could haul their superiors into court, and could violate the proper hierarchies of respect! The Great Qing Code made it clear that champerty, maintenance, barratry, pettifoggery—whatever name you used to describe what Tian did—were crimes.

But Tian understood the yamen courts were parts of a complex machine. Like the watermills that dotted the Yangtze River, complicated machines had patterns, gears, and levers. They could be nudged and pushed to do things, provided you were clever. As much as the scholars and merchants hated Tian, sometimes they also sought his help, and paid him handsomely for it, too.

"I can't pay you much."

Tian chuckled. "The rich pay my fee when they use my services but hate me for it. In your case, it's payment enough to see this moneyed cousin of yours foiled."

Tian accompanied Li to the yamen court. Along the way, they passed the town square, where a few soldiers were putting up posters of wanted men.

Li glanced at the posters and slowed down. "Wait, I think I may know—"

"Shush!" Tian pulled her along. "Are you crazy? Those aren't the magistrate's bailiffs, but real Imperial soldiers. How can you possibly recognize a man wanted by the Emperor?"

"But—"

"I'm sure you're mistaken. If one of them hears you, even the greatest litigation master in China won't be able to help you. You have trouble enough. When it comes to politics, it's best to see no evil, hear no evil, speak no evil."

*That's a philosophy a lot of my monkeys used to share*, said the Monkey King. *But I disagree with it.*

*You would, you perpetual rebel*, thought Tian Haoli. *But you can grow a new head when it's cut off, a luxury most of us don't share.*

Outside the yamen court, Tian picked up the drumstick and began to beat the Drum of Justice, petitioning the court to hear his complaint.

Half an hour later, an angry Magistrate Yi stared at the two people kneeling on the paved-stone floor below the dais: the widow trembling in fear, and that troublemaker, Tian, his back straight with a false look of respect on his face. Magistrate Yi had hoped to take the day off to enjoy the company of a pretty girl at one of the blue houses, but here he was, forced to work. He had a good mind to order both of them flogged right away, but he had to at least keep up the appearance of being a caring magistrate lest one of his disloyal underlings make a report to the judicial inspector.

"What is your complaint, guileful peasant?" asked the magistrate, gritting his teeth.

Tian shuffled forward on his knees and kowtowed. "Oh, Most Honored Magistrate," he began—Magistrate Yi wondered how Tian managed to make the phrase sound almost like an insult—"Widow Li cries out for justice, justice, justice!"

"And why are *you* here?"

"I'm Li Xiaoyi's cousin, here to help her speak, for she is distraught over how she's been treated."

Magistrate Yi fumed. This Tian Haoli always claimed to be related to the litigant to justify his presence in court and avoid the charge of being a litigating hooligan. He slammed his hardwood ruler, the symbol of his authority, against the table. "You lie! How many cousins can you possibly have?"

"I lie not."

"I warn you, if you can't prove this relation in the records of the Li clan shrine, I'll have you given forty strokes of the cane." Magistrate Yi was pleased with himself, thinking that he had finally come up with a way to best the crafty litigation master. He gave a meaningful look to the bailiffs standing to the sides of the court, and they pounded their staffs against the ground rhythmically, emphasizing the threat.

But Tian seemed not worried at all. "Most Sagacious Magistrate, it was Confucius who said that 'Within the Four Seas, all men are brothers.' If all men were brothers at the time of Confucius, then it stands to reason that being descended from them, Li Xiaoyi and I are related. With all due respect, surely, Your Honor isn't suggesting that the genealogical records of the Li family are more authoritative than the words of the Great Sage?"

Magistrate Yi's face turned red, but he could not think of an answer. Oh, how he wished he could find some excuse to punish this sharp-tongued *songgun*, who always seemed to turn black into white and right into wrong. The Emperor needed better laws to deal with men like him.

"Let's move on." The magistrate took a deep breath to calm himself. "What is this injustice she claims? Her cousin Jie read me the contract. It's perfectly clear what happened."

"I'm afraid there's been a mistake," Tian said. "I ask that the contract be brought so it can be examined again."

Magistrate Yi sent one of the bailiffs to bring back the wealthy cousin with the contract. Everyone in court, including Widow Li, looked at Tian in puzzlement, unsure what he planned. But Tian simply stroked his beard, appearing to be without a care in the world.

*You do have a plan, yes?* said the Monkey King.

*Not really. I'm just playing for time.*

*Well,* said Monkey, *I always like to turn my enemies' weapons against them. Did I tell you about the time I burned Nezha with his own fire-wheels?*

Tian dipped his hand inside his robe, where he kept his writing kit.

The bailiff brought back a confused, sweating Jie, who had been interrupted during a luxurious meal of swallow-nest soup. His face was still greasy as he hadn't even gotten a chance to wipe himself. Jie knelt before the magistrate next to Tian and Li and lifted the contract above his head for the bailiff.

"Show it to Tian," the magistrate ordered.

Tian accepted the contract and began to read it. He nodded his head from time to time, as though the contract was the most fascinating poetry.

Though the legalese was long and intricate, the key phrase was only eight characters long:

上賣莊稼，下賣田地

The mortgage was structured as a sale with a right of redemption, and this part provided that the widow sold her cousin "the crops above, and the field below."

"Interesting, most interesting," said Tian as he held the contract and continued to move his head about rhythmically.

Magistrate Yi knew he was being baited, yet he couldn't help but ask, "*What* is so interesting?"

"Oh Great, Glorious Magistrate, you who reflect the truth like a perfect mirror, you must read the contract yourself."

Confused, Magistrate Yi had the bailiff bring him the contract. After a few moments, his eyes bulged out. Right there, in clear black characters, was the key phrase describing the sale:

上賣莊稼，不賣田地

"The crops above, but *not* the field," muttered the magistrate.

Well, the case was clear. The contract did not say what Jie claimed. All that Jie had a right to were the crops, but not the field itself. Magistrate Yi had no idea how this could have happened, but his embarrassed fury needed an outlet. The sweaty, greasy-faced Jie was the first thing he laid his eyes on.

"How dare you lie to me?" Yi shouted, slamming his ruler down on the table. "Are you trying to make me look like a fool?"

It was now Jie's turn to shake like a leaf in the wind, unable to speak.

"Oh, now you have nothing to say? You're convicted of obstruction of justice, lying to an Imperial official, and attempting to defraud another of her property. I sentence you to a hundred and twenty strokes of the cane and confiscation of half of your property."

"Mercy, mercy! I don't know what happened—" The piteous cries of Jie faded as the bailiffs dragged him out of the yamen to jail.

Litigation Master Tian's face was impassive, but inside he smiled and thanked Monkey. Discreetly, he rubbed the tip of his finger against his robe to eliminate the evidence of his trick.

A week later, Tian Haoli was awakened from another banquet-dream with the Monkey King by persistent knocking. He opened the door to find Li Xiaoyi standing there, her pale face drained of blood.

"What's the matter? Is your cousin again—"

"Master Tian, I need your help." Her voice was barely more than a whisper. "It's my brother."

"Is it a gambling debt? A fight with a rich man? Did he make a bad deal? Was he—"

"Please! You have to come with me!"

Tian Haoli was going to say no because a clever *songshi* never got involved in cases he didn't understand—a quick way to end a career. But the look on Li's face softened his resolve. "All right. Lead the way."

Tian made sure that there was no one watching before he slipped inside Li Xiaoyi's hut. Though he didn't have much of a reputation to worry about, Xiaoyi didn't need the village gossips wagging their tongues.

Inside, a long, crimson streak could be seen across the packed-earth floor, leading from the doorway to the bed against the far wall. A man lay asleep on the bed, bloody bandages around his legs and left shoulder. Xiaoyi's two children, both girls, huddled in a shadowy corner of the hut, their mistrustful eyes peeking out at Tian.

One glance at the man's face told Tian all he needed to know: it was the same face on those posters the soldiers were putting up.

Tian Haoli sighed. "Xiaoyi, what kind of trouble have you brought me now?"

Gently, Xiaoyi shook her brother, Xiaojing, awake. He became alert almost immediately, a man used to light sleep and danger on the road.

"Xiaoyi tells me that you can help me," the man said, gazing at Tian intently.

Tian rubbed his chin as he appraised Xiaojing. "I don't know."

"I can pay." Xiaojing struggled to turn on the bed and lifted a corner of a cloth bundle. Tian could see the glint of silver underneath.

"I make no promises. Not every disease has a cure, and not every fugitive can find a loophole. It depends on who's after you and why." Tian walked closer and bent down to examine the promised payment, but the tattoos on Xiaojing's scarred face, signs that he was a convicted criminal, caught his attention. "You were sentenced to exile."

"Yes, ten years ago, right after Xiaoyi's marriage."

"If you have enough money, there are doctors that can do something about those tattoos, though you won't look very handsome afterwards."

"I'm not very worried about looks right now."

"What was it for?"

Xiaojing laughed and nodded at the table next to the window, upon which a thin book lay open. The wind fluttered its pages. "If you're as good as my sister says, you can probably figure it out."

Tian glanced at the book and then turned back to Xiaojing.

"You were exiled to the border near Vietnam," Tian said to himself as he deciphered the tattoos. "Eleven years ago . . . the breeze fluttering the pages . . . ah, you must have been a servant of Xu Jun, the Hanlin Academy scholar."

Eleven years ago, during the reign of the Yongzheng Emperor, someone had whispered in the Emperor's ear that the great scholar Xu Jun was plotting rebellion against the Manchu rulers. But when the Imperial guards seized Xu's house and ransacked it, they could find nothing incriminating.

However, the Emperor could never be wrong, and so his legal advisors had to devise a way to convict Xu. Their solution was to point at one of Xu's seemingly innocuous lyric poems:

清風不識字，何故亂翻書

*Breeze, you know not how to read,*
*So why do you mess with my book?*

The first character in the word for "breeze," *qing*, was the same as the name of the dynasty. The clever legalists serving the Emperor—and Tian did have a begrudging professional admiration for their skill—construed it as a treasonous composition mocking the Manchu rulers as uncultured and illiterate. Xu and his family were sentenced to death, his servants exiled.

"Xu's crime was great, but it has been more than ten years." Tian paced beside the bed. "If you simply broke the terms of your exile, it might not be too difficult to bribe the right officials and commanders to look the other way."

"The men after me cannot be bribed."

"Oh?" Tian looked at the bandaged wounds covering the man's body. "You mean . . . the Blood Drops."

Xiaojing nodded.

The Blood Drops were the Emperor's eyes and talons. They moved through the dark alleys of cities like ghosts and melted into the streaming caravans on roads and canals, hunting for signs of treason. They were the reason that teahouses posted signs for patrons to avoid talk of politics and neighbors looked around and whispered when they complained about taxes. They listened, watched, and sometimes came to people's doors in the middle of the night, and those they visited were never seen again.

Tian waved his arms impatiently. "You and Xiaoyi are wasting my time. If the Blood Drops are after you, I can do nothing. Not if I want to keep my head attached to my neck." Tian headed for the door of the hut.

"I'm not asking you to save me," said Xiaojing.

Tian paused.

"Eleven years ago, when they came to arrest Master Xu, he gave me a book and told me it was more important than his life, than his family. I kept the book hidden and took it into exile with me.

"A month ago, two men came to my house, asking me to turn over everything I had from my dead master. Their accents told me they were from Beijing, and I saw in their eyes the cold stare of the Emperor's falcons. I let them in and told them to look around, but while they were distracted with my chests and drawers, I escaped with the book.

"I've been on the run ever since, and a few times they almost caught me, leaving me with these wounds. The book they're after is over there on the table. *That*'s what I want you to save."

Tian hesitated by the door. He was used to bribing yamen clerks and prison guards and debating Magistrate Yi. He liked playing games with words and drinking cheap wine and bitter tea. What business did a lowly *songgun* have with the Emperor and the intrigue of the Court?

*I was once happy in Fruit-and-Flower Mountain, spending all day in play with my fellow monkeys*, said the Monkey King. *Sometimes I wish I hadn't been so curious about what lay in the wider world.*

But Tian was curious, and he walked over to the table and picked up the book. *An Account of Ten Days at Yangzhou*, it said, by Wang Xiuchu.

A hundred years earlier, in 1645, after claiming the Ming Chinese capital of Beijing, the Manchu Army was intent on completing its conquest of China.

Prince Dodo and his forces came to Yangzhou, a wealthy city of salt merchants and painted pavilions, at the meeting point of the Yangtze River and the Grand Canal. The Chinese commander, Grand Secretary Shi Kefa, vowed to resist to the utmost. He rallied the city's residents to reinforce the walls and tried to unite the remaining Ming warlords and militias.

His efforts came to naught on May 20, 1645, when the Manchu forces broke through the city walls after a seven-day siege. Shi Kefa was executed after refusing to surrender. To punish the residents of Yangzhou and to teach the rest of China a lesson about the price of resisting the Manchu Army, Prince Dodo gave the order to slaughter the entire population of the city.

One of the residents, Wang Xiuchu, survived by moving from hiding place to hiding place and bribing the soldiers with whatever he had. He also recorded what he saw:

*One Manchu soldier with a sword was in the lead, another with a lance was in the back, and a third roamed in the middle to prevent the captives from escaping. The three of them herded dozens of captives like dogs and sheep. If any captive walked too slow, they would beat him immediately, or else kill him on the spot.*

*The women were strung together with ropes, like a strand of pearls. They stumbled as they walked through the mud, and filth covered their bodies and clothes. Babies were everywhere on the ground, and as horses and people trampled over them, their brains and organs mixed into the earth, and the howling of the dying filled the air.*

*Every gutter or pond we passed was filled with corpses, their arms and legs entangled. The blood mixing with the green water turned into a painter's palette. So many bodies filled the canal that it turned into flat ground.*

The mass massacre, raping, pillaging, and burning of the city lasted six days.

*On the second day of the lunar month, the new government ordered all the temples to cremate the bodies. The temples had sheltered many women, though many had also died from hunger and fright. The final records of the cremations included hundreds of thousands of bodies, though this figure does not include all those who had committed suicide by jumping into wells or canals or through self-immolation and hanging to avoid a worse fate. . . .*

*On the fourth day of the lunar month, the weather finally turned sunny. The bodies piled by the roadside, having soaked in rainwater, had inflated and the skin on them was a bluish black and stretched taut like the surface of a drum. The flesh inside rotted and the stench was overwhelming. As the sun baked the bodies, the smell grew worse. Everywhere in Yangzhou, the survivors were cremating bodies. The smoke permeated inside all the houses and formed a miasma. The smell of rotting bodies could be detected a hundred li away.*

Tian's hands trembled as he turned over the last page.

"Now you see why the Blood Drops are after me," said Xiaojing, his voice weary. "The Manchus have insisted that the Yangzhou Massacre is a myth, and anyone speaking of it is guilty of treason. But here is an eyewitness account that will reveal their throne as built on a foundation of blood and skulls."

Tian closed his eyes and thought about Yangzhou, with its teahouses full of indolent scholars arguing with singing girls about rhyme schemes, with its palatial mansions full of richly-robed merchants celebrating another good trading season, with its hundreds of thousands of inhabitants happily praying for the Manchu Emperor's health. Did they know that each day, as they went to the markets and laughed and sang and praised this golden age they lived in, they were treading on the bones of the dead, they were mocking the dying cries of the departed, they were denying the memories of ghosts? He himself had not even believed the stories whispered in his childhood about Yangzhou's past, and he was quite sure that most young men in Yangzhou now have never even heard of them.

Now that he knew the truth, could he allow the ghosts to continue to be silenced?

But then he also thought about the special prisons the Blood Drops maintained, the devious tortures designed to prolong the journey from life to death, the ways that the Manchu Emperors always got what they wanted in the end. The Emperor's noble Banners had succeeded in forcing all the Chinese to shave their heads and wear queues to show submission to the Manchus, and to abandon their *hanfu* for Manchu clothing on pain of death. They had cut the Chinese off from their past, made them a people adrift without the anchor of their memories. They were more powerful than the Jade Emperor and ten thousand heavenly soldiers.

It would be so easy for them to erase this book, to erase him, a lowly *songgun*, from the world, like a momentary ripple across a placid pond.

Let others have their fill of daring deeds; he was a survivor.

"I'm sorry," Tian said to Xiaojing, his voice low and hoarse. "I can't help you."

Tian Haoli sat down at his table to eat a bowl of noodles. He had flavored it with fresh lotus seeds and bamboo shoots, and the fragrance was usually refreshing, perfect for a late lunch.

The Monkey King appeared in the seat opposite him: fierce eyes, wide mouth, a purple cape that declared him to be the Sage Equal to Heaven, rebel against the Jade Emperor.

This didn't happen often. Usually Monkey spoke to Tian only in his mind.

"You think you're not a hero," the Monkey King said.

"That's right," replied Tian. He tried to keep the defensiveness out of his voice. "I'm just an ordinary man making a living by scrounging for crumbs in the cracks of the law, happy to have enough to eat and a few coppers left for drink. I just want to live."

"I'm not a hero either," the Monkey King said. "I just did my job when needed."

"Ha!" said Tian. "I know what you're trying to do, but it's not going to work. Your job was to protect the holiest monk on a perilous journey, and your qualifications consisted of peerless strength and boundless magic. You could call on the aid of the Buddha and Guanyin, the Goddess of Mercy, whenever you needed to. Don't you compare yourself to me."

"Fine. Do you know of *any* heroes?"

Tian slurped some noodles and pondered the question. What he had read that morning was fresh in his mind. "I guess Grand Secretary Shi Kefa was a hero."

"How? He promised the people of Yangzhou that as long as he lived, he would not let harm come to them, and yet when the city fell, he tried to escape on his own. He seems to me more a coward than a hero."

Tian put down his bowl. "That's not fair. He held the city when he had no reinforcements or aid. He pacified the warlords harassing the people in Yang-zhou and rallied them to their defense. In the end, despite a moment of weak-ness, he willingly gave his life for the city, and you can't ask for more than that."

The Monkey King snorted contemptuously. "Of course you can. He should have seen that fighting was futile. If he hadn't resisted the Manchu invaders and instead surrendered the city, maybe not so many would have died. If he hadn't refused to bow down to the Manchus, maybe he wouldn't have been killed." The Monkey King smirked. "Maybe he wasn't very smart and didn't know how to survive."

Blood rushed to Tian's face. He stood up and pointed a finger at the Monkey King. "Don't you talk about him that way. Who's to say that had he surrendered, the Manchus wouldn't have slaughtered the city anyway? You think lying down before a conquering army bent on rape and pillage is the right thing to do? To turn your argument around, the heavy resistance in Yangzhou slowed the Manchu Army and might have allowed many people to escape to safety in the south, and the city's defiance might have made the Manchus willing to give better terms to those who did surrender later. Grand Secretary Shi was a real hero!"

The Monkey King laughed. "Listen to you, arguing like you are in Magistrate Yi's yamen. You're awfully worked up about a man dead for a hundred years."

"I won't let you denigrate his memory that way, even if you're the Sage Equal to Heaven."

The Monkey King's face turned serious. "You speak of memory. What do you think about Wang Xiuchu, who wrote the book you read?"

"He was just an ordinary man like me, surviving by bribes and hiding from danger."

"Yet he recorded what he saw, so that a hundred years later the men and women who died in those ten days can be remembered. Writing that book was a brave thing to do—look at how the Manchus are hunting down someone today just for *reading* it. I think he was a hero, too."

After a moment, Tian nodded. "I hadn't thought about it that way, but you're right."

"There are no heroes, Tian Haoli. Grand Secretary Shi was both courageous and cowardly, capable and foolish. Wang Xiuchu was both an opportunistic survivor and a man of greatness of spirit. I'm mostly selfish and vain, but sometimes even I surprise myself. We're all just ordinary men—well, I'm an ordinary demon—faced with extraordinary choices. In those moments, sometimes heroic ideals demand that we become their avatars."

Tian sat down and closed his eyes. "I'm just an old and frightened man, Monkey. I don't know what to do."

"Sure you do. You just have to accept it."

"Why me? What if I don't want to?"

The Monkey King's face turned somber, and his voice grew faint. "Those men and women of Yangzhou died a hundred years ago, Tian Haoli, and nothing can be done to change that. But the past lives on in the form of memories, and those in power are always going to want to erase and silence the past, to bury the ghosts. Now that you know about that past, you're no longer an innocent bystander. If you do not act, you're complicit with the Emperor and his Blood

Drops in this new act of violence, this deed of erasure. Like Wang Xiuchu, you're now a witness. Like him, you must choose what to do. You must decide if, on the day you die, you will regret your choice."

The figure of the Monkey King faded away, and Tian was left alone in his hut, remembering.

"I have written a letter to an old friend in Ningbo," said Tian. "Bring it with you to the address on the envelope. He's a good surgeon and will erase these tattoos from your face as a favor to me."

"Thank you," said Li Xiaojing. "I will destroy the letter as soon as I can, knowing how much danger this brings you. Please accept this as payment." He turned to his bundle and retrieved five taels of silver.

Tian held up a hand. "No, you'll need all the money you can get." He handed over a small bundle. "It's not much, but it's all I have saved."

Li Xiaojing and Li Xiaoyi both looked at the litigation master, not understanding.

Tian continued. "Xiaoyi and the children can't stay here in Sanli because someone will surely report that she harbored a fugitive when the Blood Drops start asking questions. No, all of you must leave immediately and go to Ningbo, where you will hire a ship to take you to Japan. Since the Manchus have sealed the coast, you will need to pay a great deal to a smuggler."

"To Japan!?"

"So long as that book is with you, there is nowhere in China where you'll be safe. Of all the states around, only Japan would dare to defy the Manchu Emperor. Only there will you and the book be safe."

Xiaojing and Xiaoyi nodded. "You will come with us, then?"

Tian gestured at his lame leg and laughed. "Having me along will only slow you down. No, I'll stay here and take my chances."

"The Blood Drops will not let you go if they suspect you helped us."

Tian smiled. "I'll come up with something. I always do."

A few days later, when Tian Haoli was just about to sit down and have his lunch, soldiers from the town garrison came to his door. They arrested him without explanation and brought him to the yamen.

Tian saw that Magistrate Yi wasn't the only one sitting behind the judging table on the dais this time. With him was another official, whose hat indicated that he came directly from Beijing. His cold eyes and lean build reminded Tian of a falcon.

*May my wits defend me again*, Tian whispered to the Monkey King in his mind.

Magistrate Yi slammed his ruler on the table. "Deceitful Tian Haoli, you're hereby accused of aiding the escape of dangerous fugitives and of plotting acts of treason against the Great Qing. Confess your crimes immediately so that you may die quickly."

Tian nodded as the magistrate finished his speech. "Most Merciful and Far-Sighted Magistrate, I have absolutely no idea what you're talking about."

"You presumptuous fool! Your usual tricks will not work this time. I have iron-clad proof that you gave comfort and aid to the traitor Li Xiaojing and read a forbidden, treasonous, false text."

"I have indeed read a book recently, but there was nothing treasonous in it."

"What?"

"It was a book about sheep herding and pearl stringing. Plus, some discussions about filling ponds and starting fires."

The other man behind the table narrowed his eyes, but Tian went on as if he had nothing to hide. "It was very technical and very boring."

"You lie!" The veins on Magistrate Yi's neck seemed about to burst.

"Most Brilliant and Perspicacious Magistrate, how can you say that I lie? Can you tell me the contents of this forbidden book, so that I may verify if I have read it?"

"You . . . you . . ." The magistrate's mouth opened and closed like the lips of a fish.

Of course Magistrate Yi wouldn't have been told what was in the book— that was the point of it being forbidden—but Tian was also counting on the fact that the man from the Blood Drops wouldn't be able to say anything either. To accuse Tian of lying about the contents of the book was to admit that the accuser had read the book, and Tian knew that no member of the Blood Drops would admit such a crime to the suspicious Manchu Emperor.

"There has been a misunderstanding," said Tian. "The book I read con-

NEBULA AWARDS SHOWCASE 2015

tained nothing that was false, which means that it can't possibly be the book that has been banned. Certainly Your Honor can see the plain and simple logic." He smiled. Surely he had found the loophole that would allow him to escape.

"Enough of this charade," the man from the Blood Drops spoke for the first time. "There's no need to bother with the law with traitors like you. On the Emperor's authority, I hereby declare you guilty without appeal and sentence you to death. If you do not wish to suffer much longer, immediately confess the whereabouts of the book and the fugitives."

Tian felt his legs go rubbery and, for a moment, he saw only darkness and heard only an echo of the Blood Drop's pronouncement: *sentence you to death.*

*I guess I've finally run out of tricks*, he thought.

*You've already made your choice*, said the Monkey King. *Now you just have to accept it.*

Besides being great spies and assassins, the Blood Drops were experts at the art of torture.

Tian screamed as they doused his limbs in boiling water.

*Tell me a story*, said Tian to the Monkey King. *Distract me so I don't give in.*

*Let me tell you about the time they cooked me in the alchemical furnace of the Jade Emperor*, said the Monkey King. *I survived by hiding among smoke and ashes.*

And Tian told his torturers a tale about how he had helped Li Xiaojing burn his useless book and saw it turn into smoke and ashes. But he had forgotten where the fire was set. Perhaps the Blood Drops could search the nearby hills thoroughly?

They burnt him with iron pokers heated until they glowed white.

*Tell me a story*, Tian screamed as he breathed in the smell of charred flesh.

*Let me tell you about the time I fought the Iron Fan Princess in the Fire Mountains*, said the Monkey King. *I tricked her by pretending to run away in fear.*

And Tian told his torturers a tale about how he had told Li Xiaojing to escape to Suzhou, famed for its many alleys and canals, as well as refined lacquer fans.

They cut his fingers off one by one.

*Tell me a story*, Tian croaked. He was weak from loss of blood.

*Let me tell you about the time they put that magical headband on me*, said the Monkey King. *I almost passed out from the pain but still I wouldn't stop cursing.*

And Tian spat in the faces of his torturers.

Tian woke up in the dim cell. It smelled of mildew and shit and piss. Rats squeaked in the corners.

He was finally going to be put to death tomorrow, as his torturers had given up. It would be death by a thousand cuts. A skilled executioner could make the victim suffer for hours before taking his final breath.

*I didn't give in, did I?* he asked the Monkey King. *I can't remember everything I told them.*

*You told them many tales, none true.*

Tian thought he should be content. Death would be a release. But he worried that he hadn't done enough. What if Li Xiaojing didn't make it to Japan? What if the book was destroyed at sea? If only there were some way to save the book so that it could *not* be lost.

*Have I told you about the time I fought Lord Erlang and confused him by transforming my shape? I turned into a sparrow, a fish, a snake, and finally a temple. My mouth was the door, my eyes the windows, my tongue the Buddha, and my tail a flagpole. Ha, that was fun. None of Lord Erlang's demons could see through my disguises.*

*I am clever with words*, thought Tian. *I am, after all, a* songgun.

The voices of children singing outside the jail cell came to him faintly. He struggled and crawled to the wall with the tiny barred window at the top and called out, "Hey, can you hear me?"

The singing stopped abruptly. After a while, a timid voice said, "We're not supposed to talk to condemned criminals. My mother says that you're dangerous and crazy."

Tian laughed. "I *am* crazy. But I know some good songs. Would you like to learn them? They're about sheep and pearls and all sorts of other fun things."

The children conferred among themselves, and one of them said, "Why not? A crazy man must have some good songs."

Tian Haoli mustered up every last bit of his strength and concentration. He thought about the words from the book:

*The three of them herded dozens of captives like dogs and sheep. If any captive walked too slow, they would beat him immediately, or else kill him on the spot. The women were strung together with ropes, like a strand of pearls.*

He thought about disguises. He thought about the way the tones differed between Mandarin and the local topolect, the way he could make puns and approximations and rhymes and shift the words and transform them until they were no longer recognizable. And he began to sing:

*The Tree of Dem herded dozens of Cap Tea*
*Like dogs and sheep.*
*If any Cap Tea walked too slow, the Wood Beet*
*Hmm'd immediately.*
*Or else a quill, slim on the dot.*
*The Why-Men were strong to gather wits & loupes*
*Like a strand of pearls.*

And the children, delighted by the nonsense, picked up the songs quickly.

They tied him to the pole on the execution platform and stripped him naked.

Tian watched the crowd. In the eyes of some, he saw pity, in others, he saw fear, and in still others, like Li Xiaoyi's cousin Jie, he saw delight at seeing the hooligan *songgun* meet this fate. But most were expectant. This execution, this horror, was entertainment.

"One last chance," the Blood Drop said. "If you confess the truth now, we will slit your throat cleanly. Otherwise, you can enjoy the next few hours."

Whispers passed through the crowd. Some tittered. Tian gazed at the bloodlust in some of the men. *You have become a slavish people*, he thought. *You have forgotten the past and become docile captives of the Emperor. You have learned to take delight in his barbarity, to believe that you live in a golden age, never bothering to look beneath the gilded surface of the Empire at its rotten, bloody foundation. You desecrate the very memory of those who died to keep you free.*

His heart was filled with despair. *Have I endured all this and thrown away my life for nothing?*

Some children in the crowd began to sing:

*The Tree of Dem herded dozens of Cap Tea*
*Like dogs and sheep.*
*If any Cap Tea walked too slow, the Wood Beet*

*Hmm'd immediately.*
*Or else a quill, slim on the dot.*
*The Why-Men were strong to gather wits & loupes*
*Like a strand of pearls.*

The Blood Drop's expression did not change. He heard nothing but the nonsense of children. True, this way, the children would not be endangered by knowing the song. But Tian also wondered if anyone would ever see through the nonsense. Had he hidden the truth too deep?

"Stubborn till the last, eh?" The Blood Drop turned to the executioner, who was sharpening his knives on the grindstone. "Make it last as long as possible."

*What have I done?* thought Tian. *They're laughing at the way I'm dying, the way I've been a fool. I've accomplished nothing except fighting for a hopeless cause.*

*Not at all*, said the Monkey King. *Li Xiaojing is safe in Japan, and the children's songs will be passed on until the whole county, the whole province, the whole country fills with their voices. Someday, perhaps not now, perhaps not in another hundred years, but someday the book will come back from Japan, or a clever scholar will finally see through the disguise in your songs as Lord Erlang finally saw through mine. And then the spark of truth will set this country aflame, and this people will awaken from their torpor. You have preserved the memories of the men and women of Yangzhou.*

The executioner began with a long, slow cut across Tian's thighs, removing chunks of flesh. Tian's scream was like that of an animal's, raw, pitiful, incoherent.

*Not much of a hero, am I?* thought Tian. *I wish I were truly brave.*

*You're an ordinary man who was given an extraordinary choice*, said the Monkey King. *Do you regret your choice?*

*No*, thought Tian. And as the pain made him delirious and reason began to desert him, he shook his head firmly. *Not at all.*

*You can't ask for more than that*, said the Monkey King. And he bowed before Tian Haoli, not the way you kowtowed to an Emperor, but the way you would bow to a great hero.

Author's Note: For more about the historical profession of *songshi* (or *songgun*), please contact the author for an unpublished paper. Some of Tian Haoli's exploits are based on folktales about the great Litigation Master Xie Fangzun collected by the anthologist Ping Heng in *Zhongguo da zhuangshi* ("Great Plaintmasters of China"), published in 1922.

For more than 250 years, *An Account of Ten Days at Yangzhou* was suppressed in China by the Manchu emperors, and the Yangzhou Massacre, along with numerous other atrocities during the Manchu Conquest, was forgotten. It was only until the decade before the Revolution of 1911 that copies of the book were brought back from Japan and republished in China. The text played a small, but important, role in the fall of the Qing and the end of Imperial rule in China. I translated the excerpts used in this story.

Due to the long suppression, which continues to some degree to this day, the true number of victims who died in Yangzhou may never be known. This story is dedicated to their memory.

# "THE WEIGHT OF THE SUNRISE"

## VYLAR KAFTAN

*Vylar Kaftan was previously nominated for a 2010 Nebula Award. "The Weight of the Sunrise" was published in* Asimov's Science Fiction.

### 1. *The Disfigured God*

So you ask for the story of your origin, beautiful boy, and why you and your father are different from those around you. You are fourteen and nearly a man. Before you choose your name, you should know yourself—and I, your grandfather, will tell you the story of you. The tale is written in the scars of my hands, and told in the blood of the Incan people.

You must imagine me younger, child—much the age that your father is now. Picture a warm December day, just before midsummer. It was 1806, though back then we did not count the years as Europeans do. Smallpox raged through the southern Land of the Four Quarters. You've seen your grandmother's pitted face; once she was considered a beauty for those telltale scars. I worked in the fields near Cusco, because I enjoyed farming. I had never liked the city. The cool soil on my hands reminded me of childhood, and of home in the northern mountains.

When the gods summoned me, I was planting late-spring tomatoes—the ones that would blossom shortly before June frost. I knelt on the terraced slopes south of Cusco, on land owned by your grandmother's clan—since as you know, I myself came from a poor potato-farming family. Each seed entered the ground lovingly; I thanked Pachimama that I could enjoy the planting and not fear the harvest. The noon sun blessed my bare head. My water jug rested nearby, with my flintlock rifle leaning against it.

The sunlight faded—but no cloud marked the sky. I looked up. Two men approached, noble in dress and bearing. They wore macaw feathers at their throats, so I knew they outranked any noble I'd ever met. Although society did not require me to bow, I stood and did so anyway.

The taller one, who wore the brighter feathers, said, "Lanchi Ronpa?"

"I am Lanchi," I said, leaving off the honorific as I often did. I disliked claiming noble status simply because my family survived smallpox, even though it was my right. I was traveling at the time and never exposed. For all I knew, smallpox would kill me if I ever caught it. Even the great physician Ronpa himself had admitted that while Inti marked certain families with the sacred scars, he would still take their children as he pleased.

The shorter man looked disdainfully at my dirty tunic and hands. I guessed he was subordinate, because he didn't speak. The first man said, "I am Amaru Aroynapa, and this is my cousin Paucar Aroynapa. We come on behalf of the Sapa Inca himself, Coniraya the Condor, Emperor of the Four Quarters. A matter of great importance has arisen. You are summoned into his presence."

My knees trembled. The Aroynapa family? Not just any nobles, but cousins to the god-emperor himself! It was only three years ago that the former Sapa Inca joined the Court of the Dead. The ruler now called Coniraya was barely a man, yet had proved his godhood through skillful combat against his brother. And now the god's mortal cousins summoned me into his presence?

"What honor could the Sapa Inca possibly wish to grant me?" I asked, my mouth dry.

"Your grandfather was British, was he not?"

"Yes," I said, "born Smith in the land of Britain, but he came here as a trader and learned our ways. He took the name—"

"And do you speak English?"

I hadn't spoken it since I was ten. My grandfather had lived in isolation on our farm, and we had always feared an edict ordering his death. He had died of digestive ills twenty years ago. "I have spoken English," I said cautiously, worried that I had forgotten it. "But the foreigners were expelled from our land forty years ago. What possible need has the Sapa Inca for that language?"

"Things have changed," said the shorter man abruptly. "Do not question the need."

"His question is intelligent, Paucar," said Amaru gently. "He will want to understand why the Sapa Inca summons him." He addressed me. "There are visitors from the northern lands. They bear a British flag, but call themselves Americans. They brought their own translator, a poor fisherman from a distant village with heritage like yours. But such a man cannot appear before a god."

I understood instantly. "And there are no true nobles who speak this language anymore."

"Exactly. There are several families with English heritage, particularly among the farmers and fishermen in the distant north. There are also several families elevated to nobility as the Ronpa, because one parent and two children proved resilient to smallpox. However, there is only one man in Cusco who has both qualities."

I put down my hoe as my palms sweated. I had never felt like I belonged in Cusco, despite my rank. It was only at manhood that my family earned a place in the capital—and that, only by chance, as smallpox swept our village. I was no more elegant than the fisherman I would replace. But I had learned some manners in the city, and of course the Sapa Inca would not speak with a fisherman. Perhaps if I went, I might spare this man the pressures I had felt since arriving—the burden I could only share with my wife, who understood my fears.

I said calmly, "If the Sapa Inca calls, then I answer gladly."

Amaru nodded. "Prepare yourself and inform your wife. Come to the palace at nightfall, where we will begin your quarantine."

I paused, concerned for my coarse appearance. "I have an embroidered tunic, perhaps—"

Paucar snorted, but Amaru gave a tiny smile. "Your clothes will be burned, Lanchi. You may as well wear what you have on now."

My face grew hot. "Of course." The Sapa Inca would shower me with clothes and jewelry, as casually as a dog sheds its hair. And that was only the beginning. No matter what came of the meeting, my life would be different forever. No man could meet a god and remain unchanged.

I shouldered my musket and water jug and headed home. I had a long walk. There were few fields near Cusco itself, since few commoners lived in the capital. In those days it was quite strange to be of Ronpa class; we existed in a world halfway between the established families and the workers. My home lay across the city. It would have been shorter to cut through, but I preferred the scenic route on the beautiful fitted stone roads, which had remained strong for four centuries. I'd heard that the roads in Europe were full of holes. It amazed me that the inventors of muskets could not build a road.

As I neared home, I recognized the scent of llama stew, which my beloved Yma had promised me for supper. I hurried toward the familiar stone house, which still felt too lavish. We had a traditional blanket door rather than the newfangled European doors, because we preferred the fresh breeze.

I pushed the blanket aside. "Yma, darling. I'm home early with news."

She looked up from her cookpot. My heart filled with contentment at the sight. My wife was as lovely as the day I gave her mother coca leaves; still sweetly shaped, like a goddess, with cornsilk hair falling to her hips. The pockmarks dotting her face proved her health and strength; no partial scarring to ruin her symmetry! My Yma had survived the pox at fifteen, which made her a good mate for a Ronpa like myself. With Inti's blessing, our children might escape death by pox.

Yma smiled, but her expression faded. "You look troubled. Is the news bad?"

"Not bad," I told her, "but unexpected."

With a peal of laughter, my little Chaska raced through the doorway, covered in cornmeal. "Papa!" she cried, hugging and kissing my arm with flour-covered lips. The joy of my life! She would be nine at Midsummer. Bright stars, her nickname meant—or planets, as we now called them, after sharing knowledge with European astronomers in the past century.

"Hello, sweet child," I said affectionately, patting her head so as not to spoil her. I pushed her away and went to my son, who crawled in his baked-earth playpen. I picked him up and swung him around once before setting him down. My heart ached to give this boy his nickname, but I didn't dare tempt the spirits to steal him. He must simply be "the baby" until his second birthday.

My wife said, "Chaska, get back to grinding." My daughter bounded out the door. Work seemed to brighten her spirits, which we thought was positive. We took great care with our daughter, as she was considered one of the prettiest girls in Cusco, and we hoped she might be chosen as a priestess someday.

"What has happened?" asked Yma, setting down her spoon.

When I told her, her eyes widened and her face grew pensive. Yma was a youngest daughter of the lower nobility, and she knew what an imperial summons meant. It could mean our family's great fortune—or the execution of us all, should I displease our ruler.

Finally she said only, "I must cut your bangs before you go. I don't want locks of your hair in the palace's power."

I nodded, even though she had cut my hair only last week. She called Chaska to stir the stew. Yma trimmed my hair neatly to eyebrow length in front and chin on the sides. She wielded the knife carefully, as if her haircut would protect me when she herself could not. Ah, my child—how I loved that woman, your honored grandmother! I miss her every day, now that she has gone to the Empire of the Sun. She was the moon to my sun, the silver to my gold—the lesser but equally important half of our pairing, as all things in this world are matched. Without her, I would have been nothing. Someday, my child, you will choose a woman yourself, and you will understand why family is the world's true gold. The greatest joy imaginable is to love another person as I did my Yma.

But that evening, I kissed my wife goodbye fearing that I might lose all happiness. I embraced both my children lovingly, regardless of what others might say about spoiling them.

I saw my city with new eyes as I crossed it that evening. I admired the square at Huacaypata, where workers prepared the vast stone tables for the Midsummer feast. I watched the lesser nobles bustle through the streets on evening calls, clad in bright wool tunics and shining feathers from the Amazon. A few even wore hats, which the Europeans had popularized, though many Incas now scorned that tradition as foreign. Yet none could argue that bright-feathered hats were practical, and thus the custom persisted in noble circles.

Cusco seemed newly fragile to me. Even as servants bathed me in the Cori-cancha's stone chambers, scouring away dirt and hard work, I could not appreciate the palace's beauty. The Americans! What could they want from us? They were a British splinter group, ruled from overseas—much the way we ruled tribes across three thousand miles of desert, rainforest, and mountains. Yet they called themselves both British subjects, and Americans.

No Incan ruler would tolerate such a thing. The leaders of conquered peoples were granted nobility in Cusco, and imperial loyalists were sent to the new lands as rulers. In this way all became Incan. I could not understand why the British did not do likewise.

And so I waited, naked and solitary, for my turn to see the god-emperor. Twelve days must pass before contact, per Ronpa's guidance. The ruler had singlehandedly saved the Incan Empire, or what was left after millions died in the 1500s. I was comfortable enough; the waiting chambers held heated bricks and fascinating mosaics. I was not allowed to touch anything, and so I sat and thought. It was hard not to think through my history lessons, to remember foolish Pizarro who attacked 80,000 Incas with only 168 Spaniards; mere horses, cannons, and armor could not daunt so many Incan warriors! The brave Atahualpa slew most of Pizarro's men, keeping seven to teach him how cannons worked.

I thought of these men, as my attendants dressed me in the finest tunic I had ever touched. But even those Spaniards, who had lived with smallpox since anyone could remember, did not know how to manage it. It was Incan science that figured out how to quarantine and sanitize. I found courage here. The gods may have tested us, but my people triumphed—and eventually took back our lost lands, until our empire was as glorious as before. This time, Incas and out-siders would meet on equal ground.

But one thing nagged me, as the servants pressed thick gold earplugs through my ears. I would be held responsible for these Americans' words. Surely they came to bargain. If they threatened the Sapa Inca, I would have to alter their tone—or the ruler might blame me for their sacrilege. Yet if the Sapa Inca knew I translated imperfectly, I might be killed for that offense too. I held an unwinnable position.

The attendants strapped a heavy gold block to my back, for no man could meet the Sapa Inca unburdened. I staggered under the weight. Unless the barbarians were perfect nobles—gentle and respectful in all ways—my fate was tied to theirs. And I had little hope that they would respect our god-emperor enough to avoid offense.

A servant led me from the waiting room. I stumbled barefoot on the tiled floor, nearly blind to my surroundings. Massive stone pillars and golden trim marked my route. I passed lines of nobles, each clad more finely than the last, wearing gold sun-masks that marked their ranks. It was like a strange dream that might vanish on waking. I waited behind three different doors, each grander than the previous, until finally the imperial crier summoned me forth.

I steeled myself. If the Sapa Inca received the Americans, then surely he must hear their request. He would want my honest translation. With aching back and pounding heart, I stumbled into the throne room. I walked what seemed like the entire length of Cusco to reach the Sapa Inca's pedestal. I pressed my body to the floor and did not lift myself until called. Even then I rose slowly and kept my eyes downcast.

Before me stood the great gold screen, carved with pumas and condors and flowers, which hid the man my eyes were unworthy to see.

## 2. The Sapa Inca Speaks

You, my grandson, have seen the throne room yourself, because of your father's accomplishments. Perhaps my story seems mundane. You must remember—I never dreamed of meeting the Sapa Inca. When I was fourteen, I still lived in the village Pitahaya, where I farmed and hunted and studied my British grandfather's Bible. I had only two dreams: to farm my own land, and to have a brother. You will not appreciate how difficult a boy's life is with two elder and two younger sisters!

So you must picture this day as if you were me, my child. When smallpox struck Pitahaya, my elder sisters had already married into other villages. I was away on my first solo hunt, preparing to become a man. My parents and younger sisters stayed home.

Imagine yourself on a hunt today—yes, I know you prefer sailing, but bear with me. You're alone, with your musket and your senses. You stalk a raptor or wildcat, and think yourself clever. You might kill a condor, as I did, and declare yourself a man. You mark your face with its blood. You walk home, proud and triumphant, after your five-day hunt.

Then you reach the village hill and find you cannot walk further. Imperial soldiers block your way. Smallpox has struck your home. Houses burn, to kill the disease, and you don't know who's inside. The soldiers tell you three-fourths of your village has died. They cannot tell you of your family. You must look to the sickly clusters, sleeping in the open air, quarantined by scarred pox survivors. You cannot join them, so you squint from a distance, wishing your eyes were those of the condor you killed.

But no. My child, you cannot imagine such madness. You no longer fear smallpox the way we did. Three days passed before I learned my family's fate. My mother recovered, but my sisters went blind. My father died moaning my name. My grandson, you will never come home to a deeply scarred family—to learn that overnight your family is newly valued as Ronpa. Your fortune is made. But at what cost! Look at your wrecked village, where women weep, where possessions burn. See your friends and neighbors, drowned by the dozens in pestilence.

Try to understand, dear boy. Because the story of you depends on this fear.

My burning village haunted me as I met the Sapa Inca, who sat unapproachable behind his solid screen. I knew he had never seen such a thing.

"You are Lanchi Ronpa," stated an imperious voice from behind the golden wall.

"Yes, Your Divinity," I answered, and flushed hot as the nobles tittered behind their masks. I was supposed to address him as Greatness; that other title meant his brother the High Priest.

Luckily, the voice sounded amused. "Lanchi Ronpa, you will translate for the Americans when they are granted entrance. Keep yourself firm at all times. Speak in your most imperial tone when you convey our words, as if you were the greatest of men. When you interpret their words, use a vulnerable tone. We command you to translate as accurately as possible."

Those words relieved me somewhat, but not entirely. The Sapa Inca might announce one thing, and do another if sufficiently angered. No one would question his fickleness. So I simply said, "I hear and obey, Your Greatness."

"Stand beside this screen to speak."

Nervously I approached the screen, which extended sideways to shield the god-emperor completely. I heard nobles whispering. No matter what else happened this day, I would be remembered as the Ronpa who stood on the highest step. My knees shook. I could not have borne seeing the Sapa Inca's face.

A woman's voice spoke softly next to me. "Lanchi Ronpa, you will also ask any question I have of these Americans when the time comes."

The Coya Inca! She was here as well. Most ruling women kept to their domestics, but this one had always been ambitious. Wife to the Sapa, she was the moon who shone beneath his daylight. I had no idea how to address her. I murmured, "I hear and obey, star of the purest sky."

The compliment seemed acceptable, as no words came from behind the screen. Thus I waited for the Americans.

Soon the imperial guards appeared, armed with every weapon known to us, from traditional bolas to modern flintlock rifles—the best our scientists had developed. We had not stumbled through centuries of poverty and war; only plagues interrupted our science. Ever since Atahualpa's reign, imperial guards remained armed at all times. One never knew when a diplomat might attack. So many warriors arrived that I could see nothing else. Then the procession parted like grain in the wind, and I saw the Americans.

My child, I tell you—I feared disappointment that they were only men, but in fact I was astonished. The Americans were five in number. All wore heavy stones on their backs. First I noticed their leader—who, at that time, I thought might be king. He had deep-set eyes like my grandfather, with ghostly irises and rust-colored eyebrows. His hair amazed me, for it was curled throughout, and aged white despite his young face. It looked like he had rolled it on sticks and slept on it while damp. I wondered why this man would arrange his hair so strangely.

But these thoughts vanished quickly—for among the Americans stood the strangest man I'd ever seen. His skin was dark as fertile soil, with hair like the black llamas that honor the creator god. Like the others, he wore strange clothing: a fine white shirt, with excess fabric gathered at his throat. His shirt was far too short, only falling to his waist, and fine wool fitted the shape of his legs. I saw no point in this; it seemed confining, but I recalled that Europeans had long dressed in this fashion. He looked younger than the leader, though perhaps that was because of the leader's white hair.

I met the dark man's gaze, though he quickly looked down. The pale man addressed me in English. I thanked Inti that he spoke slowly, which helped me. He said, "Praise God that we have arrived here to meet you, and that you have welcomed us. We are Americans, and currently subjects of the British Empire. In the name of the thirteen American colonies, I greet you and request that we negotiate."

I paused before translating "God"—did he mean Inti or did he mean the character from British mythology? I finally translated as "divinity," and I think the Sapa Inca took it as meaning the true gods.

The court scribe said, "State your name, title, and rank for the records."

"I am Ambassador John Fernando Loddington de Godoy. As you request my rank, I will state that my father owns an enormous farm in Virginia, which is the most proud and courageous of the American lands. My mother was Spanish-born of noble blood, and thus my titling is to Catalan lands. In America my nobility comes from the amount of land I own. You must forgive my slow response. American ranks are understood very differently."

I wondered how Americans recognized their nobles, but it was not my role to ask. I translated his words. The scribe took notes and said, "You may address the Sapa Inca. He will respond only if he pleases. When you are finished, you must leave, whether or not he has spoken."

Loddington looked at the screen. I saw his distrust; he clearly lacked confidence that any man sat there at all, let alone the Sapa Inca. Yet he recognized his place, and his words showed his cleverness.

He said, "I am pleased that the Sapa Inca considered our proposal worthy, and that he would bring his most honored presence to this meeting so that he might hear with his own ears and respond with his own voice. Though we had chosen our translator and prepared ourselves accordingly, his great wisdom moved him to choose his own man. Indeed, what effective ruler could trust a translator who was not self-selected and aligned with his interests?"

By this, I learned not to underestimate this man. I felt uncomfortable translating the last part, because it might inspire the Sapa Inca to ensure that I was in fact perfectly aligned. I worried that this might force the marriage of my daughter to an imperial cousin, perhaps within the week. You may think this an overreaction—but that is precisely the power the ruler held, and he might on a whim raise my fortune and deprive my daughter of her free choice. At any rate, I saw Loddington's intent. He had both complimented and condemned the man in the same words—and ensured that the Sapa Inca would prove his presence with his own voice.

Our ruler did precisely as Loddington intended. The voice from the screen spoke with the strength of a mountain storm. "We are most curious about your intent. Why have you come to this land? What could your impoverished people offer us?"

"We bring relief from the smallpox which devastates your empire."

"A cure?" I blurted out, forgetting myself.

"Better than a cure. We bring something that will make you—" and here he spoke a word I did not know.

I meant to clarify, but the scribe interrupted me and said, "Translate immediately for the Sapa Inca."

"I am trying," I said in Quechua, "but I must understand properly first." I addressed Loddington in English. "What does this word mean? Say it again?"

"*Immune*," he said clearly. "Smallpox will never affect you. This is what happens after a person receives the vaccine."

That last word was also unfamiliar, but I didn't need a definition. This *vaccine* was a brilliant device that could save my people. My heart lifted at the thought. What *was* a vaccine? Perhaps a gift, or an item? My imagination suggested a suit of golden armor, with gaps too small for a pustule to cross. I wondered how many men could wear it.

But of course I must translate, and so I said in Quechua, "He offers something called *vaccine*, which he says will prevent smallpox from affecting a person. They will not sicken."

"Not sicken?" repeated the Sapa Inca, clearly surprised. All the nobles whispered at once. Words swelled among the crowd and flowed outward from the lower palace, like water cascading down a hillside.

"That is his claim, Your Greatness," I said.

"Convey neither surprise nor interest. Ask how this *vaccine* works."

I did so, and Loddington smiled in a familiar way. A man smiles like that when he knows he will win the coming battle. But, my grandson: remember that an unseen battle has no certain victor, for time and terrain will vary the outcome.

Loddington said, "Surely Your Greatness will understand that the precise method of conveying the vaccine cannot be shared without guaranteed payment."

At my translation, the Sapa Inca said, "Explain how the vaccine works. We cannot believe anything known to science would stop the illness."

Loddington's response surprised me greatly. He said, "Bring twenty healthy men to my camp outside Cusco, and let them stay five days. I will give them the vaccine. Then send them to a village where smallpox rages. Have them share drinks with the infected. Your men will remain whole."

I couldn't believe what I heard. All men knew that sharing a drink with an infected person meant exposure; even breathing air might contaminate a man. Before I translated, I asked Loddington, "What is this vaccine? The Sapa Inca will be more tolerant if he has some idea of its nature. Is it a mask, or . . . a charm perhaps? Or maybe a kind of healing earth? How do you know it will work on our people?"

Loddington chuckled and said, "It's like teaching a boy to shoot a bird. When the boy grows up, he can shoot a lion. I could not show you the vaccine even if I wished to; it is so small that a beetle wearing spectacles could not see it."

I blew my breath out my cheek, thinking perhaps the man was mad—but I translated these words for my audience. I knew what lions were from the Bible, but I used the word *puma* for simplicity. At my speech, even more murmurs rose from the nobles. Cusco would discuss this day for years to come.

The Sapa Inca remained silent for a long time. I heard the Coya Inca whispering, but I couldn't make out her words. Finally the Sapa Inca said, "Lanchi Ronpa, are you sure you understand this man?"

"Yes, Your Greatness."

"Ask him—if this vaccine proves effective, how many men could we protect?"

Upon hearing this request, Loddington replied boldly, "Your Greatness, I will teach your doctors how to protect every man, woman, and child in the Four

Quarters. With the vaccine, your doctors can save your great Empire from this terrible scourge."

As I considered this, he added, "Think of what you might become, if you cast off the Spanish plague. Your empire even now surpasses those of Britain and Spain, including their New World holdings. France is a distant contender—and believe me, I have patrolled our western border and dealt with many Frenchmen. The world could lie at your feet. The Inca could expand northwards and expel Spain from the California Territory and Mexico. We offer you the chance to seize these rich lands from their overseas masters, that they may serve Incan glory instead."

As soon as I dared, I translated so I would not miss any nuance. It was difficult to keep it all together. I was thinking about how, after the worst of the 16th century plagues, we Incas had needed two hundred years just to recover our former size. The reconquest of the southern lands had required huge expense and effort—slowed by smallpox. We'd lost time in quarantining victims and performing medical experiments. We'd grown skilled at limiting the disease's reach, but made no progress on understanding its cause. If those great minds researching smallpox could be transferred to the project of Incan expansion—!

It seemed the Sapa Inca thought as I did, for his next question was, "If this *vaccine* proves effective, what is its price?"

Most diplomats would have hedged their answer, but Loddington proved a bolder man. He said, "Four thousand times my own weight in gold, and a peace treaty between our nations."

I was certain I'd misheard that, so I clarified the number with him. But I had indeed heard correctly. I conveyed the request to the Sapa Inca, thinking he'd laugh the American out of the room. Gold belonged to Inti; we valued it for spiritual power and not as a bargaining tool. But the Sapa Inca said nothing, even though the nobles shouted their outrage.

After some time, the Sapa Inca replied, "That is the weight of the sunrise itself."

"That is our price," said Loddington firmly.

"As a mere subject, you have no right to speak for Britain and thus cannot offer any such bargain. Furthermore, if you truly possess such a scientific miracle, any man with humanitarian values would offer it for only the cost of his voyage and supplies, plus some incidental reward."

"To your second point—if I acted on my own free will, then a humanitarian mission might happen, which would assure me the richest seat in Heaven. But I represent the thirteen American Colonies under British rule, and in their name, I ask such an enormous price. For you see, we wish our nation free of British rule. We desire a land of free men who decide their own affairs, rather than suffer rule from afar. And the price of this vaccine would fund our war against Britain—who taxes us unfairly and strips our resources, while giving nothing in return. You must understand—our overseas tyrants are nothing like what you've seen in your Empire's history. Here in the Four Quarters, the government cares for its people. Tales abound in our history books of how the Sapa Inca provides new clothing for every bride and groom in the land. Surely you understand why men must pursue fair treatment from their leaders."

I prayed for him to fall silent so I could catch up. Even a polite wave of my hand had not cued him to stop. I tried my best, although I stumbled on the part about rebelling against rulers. I thought surely the Sapa Inca would find this man and his ideas threatening, but once again, the ruler remained silent for a long time.

As we waited, Loddington spoke again. "It is a most reasonable price for—"

The Sapa Inca interrupted with, "What if we killed you and took this vaccine?"

I translated uncomfortably, but Loddington didn't blink. "You don't even know what it looks like, much less how to use it. If we thought you did, we would destroy it before you came close. I do not fear your empty threat."

More silence, and then the Sapa Inca said, "State the full terms of the agreement."

"We ask four thousand times my weight in gold, plus a permanent peace treaty between our nations. We intend to claim all land west of us, up to a river called the Mississippi."

The Sapa Inca did not respond, so Loddington said, "I can show Your Greatness this river on a map if necessary."

"We know where it is," said the Sapa Inca.

Before I could translate that response, Loddington continued smoothly, perhaps understanding the Sapa Inca's tone. "You may claim all land west of the Mississippi, though Spain might challenge you. But Spain is chaotic and impoverished right now, as is Britain. I'm sure you've followed the troubles in their lands."

Even I saw the true nature of this game. If we distracted Spain in the northern lands, they couldn't help Britain defend against the American rebellion. Both wars would more likely succeed. I translated this proposal for the Sapa Inca, and Loddington continued, "Surely you of all people would—"

The Sapa Inca interrupted with, "Silence. We are thinking."

The room fell silent for some time, aside from nobles whispering. I watched Loddington's llama-haired companion. Although he was taller, and bore himself like a man, I thought after a close look that perhaps he was yet a boy. He was certainly no older than seventeen, and I thought he might be as young as fourteen—just on the threshold of manhood. I wondered why he accompanied Loddington. Perhaps he was a servant? His stance indicated deference, as did his positioning. The boy fascinated me, even then. I suppose that Inti himself signaled how my fate lay entwined with this almost-grown boy, in a way that none could foresee. At the time I thought to myself he was the lesser of the pair with Loddington, for all great things were paired, and perhaps that included Americans.

Loddington shifted on his feet. He was impatient—a fact that my people might use against him, if necessary. I wondered how expensive the Sapa Inca found this proposal. Our ruler was wealthy beyond any earthly standard—but four thousand times the weight of a man? And to insist on payment in gold, which should be too holy for common transaction! I thought that even if the Sapa Inca considered the sum astronomical, he wouldn't dare show it.

After what seemed like hours, the living god-emperor of the Incan people pronounced his decision.

"We will provide these twenty men as requested. You will give them this vaccine and we will expose them to smallpox. When you have proven your claim, you will receive half the amount you request, paid in silver."

"Half!" shouted Loddington, then regained himself. "Half is simply not enough," he said. "And our payment must be in gold. Our creditors will not accept silver. If you do not want this vaccine, then I will go home."

"You are a fool to throw away so much wealth," said the Sapa Inca.

"We will find resources through other means," said Loddington.

"You would kill innocent men, women, and children for the sake of greed?" Loddington's face darkened, and he said, "I would save each and every citizen under threat. It is you who would kill them by refusing this deal."

I cringed as I translated this, carefully specifying that *he* said these things, not I. After a long silence, the Sapa Inca said, "One-fourth your requested price in gold when you prove your claim, and another one-fourth half a year after this vaccine continues to be effective."

Ah, the wisdom of the gods indeed! Loddington countered with, "One-fourth when the vaccine proves effective, and the remaining three-fourths at the half-year mark."

"You are dismissed," said the Sapa Inca coldly.

To my surprise, Loddington shrugged and smiled. He bowed deeply and turned to his dark-skinned companion. "Come, Marco," he said. "We have a long voyage ahead of us."

Loddington strode down the long hallway, chin lifted like an emperor. His party followed. Every noble's head turned to follow them. I heard loud whispering behind the screen—this time an unknown man's voice, along with the two rulers. Loddington had nearly left when the Sapa Inca commanded, "Call out for him to stop."

"Stop!" I shouted. Loddington paused near the door, tilting his head. But he didn't turn around. He gave no indication he would hear any more. I realized that I had met a rare creature: a man to whom the living god himself must submit.

The Sapa Inca said, "One-half when the vaccine proves effective, and the other half a year from that day. The full amount that you request, paid in gold."

Loddington turned on the threshold, and smiled. His face reminded me of a raptor diving toward prey. "And the peace treaty?"

"As requested, provided it cover aggression by either nation."

"Agreed," said Loddington smoothly, "by power vested in me from the Governor of Virginia and the General of the American Revolutionary Army. Shall we formalize in writing?"

The rest of the day—and then the week—fell to writing endless documents. The scribes took care of the Quechua versions, and Loddington wrote the English ones. I had to catch discrepancies, which twisted my stomach. Too many papers and not enough time! Luckily English and Quechua shared an alphabet, as we'd taken the Spanish letters—but still I felt overwhelmed. No one could help me; even another English-speaker offered little help, as those few men were illiterate peasants.

I was not called to further meetings, as they mostly consisted of Coniraya with his chief advisors. I did hear about the changing plans, though. The first plan was to test the vaccine on criminals, in case the American intended to attack us with poison. Because we do not keep prisons, this required bringing in criminals who'd committed two crimes and would normally be killed outright. They were kept under strict guard, until someone realized that of course the guards could not accompany the criminals so closely to an infected village and ensure proper exposure.

Attention turned to those loyal men who would volunteer for this task, and to my surprise, twenty were found. I suspected that the Sapa Inca had ordered compliance, and they dared not disobey, but I was not privy to these discussions. Most likely many llamas died as the High Priest examined their entrails, and runners wore themselves out relaying messages between the Sapa Inca and his spiritual advisor. I was notified that the village chosen for the test was Sayacmarca, and that several pox survivors would accompany these men, in order to assist should they fall ill.

Thus I learned that my wife Yma would go with these volunteers, as one volunteer was a widow who required a female companion. I supposed this was the Coya Inca's doing; it made sense to ensure the vaccine worked on women too, but I wished anyone other than my wife might go. My family was already entangled too far above our station. Great harm came to those who mingled with too-powerful people. Yma would go, and endure a twelve-day quarantine before her return. I was assured that my children would be cared for in her absence, as I was needed at the palace—and in particular that my lovely Chaska would join the priestesses, as a reward from the Sapa Inca. Yes, I was assured.

So you will understand, dear child, my dead panic when I heard of the Sapa Inca's plans to appease the gods. You see, Amaru and Paucar—his cousins who had come to me earlier—paid me a visit, shortly into this time of paperwork. I drowned in scrolls, with aching eyes and head. The windowless room was stuffy and hot, and all I could think of was seeing my wife and children again. But then Amaru told me of my next task as translator.

"The Sapa Inca awaits the results from Sayacmarca. Meanwhile, he instructs us to take the American leader and his servant to Machu Picchu and show them that palace's glory. Their entourage will remain in the palace as honored guests, under guard."

"Machu Picchu!" I exclaimed, setting down my papers. "No one sees Machu Picchu except the most——"

"Even I have not seen it," interrupted Paucar, "and I believe the American does not belong there. But this is the order and so we shall obey."

"I believe," said Amaru quietly, "that the intent is to impress the man. But yes, the fact that our cousin would allow such savage eyes into a holy place—I think that Coniraya already believes this vaccine will work, and he wants nothing to stop this deal. Perhaps he hopes that an impressed American will show mercy in his dealings."

I shook my head. "This is all amazing to me," I said. "I have never dreamed of visiting Machu Picchu."

Amaru said, "We will meet the High Priest there. I believe Ahuapauti wishes to talk to the Americans without his brother present."

I knew he meant the Sapa Inca, for then as now, the Sapa and Coya and High Priest were all siblings or at least cousins—and those three were full siblings, which was most unusual. I asked, "What do you suppose the High Priest thinks of Loddington?"

Paucar snorted. "You know as much as we do. You translated his every word."

I blinked, startled. The High Priest had been speaking in the throne room, as if he ruled the land? I had heard two different male voices behind the screen, along with the female. It was said that Ahuapauti as the elder brother always coveted the throne, despite losing to Coniraya in combat. Perhaps there had been an arrangement between them that they might share governance, and their sister would be wife to both.

"Does Ahuapauti rule this land then?" I asked, feeling like an ignorant villager.

Amaru said, "The rumor around court is that the Sapa Inca defers to the High Priest in all complex and unusual matters. He spends his time listening, rather than speaking, so he can accurately assess the situation. There are some who feel that this encourages the High Priest to desire too much power, but others think the brothers found an effective balance."

Paucar added, "Some say the Coya Inca prefers her elder brother, but no one says this unless he wants to be thrown off a mountaintop."

Amaru narrowed his eyes at his cousin, then continued, "However, the Sapa Inca makes all the decisions, including the plan for a hundredfold sacrifice on Atun Cusqui."

"A hundredfold!" I exclaimed, for normally only six boys and six girls were married at the festival.

"Yes. Six hundred boys and six hundred girls, aged nine to thirteen, will be married and then given to the gods near Lake Titicaca. The Sapa Inca believes we must increase our sacrifice as penance for spending our gold, which is Inti's sweat that we have earned."

I hardly heard his words, for my world collapsed around me. My family was being discussed in every noble household by now. Any hope of obscurity was gone. My beautiful Chaska—my darling daughter, admired by all around me, would surely be targeted for those marriages. She could hardly escape such a huge gathering of children. My daughter would be crowned with flowers—and then killed by a penitent priest.

I had never liked the festival sacrifices, but Inti demanded them, and who could question a god's will? And now the sacrifices seemed nightmarish. What god would ask this of a father? I turned away, that these men would not see my pain. I was trapped between two terrible outcomes. If the Sapa Inca consummated this trade, it would cost me my daughter—and hundreds of other daughters and sons. Yet if he rejected it, how many children would die from smallpox? Perhaps twelve hundred lives was a bargain indeed.

I had no answer then, and no answer now. At that moment, I desperately wished for my child's sweet face and her arms thrown about me.

## 3. Machu Picchu

Let me tell you, child, of how smallpox strikes. This is the tale told to me by your grandmother Yma, from when she was fifteen.

Put yourself here, with your grandmother. You're lying on your reed mat in your house's loft. It's summer and you're far too warm. You hear your parents talking below, of how smallpox has swept through villages too close to Cusco. They talk of rumors, how a man escaped quarantine. This man, you think, may be in Cusco now, infecting the millions gathered here.

The thought makes your forehead sweat. You shiver. And you think, *I am scaring myself*, but you know you can't sicken yourself with a thought. Still, your stomach twists and your back hurts, which could be from weaving wool today. And there's a lump in your cheek, which you run your tongue over, which might be where you burned yourself on supper. Perhaps you should show your father this lump, or not—why worry over nothing?—but you decide you should. You try to stand up, but the world spins. So you crawl, and fall against your hand—and where did you get those two blisters on your cheek? You're sure they're new, those two dots like the sun and the moon. You call for your parents, but your voice is weak.

And your parents come, and wrap you in blankets, but you hear soldiers surrounding your house. This must be quarantine—it happened once before, in childhood. But that was other children, not *you* who lay here, sweating and shaking, your tongue swollen like boiled squash. A hot red rash blisters all your skin. A scarred stranger brings you water, and you drink, and the stranger is gone and back again. You call for your parents, but they do not come. All around you the city of Cusco is silent, except for cries of pain and death. You do not know what happens next.

In time you come to your senses, not knowing the day or week, and the stranger is someone else. You're feeble as a newborn pup and your face is scarred like baked earth. You ask for your parents, but the stranger shakes his head. You wail as grief consumes you. And this house is yours now, empty and cold.

And that house is this house, where now we sit and I tell you the story of you. That plague was in 1793, when one-fifth of Cusco perished by smallpox— and still that toll was better than 16th-century plagues, where nine of ten might die. It's a miracle that we survived at all, Inti's blessing that the physician Ronpa discovered quarantine. Even the Europeans who brought this horror could not destroy the Incan Empire at its height. Though had the Spanish fully assaulted us in the earliest years, it might have been different, child—so very different.

So you see the choice we faced in 1806, my dear grandson, and why it mattered. Smallpox crippled us. It forced a twelve-day quarantine for all travelers. Without smallpox, our Empire could explode northward, taking the Spanish lands and all their wealth. We could replenish any funds we'd spent to get this vaccine. But everything relied on the vaccine doing what the Americans promised.

We went to Machu Picchu on litters carried by imperial runners, and we had scarcely begun our journey before Amaru ordered his runners to carry him close to me. The Americans were far behind us; I had no doubt they were being reminded of their place.

Amaru said, "I'm told that when the twenty volunteers reported to Loddington's camp, he blindfolded them and separated them from their sighted companions. He brought them into a tent and promised that the vaccine would hurt only briefly, and they would sicken slightly but recover within three days. Then they would journey to Sayacmarca. Five volunteers quit at this point. I believe they preferred to risk the Sapa Inca's wrath over sickness."

Intrigued, I asked, "What did he do to them?"

"None are sure," said Amaru. "All reported a stab in the arm, as with a cactus. The woman declared it was a sewing needle she felt. Several heard labored breathing and coughs—small coughs, like a child. One man reported the stench of stale urine and feces, as if someone had perhaps lain in them for some time."

I considered the mystery and had no ideas. "And did they sicken?"

"Yes," said my companion, as if thinking aloud to himself. "They became ill, though not with smallpox. All had to wait in these tents for three days. The smallpox survivors who had come with them were forbidden to enter the tents, and witnessed nothing. But these volunteers all emerged with slight scars, mostly on their hands."

"As with smallpox."

"No, nothing like. The scars were so mild they might have been caused by childhood injury. They reported feeling feverish, and blistering a bit—but with larger blisters, they said, based on talking with the smallpox survivors."

I glanced backward where the Americans rode. "And now they will not get smallpox?"

"So he claims. They are traveling to Sayacmarca now. I am sure that word will come from that village before the volunteers return; the Emperor has of course assigned smallpox survivors as runners."

And their clothes would be burned before they met the next runner, and their hair shaved off. No chances could be taken. With a start, I realized my wife would lose her beautiful hair, and this was only the beginning of changes for my family.

I realized Amaru had addressed me while I was lost in thought, and I asked his pardon. "Again, please?"

"I said—befriend this American. Get him to trust you. I must play the arrogant noble, but he will relax around a man of more ordinary rank. Find out what this vaccine is, if you can. If nothing else, learn what moves him, so that we might leverage it against him if needed."

"I will try," I murmured, feeling pressured.

Shortly we crossed the holy bridge over the Urubamba, and stopped to let our carriers rest. Amaru and Paucar offered coca leaves to the river, since this site lay on the sacred lines. Amaru gave me two small leaves and I understood his intent.

I took the leaves to Loddington and his companion. Loddington looked quite pale from his travels, though his servant appeared wide-eyed and excited. Up close, I saw that Loddington's coiled white hair was actually a fitted item that sat atop his head, like a hat. Small tufts of red-brown locks peeked out underneath. How peculiar, to wear hair as a hat. I wondered if the boy's llama hair was also a hat, but it looked natural.

Bowing slightly, I offered the two leaves on an outstretched palm.

"What are these?" asked Loddington.

"Coca leaves," I told him. "They will help you adjust to the mountain air."

Loddington grabbed both leaves and stuffed them in his mouth. Surprised, I looked at his companion, but the boy seemed to expect this behavior. I had meant one for each man, but indeed the boy seemed healthier. I knew from my grandfather that some men found our air easier than others.

"I am called Lanchi Ronpa," I told them. "Lanchi is my name, and Ronpa is where my father's name should be—but because some of my family survived smallpox, we are children of Ronpa, the great physician who became Sapa Inca. He is the disfigured god of our people."

"I know Ronpa," said Loddington. "Without him, Incan civilization would have collapsed. You owe him a great debt. Actually, some of our modern science is based on his work. For a man who didn't know what a germ was, he did an amazing job protecting your people."

I didn't know what a *germ* was either, but felt reluctant to ask. "We will meet Ronpa at Machu Picchu. He lives there along with all other past rulers."

Loddington gave me a strange look. I figured he might not understand that our god-emperors were immortal, but he didn't question me further. Personally, I was excited beyond belief that I would see the mummies of Ronpa and Atahualpa and our other great leaders. Loddington's color improved greatly with the coca leaves, and he asked me, "How is it that you speak English?"

"My grandfather was a British merchant. He came to these lands before the Expulsion and married here."

"Oh, he went native. I see. Our previous translator had a similar story, but his English was better. I'm sorry, that was rude of me. I prefer to speak my mind. Diplomacy tires me."

The boy smiled at this, but didn't say anything. He picked up a fan and created a small breeze for Loddington. I liked the way this boy kept his own counsel and never spoke out of turn. Suddenly I wondered if he was mute. I asked him, "What's your name?"

He looked away shyly. Loddington said, "Go on, boy. Answer the man."

"Marco," he said, quietly but clearly. I noticed that his jawline was nearly as square as Loddington's, and both Americans had hooked noses. They bore a certain barbaric look; they resembled coarse peasants rather than elegant nobles. Despite their oddness, I felt more comfortable with them than the wealthiest of Incan society.

Loddington said, "Named him for the famous explorer who opened China. His mama still cooks for my family back in Virginia. He's here to help me carry out my work. And he helped sail the ship here. Smart boy, he is. Natural on the water. Shame he's a mulatto, or he'd be a captain by now!"

"What is a *mulatto*?" I asked.

Loddington grinned at me. "Dark enough for a houseboy, but white enough you won't lose him at night!"

I didn't understand his riddle, so I asked, "And his family works for you?"

"Close enough," Loddington replied. "He was born into our household. Marco was always special to Father."

"Ah!" I said, understanding. I looked at their faces again and saw proof. "You are brothers!"

Marco's eyes widened like a startled cat's. Loddington's face grew tight. "We are not brothers," he said stiffly. "My mother is a Spanish-born lady of the noble house of de Godoy, who gave up her privilege to marry my father in the New World. Her bloodline traces back to cousins of Queen Isabella three centuries ago. Marco is my manservant and his mother is from Africa."

My heart pounded. Clearly I had offended Loddington in some major way. Marco ducked his head and busied himself with a strange leather bag, as if the contents needed immediate inspection. I quickly said, "Please forgive any offense I have caused. You must understand, my knowledge of English is limited to reading my grandfather's Bible and speaking with him, and my knowledge of America is almost nothing. I do not have the education that Incan nobles receive, for I was raised on a farm and I achieved my status through luck. I regret the insult and ask only that you let me learn from you. I may not be born into privilege as you are, but I have worked hard to improve myself."

I felt I hadn't said any magic words. But perhaps Loddington regained control of himself, because he said, "Please forgive my temper. I am very proud of my father and I'm sure you can understand that."

"What man should feel less for his father?" I asked, smiling at Marco to show I meant no harm. "I have a baby son myself, along with an older daughter, and I pray myself worthy of my boy's respect."

"Please do join us in our carrier," said Loddington. "I would like to learn more of the Incan people. I read widely before I came here, but naturally our histories are sparse after the Expulsion. How is it that your grandfather stayed here through the wrath of the Sapa Inca?"

Gratefully, I joined him and Marco, where we passed the remaining ride in pleasant talk. I told them of how my grandfather had become so Incan in his ways that the villagers accepted him, and the soldiers from Cusco had never forced him out. A handful of men had escaped the Expulsion in this way. I improved my accent by copying Loddington's speech—a longer sound than I was used to, deeper in the throat, with r's that carried longer than seemed necessary. I thought then that I must be out of practice with English, though later I learned that Americans speak differently.

I told him how I farmed some land with my wife's family. He seemed very interested in our terraced landscapes, and I was able to point out several well-built ones on our journey, where peasants farmed food for the magnificent imperial palace at Machu Picchu. I learned that his two loves were farming and sailing; his crop was tobacco, which was a luxury in my land, and his waters were the sea called Atlantic. I asked how he managed both enterprises, and he said, "My wife manages the plantation and my men work the fields," by which I concluded American families must be as broad and complex as our own.

At one point on our journey, we crossed a thick stone bridge over a narrow stream. I noticed Marco eyeing the water hungrily, as if he wished to explore where its merry waters led. I leaned over and said, "We have reed rafts, if you wish at some point to travel the land with Imperial companions."

Marco grinned and glanced at Loddington, who shrugged. Marco said, "I don't think I'll have time for an adventure."

Loddington said, "We'll be here a while, Marco, and traveling great distances to vaccinate the people. It's possible you'll get your wish."

"You're that sure of your vaccine?" I asked.

"Positive. It works. I have no fear as we head to your famed palace—although I note how easily we might mysteriously disappear on our way there, or back. Your ruler is no fool."

I couldn't think of a diplomatic answer, so I just said, "You're wise to see it."

By afternoon we'd reached a narrow path, from which Machu Picchu rose in the distance. A leafy canopy shaded us from the sun's rays. On our left rose a vast stone wall; on the right the cliff dropped away to sheer rock and a distant crevice. Though I was used to the mountain heights, the sight floored me; no man could look down and forget his place in Viracocha's creation. Loddington gave it the barest glance before settling back into comfort. Marco stared downwards, his eyes dancing like wild men. Slowly our carriers marched, step by step, toward this most sacred palace. It felt like the trees sank as we climbed.

As the palace drew into view, Marco's jaw dropped. Energy rushed through me, as if the gods themselves spoke in my body and declared me worthy. Never in my life had I dreamed of seeing this miracle, this beautiful jewel on the mask of the Incan people—me, from humble origins, whom fate had vaulted into this place. Even Loddington's eyebrows went up at the sun-drenched stones, shaped into perfection over three centuries ago and faultless ever since.

Now my child, let me tell you: though you have seen Machu Picchu before, you have not seen it through my eyes—on that day shortly before Midsummer, when the sun honored this incredible creation. You have run through its corridors with the sons of the Sapa Inca himself. To you perhaps Machu Picchu is a happy childhood memory, a place where noble cousins might play hide and seek with you. You have run your hands along the stones' fitted edges, feeling no gap—yes, the palace proves the Incan mastery of stonework, before we'd ever heard of Europe or smallpox. Can you believe, child, that even today the Americans spread plaster on their stones, like thick llama guts, to glue their walls together?

Ah, our Incan engineers, they surpassed even the modern European artisan! They built seventeen channels to splash water through the palace and siphon away the rainy season, so that the palace would never flood or erode. They reshaped the ground under this palace into graveled terraces, that the water might restore the earth. All of this, done in a few decades—solely because the Sapa Inca Pachacuti demanded it, and a god's bidding must be done without question. Men gave their lives to ensure Machu Picchu would merit its holy location—for why else build a magnificent palace in the most unreachable mountains, other than to prove that one can?

And those were my thoughts as we arrived—that Machu Picchu represented the peak accomplishment for the early Empire, before the European diseases wasted us so deeply that we spent a century regaining our lands. But Cusco and Machu Picchu had remained ours always, their glory crowning our legacy.

I remained silent until our carriers reached the palace entrance, for I did not wish to disturb anyone's thoughts. Marco drank in the sights like woolen yarn with dye; he looked as if he were memorizing everything he saw, as if it could sustain him through a lean period surrounded by white walls. Loddington's eyes swept the plaza, from the gold-leaf pumas and carved birds to the massive stone pillars that marked the first step. Terraces rose above us like earthen warriors. Water splashed through the channels, and I knelt to refresh myself with a drink.

I did not fear tainting the water, for this was the lowest point. Only the Sapa Inca could drink from the heights.

Amaru and Paucar drew near, and Amaru addressed Loddington. "This is the imperial palace of Machu Picchu, summer home of the Sapa Inca himself. He has instructed us to show you the palace in all its glory."

"I thank you for the privilege," said Loddington, but I detected a note of humor in his voice. I couldn't understand it.

Amaru and Paucar led our little processional, with Loddington following, and Marco and myself in back. Eight armed guards accompanied us, stone-faced and attentive; we Incas held a long memory after the treacherous Pizarro. Personally, I felt no danger that the Americans might harm us, but caution was wise.

We toured endless terraces and plazas, each more glorious than the last, lined with so many gold-leaf cornstalks I went cross-eyed. So much glamor overwhelmed me. I appreciated the beauty of isolated fountains, and the occasional secluded passage—but I thanked Inti for not making me Sapa Inca, for I think I would have perished of richness.

Amaru discussed the palace's history, and Paucar commented on its architecture. I learned much as I translated for the Americans, but mostly I spoke to Marco. He listened with shining eyes, as if I narrated legends rather than history. Loddington listened too, but his eyes were distant, and in time he drifted away to study the delicate gold sculptures lining the pools and archways.

Amaru said, "We understand that gold is valuable in every known nation. Europeans—and Americans, it seems—trade it for earthly goods and services. But we consider it spiritual currency. Gold buys honor in Inti's eyes; it is created by the sun itself, and is holy. Thus why Machu Picchu is laden with the sun's sweat; it marks the hard work done to honor our Sapa Inca and the god Inti himself."

When I had translated this, Marco asked, "What do you use for money?"

Amaru answered, "We have bartered since the early days of the Empire. When Europeans arrived, they nearly destroyed us—but our Empire survived, and eventually welcomed the Europeans. We quickly saw the value of a single tradable item, useful in any context. So the Sapa Inca—this was Ronpa's reign, in 1543—declared silver as our currency. Gold is reserved for religious and imperial use. Of course some nobles buy and sell gold, but it is not demeaned with everyday economic use."

"So if you pay us in gold," said Marco thoughtfully, "it's like selling us a piece of heaven."

"Marco!" exclaimed Loddington. "Come here. I need you immediately."

The boy went to his leader, and Amaru asked me quietly, "Have you learned anything of interest yet?"

"No," I said, worrying that I'd been given a too-difficult task. I couldn't see why Loddington might tell me anything surprising. He seemed too smart a man to reveal any clues to his thinking.

"Unless I miss my guess, he will open to you," said Amaru, smiling. "Keep translating for me, please."

I bowed slightly, still bothered by Marco's words. It was true—if we paid in gold, we were selling our gods for the people's health. No wonder the Sapa Inca felt we should make a hundredfold child sacrifice. Without that additional gift, the gods would be angry at our heathen choice—and a new illness might strike us down.

We headed next to the great Temple of the Three Windows, where all the former Sapa Incas lived. Their lovingly-wrapped mummies once lived in the Coricancha to advise the Sapa Inca, but they had been moved here in 1766 for peace and privacy. Now I felt Machu Picchu's true power, and my knees grew weak. Amaru led us through winding passages towards the rulers' alcoves, and he chose Ronpa's nook first.

I admired Ronpa's clean wrappings, and I imagined the living god standing before us. Amaru droned on and on, describing the complex family relationships among the various rulers—most were cousins of some fashion—and stressing the importance of good imperial heritage. I translated mindlessly; family terms and names were easy, without nuance, and could vanish from my head once spoken. Loddington looked exceptionally bored during this part, and even Marco's eyes dulled a bit. As I explained how the Sapa Inca and the High Priest were often brothers, and the current Coya Inca was their sister, Loddington snapped to attention.

"Do you mean to tell me that your rulers are siblings?" he asked.

"Yes," I said, taken aback. "It's always been this way."

Loddington looked like he wanted to say something angry, but he controlled himself with tight lips and narrow eyes. Marco just looked confused, as if he couldn't understand how such a thing were possible. Amaru asked, "Is there a problem?"

"They wished to clarify my translation," I said.

"Ah," he said. "We will tour the upper fountains and the plaza next, and then we can rest. I suspect our guests need it."

Indeed, Loddington looked exhausted, and even Marco looked worn down. But Amaru spent the entire afternoon lecturing on the sights at Machu Picchu. I thought my eyes couldn't handle any more gold. As the sun dropped lower, Amaru stopped in a room with a lovely window, which framed a dropaway landscape of the valley and the setting sun. I couldn't even appreciate it anymore; I was numb with awe.

"You may rest here," he told the Americans. "Lanchi will stay in case you need anything. Paucar and I will attend to the High Priest." He handed me two more coca leaves and departed.

When we were alone, Loddington sat on a bench and took a deep breath, looking pale. Marco sat next to him and leaned against the wall. Marco had carried all of Loddington's bundles up hundreds of flights of stairs, so I offered him the coca leaves. He took them and offered both to Loddington, who glanced at me and chose only one leaf.

He chewed it roughly, like it angered him. "Royalty is the same anywhere you look," he said.

I wasn't sure if he addressed Marco or me. When the boy didn't answer, I said, "How do the royals act in the colonies where you live?"

"Uppity. They think they own us. Nobles think it's all about the family you're born into. Did you hear him going on about the lineage of each ruler? It's like that heritage mattered more than what the man actually did."

I thought this odd from a man so proud of his noble Spanish mother, but didn't say so. "According to legend, we Incas appeared on earth at the end of a golden rod," I told him. "The nobles ensure that our rulers always connect back to Manco Inca and the other seven original people."

"What does it matter, though? A man's worth is in his deeds. It doesn't matter if he was born a king or a shoemaker. A good man proves his worth regardless of his station."

"That much is true," I agreed. "I have known peasants who were kinder than I deserved, and nobles who angered at nothing."

"That's what I mean," said Loddington. "Do you think these nobles deserve all this wealth? Look at the gold in this place. Every man in your nation could be rich. Yet your people toil in the fields to support the Sapa Inca, and they have no say in their future. Do you think that's fair?"

"The Sapa Inca deserves the best of everything," I told him. "The gods choose him to rule us, and he must lack for nothing."

"But why should an ordinary man suffer to offer him such tremendous wealth? When there is no chance of that man becoming noble himself, unless disease should spare his family, as happened to you?"

"It's an interesting question," I said cautiously, as Amaru's wisdom dawned on me. "It is true that a man can find great strength by doing things for himself. Many nobles don't understand this."

"Exactly," said Loddington. "Marco, fetch me some water from that fountain, will you? I've developed enough great strength for a week after those stairs."

"Most nobles are born with everything—all that they might want, and they never question that. I have more humble origins, and I still feel awkward among them."

"Really?" asked Loddington, sounding interested. Marco slipped a cup out of his pack and filled it with water. "How did you arrive at court?"

"I'm not really part of court," I said. I told him of the day I left for a hunt, and came back a man. When I reached the part about my younger sisters contracting smallpox, he listened very acutely. A bird flew in the window and he barely noticed; he listened as I described the horror of finding my sisters maimed and my father dead.

"That must have been a nightmare," he said quietly, sipping water. "You're lucky you were never exposed to the disease. It might have killed you. God willing, your Sapa Inca will make this deal, and spare your people such suffering. Smallpox has always been cruel, but particularly so to your people. No one knows why."

"I sincerely hope the vaccine will work for us," I said, "though my heart aches at my personal grief, should that be true."

"How so?"

I was torn by uncertainty. I wanted to tell him about the Sapa Inca's plan to sacrifice twelve hundred children at Atun Cusqui, and that my Chaska was likely to be chosen for this honor. On one hand, Amaru had instructed me to befriend the man and learn his secrets, and what better way to open a man than to open oneself? Yet on the other, perhaps in discussing the true cost of his demand, I would harm future negotiations.

I'm not sure what decided me. I think something in Marco's face moved me to share my fears, something about his innocence mixed with excitement. Somewhere, I thought, this boy's mother has released him into the world to become a man, and she must miss him terribly. Besides, perhaps if Loddington knew the full consequences, he might lower his price. Surely a mere thousand times his own weight in gold would buy a whole kingdom.

So I told Loddington and Marco of their vaccine's ultimate cost, and Loddington's face turned solid white. He stood and paced the room, then leaned against the window looking at the view.

"That's horrible," whispered Marco. "Those poor kids—they're killed? For what purpose?"

"To appease the gods," I said. "Because if we pay the price requested, we are spending divinity itself. Gold is not money to us."

"Barbarians," said Loddington, almost inaudibly.

Now I feared I had done terrible damage. I said, "Perhaps there is another way that my nation could pay, with silver? Or a smaller amount, or—"

"Silver would be too heavy in the amount I need," he said. "I can't transport it. Besides, it's useless for backing our money. Military service wouldn't help either; you don't know our terrain the way we do, and— Ugh! Child sacrifice and incestuous marriage. Jesus protect us."

Greatly worried, I said, "Perhaps the Sapa Inca will change his plan, or—"

"It's not my business," he said sharply. "My job is to make this deal and fund our war. There's more than twelve hundred American children praying for me to succeed. They're praying for an independent land, free of unfair tax policies and royal meddling—a land of brotherhood and equality. And in my homeland, each of those children has value for who they are. Any boy can work hard and be a landowner, like my father did to earn his plantation. And that's a cause worth fighting for, even if the price is far too high. Every life has value—even if the Sapa Inca cannot understand that. But you understand, I think."

His speech moved me, despite my fears. I thought then that despite his rough manners, this kind of man made history—and if indeed he planned to free his home from British oppressors, this he would do at whatever cost. His word "brotherhood" rang through my ears. I had always wished for a brother, squeezed as I was between sisters. A man like Loddington would make a fine brother, so self-possessed and strong in his convictions.

"It sounds like a marvelous land," I told him. "I would like to see what would happen if the worthy were allowed to be wealthy."

"So would I," said Loddington, staring out into the valley. "I would like to see that very much."

Something in his manner troubled me, like I'd glimpsed a cat's yellow eyes in the night.

## 4. The Condor's Brother

My grandson, today you should reflect on what it means to be a man. The story of you includes several great men, and several who failed to achieve such greatness. Your story also describes men with mixed motives—both good and evil, as many men are in the end. Most men who have walked the earth since time began appear in this tale, in one form or another, and I leave you to judge their hearts.

That evening, we were summoned to the Temple of the Three Windows, where we learned that the High Priest would consult the gods. Loddington and Marco had rested well by this point. So we headed to the temple, our steps light upon the stone. Since the summer solstice would occur in only three days, the sun hovered well into the evening, and it felt like darkness would never touch this glorious place.

In the temple, hundreds of priestesses washed and scented us. This was the role I hoped my little Chaska might play someday, if she lived to see adulthood, and I prayed quietly as the women combed my hair. One offered me a mug of chicha, the sacred wine brewed from spit and corn, and I drank deeply. Loddington submitted to their care without much reaction. Marco seemed very interested in admiring the lovely priestesses, who represented the best of Incan beauty.

During the preparations, Amaru pulled me aside and said, "It is said that tonight the High Priest determines whether the bargain offered is satisfactory, and whether a great sacrifice is required at Atun Cusqui."

"I hope the omens are good," I said.

"So do we all," he said. "Some are troubled, including myself. It is unwise that the High Priest should openly question the Sapa Inca's will. It's one thing to speak from his chair sometimes, but another entirely to consult the gods about another god's decision."

Astonished at Amaru's openness, I looked at his hands, which folded and unfolded in front of him. I decided he must be nervous, and perhaps even looking to someone as unimportant as myself for guidance. Perhaps he could talk to me without worrying which nobles might hear of his concerns. I said, "Maybe the gods will confirm the Sapa Inca's decision."

"I hope so," he said distractedly, and left for another room. Meanwhile, I hoped with all my heart that the entrails would say otherwise, that I might not worry about my daughter's fate, entangled with the fates of other children in the Four Quarters.

We gathered outside the Temple, and Amaru deferred to his cousin Paucar, who apparently held higher religious education and experience. Paucar instructed me, "The High Priest will consult a llama's entrails about the American proposal. The Americans must stand quietly near the consultation and not disrupt it. Translate some basics for them, but don't give too much detail. They are not allowed to understand too well. The ceremony will be held on the outside altar so that the barbarians do not see this most sacred place."

I had no idea how to combine that instruction with Amaru's direction to be forthright with the Americans, so I decided to pretend I understood little of what happened. It turned out that I did not need to pretend; in fact the ceremony was nothing like the public festivals I had attended.

A row of priests wearing speckled gold masks stood next to the golden altar. They chanted low words I couldn't understand, though I heard the names of Inti and Viracocha and many others. I glanced at Paucar, who stood on the far side of Loddington and Marco. His head remained bowed and he chanted along with the priests.

A priest brought in a hooded condor; its wings were clipped, so it could not fly away. They chained its foot to a perch over the altar. I guessed they meant it to represent the Condor, as the Sapa Inca Coniraya had been known in his younger days, fighting for the rule of our land. I thought it odd that the bird would be chained to the post, symbolically, but I was no priest and I supposed it necessary for the ritual.

Another priest led a young llama to the altar. He pushed her down on the stained gold slits that lined the cutting surface. She bleated loudly. Strong men strapped her down on her back, tying her forelegs together, and then her hind legs. I glanced over at Loddington, who watched with mild distaste, and at Marco beyond him, who looked worried.

"Marco," I said quietly, "you may wish to look away for a while."

"I can handle it," he said stubbornly—and he did, for when a priest slashed her belly, and the intestines sprung forth like writhing maggots, it was Marco who remained stoic, and Loddington who blanched. The smell of rotten vegetation and llama manure curled my nose hairs, and even though I'd slaughtered my share of animals in the fields, I had always disliked the task.

The High Priest stepped out from the shadows, wearing a fancy gold mask with rays scattering from his face, so large that two priests mirrored his every move just to support the sides. He plunged a fist into the llama's guts and lifted forth a bloody mass. He examined it from all sides like a jeweler examining turquoise, and then shoved it back into the body. Other intestines bulged as he smoothed down the belly.

"What does it say?" whispered the ever-curious Marco.

"I have no idea," I said honestly. I glanced up at the roof's edge, looking at the stars. The roof here stood high above us, with irregularly-shaped stones carved in interesting patterns. Something felt wrong to me, but I couldn't place it. By now, the night fell blackly over us. I saw only hundreds of torches circling the altar, and the stars beyond the rooftop. I thought of Chaska then, my bright-star planet, and looked towards the sight that had inspired her nickname. The light blinked into view, vanished, then blinked back. Mystified, I stared at the sky. How could a planet vanish?

Too late I realized what I was seeing. "Look out!" I shouted, heedless of the ceremony. I leaped forward and pushed Loddington as the boulder tumbled off the roof towards us.

My grandson, picture these events happening now. Imagine time moves like water, and air hardens to rock. I cannot speak; my lungs are full of stones. Loddington leaps away like me—but says nothing. His silence is an accusation. Time itself slows to witness the crime. Loddington stands idle, not reaching for this boy who shares his father—his brother, whose face speaks the truth. The boulder is falling, and I cannot save Marco. But one man can help—*does* help. To this day I bless him, and trust Inti to warm his spirit in the brightest sunlight.

Time restored itself. Marco lay face down, thrown from the boulder with mere scrapes, but Paucar's legs lay crushed beneath the rock. Paucar still lived— though later I learned not for long. Priests rushed him away for treatment. He said nothing to me as he passed, nor I to him. How I wish I could speak now, to thank him for his courage! I don't know what moved him—but Paucar was a great man, worthy of his birth. And thus you know a man's measure: how he dies is how he lived. Loddington's empty claims of brotherhood echoed in my mind. *This* was how he treated a brother: by ignoring a threat to his brother's welfare, since it bothered him not at all. He was no brother, but a snake.

The rest of the night blurred. We were whisked away to sleep on reed mats, all in one room. I slept fitfully, dreaming of Paucar's crushed legs, and of llama entrails spilling the fate of my people and my child. In my dreams the entrails snarled my wrists and ankles. I tried to run a long road through the Empire, but I slipped on blood and fell nonstop through the night.

Near midnight, someone shook my shoulder. I woke quickly and saw Marco's face, silhouetted by moonlight through the window. I sat up and he lifted a finger to his lips. He pointed at Loddington, who slept soundly.

"What is it?" I asked.

"Thank you for saving our lives," he said simply. "I wanted to tell you myself. I'm sorry about the man who was so gravely injured."

"Marco," I said, worried, "why did your companion not save you when he could have?"

"He surely meant to," said the boy defensively. "He was startled and not thinking."

I looked at him, realizing that some part of him needed to preserve this lie. "You *are* half-brothers, are you not? Is it so different in America that half-brothers are not kin?"

"His father lay with my mother," the boy said, with great shame, "and surely here too that is a crime, if a man and woman are not married."

Ah, illegitimacy! Finally I understood why Loddington did not acknowledge his brother. Or so I thought, at the time. "So then you will leave once you are fully a man, and build your own life away from the accusations written on your face."

Marco said, "I must stay with John Fernando, unless he sells me elsewhere. I am surprised he did not do so upon his father's death, but perhaps he humors his sister who cherishes me. He is decent to me; he never beats me nor insults me."

"Sells you?" I asked, wondering if this word held a modern meaning I did not know.

Marco's eyes flickered. "John Fernando may sell me to another man as he pleases, and I would serve that man as I do him."

Oh my child, so much of the world I did not understand then! I thought merely of brotherhood, and America as Loddington claimed it: a land where any man might fight for his freedom to live as he pleased. In my mind I reconciled this image with Marco's words by thinking that servants might change lords for better pay—but the cracks in the mirror already glimmered. I knew even then that Loddington's brotherhood was as shoddy in spirit as he.

So I said to Marco, "Dear boy, I would be proud to know you as servant, or free man, or brother—whichever role Inti would give you in the Land of the Four Quarters, for I admire your spirit. I am delighted that you were uninjured today."

Marco smiled at that, and clasped my hand. "Someday, Lanchi, I would like to name a ship for you." He lay down to sleep again, and I did the same, resting uneasily through the night.

In the morning Amaru came, his face lined with grief and pain. He beckoned me out of the room, and I hastened to follow. He said, "I trust you are well and whole."

"By Inti's grace, I am," I said. "I am sorry for your hardship. But Paucar saved Marco's life."

"If my cousin lives, he will be crippled," said Amaru. "I pray that the boy proves worthwhile."

I attributed the unkindness to lack of sleep and his deep suffering. "All lives have value, and Paucar is a hero to that child," I told him.

I wasn't sure my words would help. We Incas loved our children so much that it hurt. In their eyes, we saw the wise adults they would become. This is why we sacrificed so many children in those days—we were returning their potential to the gods. But any doubts on this practice are a modern anachronism; in those days, we gave children to the gods, and none questioned it.

Amaru smiled sadly. "I also like the boy's spirit, but I would rather have my cousin," he said. "But I come bearing news. The vaccine works and the Sapa Inca is pleased with the results. All the volunteers remained in Sayacmarca, shared drinks with the victims, and walked out unscathed."

"By the sunrise, a true miracle," I whispered. Indeed, I had not believed it until that very moment! With such treatment, I could keep my children and myself safe from the dread disease—and every father in Cusco could do likewise. My heart surged with desire to see my family, but fell again as I remembered what this news meant. A working vaccine meant the Sapa Inca would surely consummate this deal with the American delegation. And that meant my Chaska's future would likely see her lying in a snowy mountain pit, dead in her flower crown.

Amaru continued, "We are to return immediately and undergo another quarantine. At that point the Sapa Inca will require translation to continue negotiations."

"And of this assassination attempt?" I asked. "Surely anyone can see what it was. I suppose a gun could not look so much like an accident."

"All the workers on the wall that day were killed," said Amaru matter-of-factly. "Rumors say that some very high-level priests may be implicated in scandal. Do not trouble yourself with such matters. Leave them to my investigation. Do not befriend the Americans any further; it would complicate matters at this point. Leave them to their business as you attend to your own."

And thus our processional wound away from Machu Picchu, and its tall pillars like teeth in the sky, as we returned to Cusco. Per Amaru's instructions, I conveyed the information, and then stayed distant from the Americans. Thus I trapped them in a silent cloud through which they could not communicate. Upon arrival in Cusco, they were taken to one area for quarantine, and I to another.

I expected that twelve days from our arrival, we would all appear once more before the Sapa Inca, or perhaps the Condor's brother speaking in his place. But on the fifth day, I heard rumor from the attendants of great unrest in the palace, and on the eighth day I smelled burning flesh in the courtyards. I could see nothing from my barren waiting room, but an attendant told me that those loyal to the High Priest were burning alive for treason. On the ninth day I heard of the execution of the High Priest Ahuapauti for treason against the gods. No one would tell me precise details—perhaps they did not know—but I deduced that it involved the attempt on the Americans' lives. The only thing I felt sure of was that my daughter's fate was sealed. The Sapa Inca Coniraya now held sole power—and he had insisted we increase the festival sacrifice.

My dear grandson, I am no priest, but it seems to me that a man who kills those who disagree with him—especially his spiritual guide—cannot then argue that his way is righteous.

I expected a quick conclusion to the business at hand, but instead I was kept a thirteenth day, then a fourteenth. On the fifteenth day of my quarantine, an unfamiliar noble came to my chambers and told me to go home until I was summoned back. I had heard that morning that the Coya Inca was permanently exiled to a remote mountain palace. If only we had known then of the complex web of treachery against the Sapa Inca and the Incan people, woven by those two high-profile lovers and siblings to our ruler! But we owe the traitors a great debt. Had they delayed their conspiracy to steal the throne, the Sapa Inca might have paid the Americans' steep price. The siblings' crimes saved the Incan people from sacrilege.

But I digress. I was surprised, but delighted about returning home. I wondered of the Americans, but knew not where they might be. When I returned to my house, there I found my wife Yma—head shaven, dressed in new clothing, but more beautiful than ever. I kissed her deeply and traced her cheekbones with my finger, the familiar bumps of her scarred skin like a blessing. Scarcely had I finished embracing her than Chaska leaped into my arms, and I hugged her as if it might be the last time. Sternly I ordered her back to chores, ignoring my own aching heart, and she obeyed without even a childish glance backward. I stroked my son's head, and he giggled as I placed him back in his pit.

The room smelled like boiled greenery; Yma was preparing yucca to ease aching joints, which she sold at the medicine market. We reconnected as man and woman will, and then lay in each other's arms, savoring each other. Then of course the daily tasks of the household called, and my son squalled for feeding, which my wife obliged.

She listened to my tale with fascination, asking many questions about the Americans. She gasped at Loddington's price, and felt even more horror than I.

"They demand money like blood," she said. "How could they steal our spirit itself? Do they not see how entire families—whole clans—are wiped by this dread disease?"

"They see," I said, "but they desire their nation of brotherhood—or so they call it."

I told her of Machu Picchu and Loddington's careless disregard for his brother, and her face crinkled with disgust. When I told her of the Sapa Inca's likely decision to sacrifice twelve hundred children, she immediately formed the same conclusion I had about Chaska. My heart sank, for she proved to me that I was not wrong.

"We could leave Cusco," she said. "Travel to the distant southern lands, and raise our family there."

"Impossible," I said. "I am now in the Sapa Inca's service as translator, and thus our family is bound to him. He would not let me leave, and we cannot run from the Imperial guards. They would find us no matter where we were."

My wife grieved here, for we had lost another daughter at birth shortly after Chaska, and she knew the pain of losing a child. I held her, and stroked her shorn hair. When she had cried, I said, "Tell me of what you witnessed in Sayacmarca."

She straightened and said, "Truly, I wish I had more to report! I saw death and torment in the stricken village, as always, and I wish I could banish those memories. But the volunteers all survived, and bear only the strange scars on their hands that marked them after their illness."

"What illness?"

"The American took them into a dwelling at his camp and made them somewhat sick for a few days. It was like a lesser version of smallpox—a kind which did not ravage their bodies, but rippled them like a pond."

"And did you see how this was done?"

"No, though I did hear a child's cry at one point."

"A child's cry?" I asked, remembering Amaru's tale of strange noises and the smell of urine. "Are you certain?"

"I am a mother," she said pointedly, and I acknowledged her talent. As I have stated, the husband is not complete without the wife; he may be the greater of the pairing, but he cannot stand alone.

I said, "It is all very strange. I cannot help but think that the Americans are being unfair in this debate. They would kill millions of Incan men, women, and children—for the sake of their rebellion against England, which is supposed to be about brotherhood. Yet they do not demonstrate this brotherhood even when the stakes are smaller. Why should I think they will behave differently on a larger scale?"

My wife nodded, saying, "It is wrong to hold us hostage against such a deadly enemy."

My dear grandson, I must tell you something. A moment comes where an idea visits your mind, straight from the gods themselves. An idea is a guest, worthy of the best hospitality. It taps on the door, or simply walks in like it lives there, and you must handle it wisely or it may depart forever. The gods had given me an idea, and let it linger for some time before I noticed it. By this point the idea had so firmly lodged into my being that it seemed part of my family, which I must protect at all costs.

"Yma," I said to my wife, "if I were to ask you where the American camp was located, how close could you bring me to that place?"

"Within arm's reach," she said, "for I paid close attention to our direction as we went, in case I became separated."

"Wise woman," I said. I did not mean to tell her my plan, because if it went poorly for me, there was a chance she could beg for mercy and claim she had no knowledge. A slim chance, for a man's family was held accountable for his misdeeds—but given her noble family, I thought her cousins might protect her from Imperial wrath.

But my precautions proved needless, for my wife asked with narrow eyes, "Lanchi Ronpa, what is it that you mean to do?"

I did not dare answer her, but stood and inspected my musket where it hung over the door. Let her think I wished to shoot the American, for that might be more honorable than what I intended. But I underestimated her—

ah, how often I did that!—for she said, "My husband, in our land, medicine is available for any man who requires it."

"This is true," I said.

"If a thief can prove that an official should have provided him with an item, and did not do so, it is the official who is executed for failing to serve."

"It is so," I admitted.

She kissed me and said, "My darling, you are on an errand of mercy. Steal this vaccine, if you can, and provide it to our people! I would consider this moral and right, and the Sapa Inca himself could not convince me otherwise."

"I fear for you, if you know what I do," I said.

She laughed. "Perhaps I shall tell you precisely where that camp was, in case you happened to want to visit that place tonight."

You see, I loved my wife with all my heart, and in that moment I loved her a hundredfold. Someday, child, I pray that you will be equally fortunate.

## 5. Ronpa's Blessing

I followed Yma's directions and approached a grove outside Cusco—an area I had not visited often. I expected Loddington's men would guard the camp that stored his precious vaccine. I did not know what I sought. I only knew it was small, and perhaps involved a sewing needle—or so Amaru had surmised, from the volunteers' reports. I feared the vaccine might be something that Loddington kept on his person, in which case I had no idea how to obtain it. Would I kill a man for this vaccine, if I felt sure it were necessary? I debated in my mind and decided that yes, I would if I must—but then I could have no argument with the gods if Chaska were chosen for sacrifice. I steeled myself for the possibility, but prayed that it would be otherwise.

And so you see, I was on a fool's errand—seeking a vaccine of unknown shape, size, and location. I pictured something like thread through a needle's eye, but knew no definitive answer. It was easy to move through the area alone; guards surrounded the camp, but they were protecting against an army encroachment, or a violent war party. The Americans likely thought that a single man like me could not possibly find and identify their vaccine. They failed to understand that a determined man—one responsible for his family's fate—possesses a fox's cunning and a raptor's strength.

I crept closer, using shady trees and leafy ferns for cover. One American started, as if he saw me; he aimed his musket briefly. A squirrel darted out, and the man relaxed, presumably thinking the animal had startled him. I thanked the squirrel, vowing to honor them later if I survived. I prayed quickly to Mama-Quilla the moon goddess to shadow my way, and then darted through a glade to my next target.

In this manner I found a path to the closest tents, and then wondered where to look first. I would not have long before someone spotted me. I knew the outside tents would hold only supplies, nothing critical—and thus I sauntered towards the central tents, hoping for some divine sign of approval to hint me in the right direction.

And there! A small cough. Despite lacking a woman's intuition, I knew that sound was a young child. I hoped not to startle the child, but a youth might be persuaded to tell me of the vaccine, if indeed they knew. And a child's declaration of an invader, if it came to that, might be tossed off as fancy and nothing more.

It was risky, but so was this whole attempt. I folded the cloth away from a tent and peeked inside.

The tent was dark, but moonlight crept in as my silent assistant. As my eyes adjusted, I saw two sleeping boys, perhaps five or six years old. Their heads pointed toward me and their feet away. Even through the forest air, they smelled of human waste. The wind rustled the leafy trees behind me, granting a moment of brighter moonlight. To my shock, I saw that these children were darker even than Marco—how was that possible?—and had the same llama-hair as he. Cousins perhaps? Iron chains with solid-looking locks wrapped their bodies. I did not know what it meant. The tent darkened again as the trees settled back. A child coughed, and I hastily withdrew.

I turned around and faced the muzzle of a musket, pointed directly at me. Behind that gun stood Marco, his eyes masked and unreadable.

I held perfectly still. The boy and I looked at each other. I had no doubt that he knew well how to use the gun, and I had no urge to test his reflexes. What I didn't know was why he had not shot me already, nor what he intended for me.

We stood that way for what seemed like a whole night, though I am sure it was only moments. After a while, I murmured, "It would be better for both of us if you made a decision."

Marco's lip quivered, but the gun stayed firm. "I'm supposed to protect the camp," he said.

"Where is Loddington?"

"He stayed in Cusco at the palace. He's refusing to leave until the Sapa Inca agrees to speak with him again, through our original translator."

We held still a bit longer, looking at each other. Finally I said, "I'm sorry you will have to think of a new name for your ship."

"Step inside that tent," ordered Marco, keeping the gun on me.

We entered the tent where the boys lay. I said, "What happens now, Marco?"

"I—I don't know," he admitted, sounding more like a child than ever before. "John Fernando said someone would probably sneak in and try to steal the vaccine, but I never expected it would be *you*, Lanchi. How—how could you be a thief?"

"In this land . . ." I said, preparing to tell him what my wife had told me, but the boy lowered his gun and looked at the ground. Of course I could have jumped him and overpowered him there, without alerting anyone, but I had no intention of doing so.

I studied him, slumped against the tent wall, and simply said, "There are so many lives at stake. I cannot see how I could stand by and watch my people die, for the sake of a foreign war with no sensible grounds."

"No grounds!" he exclaimed. "John Fernando fights for the freedom of Americans, to live their lives as they choose."

"So he says," I said as gently as possible, "but his actions show the lie."

"That's not true!"

"Does he fight for your freedom?"

"It's different for me," he admitted, "and these other slaves."

I knew what slaves were, of course; even my grandfather's Bible mentioned them. I had always felt sorry for them in the stories. And many things made sense to me now, about Marco and the way Loddington treated him. "Who are these boys?" I asked.

"They are the carriers of the vaccine," he told me. "I help John Fernando with his medical work. We brought with us five dozen slave boys from the auction. We have kept the vaccine alive by transmitting it through them, two boys at a time. This is why John Fernando so urgently insists on seeing the Sapa Inca; it has taken far longer for him to negotiate the deal than he thought possible. If the last boy heals before the vaccine is transferred, then all is lost to us."

"What *is* the vaccine?" I asked. "Each boy carries it separately?"

At this Marco smiled, and said, "It is very clever indeed. It is a disease called cowpox, which comes from Britain and infects some farmers and milkmaids who work with the animals. A person with cowpox sickens, but heals again—and once the body has witnessed cowpox, it guards well against smallpox! The terrible germ cannot touch the man, for the body now understands the threat and will not let it take hold."

So simple! So marvelous! You see, the principle of vaccination had been known to the Incan people since the beginning of time. It was written in our pairings of greater and lesser, of sun and moon, of husband and wife. There was the greater disease and the lesser, and neither was complete without the other.

I said to Marco, "So how does one pass the disease? Will I contract it, having been here?"

"No," said Marco, "I must vaccinate a person, or John Fernando does, by extracting pus from a cowpox blister and injecting it into a new person."

"Then if this is not done before those blisters heal . . ." I said, understanding finally.

Marco blurted out, "Lanchi, why did you come here? I wish you hadn't. I don't want to kill you, but I cannot let you leave. What can I do?"

"You can vaccinate me," I said, "and let me leave. Speak no word to Loddington, or just say you never saw me."

"I can't," protested Marco. "He will know. He always knows. I cannot be free of him."

"Then you can come with me," I said, "for I admire your courage and honesty. I see the fine man you are becoming—and nearly are."

His eyes brightened, and I knew he was intrigued. Still, I saw he was unconvinced. He said, "John Fernando has been kind to me . . ."

"I expect he treats you like gold. He is most careful with his possessions," I remarked. "Though a lump of gold cannot withstand a falling boulder."

Anger flashed through Marco's eyes, and I thought he might shoot me after all. Then he said, "I have nowhere to go and I don't know this land. I would do no better in your service."

"Then come with me as a son," I told him. "I would welcome you into my family. Here you are considered a man at fifteen, when you take a new name. I will teach you the Quechua language. And I will trade goods until I can give you an adventure such as you desire. You will be your own master."

Marco cried silently, and his body shook. I knelt to embrace him, and said, "We don't have much time. Quickly—give me the vaccine. I will carry it in my own body."

"I can't leave the boys," he said. "There's nearly sixty of them, lying in their own filth and chained to beds. They cry at night, and I can't soothe them. Some are as young as three. They call for their mothers but none are here."

My heart ached for these poor children, who could not understand their role here. "Where did they all come from?"

"They are field boys, chosen for sturdiness. I believe John Fernando plans to sell them back to the auction when he returns home—whichever ones survive. Three children died on our voyage here."

"I don't see how we can free them all," I said slowly.

"I cannot leave them here," insisted Marco. "I could not walk away knowing their future. If I stay, I might at least persuade John Fernando to sell them to known houses, who might care for these boys."

"We must find a way," I said. "There are many childless families who would be grateful to adopt a son—even one not from the Four Quarters. In the older days of the empire we commonly adopted children from conquered regions. These boys cannot go back with him." But I was thinking—how could we possibly get them all out? Marco could have crept away with me unnoticed, but not five dozen children.

I considered for some time, and then asked Marco, "Have you ever de-fanged a snake?"

We implemented our plan quickly. Marco infected me with cowpox and gave me ten needles to transfer the disease. I promised him that we would meet again soon, and he must remain quiet until that time. He distracted a guard so I could slip away unnoticed.

I returned to my wife and told her the whole story. Concerned, she sent me to bed, and insisted I rest so as not to worsen my fever. Within days I developed a rash on my hands and arms, and yellow blisters that ached to touch. My wife said it was indeed the same illness that she had seen on her visit to the camp, and at my direction, she carefully extracted the pus and injected both our children.

Oh, how hard it was to infect them, even knowing the benefits! As they sickened, I started healing; the hardest part was disguising our efforts from our neighbors, for I feared that if they discovered our illness, soldiers would quarantine the house and alert Loddington to my plan. Our daughter we persuaded to be as silent as possible, but our son did not understand, and he wailed with pain. I thought of the boys in Loddington's camp, not much older than he. I did not know what would happen to Marco—and just as bad, I feared that someone would notice us. An official quarantine would lose us precious time. We could not afford to let the last blister heal before we had transferred the precious disease to other people.

Though I was not entirely well, I decided it was critical to accelerate my plan. I asked my wife to beg favor at the palace, using any rank or pleas she could think of, to get a message to the wise Amaru—on whom all my hopes rested. With all the political chaos, I was unsure that she would succeed. But my good wife persisted, and after spending a day and a sleepless night pleading for audience, she found a servant willing to bear her message.

And so on that next night, as my body healed and my children lay ill— Amaru came alone, and at night. He was plainly dressed and wore no mask, which might call attention to himself.

When I told him my tale, his face darkened with anger. For a moment I wondered if it might be directed at myself, for thievery, but that was mere anxiety. Amaru finally said, "So this vaccine is now in the possession of the Incan people. We have no more need for this greedy bargainer."

"I do not wish to see him killed," I said hesitantly, wondering if that was his thought.

"Nor I," he said, "for the Americans might not take kindly to that. Yet I also do not wish to see him profit on the suffering of others, even if they are mere children."

"We can refuse his deal now, provided we keep the vaccine alive in our people."

"Refuse his deal, certainly. He has negotiated in bad faith. There are worse punishments for a man such as he," said Amaru.

And with that, we discussed a plan.

The next day, Amaru and I visited Loddington, where he had encamped in the palace's waiting chambers. He was speaking in broken Spanish to anyone who understood and would listen, begging for audience with the Sapa Inca. I kept my hands clasped behind my back. When he saw me, his face brightened with a generous smile.

"Lanchi Ronpa!" he exclaimed. "I asked for you, but no one would bring you."

Amaru said, "The Sapa Inca is unavailable, but he has authorized me to finalize our bargain. Here is a measure of faith." He opened his purse and poured out golden beads, more than I had ever owned myself, which tumbled into Loddington's hands and scattered across the floor. He crawled around after them, scooping up handfuls like a monkey gathering food.

Amaru said, "I have gathered more, and my warriors will bring it to your camp. Let us go there, and we will bring you—as promised—at least a tenth of what you requested, with the remainder to follow tomorrow. We would bring the entire amount today, but it is simply too much gold; the warriors must return tomorrow with it."

At my translation, Loddington's eyes narrowed. "This is a sudden change of direction for the Sapa Inca."

"He is busy," said Amaru smoothly. "He deals with matters of state and cannot attend directly to this business. He does desire the vaccine, now that it's been proven."

Loddington looked directly at me and said, "Lanchi, tell me the truth. Is the Sapa Inca really ready for the vaccine?"

"I assure you," I said, choosing my words carefully, "that the Sapa Inca will be delighted to know the secret of this vaccine."

Loddington smiled and got to his feet. "Then we shall do business together," he said. "Come, let us go to my camp."

And so we went, a processional of warriors led by the American, who did not know he was already defeated. Loddington led the parade on an imperial riding-llama, his head held high, as if he ruled all the land. I kept to the middle, not wanting him to see my hands, to know his ruin was already upon him.

When we arrived at the camp, Amaru murmured to me, "Here we go. Good luck." He assumed a haughty expression and said, "An emissary of the Sapa Inca requires all people in the visited realm to present themselves and stand forth for viewing."

I translated these words for Loddington and added, "All men may of course retain their weapons; we know you are not a fool."

Marco stepped out, carrying his musket. "What's going on?" he asked me.

I addressed him directly. "The Sapa Inca's representative asks that all persons be visible as he enters."

Marco glanced at Loddington, who said, "Humor them, Marco. They bring gold in exchange for our vaccine."

Marco looked at me, but to his credit did not show surprise. Around twenty American men appeared from the woods, all heavily armed, ready to shoot us. Amaru subtly dug his knee into his llama, and the beast reared back and spat.

"There are more," he said calmly, which I translated.

I added, "You had best bring forth all persons here, since the llama smells the presence of many who remain unseen."

Loddington frowned, then signaled with his hand. Ten more American men slid into view. Clever man. But Marco had caught on, and said, "John Fernando, shall I bring all the—"

"No!" exclaimed Loddington. "This is my encampment. Now let us close this deal."

Amaru said, "You have not been honest with us. I can smell the children as clearly as this llama can."

At these words, Loddington paled, and Marco ran off to open several tents. He flung aside canvas to show the children huddled together like clustered pebbles, staring at us with enormous eyes. Amaru frowned at the sight. He said, "Who are these children?"

"They help me with the vaccine," said Loddington angrily. "They are my property."

I counted our warriors. We had nearly a hundred men. Amaru had enough wealth to command an army. "Come here, Marco," I said. The boy came, and I grasped his shoulders firmly like a father.

Amaru waved his hand commandingly, and I addressed Loddington. "The Sapa Inca has changed his mind," I said. "He wishes to buy your children instead of the vaccine. That purse which his emissary gave you is more than the amount you paid for them. These children will now be the Sapa Inca's subjects in the Land of the Four Quarters."

"But . . ." Loddington sputtered, "but—why?"

"The Sapa Inca's word is law, and his representative merely implements it. We do not question his decisions and neither can you."

"But they are mine!"

"These children were free the moment they stepped onto our soil," I told him. "Any damage to your finances is repaid with gold. A few beads in exchange for a few children, clearly neglected. How could that not satisfy you?"

"You will never get the vaccine," said Loddington, his face red with anger. I could tell he wished to order an attack, but didn't dare, in the face of so many armed Incan warriors.

Marco spoke up defiantly. "They already have it," he said. "Look at Lanchi's hands."

I held them up. Loddington stared in disbelief. I feared he might order me shot, regardless of consequence, but Marco added, "By now he has transferred the vaccine to others, and those others can be used for vaccines. Most likely they already have been."

"You may leave this land," said Amaru. "Our deal is done."

"You—you *thieves*," Loddington screamed. "You have stolen what is mine!"

"You have tried to sell what should be any man's," I said. "It is not a crime to take it."

Loddington suddenly went white. He raised his gun and aimed at Marco. Before anyone could react, he shot. Marco reeled back, collapsing against the llama. Four Incan warriors shot Loddington where he stood, but I held Marco, pressing his shoulder where blood poured out. I hardly noticed Loddington fall, nor his men staring in shock. We are all lucky they did not shoot back; perhaps they too had some doubts about the circumstances. Or perhaps the gods guided our hands that day. I cannot say, nor can any man.

"Marco!" I shouted.

"It is—" he gasped for breath— "It is not so bad. Bind the wound tightly."

I ripped my tunic and obeyed. Oh my grandson, my heart broke—I thought I would lose Marco. But I crushed his hand in mine, and said, "Marco—stay strong. Let my hand keep you in this world. My hand, which you have marked with a blessing—stay here with your gift, and with me."

Marco smiled through his pain, and I thought that this boy had much left to do. He would not leave this world—not yet.

And he did not, for you know who Marco became.

So my child, that is the story of you, which I tell you on your fifteenth birthday that you might know yourself. And you know the rest of the tale—how the Americans fought their war without our funding and achieved their freedom anyway, though they still suffer the schism of slavery in a so-called free land. The boys we freed from Loddington were adopted into the Empire; the childless Amaru and his wife adopted three boys themselves, and rewarded me richly. I built a school with those funds, so that all boys might attend and learn.

Marco stayed in the Land of the Four Quarters and became my son. He took my name, and then traveled the seas to foreign lands as the great explorer Marco Ronpa. Your father opened the prosperous trade we now share with China, by sailing the *Lanchi* across the vast ocean. All this shortly after marrying my darling Chaska, now a beautiful woman in her own right, who had honorably left the temple for love's sake. Your father gave you his features and his voice, and blessed you with your proud strong face—the face I love as much as my wife's and my children's and my own, for you belong to the Incan people with all your soul. Someday I expect you will explore further than your father, in our faster modern ships, and visit your grandmother's homelands in Africa. But that day is not here, and you, my grandson, must find your own destiny.

And my child—the interesting thing about China is that they'd already solved the smallpox problem with a technique called variolation, which they'd learned from India. But our vaccination was safer and more effective, and Marco found that technology vital in opening China to trade. But that is another story, child, and not the story of you. Sleep now, and in the morning you must tell me your new name, the one that marks you a man in the Land of the Four Quarters.

NEBULA AWARD WINNER
BEST NOVEL

# EXCERPT FROM *ANCILLARY JUSTICE*

## ANN LECKIE

*Ann Leckie's debut novel* Ancillary Justice *also won the Hugo Award, the Arthur C. Clarke Award, the Locus Award, and the British Science Fiction Association Award. It was published by Orbit.*

1

The body lay naked and facedown, a deathly gray, spatters of blood staining the snow around it. It was minus fifteen degrees Celsius and a storm had passed just hours before. The snow stretched smooth in the wan sunrise, only a few tracks leading into a nearby ice-block building. A tavern. Or what passed for a tavern in this town.

There was something itchingly familiar about that outthrown arm, the line from shoulder down to hip. But it was hardly possible I knew this person. I didn't know anyone here. This was the icy back end of a cold and isolated planet, as far from Radchaai ideas of civilization as it was possible to be. I was only here, on this planet, in this town, because I had urgent business of my own. Bodies in the street were none of my concern.

Sometimes I don't know why I do the things I do. Even after all this time it's still a new thing for me not to know, not to have orders to follow from one moment to the next. So I can't explain to you why I stopped and with one foot lifted the naked shoulder so I could see the person's face.

Frozen, bruised, and bloody as she was, I knew her. Her name was Seivarden

Vendaai, and a long time ago she had been one of my officers, a young lieutenant, eventually promoted to her own command, another ship. I had thought her a thousand years dead, but she was, undeniably, here. I crouched down and felt for a pulse, for the faintest stir of breath.

Still alive.

Seivarden Vendaai was no concern of mine anymore, wasn't my responsibility. And she had never been one of my favorite officers. I had obeyed her orders, of course, and she had never abused any ancillaries, never harmed any of my segments (as the occasional officer did). I had no reason to think badly of her. On the contrary, her manners were those of an educated, well-bred person of good family. Not toward me, of course—I wasn't a person, I was a piece of equipment, a part of the ship. But I had never particularly cared for her.

I rose and went into the tavern. The place was dark, the white of the ice walls long since covered over with grime or worse. The air smelled of alcohol and vomit. A barkeep stood behind a high bench. She was a native—short and fat, pale and wide-eyed. Three patrons sprawled in seats at a dirty table. Despite the cold they wore only trousers and quilted shirts—it was spring in this hemisphere of Nilt and they were enjoying the warm spell. They pretended not to see me, though they had certainly noticed me in the street and knew what motivated my entrance. Likely one or more of them had been involved; Seivarden hadn't been out there long, or she'd have been dead.

"I'll rent a sledge," I said, "and buy a hypothermia kit."

Behind me one of the patrons chuckled and said, voice mocking, "Aren't you a tough little girl."

I turned to look at her, to study her face. She was taller than most Nilters, but fat and pale as any of them. She out-bulked me, but I was taller, and I was also considerably stronger than I looked. She didn't realize what she was playing with. She was probably male, to judge from the angular mazelike patterns quilting her shirt. I wasn't entirely certain. It wouldn't have mattered, if I had been in Radch space. Radchaai don't care much about gender, and the language they speak—my own first language—doesn't mark gender in any way. This language we were speaking now did, and I could make trouble for myself if I used the wrong forms. It didn't help that cues meant to distinguish gender changed from place to place, sometimes radically, and rarely made much sense to me.

I decided to say nothing. After a couple of seconds she suddenly found something interesting in the tabletop. I could have killed her, right there, without much effort. I found the idea attractive. But right now Seivarden was my first priority. I turned back to the barkeep.

Slouching negligently she said, as though there had been no interruption, "What kind of place you think this is?"

"The kind of place," I said, still safely in linguistic territory that needed no gender marking, "that will rent me a sledge and sell me a hypothermia kit. How much?"

"Two hundred shen." At least twice the going rate, I was sure. "For the sledge. Out back. You'll have to get it yourself. Another hundred for the kit."

"Complete," I said. "Not used."

She pulled one out from under the bench, and the seal looked undamaged. "Your buddy out there had a tab."

Maybe a lie. Maybe not. Either way the number would be pure fiction. "How much?"

"Three hundred fifty."

I could find a way to keep avoiding referring to the barkeep's gender. Or I could guess. It was, at worst, a fifty-fifty chance. "You're very trusting," I said, guessing *male*, "to let such an indigent"— I knew Seivarden was male, that one was easy—"run up such a debt." The barkeep said nothing. "Six hundred and fifty covers all of it?"

"Yeah," said the barkeep. "Pretty much."

"No, all of it. We will agree now. And if anyone comes after me later demanding more, or tries to rob me, they die."

Silence. Then the sound behind me of someone spitting. "Radchaai scum."

"I'm not Radchaai." Which was true. You have to be human to be Radchaai.

"*He* is," said the barkeep, with the smallest shrug toward the door. "You don't have the accent but you stink like Radchaai."

"That's the swill you serve your customers." Hoots from the patrons behind me. I reached into a pocket, pulled out a handful of chits, and tossed them on the bench. "Keep the change." I turned to leave.

"Your money better be good."

"Your sledge had better be out back where you said." And I left.

The hypothermia kit first. I rolled Seivarden over. Then I tore the seal on the kit, snapped an internal off the card, and pushed it into her bloody, half-frozen mouth. Once the indicator on the card showed green I unfolded the thin wrap, made sure of the charge, wound it around her, and switched it on. Then I went around back for the sledge.

No one was waiting for me, which was fortunate. I didn't want to leave bodies behind just yet, I hadn't come here to cause trouble. I towed the sledge around front, loaded Seivarden onto it, and considered taking my outer coat off and laying it on her, but in the end I decided it wouldn't be that much of an improvement over the hypothermia wrap alone. I powered up the sledge and was off.

I rented a room at the edge of town, one of a dozen two-meter cubes of grimy, gray-green prefab plastic. No bedding, and blankets cost extra, as did heat. I paid—I had already wasted a ridiculous amount of money bringing Seivarden out of the snow.

I cleaned the blood off her as best I could, checked her pulse (still there) and temperature (rising). Once I would have known her core temperature without even thinking, her heart rate, blood oxygen, hormone levels. I would have seen any and every injury merely by wishing it. Now I was blind. Clearly she'd been beaten—her face was swollen, her torso bruised.

The hypothermia kit came with a very basic corrective, but only one, and only suitable for first aid. Seivarden might have internal injuries or severe head trauma, and I was only capable of fixing cuts or sprains. With any luck, the cold and the bruises were all I had to deal with. But I didn't have much medical knowledge, not anymore. Any diagnosis I could make would be of the most basic sort.

I pushed another internal down her throat. Another check—her skin was no more chill than one would expect, considering, and she didn't seem clammy. Her color, given the bruises, was returning to a more normal brown. I brought in a container of snow to melt, set it in a corner where I hoped she wouldn't kick it over if she woke, and then went out, locking the door behind me.

The sun had risen higher in the sky, but the light was hardly any stronger. By now more tracks marred the even snow of last night's storm, and one or two Nilters were about. I hauled the sledge back to the tavern, parked it behind. No one accosted me, no sounds came from the dark doorway. I headed for the center of town.

People were abroad, doing business. Fat, pale children in trousers and quilted shirts kicked snow at each other, and then stopped and stared with large surprised-looking eyes when they saw me. The adults pretended I didn't exist, but their eyes turned toward me as they passed. I went into a shop, going from what passed for daylight here to dimness, into a chill just barely five degrees warmer than outside.

A dozen people stood around talking, but instant silence descended as soon as I entered. I realized that I had no expression on my face, and set my facial muscles to something pleasant and noncommittal.

"What do you want?" growled the shopkeeper.

"Surely these others are before me." Hoping as I spoke that it was a mixed-gender group, as my sentence indicated. I received only silence in response. "I would like four loaves of bread and a slab of fat. Also two hypothermia kits and two general-purpose correctives, if such a thing is available."

"I've got tens, twenties, and thirties."

"Thirties, please."

She stacked my purchases on the counter. "Three hundred seventy-five." There was a cough from someone behind me—I was being overcharged again.

I paid and left. The children were still huddled, laughing, in the street. The adults still passed me as though I weren't there. I made one more stop— Seivarden would need clothes. Then I returned to the room.

Seivarden was still unconscious, and there were still no signs of shock as far as I could see. The snow in the container had mostly melted, and I put half of one brick-hard loaf of bread in it to soak.

A head injury and internal organ damage were the most dangerous possibilities. I broke open the two correctives I'd just bought and lifted the blanket to lay one across Seivarden's abdomen, watched it puddle and stretch and then harden into a clear shell. The other I held to the side of her face that seemed the most bruised. When that one had hardened, I took off my outer coat and lay down and slept.

Slightly more than seven and a half hours later, Seivarden stirred and I woke. "Are you awake?" I asked. The corrective I'd applied held one eye closed, and one half of her mouth, but the bruising and the swelling all over her face was much reduced. I considered for a moment what would be the right facial expression, and made it. "I found you in the snow, in front of a tavern. You looked like you needed help." She gave a faint rasp of breath but didn't turn her head toward me. "Are you hungry?" No answer, just a vacant stare. "Did you hit your head?"

"No," she said, quiet, her face relaxed and slack.

"Are you hungry?"

"No."

"When did you eat last?"

"I don't know." Her voice was calm, without inflection.

I pulled her upright and propped her against the gray-green wall, gingerly, not wanting to cause more injury, wary of her slumping over. She stayed sitting, so I slowly spooned some bread-and-water mush into her mouth, working cautiously around the corrective. "Swallow," I said, and she did. I gave her half of what was in the bowl that way and then I ate the rest myself, and brought in another pan of snow.

She watched me put another half-loaf of hard bread in the pan, but said nothing, her face still placid. "What's your name?" I asked. No answer.

She'd taken kef, I guessed. Most people will tell you that kef suppresses emotion, which it does, but that's not all it does. There was a time when I could have explained exactly what kef does, and how, but I'm not what I once was.

As far as I knew, people took kef so they could stop feeling something. Or because they believed that, emotions out of the way, supreme rationality would result, utter logic, true enlightenment. But it doesn't work that way.

Pulling Seivarden out of the snow had cost me time and money that I could ill afford, and for what? Left to her own devices she would find herself another hit or three of kef, and she would find her way into another place like that grimy tavern and get herself well and truly killed. If that was what she wanted I had no right to prevent her. But if she had wanted to die, why hadn't she done the thing cleanly, registered her intention and gone to the medic as anyone would? I didn't understand.

There was a good deal I didn't understand, and nineteen years pretending to be human hadn't taught me as much as I'd thought.

*For my parents, Mary P. and David N. Dietzler, who didn't live to see this book but were always sure it would exist.*

# FINDING FRQNKIE:
# REMEMBERING FRANK M. ROBINSON

## ROBIN WAYNE BAILEY

Early Sunday morning on June 30, 2014, my longtime friend and mentor, Frank M. Robinson, known to many of us as "Frqnkie," passed away. It was Gay Pride Weekend in San Francisco, and Frank would have approved of the timing. He had the largest parade in the country to send him on his way.

Frank Robinson, born 1926, was also a longtime member of the Science Fiction and Fantasy Writers of America. More, he was chosen to receive an honor as "Distinguished Guest" at the 2014 Nebula Awards ceremonies, an honor quite shamefully overlooked as the evening went on and the various other awards were presented. Due to sudden ill health, Frank was unable to attend the event. He had hoped right up until the last moment to attend for just a day, but that was not to be. Finally, realizing that he would not have the strength, he prepared a brief acceptance speech, but only after the ceremonies ended were we able to get his remarks out to the public via the SFWA.org website. Here are those remarks.

*Some time ago a group of aeronautical engineers were asked if they had ever read any of Bob Heinlein's SF books for kids. 90 % of them raised their hands. Some years later, I later interviewed Arthur C. Clarke for* Playboy *and he asked me half a dozen science questions. The last one was more of a parable than a question: What was the one thing could a fish never conceive of? The answer was "Fire!" The parable was that there were things in the universe of which man could never conceive of. It occurred to me then that science fiction and its writers were the imagination of this world. I still think that. All of you writers are a part of that imagination, and each and every one of you deserves a gold star. I can't write much more—I'm crying as I write this.*

*—Frank M. Robinson*

I first met Frank some thirty-five years ago when I was selling my very first stories. Wilson "Bob" Tucker introduced us. The two had known each other since they were both youngsters. Frank and Bob became the grandfathers I never had. Bob taught me what it meant to be a fan and Frank taught me important lessons about how to be a professional. *"Stop thinking of yourself as a science fiction writer,"* he once told me, *"and start thinking of yourself as a writer."*

He exemplified that lesson. Frank moved with elegant ease from novels to short stories, from thrillers and mysteries to science fiction and non-fiction. He frequently blended genres. His first novel, *The Power* (1956), and its later sort-of-sequel, *Waiting* (2000), both mingled equal parts science fiction and mystery-thriller to potent effect. Both books also received high accolades. George Pal turned *The Power* into a very successful film starring George Hamilton, Michael Rennie and Suzanne Pleshette; National Public Radio named *Waiting*, upon its release, as one of its Notable Books and Best Summer Reads. Frank also gave us two highly praised non-fiction books, *Pulp Culture: The Art of the Fiction Magazines* (2001) and *Science Fiction of the 20th Century* (1999), both highly prized by collectors and genre historians. His science fiction novel, *The Dark Beyond the Stars* (1991) won one of the first Lambda Literary Awards ever presented to a work of science fiction and, to my knowledge, it has never gone out of print.

In 1971, working with his friend and collaborator, Thomas N. Scortia, Frank hit the literary jack-pot when their novel, *The Glass Inferno*, came to the attention of famed producer, Irwin Allen. Allen, as Frank often told it, was looking for a "big hit" to follow his mega-hit, *The Poseidon Adventure*. In a tale both hilarious and too convoluted to recount here, their novel and a similar novel, *The Tower*, by Richard Martin Stern, were combined into one screenplay and became an even bigger mega-hit film, *The Towering Inferno*. That movie established Frank as a writerly force. He and Scortia would go on to produce other highly successful works, such as *Blow-Out*, *The Nightmare Factor*, *The Prometheus Crisis*, and *The Gold Crew*, which was translated into film as *The Fifth Missile*.

Although Frank wrote in a wide variety of other arenas with collaborators and alone, his love of science fiction was life-long. At age sixteen, he began work as an office boy at Ziff-Davis in Chicago where he met and got to know legendary editors Ray Palmer and Howard Browne. He called that job "the closest I've ever come to Nirvana." Frank also talked about how, times being hard for everyone, he would smuggle the science fiction magazines out of the offices under his jacket to read and devour. At the same time, he found his way into Chicago and Illinois fandom. Throughout his life, he was a reader and collector of pulp magazines, books, and art, amassing over time one of the finest pulp collections in the world. As he used to say, "I never met a mint-condition pulp magazine I didn't like."

While still in Chicago, he also worked for a number of "men's" magazines, such as *Rogue*, *Cavalier*, and *Playboy*. He spoke most fondly of his time at *Playboy* where he wrote and edited the famous "Playboy Advisor" column. He once joked to me that the two most successful sex advice columnists of all time—himself and Seattle's Dan Savage—were both gay men.

That's right, Frank was gay. No secret to anyone who knew him, really. I mentioned at the beginning of this appreciation that among his friends he often spelled his name stylistically with the letter "q." It was his way, in less tolerant times, of acknowledging his sexuality. Frank was a quiet and unassuming activist who never really sought the spotlight he so richly deserved. I asked him about that once. He said, "I just don't carry a bull-horn in my pocket." He didn't need a bull-horn. Frank had the Power of Words. In underground newspapers, he chronicled the early gay rights movement in Chicago and across America. As a speech-writer for San Francisco city supervisor, Harvey Milk, he helped to change the world.

I visited Frank as often as I could and spoke with him regularly by phone. I'll never forget the morning he called me up, shouting into the phone, "Robin! They're making a movie—and I'm in it!" Frank sounded like a little kid that morning, a little kid with a very deep and rumbling voice, but a kid brimming with excitement. That movie was *Milk*, starring Sean Penn, James Franco, and

Emil Hirsh. As he explained to me, the producers first approached him about serving as a technical advisor, because Frank had known Harvey Milk closely, been in the camera shop, and lived in the Castro through that period of time. However, they soon made him an "extra" on the set, a sort of ageless "everyman" appearing in the crowds in key scenes. Then, in one of those scenes, Franco began feeding Frank lines. Those lines wound up on the cutting room floor, but they were enough to earn Frank SAG membership, and he was dancing again about that.

Those were very happy days for Frank. He called every other evening with news from the set or to tell me he was cooking fried chicken dinner for Sean Penn or that Dustin Lance Black was in his living room. Frank was clearly star-struck without ever seeming to realize that in his own right he was one of the stars. If you have access to the DVD version of the film, watch the extra features where you'll find an extended interview with Frank.

I called Frank one of my grandfathers. During my very first visit to his home, he and I were strolling around the Castro, and he eventually guided me into A Different Light, which was one of the great gay bookstores in the neighborhood. The clerk, who knew Frank well, hurried to greet us, asking as he turned to me, "Is this your grandson?" Frank barked his trade-mark short laugh. "Hah!" I looked up at him and meekly asked in front of the clerk if it was okay if I called him "Grand-dad." Frank grinned a crooked grin and answered *sotto voce*, "Well, all right, but not too loud and not in public." It became one of our personal jokes.

In 1994, while I was serving SFWA as Central-South regional director, I proposed that the organization establish a way to honor older writers who had once had an impact on the field but who had, over the years, faded from the limelight. We had often heard Heinlein's famous admonition to "pay it forward." I felt strongly that it was also important that we "pay it backward." I suggested a program that sought out older writers and brought them back into the spotlight, particularly at the Nebula Awards. Ann Crispin coined the name, *Author Emeritus*, and it stuck. The following year, 1995, we brought Emil Petaja to New York to honor him as our first Author Emeritus. As it turned out, Emil Petaja also lived in the Castro only a few blocks from Frank, and although Frank only knew Emil slightly, I invited him to introduce the very first AE. Frank made a magnificently touching presentation, and Emil was thrilled. That was a fine and shining moment for SFWA.

Years later, when President Steven Gould consulted me about a 2014 Author Emeritus presentation and suggested Frank, I enthusiastically agreed. I only had one qualm, that I thought it was time to drop the title, *Author Emeritus*. In too many minds for too many reasons, it had come to be regarded as a sort of Junior Grand Master, something it was never intended to be. Steve and the Board of Directors settled on "Distinguished Guest." Perfect. It feels a bit poignant, though, that Frank, who was integral when we launched the *Author Emeritus* program, also played his role as we phased it out.

I stayed at Frank's home many times over the years and traveled with him on several occasions, usually to Nebula Awards events. In June, on the Sunday afternoon following the San Jose frolic, I saw him for the last time just a couple of weeks before his passing. His honor and acceptance speech were shamefully overlooked at the ceremony, so along with my partner Ron Davis and fellow writer Bob Angell, we resolved to take a train to San Francisco, along with the award, and make our own private presentation. We brought him his award, a couple of copies of the *SFWA Bulletin* special Nebulas edition, and two extra copies of *Through My Glasses Darkly* (2002), a collection of his short work that I had selected and edited with him. Those last hours were bittersweet, because I sensed that I would not see him again. While Ron, Bob, and Frank's assistant Brian Kamps prepared dinner, Frank and I sat on a couch and talked. He held my hand the entire time, which was uncharacteristic, because Frank was never much for open displays of affection. He said himself that he was of that generation when it was hard to do so.

On August 8, 2014, a memorial service took place at the Women's Building in the Market District. Over a hundred people turned out to say goodbye and to honor Frank's memory. The following Saturday morning, August 9, a number of them boarded a yacht to sail around San Francisco Bay. It was Frank's eighty-eighth birthday, and the group sang "Happy Birthday" as they scattered his ashes on the water.

## ANDRE NORTON AWARD FOR YOUNG ADULT SCIENCE FICTION AND FANTASY WINNER

# EXCERPT FROM *SISTER MINE*

## NALO HOPKINSON

*The Andre Norton Award for Young Adult Science Fiction and Fantasy is presented to the best young adult science fiction or fantasy book, in parallel with the annual Nebula Awards.* Sister Mine *was first published by Grand Central Publishing.*

We'd had to be cut free of our mother's womb. She'd never have been able to push the two-headed sport that was me and Abby out the usual way. Mom was still human at the time. My dad's family hadn't yet exiled her to the waters.

After the C-section, just for a few days, she was kind of sidelined while she recovered. That gave Dad's family the opening they needed to move in and take over. 'Cause from their perspective, things were a mess. Abby and I were fused, you see. Conjoined twins. Abby's head, torso and left arm protruded from my chest. We shared a liver, both kidneys, and three and three-quarters legs between us. We had two stomachs, two hearts and four lungs, and enough colon for us each to have a viable section, come to that. Abby and I could have lived as we were, conjoined. Between us, we had what we needed. But here's the real kicker; Abby had the magic, I didn't. Far as the Family was concerned, Abby was one of them, though cursed, as I was, with the tragic flaw of mortality. Abby and me, my mom brought us that gift.

You might say that my dad married outside the family. To hear some of them tell it, outside the species. Most of his family would barely give Mom the time of day while she was still around, despite the fact that she and her kin had done steward service to them for centuries. Or rather, because of it. Dad's family could have stood it if she were just some dalliance of Dad's, a bit of booty call. Even love might have been OK, if they'd kept it to a dull roar. Wouldn't have been the first time that a celestial had knocked boots with the help. But no, Mom and Dad had to go and breed.

With Mom unable to interfere for the time being, Dad's family decided that obviously, the human doctors of the hospital where we were born had to surgically separate Abby and me. They put pressure on my dad till he agreed to it. They're not really venal, that lot, just too big for their britches. They've been emissaries of the Big Boss for so long that they forget they aren't gods themselves, just glorified overseers. But overseers with serious power. Mom's kin didn't say boo. They knew damned well that they didn't have the cash to buy that much trouble.

The second we were separated, Abby began to die. There was something vital she needed that my body'd been supplying. No one could tell exactly what, but we were losing her.

There's a guardian that attends births and deaths. He keeps his eye on the young and on the old; the former having so recently left the other world for this one, and the latter soon to depart that way again. That guardian, you might say that he's a border guard. It's his job to send the living on their way, and the dead on theirs. If it's not your time, you're not going anywhere. He was there, ready to do his job, when Abby and I were born, the semi-celestial child and her human donkey of a sister. Now it was time for him to escort her back across the barrier between the quick and the dead. He lingered over our cribs in Intensive Care for an instant. He smiled at us both, chucked us under our tiny chins. He thought we were kinda cute. Then he kissed us each on the forehead and gently picked Abby up, cradled her in his arms. My dad, grieving, watched him. The guardian gave him a rueful look. Have I mentioned that the guardian is our uncle? Dad's brother? He took Abby, leaving my dad to weep at my bedside.

The guardian should have carried Abby to the crossroads right away. Instead, he took her to my mom's room. He'd taken a shine to Mom, Uncle had. A real shine. The kind that sets brother against brother, starts family feuds.

Mom was still dopey from the anaesthetic, but uncle took care of that. Plain ol' unconsciousness was no challenge for the being who shuttled humans from life to death like beads on an abacus. Even in her half-sleep she'd been begging to see her babies, and now she was fully awake. This was her first time seeing Abby, but when she clapped eyes on my uncle carrying a gasping bundle whose little mouth pursed like my dad's, she figured out pretty quickly that the baby was one of hers.

The guardian's impartial. He has to be. Normally he wouldn't be put in the position of herding family across the borders between life and death, since the rest of that lot don't die. Not permanently, anyway.

Mom begged him for Abby's life.

He replied, "There isn't enough of her to survive on this side of the gate."

Mom was having none of it. She began to make promises. But what does a human have to offer a demigod? She tried to swear her lifelong obedience. Uncle shook his head. In a way, he already had that, from every mortal on this plane and the next. But he didn't leave with Abby. Mom's arms ached to hold her baby. She promised sex, the best he'd had, and he's had some good stuff. He's not just Lord of the Grave, my uncle. All that borning and dying business has given him a taste for some of the sweetest gifts of the flesh. My mom was fine, they tell me. All blackberry sweet juice. And she knew what to do with what she had. How d'you think she managed to catch the eye of not just one celestial, but two?

Thing is, Uncle, for all his lechery, is pretty professional about his job. He shook his head, turned towards the door. But Mom spied the tear twinkling in his eye, and she knew she'd underestimated him. Sure, he liked doing the nasty plenty well, but—"Save her," Mom said wildly. "And I'll love you."

Uncle stopped, one hand on the door's crash bar, the other supporting Abby's one-and-three-quarters-legged little rump. He knows lies, Uncle does. There's a propaganda machine that makes him out to be the prince of them, but that's some bullshit. Those are the same people that won't let their kids borrow fiction from the libraries. Stories aren't lies, people. Some of them are truer than any autobiography. But Uncle does know how lies taste; refined sugar-sweet, not molasses-sweet like truth, with its sulfurous backbite. Mom was telling the truth; the room was treacly with it. If he saved her daughter, she would love him. She would love Death itself, fiercely and hotly. What parent wouldn't, under the circumstances?

Uncle looked down at the child he was holding, at her piecemeal body and oddly canted face. Her jaundiced skin going blue. She had my mom's eyes. We both do. Uncle turned. Mom reached her hand out, took his in it, her eyes brimming with hope, with love enough to fight for her child, and more.

Uncle whispered, "I can't do it. She needs organs, tissues that I can't give her. I'm a ferryman. I can't make her live."

"Allyou need me for that," said my dad. He walked into Mom's room. Uncle tried to snatch his hand away from Mom's, but she held on and looked Dad full in the face. A mother's love is fierce with pride, and Mom was never one for regrets.

Dad read the signs of what had gone on between them, like spoor in the room. "You want this?" he asked Mom.

"Yes."

"Brother mine," said Dad, "give me my child." His two eyes made four with Uncle's. In that moment, Dad's eyes in his bark-brown face were green, the bright green of new spring leaves. Gently, Uncle handed Abby over. Gently, Dad took her. His first time holding his baby. That was the moment that Uncle violated the border between this side and the next, for once he had taken a soul to himself, he wasn't ever supposed to hand it over until he had delivered it to its destination.

If Uncle is a ferryman between the worlds, Dad is a gardener. His talents are growing, grafting, and pruning. "Lewwe go then, nuh?" said Dad to his brother.

"What?" said Mom. "Where're you taking her?"

Dad replied, his voice full of loss, "Can't fix her up here. We have to go to the next side. You stay and see to Makeda." He tried on a smile. "We going to bring her sister back to you before you could say Jack Mandora."

Uncle embraced Dad. Their circled arms protected Abby. Mom had to look away from the brothers then. Their aspects were already changing, preparing to cross over to the other side. Mortals cannot look upon that celestial shift for long. It's like looking directly into the sun. Between the glory that was the brothers, dying Abby was a fleeting scrap of dull flesh. Then the three were gone. Mom clambered back into her bed, closed her eyes, and prayed for both her children. No point imploring the Big Boss. He has more important things to look after. As so many claypickens do, Mom prayed to the celestials more directly involved in the affairs of this plane: in this case, to her lover and to his brother.

Baby Abby came back to us from the other side a living being who could grow and thrive on her own. Of course the Family knew immediately what the brothers had done. Abby shouldn't have been alive. Those were some big-ass laws they broke. There were to be consequences. Since Dad had been willing to do all that for a human, they made him into one. They stripped his godsoul away from him, leaving him purely claypicken. (You do realize that Dad and his family had been among the first humans of the world? When the Big Boss decided he wanted some managerial staff, they volunteered for the job.) Dad would have to spend a whole human lifetime with only the tricksy pinch of mojo that claypickens can sometimes muster if they chance upon exactly the right charms, potions, and prayers in exactly the right configuration at exactly the right time. His godsoul would return to him when the flesh body died.

After all, we would need someone to look after us until we were grown; someone who wasn't too busy looking after every other living thing. Because Grandma Ocean had seen to Mom. Grandma's province is the waters of the world, salt and sweet both. She tossed Mom over her shoulder into one of them, and didn't even look back to see which one she'd landed in. She didn't deprive my mother of life, but of the beautiful form with which, Grandma convinced herself, Mom had bewitched her sons. Loch Ness has Nessie, its monster of fame and fable. Okanagan Lake has Naitaka, aka Ogopogo, a snake demon. As with them, no one has ever found proof that the monster that people began sighting in Lake Ontario just under thirty years ago really exists. She does have a name, though, and it's Cora. I call her Mom, or I would, if I ever met her.

And Uncle Jack? Or John, or whichever of his monikers he chose to use at any given time? Well, his family couldn't do anything incapacitating to him, as they had to Dad. If they did, it would bung up the claypicken wheel of life and death. No one would be able to get on or off, and pretty soon the Big Boss would come looking for the cause of the constipation, and though he (or she, or they, or it) might or might not be green, they say he's a big fella, bigger than all Creation, and you sure as hell wouldn't like him when he was angry.

So for his transgressions against the tabus of death and life, the Family punished my Uncle in the worst way they could think of; they left him unharmed. His curse was to carry the knowledge of the fate he had helped bring down on his dear brother and on my mother.

That's how the story went that Uncle used to tell me and Abby when we were kids and he was babysitting and had run out of other ways to keep us occupied. He made it sound almost jolly. At least romantic. Because Uncle likes to keep things lighthearted. It's important to him to always have a smile on his face. It keeps his spirits up, and sometimes it prevents people from being too scared when it's their time and he shows up to ferry them over to the other side. Though sometimes his death's-head grin just makes them shit their pants with terror. But, as Uncle says, you win some, you lose some.

# ABOUT THE DAMON KNIGHT MEMORIAL GRAND MASTER AWARD

In addition to giving the Nebula Awards each year, SFWA also may present the Damon Knight Grand Master Award to a living author for a lifetime of achievement in science fiction and/or fantasy. In accordance with SFWA's bylaws, the president shall have the power, at his or her discretion, to call for the presentation of the Grand Master Award. Nominations for the Damon Knight Memorial Grand Master Award are solicited from the officers, with the advice of participating past presidents, who vote with the officers to determine the recipient.

There have been thirty Grand Masters since the award was founded in 1975. Samuel R. Delany is the most recent.

| 1975 | Robert A. Heinlein (1907–1988) |
| 1976 | Jack Williamson (1908–2006) |
| 1977 | Clifford D. Simak (1904–1988) |
| 1979 | L. Sprague de Camp (1907–2000) |
| 1981 | Fritz Leiber (1910–1992) |
| 1984 | Andre Norton (1912–2005) |
| 1986 | Arthur C. Clarke (1917–2008) |
| 1987 | Isaac Asimov (1920–1992) |
| 1988 | Alfred Bester (1913–1987) |
| 1989 | Ray Bradbury (1920–2012) |
| 1991 | Lester del Rey (1915–1993) |
| 1993 | Frederik Pohl (1919–2013) |
| 1995 | Damon Knight (1922–2002) |
| 1996 | A. E. van Vogt (1912–2000) |
| 1997 | Jack Vance (1916–2013) |
| 1998 | Poul Anderson (1926–2001) |
| 1999 | Hal Clement (Harry Stubbs) (1922–2003) |

2000    Brian W. Aldiss (1925–)

2001    Philip José Farmer (1918–2009)

2003    Ursula K. Le Guin (1929–)

2004    Robert Silverberg (1935–)

2005    Anne McCaffrey (1926–2011)

2006    Harlan Ellison (1934–)

2007    James Gunn (1923–)

2008    Michael Moorcock (1939–)

2009    Harry Harrison (1925–2012)

2010    Joe Haldeman (1943–)

2011    Connie Willis (1945–)

2012    Gene Wolfe (1931–)

2013    Samuel R. Delany (1942–)

# "A LIFE CONSIDERED AS A PRISM OF EVER-PRECIOUS LIGHT: AN APPRECIATION OF SAMUEL R. DELANY"

## NALO HOPKINSON

I'm honoured and tickled to be writing an appreciation for Samuel (Chip) R. Delany, SFWA's 2013 Grand Master. I doubt I would be a published SF/F writer if it weren't for him. I doubt I'm alone in that. His writing excites me. It fills my brain with thoughts and mirrored neuron responses, and teaches me about writing. I was lucky enough to have him as a teacher when I attended Clarion in 1995, but I held his work in high esteem long before that.

So: what is there to appreciate about Chip and his works? (And by "works" I mean the whole package; writing, teaching, activism, and being:

I appreciate Chip's frankness and particularity about sex, sensuality, and sexuality, especially gay black male sexuality. Especially that it happens so often in science fictional contexts, still a rare occurrence in the genre. When I, a Caribbean black reader, was in my 20's—I'm 53 now—my literary world was comprised of science fiction/fantasy, Caribbean literature, erotica/porn, black literature, and everything else. I read bits of all of it, but primarily SF/F and probably porn, which meant that I read a lot of stories about white people having fantastical adventures. And that was fine at first, because I was fortunate enough to have other literatures and other experiences of the world around me. For many years, I didn't notice that the fiction I loved didn't seem to much love me back. (It's coming around.) When I read Chip's genre-busting novel *Dhalgren*, it was a revelation. It was full of the future, and the future was full of people of colour and jamette[1] people living lives and having raunchy sex right alongside the white folks. And the sex was hella queer. I was straight-identified at the time, and I'm middle class. Not that it mattered when it came to *Dhalgren*. It was as though science fiction and James Baldwin had made a love child, and it was that novel. *Dhalgren* brought three of my worlds into conjunction, and in doing so, made me more real. It put people like me on the page right smack dab in the centre of my beloved science fiction. It made me realize that truth is not always absolute. It made me consider whose truths get told, and why. It showed me what the novel is capable of, in ways I had vaguely apprehended before from other groundbreaking novels, but had never really lived in until *Dhalgren*. It made me long for more of that experience.

And Chip is still bringing it. In 2014, at the Nebula Awards weekend in San Jose, Chip gave a reading from his recent novel, *Through the Valley of the Nest of Spiders*. (I haven't finished reading my copy yet. The variety of ingested bodily fluids in the first few pages is giving me pause. Shouldn't have started reading it while I was eating breakfast! But I will persevere.) At Chip's reading, I was in the back, holding hands with my primary partner, David. One of us is female, the other male, but we're both black, both writers, both queer-identified. We're used to living at-risk lives in racialized bodies. That evening, we sat and snuggled in happy tears as Chip read about a community of black men, simultaneously utterly average and utterly unique, daring to live, love, and fuck each other. Surviving the life. One of the best fairy stories ever; the kind that sometimes manages to come true. And yes, the pun is deliberate.

As well as in queer male lives, Chip's pride in blackness is a healing balm against the myriad cuts of daily existence as a black person in a society that brays that you are stupid, ugly, criminal, a despoiler, a thug, a problem. There are many who do this work of necessary healing. Chip is one of them. I appreciate his insistence in putting blackness and working class sensibilities (not the same thing, yet there are places of overlap) on the page at a time when little of that was happening in SF/F. I have to also praise the editors who have had the stones to publish his work. The genre would be poorer had that not happened.

---

1. Trinidad creole: "underclass." From the French "le diamètre," meaning beneath the diametre of respectability.

I appreciate Chip's sense of humour and playfulness; for instance, the ending of *The Madman*, when you find out how the two men live their lives together. Rarely has something so stank made me giggle so much. The character of Raven in *Tales of Nevèrÿon* with her matter-of-fact, norm-flipping monologues on what menstruation is for, how to keep from getting pregnant, and why men have those floppy, delicate "scars of Eif'h" hanging between their thighs. I howled with laughter. Thanks to Raven, I also discovered places where gender norms had sunk their claws into me and began to yank them out.

I appreciate Chip's joy in life and his willingness to be silly. One Readercon, he spent hours with a bunch of other con-goers in a hot, stuffy room, playing Mafia. (For those who don't know it, Mafia is kind of like Murder in the Dark meets "Who Goes There?") I will never forget the sight of Chip, having just won the round by killing everyone, doing the Ex Tempore Evil Elf Dance of Villainy.

I appreciate the sheer, dense beauty of his language. Sometimes the density is in the deep investigation of the physicality of a moment, second by second, as it gets your own senses buzzing. Sometimes it's in the way he reframes your way of thinking about something so that you'll never see it quite the same way again. (See Raven and the scars of Eif'h.)

His creative daring. He's unafraid to insert a lecture on a non-fictional topic into the middle of a fictional narrative. To get intensely personal, as in his memoir *The Motion of Light On Water*. To write in forms considered déclassé, such as porn and comics. To take on the fictional persona of a female academic —K. Leslie Steiner—to rigorously critique his own work. Who *does* that?

His generosity. Chip uses complicated sentences in his writing, but in person, speaks in simpler language. He has a knack of assuming everyone is capable of complex analysis while simultaneously taking people as he finds them. Many years ago, I wrote a mostly inept review of his novel *The Madman*. I knew it was inadequate to the novel but at the time, I couldn't articulate why, or figure out how to fix it. When I mentioned my review to Chip at Clarion in 1995, replied that he'd read it and liked it because it was positive; a tactful acknowledgement that the value of my review was not its critical analysis but its enthusiasm, because he enjoyed hearing his work praised. The generosity wasn't just in his tact, but in his using it to tell the truth. I have often seen him tell someone a hard truth. I have never seen him be disrespectful about it.

Though I also appreciate that he has stopped telling Clarion students which of them will and won't be writers. It was something he was still doing at my Clarion in 1995. I don't remember what he told me, though. I suspect I deliberately blanked on it, because if he said "writer," I feared I'd be too overawed to try for it. And I'd made up my mind that if he said "non-writer," I'd just have to do my utmost to prove him wrong.

Chip does love his students. At the end of Fred Barney Taylor's documentary *The Polymath, or The Life and Opinions of Samuel R. Delany, Gentleman*, Chip tells a story about urging a group of his students to raise their hands in class even if to say they don't know the answer. Because every time they remain silent, he told them, they learn something. They learn not to speak for themselves, not to ask for a raise. They learn to keep quiet and "take it." Then he says to the interviewer, "Because you need to teach people . . ." and bursts into tears as he continues, "that they are important enough to say what they have to say."

I appreciate Chip's activism on a number of fronts. His essay on racism in science fiction community is a teaching tool for those who don't understand systemic racism, who think that racism is a white guy spewing hateful epithets, who believe that because they don't hate people of colour, they are incapable of perpetuating racism. With his skills of analysis and his frankness about his personal life, he was uniquely placed to write the non-fiction book *Times Square Red Times Square Blue*. In it, he decries New York City's closing down of the porn theatres in Times Square with the frank perspective of someone who's frequented them for sex. He describes the theatres as sexual spaces, precious because they facilitated a dissolving of class, race, sexuality, and gender barriers. I appreciate Chip's insistence that all aspects of life can be spoken and are deserving of contemplation.

And oh, my God, his writing. His beautiful, thick, raunchy, rambling, misbehaved, surprising, delightful, funky, thoughtful books, essays, and stories. They are the reason so many in the audience at the Nebula Awards hollered with joy at seeing Samuel R. Delany accept the SFWA Grand Master Award from Connie Willis.

To Chip,
With love,
your student.

## DAMON KNIGHT MEMORIAL
## GRAND MASTER: SAMUEL R. DELANY

# "TIME CONSIDERED AS A HELIX OF SEMI-PRECIOUS STONES"

Lay ordinate and abscissa on the century. Now cut me a quadrant. Third quadrant if you please. I was born in 'fifty. Here it's 'seventy-five.

At sixteen they let me leave the orphanage. Dragging the name they'd hung me with (Harold Clancy Everet, and me a mere lad—how many monickers have I had since; but don't worry, you'll recognize my smoke) over the hills of East Vermont, I came to a decision:

Me and Pa Michaels, who had belligerently given me a job at the request of *The Official* looking *Document* with which the orphanage sends you packing, were running Pa Michaels' dairy farm, i.e., thirteen thousand three hundred sixty-two piebald Guernseys all asleep in their stainless coffins, nourished and drugged by pink liquid flowing in clear plastic veins (stuff is sticky and messes up your hands), exercised with electric pulsers that make their muscles quiver, them not half-awake, and the milk just a-pouring down into stainless cisterns. Anyway. The Decision (as I stood there in the fields one afternoon like the Man with the Hoe, exhausted with three hard hours of physical labor, contemplating the machinery of the universe through the fog of fatigue): With all of Earth, and Mars, and the Outer Satellites filled up with people and what-all, there had to be something more than this. I decided to get some.

So I stole a couple of Pa's credit cards, one of his helicopters, and a bottle of white lightning the geezer made himself, and took off. Ever try to land a stolen helicopter on the roof of the Pan Am building, drunk? Jail, schmail, and some hard knocks later I had attained to wisdom. But remember this o best beloved: I have done three honest hours on a dairy farm less than ten years back. And nobody but nobody has ever called me Harold Clancy Everet again.

Hank Culafroy Eckles (redheaded, a bit vague, six-foot-two) strolled out of the baggage room at the spaceport, carrying a lot of things that weren't his in a small briefcase.

Beside him the Business Man was saying, "You young fellows today upset me. Go back to Bellona, I say. Just because you got into trouble with that little blonde you were telling me about is no reason to leap worlds, come on all glum. Even quit your job!"

Hank stops and grins weakly: "Well . . ."

"Now I admit, you have your real needs, which maybe we older folks don't understand, but you have to show some responsibility toward . . ." He notices Hank has stopped in front of a door marked MEN. "Oh. Well. Eh." He grins strongly. "I've enjoyed meeting you, Hank. It's always nice when you meet somebody worth talking to on these damned crossings. So long."

Out same door, ten minutes later, comes Harmony C. Eventide, six-foot even (one of the false heels was cracked, so I stuck both of them under a lot of paper towels), brown hair (not even my hair dresser knows for sure), oh so dapper and of his time, attired in the bad taste that is oh so tasteful, a sort of man with whom no Business Men would start a conversation. Took the regulation 'copter from the port over to the Pan Am building (Yeah. Really. Drunk.), came out of Grand Central Station, and strode along Forty-Second toward Eighth Avenue, with a lot of things that weren't mine in a small briefcase.

The evening is carved from light.

Crossed the plastiplex pavements of the Great White Way—I think it makes people look weird, all that white light under their chins—and skirted the crowds coming up in elevators from the subway, the sub-subway, and the sub-sub-sub (eighteen and first week out of jail, I hung around here, snatching stuff from people—but daintily, daintily, so they never knew they'd been snatched), bulled my way through a crowd of giggling, goo-chewing school-girls with flashing lights in their hair, all very embarrassed at wearing transparent plastic blouses which had just been made legal again (I hear the breast has been scene [as opposed to obscene] on and off since the seventeenth century) so I stared appreciatively; they giggled some more. I thought, Christ, when I was that age, I was on a goddamn dairy farm, and took the thought no further.

The ribbon of news lights looping the triangular structure of Communication, Inc., explained in Basic English how Senator Regina Abolafia was preparing to begin her investigation of Organized Crime in the City. Days I'm so happy I'm disorganized I couldn't begin to tell.

Near Ninth Avenue I took my briefcase into a long, crowded bar. I hadn't been in New York for two years, but on my last trip through ofttimes a man used to hang out here who had real talent for getting rid of things that weren't mine profitably, safely, fast. No idea what the chances were I'd find him. I pushed among a lot of guys drinking beer. Here and there were a number of well-escorted old bags wearing last month's latest. Scarfs of smoke gentled through the noise. I don't like such places. Those there younger than me were all morphadine heads or feebleminded. Those older only wished more younger ones would come. I pried my way to the bar and tried to get the attention of one of the little men in white coats.

The lack of noise behind me made me glance back.

She wore a sheath of veiling closed at the neck and wrists with huge brass pins (oh so tastefully on the border of taste); her left arm was bare, her right covered with chiffon like wine. She had it down a lot better than I did. But such an ostentatious demonstration of one's understanding of the finer points was absolutely out of place in a place like this. People were making a great show of not noticing. She pointed to her wrist, blood-colored nail indexing a yellow-orange fragment in the brass claw of her wristlet. "Do you know what this is, Mr. Eldrich?" she asked; at the same time the veil across her face cleared, and her eyes were ice; her brows, black.

Three thoughts: (One) She is a lady of fashion, because coming in from Bellona I'd read the Delta coverage of the "fading fabrics" whose hue and opacity were controlled by cunning jewels at the wrist. (Two) During my last trip through, when I was younger and Harry Calamine Eldrich, I didn't do anything *too* illegal (though one loses track of these things); still I didn't believe I could be dragged off to the calaboose for anything more than thirty days under that name. (Three) The stone she pointed to . . .

". . . Jasper?" I asked.

She waited for me to say more; I waited for her to give me reason to let on I knew what she was waiting for. (When I was in jail, Henry James was my favorite author. He really was.)

"Jasper," she confirmed.

"—Jasper . . ." I reopened the ambiguity she had tried so hard to dispel.

". . . Jasper—" But she was already faltering, suspecting I suspected her certainty to be ill-founded.

"Okay, Jasper." But from her face I knew she had seen in my face a look that had finally revealed I knew she knew I knew.

"Just whom have you got me confused with, ma'am?" Jasper, this month, is the Word.

Jasper is the pass/code/warning that the Singers of the Cities (who last month sang "Opal" from their divine injuries; and on Mars I'd heard the Word and used it thrice, along with devious imitations, to fix possession of what was not rightfully my own; and even there I pondered Singers and their wounds) relay by word of mouth for that loose and roguish fraternity with which I have been involved (in various guises) these nine years. It goes out new every thirty days; and within hours every brother knows it, throughout six worlds and worldlets. Usually it's grunted at you by some blood-soaked bastard staggering into your arms from a dark doorway; hissed at you as you pass a shadowed alley; scrawled on a paper scrap pressed into your palm by some nasty-grimy moving too fast through the crowd. And this month, it was: Jasper.

Here are some alternate translations:

Help!

or

I need help!

or

I can help you!

or

You are being watched!

or

They're not watching now, so *move*!

Final point of syntax: If the Word is used properly, you should never have to think twice about what it means in a given situation. Fine point of usage: Never trust anyone who uses it improperly.

I waited for her to finish waiting.

She opened a wallet in front of me. "Chief of Special Services Department

Maudline Hinkle," she read without looking at what it said below the silver badge.

"You have that very well," I said, "Maud." Then I frowned. "Hinkle?"

"Me."

"I know you're not going to believe this, Maud. You look like a woman who has no patience with her mistakes. But my name is Eventide. Not Eldrich. Harmony C. Eventide. And isn't it lucky for all and sundry that the Word changes tonight?" Passed the way it is, the Word is no big secret to the cops. But I've met policemen up to a week after change date who were not privy.

"Well, then: Harmony. I want to talk to you." I raised an eyebrow.

She raised one back and said, "Look, if you want to be called Henrietta, it's all right by me. But you listen."

"What do you want to talk about?"

"Crime, Mr. . . . ?"

"Eventide. I'm going to call you Maud, so you might as well call me Harmony. It really *is* my name."

Maud smiled. She wasn't a young woman. I think she even had a few years on Business Man. But she used makeup better than he did. "I probably know more about crime than you do," she said. "In fact I wouldn't be surprised if you hadn't even heard of my branch of the police department. What does Special Services mean to you?"

"That's right, I've never heard of it."

"You've been more or less avoiding the Regular Service with alacrity for the past seven years."

"Oh, Maud, really—"

"Special Services is reserved for people whose nuisance value has suddenly taken a sharp rise . . . a sharp enough rise to make our little lights start blinking."

"Surely I haven't done anything so dreadful that—"

"We don't look at what you do. A computer does that for us. We simply keep checking the first derivative of the graphed-out curve that bears your number. Your slope is rising sharply."

"Not even the dignity of a name—"

"We're the most efficient department in the Police Organization. Take it as bragging if you wish. Or just a piece of information."

"Well, well, well," I said. "Have a drink?" The little man in the white coat left us two, looked puzzled at Maud's finery, then went to do something else.

"Thanks." She downed half her glass like someone stauncher than that wrist would indicate. "It doesn't pay to go after most criminals. Take your big-time racketeers, Farnesworth, the Hawk, Blavatskia. Take your little snatch-purses, small-time pushers, housebreakers, or vice-impresarios. Both at the top and the bottom of the scale, their incomes are pretty stable. They don't really upset the social boat. Regular Services handles them both. They think they do a good job. We're not going to argue. But say a little pusher starts to become a big-time pusher; a medium-sized vice-impresario sets his sights on becoming a full-fledged racketeer; that's when you get problems with socially unpleasant repercussions. That's when Special Services arrive. We have a couple of techniques that work remarkably well."

"You're going to tell me about them, aren't you?"

"They work better that way," she said. "One of them is hologramic information storage. Do you know what happens when you cut a hologram plate in half?"

"The three-dimensional image is . . . cut in half?"

She shook her head. "You get the whole image, only fuzzier, slightly out of focus."

"Now I didn't know that."

"And if you cut it in half again, it just gets fuzzier still. But even if you have a square centimeter of the original hologram, you still have the whole image—unrecognizable but complete."

I mumbled some appreciative *m*'s.

"Each pinpoint of photographic emulsion on a hologram plate, unlike a photograph, gives information about the entire scene being hologrammed. By analogy, hologramic information storage simply means that each bit of information we have—about you, let us say—relates to your entire career, your overall situation, the complete set of tensions between you and your environment. Specific facts about specific misdemeanors or felonies we leave to Regular Services. As soon as we have enough of our kind of data, our method is vastly more efficient for keeping track—even predicting—where you are or what you may be up to."

"Fascinating," I said. "One of the most amazing paranoid syndromes I've ever run up against. I mean just starting a conversation with someone in a bar. Often, in a hospital situation, I've encountered stranger—"

"In your past," she said matter-of-factly, "I see cows and helicopters. In your not too distant future, there are helicopters and hawks."

"And tell me, oh Good Witch of the West, just how—" Then I got all upset inside. Because nobody is supposed to know about that stint with Pa Michaels save thee and me. Even the Regular Service, who pulled me, out of my head, from that whirlybird bouncing toward the edge of the Pan Am, never got that one from me. I'd eaten the credit cards when I saw them waiting, and the serial numbers had been filed off everything that could have had a serial number on it by someone more competent than I: good Mister Michaels had boasted to me, my first lonely, drunken night at the farm, how he'd gotten the thing in hot from New Hampshire.

"But why—" it appalls me the clichés to which anxiety will drive us—"are you telling me all this?"

She smiled, and her smile faded behind her veil. "Information is only meaningful when shared," said a voice that was hers from the place of her face.

"Hey, look, I—"

"You may be coming into quite a bit of money soon. If I can calculate right, I will have a helicopter full of the city's finest arriving to take you away as you accept it into your hot little hands. That is a piece of information . . ." She stepped back. Someone stepped between us.

"Hey, Maud—"

"You can do whatever you want with it."

The bar was crowded enough so that to move quickly was to make enemies. I don't know—I lost her and made enemies. Some weird characters there: with greasy hair that hung in spikes, and three of them had dragons tattooed on their scrawny shoulders, still another with an eye patch, and yet another raked nails black with pitch at my cheek (we're two minutes into a vicious free-for-all, case you missed the transition. I did) and some of the women were screaming. I hit and ducked, and then the tenor of the brouhaha changed. Somebody sang "Jasper!" the way she is supposed to be sung. And it meant the heat (the ordinary, bungling Regular Service I had been eluding these seven years) were on their way. The brawl spilled into the street. I got between two nasty-grimies who were doing things appropriate with one another, but made the edge of the crowd with no more wounds than could be racked up to shaving. The fight had broken into sections. I left one and ran into another that, I realized a moment later, was merely a ring of people standing around somebody who had apparently gotten really messed.

Someone was holding people back.

Somebody else was turning him over.

Curled up in a puddle of blood was the little guy I hadn't seen in two years who used to be so good at getting rid of things not mine.

Trying not to hit people with my briefcase, I ducked between the hub and the bub. When I saw my first ordinary policeman, I tried very hard to look like somebody who had just stepped up to see what the rumpus was.

It worked.

I turned down Ninth Avenue and got three steps into an inconspicuous but rapid lope—

"Hey, wait! Wait up there . . ."

I recognized the voice (after two years, coming at me just like that, I recognized it) but kept going.

"Wait. It's me, Hawk!" And I stopped.

You haven't heard his name before in this story; Maud mentioned *the* Hawk, who is a multimillionaire racketeer basing his operations on a part of Mars I've never been to (though he has his claws sunk to the spurs in illegalities throughout the system) and somebody else entirely.

I took three steps back toward the doorway.

A boy's laugh there: "Oh, man. You look like you just did something you shouldn't."

"Hawk?" I asked the shadow.

He was still the age when two years' absence means an inch or so taller.

"You're still hanging around here?" I asked.

"Sometimes."

He was an amazing kid.

"Look, Hawk, I got to get out of here." I glanced back at the rumpus.

"Get." He stepped down. "Can I come, too?"

Funny. "Yeah." It makes me feel very funny, him asking that. "Come on."

By the streetlamp half a block down, I saw his hair was still pale as split pine. He could have been a nasty-grimy: very dirty black denim jacket, no shirt beneath; very ripe pair of black jeans—I mean in the dark you could tell. He went barefoot; and the only way you can tell on a dark street someone's been going barefoot for days in New York is to know already. As we reached the corner, he grinned up at me under the streetlamp and shrugged his jacket together over the welts and furrows marring his chest and belly. His eyes were very green. Do you recognize him? If by some failure of information dispersal throughout the worlds and worldlets you haven't, walking beside me beside the Hudson was Hawk the Singer.

"Hey, how long have you been back?"

"A few hours," I told him.

"What'd you bring?"

"Really want to know?"

He shoved his hands into his pockets and cocked his head. "Sure."

I made the sound of an adult exasperated by a child. "All right."

We had been walking the waterfront for a block now; there was nobody about. "Sit down." So he straddled the beam along the siding, one filthy foot dangling above the flashing black Hudson. I sat in front of him and ran my thumb around the edge of the briefcase.

Hawk hunched his shoulders and leaned. "Hey . . ." He flashed green questioning at me. "Can I touch?"

I shrugged. "Go ahead."

He grubbed among them with fingers that were all knuckle and bitten nail. He picked two up, put them down, picked up three others. "Hey!" he whispered. "How much are all these worth?"

"About ten times more than I hope to get. I have to get rid of them fast."

He glanced down past his toes. "You could always throw them in the river."

"Don't be dense. I was looking for a guy who used to hang around that bar. He was pretty efficient." And half the Hudson away a water-bound foil skimmed above the foam. On her deck were parked a dozen helicopters—being ferried up to the Patrol Field near Verrazzano, no doubt. For moments I looked back and forth between the boy and the transport, getting all paranoid about Maud. But the boat *mmmmed* into the darkness. "My man got a little cut up this evening."

Hawk put the tips of his fingers in his pockets and shifted his position.

"Which leaves me uptight. I didn't think he'd take them all, but at least he could have turned me on to some other people who might."

"I'm going to a party later on this evening-" he paused to gnaw on the wreck of his little fingernail—"where you might be able to sell them. Alexis Spinnel is having a party for Regina Abolafia at Tower Top."

"Tower Top . . . ?" It had been a while since I palled around with Hawk. Hell's Kitchen at ten; Tower Top at midnight

"I'm just going because Edna Silem will be there." Edna Silem is New York's eldest Singer.

Senator Abolafia's name had ribboned above me in lights once that evening. And somewhere among the endless magazines I'd perused coming in from Mars, I remembered Alexis Spinnel's name sharing a paragraph with an awful lot of money.

"I'd like to see Edna again," I said offhandedly. "But she wouldn't remember me." Folk like Spinnel and his social ilk have a little game, I'd discovered during the first leg of my acquaintance with Hawk. He who can get the most Singers of the City under one roof wins. There are five Singers of New York (a tie for second place with Lux on Iapetus). Tokyo leads with seven. "It's a two-Singer party?"

"More likely four . . . if I go."

The inaugural ball for the mayor gets four. I raised the appropriate eyebrow.

"I have to pick up the Word from Edna. It changes tonight."

"All right," I said. "I don't know what you have in mind, but I'm game." I closed the case.

We walked back toward Times Square. When we got to Eighth Avenue and the first of the plastiplex, Hawk stopped. "Wait a minute," he said. Then he buttoned his jacket up to his neck. "Okay."

Strolling through the streets of New York with a Singer (two years back I'd spent much time wondering if that was wise for a man of my profession) is probably the best camouflage possible for a man of my profession. Think of the last time you glimpsed your favorite Tri-D star turning the corner of Fifty-seventh. Now be honest. Would you really recognize the little guy in the tweed jacket half a pace behind him?

Half the people we passed in Times Square recognized him. With his youth, funereal garb, black feet and ash-pale hair, he was easily the most colorful of Singers. Smiles; narrowed eyes; very few actually pointed or stared.

"Just exactly who is going to be there who might be able to take this stuff off my hands?"

"Well, Alexis prides himself on being something of an adventurer. They might just take his fancy. And he can give you more than you can get peddling them in the street."

"You'll tell him they're all hot?"

"It will probably make the idea that much more intriguing. He's a creep."

"You say so, friend."

We went down into the sub-sub. The man at the change booth started to take Hawk's coin, then looked up. He began three or four words that were unintelligible inside his grin, then just gestured us through.

"Oh," Hawk said, "thank you," with ingenuous surprise, as though this were the first, delightful time such a thing had happened. (Two years ago he had told me sagely, "As soon as I start looking like I expect it, it'll stop happening." I was still impressed by the way he wore his notoriety. The time I'd met Edna Silem, and I'd mentioned this, she said with the same ingenuousness, "But that's what we're chosen for.")

In the bright car we sat on the long seat. Hawk's hands were beside him; one foot rested on the other. Down from us a gaggle of bright-bloused goochewers giggled and pointed and tried not to be noticed at it. Hawk didn't look at all, and I tried not to be noticed looking.

Dark patterns rushed the window.

Things below the gray floor hummed.

Once a lurch.

Leaning once, we came out of the ground.

Outside, the city tried on its thousand sequins, then threw them away behind the trees of Ft. Tryon. Suddenly the windows across from us grew bright scales. Behind them girders reeled by. We got out on the platform under a light rain. The sign said TWELVE TOWERS STATION.

By the time we reached the street, however, the shower had stopped. Leaves above the wall shed water down the brick. "If I'd known I was bringing someone, I'd have had Alex send a car for us. I told him it was fifty-fifty I'd come."

"Are you sure it's all right for me to tag along then?"

"Didn't you come up here with me once before?"

"I've even been up here once before that," I said. "Do you still think it's . . ."

He gave me a withering look. Well; Spinnel would be delighted to have Hawk even if he dragged along a whole gang of real nastygrimies—Singers are famous for that sort of thing. With one more or less presentable thief, Spinnel was getting off light. Beside us rocks broke away into the city. Behind the gate to our left the gardens rolled up toward the first of the towers. The twelve immense luxury apartment buildings menaced the lower clouds.

"Hawk the Singer," Hawk the Singer said into the speaker at the side of the gate. *Clang* and tic-tic-tic and *Clang*. We walked up to the path to the doors and doors of glass.

A cluster of men and women in evening dress were coming out. Three tiers of doors away they saw us. You could see them frowning at the guttersnipe who'd somehow gotten into the lobby (for a moment I thought one of them was Maud because she wore a sheath of the fading fabric, but she turned; beneath her veil her face was dark as roasted coffee); one of the men recognized him, said something to the others. When they passed us, they were smiling. Hawk paid about as much attention to them as he had to the girls on the subway. But when they'd passed, he said, "One of those guys was looking at you."

"Yeah. I saw."

"Do you know why?"

"He was trying to figure out whether we'd met before."

"Had you?"

I nodded. "Right about where I met you, only back when I'd just gotten out of jail. I told you I'd been here once before."

"Oh."

Blue carpet covered three-quarters of the lobby. A great pool filled the rest in which a row of twelve-foot trellises stood, crowned with flaming braziers. The lobby itself was three stories high, domed and mirror-tiled.

Twisting smoke curled toward the ornate grill. Broken reflections sagged and recovered on the walls.

The elevator door folded about us its foil petals. There was the distinct feeling of not moving while seventy-five stories shucked down around us.

We got out on the landscaped roof garden. A very tanned, very blond man wearing an apricot jumpsuit, from the collar of which emerged a black turtle-neck dicky, came down the rocks (artificial) between the ferns (real) growing along the stream (real water; phony current).

"Hello! Hello!" Pause. "I'm terribly glad you decided to come after all." Pause. "For a while I thought you weren't going to make it." The Pauses were to allow Hawk to introduce me. I was dressed so that Spinnel had no way of telling whether I was a miscellaneous Nobel laureate that Hawk happened to have been dining with, or a varlet whose manners and morals were even lower than mine happen to be.

"Shall I take your jacket?" Alexis offered.

Which meant he didn't know Hawk as well as he would like people to think. But I guess he was sensitive enough to realize from the little cold things that happened in the boy's face that he should forget his offer.

He nodded to me, smiling—about all he could do—and we strolled toward the gathering.

Edna Silem was sitting on a transparent inflated hassock. She leaned forward, holding her drink in both hands, arguing politics with the people sitting on the grass before her. She was the first person I recognized (hair of tarnished silver; voice of scrap brass). Jutting from the cuffs of her mannish suit, her wrinkled hands about her goblet, shaking with the intensity of the pronouncements, were heavy with stones and silver. As I ran my eyes back to Hawk, I saw half a dozen whose names/faces sold magazines, music, sent people to the theater (the drama critic for *Delta*, wouldn't you know), and even the mathematician from Princeton I'd read about a few months ago who'd come up with the "quasar/quark" explanation. There was one woman my eyes kept returning to. On glance three I recognized her as the New Fascistas' most promising candidate for president, Senator Abolafia. Her arms were folded, and she was listening intently to the discussion that had narrowed to Edna and an overly gregarious younger man whose eyes were puffy from what could have been the recent acquisition of contact lenses.

"But don't you feel, Mrs. Silem, that—"

"You must remember when you make predictions like that—"

"Mrs. Silem, I've seen statistics that—"

"You *must* remember—" her voice tensed, lowered till the silence between the words was as rich as the voice was sparse and metallic—"that if everything, *everything* were known, statistical estimates would be unnecessary. The science of probability gives mathematical expression to our ignorance, not to our wisdom," which I was thinking was an interesting second installment to Maud's lecture, when Edna looked up and exclaimed, "Why, Hawk!"

Everyone turned.

"I *am* glad to see you. Lewis, Ann," she called: there were two other Singers there already (he dark, she pale, both tree-slender; their faces made you think of pools without drain or tribute come upon in the forest, clear and very still; husband and wife, they had been made Singers together the day before their marriage six years ago), "he hasn't deserted us after all!" Edna stood, extended her arm over the heads of the people sitting, and barked across her knuckles as though her voice were a pool cue. "Hawk, there are people here arguing with me who don't know nearly as much as you about the subject. You'd be on my side, now wouldn't you—"

"Mrs. Silem, I didn't mean to—" from the floor.

Then her arms swung six degrees, her fingers, eyes, and mouth opened. "You!" Me. "My dear, if there's anyone I never expected to see here! Why it's been almost two years, hasn't it?" Bless Edna; the place where she and Hawk and I had spent a long, beery evening together had more resembled that bar than Tower Top. "Where have you been keeping yourself?"

"Mars, mostly," I admitted. "Actually I just came back today." It's so much fun to be able to say things like that in a place like this.

"Hawk—both of you—" (which meant either she had forgotten my name, or she remembered me well enough not to abuse it—) "come over here and help me drink up Alexis' good liquor." I tried not to grin as we walked toward her. If she remembered anything, she certainly recalled my line of business and must have been enjoying this as much as I was.

Relief spread Alexis' face: he knew now I was *someone* if not *which* someone I was.

As we passed Lewis and Ann, Hawk gave the two Singers one of his luminous grins. They returned shadowed smiles. Lewis nodded. Ann made a move to touch his arm, but left the motion unconcluded; and the company noted the interchange.

Having found out what we wanted, Alex was preparing large glasses of it over crushed ice when the puffy-eyed gentleman stepped up for a refill. "But, Mrs. Silem, then what do you feel validly opposes such political abuses?"

Regina Abolafia wore a white silk suit. Nails, lips, and hair were one copper color; and on her breast was a worked copper pin. It's always fascinated me to watch people used to being the center thrust to the side. She swirled her glass, listening.

"I oppose them," Edna said. "Hawk opposes them. Lewis and Ann oppose them. We, ultimately, are what you have." And her voice had taken on that authoritative resonance only Singers can assume.

Then Hawk's laugh snarled through the conversational fabric.

We turned.

He'd sat cross-legged near the hedge. "Look . . ." he whispered. Now people's gazes followed his. He was looking at Lewis and Ann. She, tall and blond, he, dark and taller, were standing very quietly, a little nervously, eyes closed (Lewis' lips were apart).

"Oh," whispered someone who should have known better, "they're going to . . ."

I watched Hawk because I'd never had a chance to observe one Singer at another's performance. He put the soles of his feet together, grasped his toes, and leaned forward, veins making blue rivers on his neck. The top button of his jacket had come loose. Two scar ends showed over his collar bone. Maybe nobody noticed but me. I saw Edna put her glass down with a look of beaming anticipatory pride. Alex, who had pressed the autobar (odd how automation has become the upper crust's way of flaunting the labor surplus) for more crushed ice, looked up, saw what was about to happen, and pushed the cutoff button. The autobar hummed to silence. A breeze (artificial or real, I couldn't tell you) came by, and the trees gave us a final *shush*.

One at a time, then in duet, then singly again, Lewis and Ann sang.

Singers are people who look at things, then go and tell people what they've seen. What makes them Singers is their ability to make people listen. That is the most magnificent oversimplification I can give. Eighty-six-year-old El Posado in Rio de Janeiro saw a block of tenements collapse, ran to the Avenida del Sol and began improvising, in rhyme and meter (not all that hard in rhyme-rich Portuguese), tears runneling his dusty cheeks, his voice clashing with the palm swards above the sunny street. Hundreds of people stopped to listen; a hundred more; and another hundred. And they told hundreds more what they had heard. Three hours later, hundreds from among them had arrived at the scene with blankets, food, money, shovels, and more incredibly, the willingness and ability to organize themselves and work within that organization. No Tri-D report of a disaster has ever produced that sort of reaction. El Posado is historically considered the first Singer. The second was Miriamne in the roofed city of Lux, who for thirty years walked through the metal streets, singing the glories of the rings of Saturn—the colonists can't look at them without aid because of the ultraviolet the rings set up. But Miriamne, with her strange cataracts, each dawn walked to the edge of the city, looked, saw, and came back to sing of what she saw. All of which would have meant nothing except that during the days she did not sing—through illness, or once she was on a visit to another city to which her fame had spread—the Lux Stock Exchange would go down, the number of violent crimes rise. Nobody could explain it. All they could do was proclaim her Singer. Why did the institution of Singers come about, springing up in just about every urban center throughout the system? Some have speculated that it was a spontaneous reaction to the mass media which blanket our lives. While Tri-D and radio and newstapes disperse information all over the worlds, they also spread a sense of alienation from first-hand experience. (How many people still go to sports events or a political rally with their little receivers plugged into their ears to let them know that what they see is really happening?) The first Singers were proclaimed by the people around them. Then, there was a period where anyone could proclaim himself a Singer who wanted to, and people either responded to him or laughed him into oblivion. But by the time I was left on the doorstep of somebody who didn't want me, most cities had more or less established an unofficial quota. When a position is left open today, the remaining Singers choose who is going to fill it. The required talents are poetic, theatrical, as well as a certain charisma that is generated in the tensions between the personality and the publicity web a Singer is immediately snared in. Before he became a Singer, Hawk had gained something of a prodigious reputation with a book of poems published when he was fifteen. He was touring universities and giving readings, but the reputation was still small enough so that he was amazed that I had ever heard of him, that evening we encountered in Central Park. (I had just spent a pleasant thirty days as a guest of the city, and it's amazing what you find in the Tombs Library.) It was a few weeks after his sixteenth birthday. His Singership was to be announced in four days, though he had been informed already. We sat by the lake till dawn while he weighed and pondered and agonized over the coming responsibility. Two years later, he's still the youngest Singer in six worlds by half a dozen years. Before becoming a Singer, a person need not have been a poet, but most are either that or actors. But the roster through the system includes a longshoreman, two university professors, an heiress to the Silitax millions (Tack it down with Silitax), and at least two persons of such dubious background that the ever-hungry-for-sensation Publicity Machine itself has agreed not to let any of it past the copy editors. But wherever their origins, these diverse and flamboyant living myths sang of love, of death, of the changing of seasons, social classes, governments, and the palace guard. They sang before large crowds, small crowds, to an individual laborer coming home from the city's docks, on slum street corners, in club cars of commuter trains, in the elegant gardens atop Twelve Towers, to Alex Spinnel's select soiree. But it has been illegal to reproduce the "Songs" of the Singers by mechanical means (including publishing the lyrics) since the institution arose, and I respect the law, I do, as only a man in my profession can. I offer the explanation then in place of Lewis' and Ann's song.

They finished, opened their eyes, stared about with expressions that could have been embarrassment, could have been contempt.

Hawk was leaning forward with a look of rapt approval. Edna was smiling politely. I had the sort of grin on my face that breaks out when you've been vastly moved and vastly pleased. Lewis and Ann had sung superbly.

Alex began to breathe again, glancing around to see what state everybody else was in, saw, and pressed the autobar, which began to hum and crush ice. No clapping, but the appreciative sounds began; people were nodding, commenting, whispering. Regina Abolafia went over to Lewis to say something. I tried to listen until Alex shoved a glass into my elbow.

"Oh, I'm sorry . . ."

I transferred my briefcase to the other hand and took the drink, smiling. When Senator Abolafia left the two Singers, they were holding hands and looking at one another a little sheepishly. They sat down again.

The party drifted in conversational groups through the gardens, through the groves. Overhead clouds the color of old chamois folded and unfolded across the moon.

For a while I stood alone in a circle of trees, listening to the music: a de Lassus two-part canon programmed for audio-generators. Recalled: an article in one of last week's large-circulation literaries, stating that it was the only way to remove the feel of the bar lines imposed by five centuries of meter on modern musicians. For another two weeks this would be acceptable entertainment. The trees circled a rock pool; but no water. Below the plastic surface, abstract lights wove and threaded in a shifting lumia.

"Excuse me . . . ?"

I turned to see Alexis, who had no drink now or idea what to do with his hands. He *was* nervous.

". . . but our young friend has told me you have something I might be interested in."

I started to lift my briefcase, but Alexis' hand came down from his ear (it had gone by belt to hair to collar already) to halt me. Nouveau riche.

"That's all right. I don't need to see them yet. In fact, I'd rather not. I have something to propose to you. I would certainly be interested in what you have if they are, indeed, as Hawk has described them. But I have a guest here who would be even more curious."

That sounded odd.

"I know that sounds odd," Alexis assessed, "but I thought you might be interested simply because of the finances involved. I am an eccentric collector who would offer you a price concomitant with what I would use them for: eccentric conversation pieces—and because of the nature of the purchase I would have to limit severely the people with whom I could converse."

I nodded.

"My guest, however, would have a great deal more use for them."

"Could you tell me who this guest is?"

"I asked Hawk, finally, who you were, and he led me to believe I was on the verge of a grave social indiscretion. It would be equally indiscreet to reveal my guest's name to you." He smiled. "But indiscretion is the better part of the fuel that keeps the social machine turning. Mr. Harvey Cadwaliter-Erickson . . ." He smiled knowingly. I have *never* been Harvey Cadwaliter-Erickson, but Hawk was always an inventive child. Then a second thought went by, viz., the tungsten magnates, the Cadwaliter-Ericksons of Tythis on Triton. Hawk was not only inventive, he was as brilliant as all the magazines and newspapers are always saying he is.

"I assume your second indiscretion will be to tell me who this mysterious guest is?"

"Well," Alex said with the smile of the canary-fattened cat, "Hawk agreed with me that *the* Hawk might well be curious as to what you have in there," (he pointed) "as indeed he is."

I frowned. Then I thought lots of small, rapid thoughts I'll articulate in due time. "*The* Hawk?"

Alex nodded.

I don't think I was actually scowling. "Would you send our young friend up here for a moment?"

"If you'd like." Alex bowed, turned. Perhaps a minute later, Hawk came up over the rocks and through the trees, grinning. When I didn't grin back, he stopped.

"*Mmmm* . . ." I began.

His head cocked.

I scratched my chin with a knuckle. ". . . Hawk," I said, "are you aware of a department of the police called Special Services?"

"I've heard of them."

"They've suddenly gotten very interested in me."

"Gee," he said with honest amazement. "They're supposed to be pretty effective."

"*Mmmm*," I reiterated.

"Say," Hawk announced, "how do you like that? My namesake is here tonight. Wouldn't you know."

"Alex doesn't miss a trick. Have you any idea *why* he's here?"

"Probably trying to make some deal with Abolafia. Her investigation starts tomorrow."

"Oh." I thought over some of those things I had thought before. "Do you know a Maud Hinkle?"

Hawk's puzzled look said "no" pretty convincingly.

"She bills herself as one of the upper echelon in the arcane organization of which I spoke."

"Yeah?"

"She ended our interview earlier this evening with a little homily about hawks and helicopters. I took our subsequent encounter as a fillip of coincidence. But now I discover that the evening has confirmed her intimations of plurality." I shook my head. "Hawk, I am suddenly catapulted into a paranoid world where the walls not only have ears, but probably eyes and long, claw-tipped fingers. Anyone about me—yea, even very you—could turn out to be a spy. I suspect every sewer grating and second-story window conceals binoculars, a tommy gun, or worse. What I just can't figure out is how these insidious forces, ubiquitous and omnipresent though they be, induced you to lure me into this intricate and diabolical—"

"Oh, cut it out!" He shook back his hair. "I didn't lure—"

"Perhaps not consciously, but Special Services has Hologramic Information Storage, and their methods are insidious and cruel—"

"I said cut it out!" And all sorts of hard little things happened again. "Do you think I'd—" Then he realized how scared I was, I guess. "Look, the Hawk isn't some small-time snatch-purse. He lives in just as paranoid a world as you're in now, only all the time. If he's here, you can be sure there are just as many of his men—eyes and ears and fingers—as there are of Maud Hickenlooper's."

"Hinkle."

"Anyway, it works both ways. No Singer's going to—Look, do you really think I would—"

And even though I knew all those hard little things were scabs over pain, I said, "Yes."

"You did something for me once, and I—"

"I gave you some more welts. That's all."

All the scabs pulled off.

"Hawk," I said. "Let me see."

He took a breath. Then he began to open the brass buttons. The flaps of his jacket fell back. The lumia colored his chest with pastel shiftings.

I felt my face wrinkle. I didn't want to look away. I drew a hissing breath instead, which was just as bad.

He looked up. "There're a lot more than when you were here last, aren't there?"

"You're going to kill yourself, Hawk."

He shrugged.

"I can't even tell which are the ones I put there anymore."

He started to point them out.

"Oh, come on," I said too sharply. And for the length of three breaths, he grew more and more uncomfortable till I saw him start to reach for the bottom button. "Boy," I said, trying to keep despair out of my voice, "why do you do it?" and ended up keeping out everything. There is nothing more despairing than a voice empty.

He shrugged, saw I didn't want that, and for a moment anger flickered in his green eyes. I didn't want that either. So he said: "Look . . . you touch a person softly, gently, and maybe you even do it with love. And, well, I guess a piece of information goes on up to the brain where something interprets it as pleasure. Maybe something up there in my head interprets the information in a way you would say is all wrong . . ."

I shook my head. "You're a Singer. Singers are supposed to be eccentric, sure; but—"

Now he was shaking his head. Then the anger opened up. And I saw an expression move from all those spots that had communicated pain through the rest of his features and vanish without ever becoming a word. Once more he looked down at the wounds that webbed his thin body.

"Button it up, boy. I'm sorry I said anything."

Halfway up the lapels, his hands stopped. "You really think I'd turn you in?"

"Button it up."

He did. Then he said, "Oh." And then, "You know, it's midnight."

"So?"

"Edna just gave me the new Word."

"Which is?"

"Agate." I nodded.

Hawk finished closing his collar. "What are you thinking about?"

"Cows."

"Cows?" Hawk asked. "What about them?"

"You ever been on a dairy farm?"

He shook his head.

"To get the most milk, you keep the cows practically in suspended animation. They're fed intravenously from a big tank that pipes nutrients out and down, branching into smaller and smaller pipes until it gets to all those high-yield semi-corpses."

"I've seen pictures."

"People."

". . . and cows?"

"You've given me the Word. And now it begins to funnel down, branching out, with me telling others and them telling still others, till by midnight tomorrow . . ."

"I'll go get the—"

"Hawk?"

He turned back. "What?"

"You say you don't think I'm going to be the victim of any hanky-panky with the mysterious forces that know more than we. Okay, that's your opinion. But as soon as I get rid of this stuff, I'm going to make the most distracting exit you've ever seen."

Two little lines bit down Hawk's forehead. "Are you sure I haven't seen this one before?"

"As a matter of fact I think you have." Now I grinned.

"Oh," Hawk said, then made a sound that had the structure of laughter but was all breath. "I'll get the Hawk."

He ducked out between the trees.

I glanced up at the lozenges of moonlight in the leaves.

I looked down at my briefcase.

Up between the rocks, stepping around the long grass, came the Hawk. He wore a gray evening suit over a gray silk turtleneck. Above his craggy face, his head was completely shaved.

NEBULA AWARDS SHOWCASE 2015

"Mr. Cadwaliter-Erickson?" He held out his hand.

I shook: small sharp bones in loose skin. "Does one call you Mr. . . . ?"

"Arty."

"Arty the Hawk?" I tried to look like I wasn't giving his gray attire the once-over.

He smiled. "Arty the Hawk. Yeah. I picked that name up when I was younger than our friend down there. Alex says you got . . . well, some things that are not exactly yours. That don't belong to you."

I nodded.

"Show them to me."

"You were told what—"

He brushed away the end of my sentence. "Come on, let me see."

He extended his hand, smiling affably as a bank clerk. I ran my thumb around the pressure-zip. The cover went *tsk*. "Tell me," I said, looking up at his head, lowered now to see what I had, "what does one do about Special Services? They seem to be after me."

The head came up. Surprise changed slowly to a craggy leer. "Why, Mr. Cadwaliter-Erickson!" He gave me the up and down openly. "Keep your income steady. Keep it steady, that's one thing you can do."

"If you buy these for anything like what they're worth, that's going to be a little difficult."

"I would imagine. I could always give you less money—"

The cover went *tsk* again.

"—or, barring that, you could try to use your head and outwit them."

"You must have outwitted them at one time or another. You may be on an even keel now, but you had to get there from somewhere else."

Arty the Hawk's nod was downright sly. "I guess you've had a run-in with Maud. Well, I suppose congratulations are in order. And condolences. I always like to do what's in order."

"You seem to know how to take care of yourself. I mean I notice you're not out there mingling with the guests."

"There are two parties going on here tonight," Arty said. "Where do you think Alex disappears off to every five minutes?"

I frowned.

"That lumia down in the rocks—" he pointed toward my feet "is a mandala of shifting hues on our ceiling. Alex—" he chuckled—"goes scuttling off under the rocks where there is a pavilion of Oriental splendor—"

"And a separate guest list at the door?"

"Regina is on both. I'm on both. So's the kid, Edna, Lewis, Ann—"

"Am I supposed to know all this?"

"Well, you came with a person on both lists. I just thought . . ." The Hawk paused.

I was coming on wrong. But a quick change artist learns fairly quick that the verisimilitude factor in imitating someone up the scale is your confidence in your unalienable right to come on wrong. "I'll tell you," I said. "How about exchanging these—" I held out the briefcase— "for some information."

"You want to know how to stay out of Maud's clutches?" He shook his head. "It would be pretty stupid of me to tell you, even if I could. Besides, you've got your family fortunes to fall back on." He beat the front of his shirt with his thumb. "Believe me, boy. Arty the Hawk didn't have that. I didn't have anything like that." His hands dropped into his pockets. "Let's see what you got."

I opened the case again.

The Hawk looked for a while. After a few moments he picked a couple up, turned them around, put them back down, put his hands back in his pockets. "I'll give you sixty thousand for them, approved credit tablets."

"What about the information I wanted?"

"I wouldn't tell you a thing." The Hawk smiled. "I wouldn't tell you the time of day."

There are very few successful thieves in this world. Still less on the other five. The will to steal is an impulse toward the absurd and tasteless. (The talents are poetic, theatrical, a certain reverse charisma . . .) But it is a will, as the will to order, power, love.

"All right," I said.

Somewhere overhead I heard a faint humming.

Arty looked at me fondly. He reached under the lapel of his jacket and took out a handful of credit tablets—the scarlet-banded tablets whose slips were ten thousand apiece. He pulled off one. Two. Three. Four.

"You can deposit this much safely—"

"Why do you think Maud is after me?"

Five. Six.

"Fine," I said.

"How about throwing in the briefcase?" Arty asked.

"Ask Alex for a paper bag. If you want, I can send them—"

"Give them here."

The humming was coming closer.

I held up the open case. Arty went in with both hands. He shoved them into his coat pockets, his pants pockets; the gray cloth was distended by angular bulges. He looked left, right. "Thanks," he said. "Thanks." Then he turned and hurried down the slope with all sorts of things in his pockets that weren't his now.

I looked up through the leaves for the noise, but I couldn't see anything.

I stooped down now and laid my case out. I pulled open the back compartment where I kept the things that did belong to me and rummaged hurriedly through.

Alex was just offering Puffy-eyes another Scotch, while the gentleman was saying, "Has anyone seen Mrs. Silem? What's that humming overhead—?" when a large woman wrapped in a veil of fading fabric tottered across the rocks, screaming.

Her hands were clawing at her covered face.

Alex sloshed soda over his sleeve, and the man said, "Oh, my God! Who's that?"

"No!" the woman shrieked. "Oh, no! Help me!" waving her wrinkled fingers, brilliant with rings.

"Don't you recognize her?" That was Hawk whispering confidentially to someone else. "It's Henrietta, Countess of Effingham." And Alex, overhearing, went hurrying to her assistance. The Countess ducked between two cacti, however, and disappeared into the high grass. But the entire party followed. They were beating about the underbrush when a balding gentleman in a black tux, bow tie, and cummerbund coughed and said in a very worried voice, "Excuse me, Mr. Spinnel?" Alex whirled.

"Mr. Spinnel, my mother . . ."

"Who are *you?*" The interruption upset Alex terribly.

The gentleman drew himself up to announce: "The Honorable Clement Effingham," and his pants leg shook for all the world as if he had started to click his heels. But articulation failed. The expression melted on his face. "Oh, I . . . my mother, Mr. Spinnel. We were downstairs at the other half of your party when she got very . . . excited. She ran up here—oh, I *told* her not to! I knew you'd be upset. But you must help me!" and then looked up.

The others looked, too.

The helicopter blacked the moon, rocking and settling below its hazy twin parasols.

"Oh, please . . ." the gentleman said. "You look over there! Perhaps she's gone back down. I've got to—" looking quickly both ways—"find her." He hurried in one direction while everyone else hurried in others.

The humming was suddenly syncopated with a crash. Roaring now, as plastic fragments from the transparent roof chattered down through the branches, clattered on the rocks . . .

I made it into the elevator and had already thumbed the edge of my briefcase clasp, when Hawk dove between the unfolding foils.

The electric eye began to swing them open. I hit DOOR CLOSE full fist. The boy staggered, banged shoulders on two walls, then got back breath and balance. "Hey, there's police getting out of that helicopter!"

"Hand-picked by Maud Hinkle herself, no doubt." I pulled the other tuft of white hair from my temple. It went into the case on top of the plastiderm gloves (wrinkled, thick blue veins, long carnelian nails) that had been Henrietta's hands, lying in the chiffon folds of her sari.

Then there was the downward tug of stopping. The Honorable Clement was still half on my face when the door opened.

Gray and gray, with an absolutely dismal expression, the Hawk swung through the doors. Behind him people were dancing in an elaborate pavilion festooned with Oriental magnificence (and a mandala of shifting hues on the ceiling). Arty beat me to DOOR CLOSE. Then he gave me an odd look.

I just sighed and finished peeling off Clem.

"The police are up there . . . ?" the Hawk reiterated.

"Arty," I said, buckling my pants, "it certainly looks that way." The car gained momentum. "You look almost as upset as Alex." I shrugged the tux jacket down my arms, turning the sleeves inside out, pulled one wrist free, and jerked off the white starched dicky with the black bow tie and stuffed it into the briefcase with all my other dickies; swung the coat around and slipped on Howard Calvin Evingston's good gray herringbone. Howard (like Hank) is a redhead (but not as curly).

The Hawk raised his bare brows when I peeled off Clement's bald pate and shook out my hair.

"I noticed you aren't carrying around all those bulky things in your pockets anymore."

"Oh, those have been taken care of," he said gruffly. "They're all right."

"Arty," I said, adjusting my voice down to Howard's security-provoking, ingenuous baritone, "it must have been my unabashed conceit that made me think that those Regular Service police were here just for me—"

The Hawk actually snarled. "They wouldn't be that unhappy if they got me, too."

And from his corner Hawk demanded, "You've got security here with you, don't you, Arty?"

"So what?"

"There's one way you can get out of this," Hawk hissed at me. His jacket had come half-open down his wrecked chest. "That's if Arty takes you out with him."

"Brilliant idea," I concluded. "You want a couple of thousand back for the service?"

The idea didn't amuse him. "I don't want anything from you." He turned to Hawk. "I need something from you, kid. Not him. Look, I wasn't prepared for Maud. If you want me to get your friend out, then you've got to do something for me."

The boy looked confused.

I thought I saw smugness on Arty's face, but the expression resolved into concern. "You've got to figure out some way to fill the lobby up with people, and fast."

I was going to ask why, but then I didn't know the extent of Arty's security. I was going to ask how, but the floor pushed up at my feet and the door swung open. "If you can't do it," the Hawk growled to Hawk, "none of us will get out of here. None of us!"

I had no idea what the kid was going to do, but when I started to follow him out into the lobby, the Hawk grabbed my arm and hissed, "Stay here, you idiot!"

I stepped back. Arty was leaning on DOOR OPEN.

Hawk sprinted toward the pool. And splashed in.

He reached the braziers on their twelve-foot tripods and began to climb. "He's going to hurt himself!" the Hawk whispered.

"Yeah," I said, but I don't think my cynicism got through. Below the great dish of fire, Hawk was fiddling. Then something under there came loose. Something else went *Clang*! And something else spurted out across the water. The fire raced along it and hit the pool, churning and roaring like hell.

A black arrow with a golden head: Hawk dove.

I bit the inside of my cheek as the alarm sounded. Four people in uniforms were coming across the blue carpet. Another group were crossing in the other direction, saw the flames, and one of the women screamed. I let out my breath, thinking carpet and walls and ceilings would be flameproof. But I kept losing focus on the idea before the sixty-odd infernal feet.

Hawk surfaced on the edge of the pool in the only clear spot left, rolled over onto the carpet, clutching his face. And rolled. And rolled. Then, came to his feet.

Another elevator spilled out a load of passengers who gaped and gasped. A crew came through the doors now with fire-fighting equipment. The alarm was still sounding.

Hawk turned to look at the dozen-odd people in the lobby. Water puddled the carpet about his drenched and shiny pants legs. Flame turned the drops on his cheek and hair to flickering copper and blood.

He banged his fists against his wet thighs, took a deep breath, and against the roar and the bells and the whispering, he Sang.

Two people ducked back into the two elevators. From a doorway half a dozen more emerged. The elevators returned half a minute later with a dozen people each. I realized the message was going through the building, there's a Singer Singing in the lobby.

The lobby filled. The flames growled, the firefighters stood around shuffling, and Hawk, feet apart on the blue rug by the burning pool, Sang, and Sang of a bar off Times Square full of thieves, morphadine-heads, brawlers, drunkards, women too old to trade what they still held out for barter, and trade just too nasty-grimy; where earlier in the evening a brawl had broken out, and an old man had been critically hurt in the fray

Arty tugged at my sleeve.

"What . . ."

"Come on," he hissed.

The elevator door closed behind us.

We ambled through the attentive listeners, stopping to watch, stopping to hear. I couldn't really do Hawk justice. A lot of that slow amble I spent wondering what sort of security Arty had:

Standing behind a couple in bathrobes who were squinting into the heat, I decided it was all very simple. Arty wanted simply to drift away through a crowd, so he'd conveniently gotten Hawk to manufacture one.

To get to the door we had to pass through practically a cordon of Regular Service policemen, who I don't think had anything to do with what might have been going on in the roof garden; they'd simply collected to see the fire and stayed for the Song. When Arty tapped one on the shoulder—"Excuse me please"—to get by, the policeman glanced at him, glanced away, then did a Mack Sennett double-take. But another policeman caught the whole interchange, touched the first on the arm, and gave him a frantic little headshake. Then both men turned very deliberately back to watch the Singer. While the earthquake in my chest stilled, I decided that the Hawk's security complex of agents and counteragents, maneuvering and machinating through the flaming lobby, must be of such finesse and intricacy that to attempt understanding was to condemn oneself to total paranoia.

Arty opened the final door.

I stepped from the last of the air-conditioning into the night. We hurried down the ramp.

"Hey, Arty . . ."

"You go that way." He pointed down the street. "I go this way."

"Eh . . . what's that way?" I pointed in my direction.

"Twelve Towers sub-sub-subway station. Look. I've got you out of there. Believe me, you're safe for the time being. Now go take a train someplace interesting. Good-bye. Go on now." Then Arty the Hawk put his fists in his pockets and hurried up the street.

I started down, keeping near the wall, expecting someone to get me with a blow-dart from a passing car, a deathray from the shrubbery.

I reached the sub.

And still nothing had happened.

Agate gave way to Malachite:

Tourmaline:

Beryl (during which month I turned twenty-six):

Porphyry:

Sapphire (that month I took the ten thousand I hadn't frittered away and invested it in The Glacier, a perfectly legitimate ice cream palace on Triton—the first and only ice cream palace on Triton—which took off like fireworks; all investors were returned eight hundred percent, no kidding. Two weeks later I'd lost half of those earnings on another set of preposterous illegalities and was feeling quite depressed, but The Glacier kept pulling them in. The new Word came by):

Cinnabar:

Turquoise:

Tiger's Eye:

Hector Calhoun Eisenhower finally buckled down and spent three months learning how to be a respectable member of the uppermiddle-class underworld. That's a novel in itself. High finance; corporate law; how to hire help: Whew! But the complexities of life have always intrigued me. I got through it. The basic rule is still the same: Observe carefully; imitate effectively.

Garnet:

Topaz (I whispered that word on the roof of the Trans-Satellite Power Station, and caused my hirelings to commit two murders. And you know? I didn't feel a thing):

Taafite:

We were nearing the end of Taafite. I'd come back to Triton on strictly Glacial business. A bright pleasant morning it was: the business went fine. I decided to take off the afternoon and go sight seeing in the Torrents.

". . . two hundred and thirty meters high," the guide announced, and everyone around me leaned on the rail and gazed up through the plastic corridor at the cliffs of frozen methane that soared through Neptune's cold green glare.

"Just a few yards down the catwalk, ladies and gentlemen, you can catch your first glimpse of the Well of This World, where over a million years ago, a mysterious force science still cannot explain caused twenty-five square miles of frozen methane to liquefy for no more than a few hours during which time a whirlpool twice the depth of Earth's Grand Canyon was caught for the ages when the temperature dropped once more to . . ."

People were moving down the corridor when I saw her smiling. My hair was black and nappy, and my skin was chestnut dark today.

I was just feeling overconfident, I guess, so I kept standing around next to her. I even contemplated coming on. Then she broke the whole thing up by suddenly turning to me and saying perfectly deadpan: "Why, if it isn't Hamlet Caliban Enobarbus!"

Old reflexes realigned my features to couple the frown of confusion with the smile of indulgence. *Pardon me, but I think you must have mistaken . . .* No, I didn't say it. "Maud," I said, "have you come here to tell me that my time has come?"

She wore several shades of blue with a large blue brooch at her shoulder, obviously glass. Still, I realized as I looked about the other tourists, she was more inconspicuous amidst their finery than I was. "No," she said. "Actually I'm on vacation. Just like you."

"No kidding?" We had dropped behind the crowd. "You are kidding."

"Special Services of Earth, while we cooperate with Special Services on other worlds, has no official jurisdiction on Triton. And since you came here with money, and most of your recorded gain in income has been through The Glacier, while Regular Services on Triton might be glad to get you, Special Services is not after you as yet." She smiled. "I haven't been to The Glacier. It would really be nice to say I'd been taken there by one of the owners. Could we go for a soda, do you think?"

The swirled sides of the Well of This World dropped away in opalescent grandeur. Tourists gazed, and the guide went on about indices of refraction, angles of incline.

"I don't think you trust me," Maud said. My look said she was right.

"Have you ever been involved with narcotics?" she asked suddenly.

I frowned.

"No, I'm serious. I want to try and explain something . . . a point of information that may make both our lives easier."

"Peripherally," I said. "I'm sure you've got down all the information in your dossiers."

"I was involved with them a good deal more than peripherally for several years," Maud said. "Before I got into Special Services, I was in the Narcotics Division of the regular force. And the people we dealt with twenty-four hours a day were drug users, drug pushers. To catch the big ones we had to make friends with the little ones. To catch the bigger ones, we had to make friends with the big. We had to keep the same hours they kept, talk the same language, for months at a time live on the same streets, in the same buildings." She stepped back from the rail to let a youngster ahead. "I had to be sent away to take the morphadine detoxification cure twice while I was on the narc squad. And I had a better record than most."

"What's your point?"

"Just this. You and I are traveling in the same circles now, if only because of our respective chosen professions. You'd be surprised how many people we already know in common. Don't be shocked when we run into each other crossing Sovereign Plaza in Bellona one day, then two weeks later wind up at the same restaurant for lunch at Lux on Iapetus. Though the circles we move in cover worlds, they *are* the same—and not that big."

"Come on." I don't think I sounded happy. "Let me treat you to that ice cream." We started back down the walkway.

"You know," Maud said, "if you do stay out of Special Services' hands here and on Earth long enough, eventually you'll be up there with a huge income growing on a steady slope. It might be a few years, but it's possible. There's no reason now for us to be *personal* enemies. You just may, someday, reach that point where Special Services loses interest in you as quarry. Oh, we'd still see each other, run into each other. We get a great deal of our information from people up there. We're in a position to help you, too, you see."

"You've been casting holograms again."

She shrugged. Her face looked positively ghostly under the pale planet. She said, when we reached the artificial lights of the city, "I did meet two friends of yours recently, Lewis and Ann."

"The Singers?" Maud nodded.

"Oh, I don't really know them well."

"They seem to know a lot about you. Perhaps through that other Singer, Hawk."

"Oh," I said again. "Did they say how he was?"

"I read that he was recovering about two months back. But nothing since then."

"That's about all I know, too," I said.

"The only time I've ever seen him," Maud said, "was right after I pulled him out."

Arty and I had gotten out of the lobby before Hawk actually finished. The next day on the newstapes I learned that when his Song was over, Hawk shrugged out of his jacket, dropped his pants, and walked back into the pool.

The firefighter crew suddenly woke up. People began running around and screaming. He'd been rescued, seventy percent of his body covered with second- and third-degree burns. I'd been industriously trying not to think about it.

"*You* pulled him out?"

"Yes. I was in the helicopter that landed on the roof," Maud said. "I thought you'd be impressed to see me."

"Oh," I said. "How did you get to pull him out?"

"Once you got going, Arty's security managed to jam the elevator service above the seventy-first floor, so we didn't get to the lobby till after you were out of the building. That's when Hawk tried to—"

"But it was you who actually saved him, though?"

"The firemen in that neighborhood hadn't had a fire in twelve years! I don't think they even know how to operate the equipment. I had my boys foam the pool, then I waded in and dragged him—"

"Oh," I said again. I had been trying hard, almost succeeding, these eleven months. I wasn't there when it happened. It wasn't my affair. Maud was saying:

"We thought we might have gotten a lead on you from him, but when I got him to the shore, he was completely out, just a mass of open, running—"

"I should have known the Special Services uses Singers, too," I said. "Everyone else does. The Word changes today, doesn't it? Lewis and Ann didn't pass on what the new one is?"

"I saw them yesterday, and the Word doesn't change for another eight hours. Besides, they wouldn't tell *me*, anyway." She glanced at me and frowned. "They really wouldn't."

"Let's go have those ice-cream sodas," I said. "We'll make small talk and listen carefully to each other while we affect an air of nonchalance. You will try to pick up things that will make it easier to catch me. I will listen for things you let slip that might make it easier for me to avoid you."

"*Um-hm.*" She nodded.

"Why did you contact me in that bar, anyway?"

Eyes of ice: "I told you, we simply travel in the same circles. We're quite likely to be in the same bar on the same night."

"I guess that's just one of the things I'm not supposed to understand, huh?"

Her smile was appropriately ambiguous. I didn't push it.


It was a very dull afternoon. I couldn't repeat one exchange from the nonsense we babbled over the cherry-peaked mountains of whipped cream. We both exerted so much energy to keep up the appearance of being amused, I doubt either one of us could see our way to picking up anything meaningful—if anything meaningful was said.

She left. I brooded some more on the charred phoenix.

The Steward of The Glacier called me into the kitchen to ask about a shipment of contraband milk (The Glacier makes all its own ice cream) that I had been able to wangle on my last trip to Earth (it's amazing how little progress there has been in dairy farming over the last ten years; it was depressingly easy to hornswoggle that bumbling Vermonter) and under the white lights and great plastic churning vats, while I tried to get things straightened out, he made some comment about the Heist Cream Emperor; that didn't do any good.

By the time the evening crowd got there, and the moog was making music, the crystal walls were blazing; and the floor show—a new addition that week—

had been cajoled into going on anyway (a trunk of costumes had gotten lost in shipment [or swiped, but I wasn't about to tell *them* that]), and wandering through the tables I, personally, had caught a very grimy little girl, obviously out of her head on morph, trying to pick up a customer's pocket book from the back of his chair—I just caught her by the wrist, made her let go, and led her to the door daintily, while she blinked at me with dilated eyes and the customer never even knew—and the floor show, having decided what the hell, were doing their act *au naturel*, and everyone was having just a high old time, I was feeling really bad.

I went outside, sat on the wide steps, and growled when I had to move aside to let people in or out. About the seventy-fifth growl, the person I growled at stopped and boomed down at me, "I thought I'd find you, if I looked hard enough! I mean if I really looked."

I looked at the hand that was flapping at my shoulder, followed the arm up to a black turtleneck where there was a beefy, bald, grinning head. "Arty," I said, "what are . . . ?" But he was still flapping and laughing with impervious *gemütlichkeit*.

"You wouldn't believe the time I had getting a picture of you, boy. Had to bribe one out of the Triton Special Services Department. That quick change bit: great gimmick. Just great!" The Hawk sat down next to me and dropped his hand on my knee. "Wonderful place you got here. I like it, like it a lot." Small bones in veined dough. "But not enough to make you an offer on it yet. You're learning fast there, though. I can tell you're learning fast. I'm going to be proud to be able to say I was the one who gave you your first big break." Arty's hand came away, and he began to knead it into the other. "If you're going to move into the big time, you have to have at least one foot planted firmly on the right side of the law. The whole idea is to make yourself indispensable to the good people. Once that's done, a good crook has the keys to all the treasure houses in the system. But I'm not telling you anything you don't already know."

"Arty," I said, "do you think the two of us should be seen together here . . . ?"

The Hawk held his hand above his lap and joggled it with a deprecating motion. "Nobody can get a picture of us. I got my men all around. I never go anywhere in public without my security. Heard you've been looking into the security business yourself," which was true. "Good idea. Very good. I like the way you're handling yourself."

"Thanks. Arty, I'm not feeling too hot this evening. I came out here to get some air . . ."

Arty's hand fluttered again. "Don't worry, I won't hang around. You're right. We shouldn't be seen. Just passing by and wanted to say hello. Just hello." He got up. "That's all." He started down the steps.

"Arty?"

He looked back.

"Sometime soon you will come back; and that time you will want to buy out my share of The Glacier, because I'll have gotten too big; and I won't want to sell because I'll think I'm big enough to fight you. So we'll be enemies for a while. You'll try to kill me. I'll try to kill you."

On his face, first the frown of confusion, then the indulgent smile. "I see you've caught on to the idea of holographic information. Very good. Good. It's the only way to outwit Maud. Make sure all your information relates to the whole scope of the situation. It's the only way to outwit me, too." He smiled, started to turn, but thought of something else. "If you can fight me off long enough and keep growing, keep your security in tiptop shape, eventually, we'll get to the point where it'll be worth both our whiles to work together again. If you can just hold out, we'll be friends again. Someday. You just watch. Just wait."

"Thanks for telling me."

The Hawk looked at his watch. "Well. Good-bye." I thought he was going to leave finally. But he glanced up again. "Have you got the new Word?"

"That's right," I said. "It went out tonight. What is it?"

The Hawk waited till the people coming down the steps were gone. He looked hastily about, then leaned toward me with hands cupped at his mouth, rasped, "Pyrite," and winked hugely. "I just got it from a gal who got it direct from Colette," (one of the three Singers of Triton). Arty turned, jounced down the steps, and shouldered his way into the crowds passing on the strip.

I sat there mulling through the year till I had to get up and walk. All walking does to my depressive moods is add the reinforcing rhythm of paranoia. By the time I was coming back, I had worked out a dilly of a delusional system: The

Hawk had already begun to weave some security-ridden plot about me, which ended when we were all trapped in some dead-end alley, and trying to get aid I called out, "Pyrite!" which would turn out not to be the Word at all but served to identify me for the man in the dark gloves with the gun/grenade/gas.

There was a cafeteria on the corner. In the light from the window, clustered over the wreck by the curb was a bunch of nastygrimies (à la Triton: chains around the wrist, bumblebee tattoo on cheek, high-heel boots on those who could afford them). Straddling the smashed headlight was the little morph-head I had ejected earlier from The Glacier.

On a whim I went up to her. "Hey . . . ?"

She looked at me from under hair like trampled straw, eyes all pupil.

"You get the new Word yet?"

She rubbed her nose, already scratch red. "Pyrite," she said. "It just came down about an hour ago."

"Who told you?"

She considered my question. "I got it from a guy, who says he got it from a guy, who came in this evening from New York, who picked it up there from a Singer named Hawk."

The three grimies nearest made a point of not looking at me.

Those farther away let themselves glance. "Oh," I said. "Oh. Thanks."

Occam's Razor, along with any real information on how security works, hones away most such paranoia. Pyrite. At a certain level in my line of work, paranoia's just an occupational disease. At least I was certain that Arty (and Maud) probably suffered from it as much as I did.

The lights were out on The Glacier's marquee. Then I remembered what I had left inside and ran up the stairs.

The door was locked. I pounded on the glass a couple of times, but everyone had gone home. And the thing that made it worse was that I could *see* it sitting on the counter of the coat-check alcove under the orange bulb. The steward had probably put it there, thinking I might arrive before everybody left. Tomorrow at noon Ho Chi Eng had to pick up his reservation for the Marigold Suite on the Interplanetary Liner *The Platinum Swan*, which left at one-thirty for Bellona. And there behind the glass doors of The Glacier, it waited with the proper wig, as well as the epicanthic folds that would halve Mr. Eng's sloe eyes of jet.

I actually thought of breaking in. But the more practical solution was to get the hotel to wake me at nine and come in with the cleaning man. I turned around and started down the steps; and the thought struck me, and made me terribly sad, so that I blinked and smiled just from reflex; it was probably just as well to leave it there till morning, because there was nothing in it that wasn't mine anyway.

*—Milford*
*July 1968*

# ABOUT THE RHYSLING AND DWARF STARS AWARDS

The Rhysling Awards are given each year by the Science Fiction Poetry Association (SFPA), in recognition of the best science fiction, fantasy, or horror poems of the year. Each year, members of SFPA nominate works that are compiled into an annual anthology; members then vote to select winners from the anthology's contents. The award is given in two categories: works of fifty or more lines are eligible for Best Long Poem, and works shorter than that are eligible for Best Short Poem. Additionally, SFPA gives the Dwarf Stars Award to a poem of ten or fewer lines.

# THE CAT STAR

## TERRY A. GAREY

if there is a Dog Star there should be
one for cats
      not lion, not leopard
although they are deserving
but a Domestic Shorthaired Cat Star
    firm in the heavens
                burning like a green-gold eye
shedding a few photons
      on a prowl through the galaxies

(I have hidden your body
    in among ground-down shale
powdered clam shell and centuries of leaf mold

bright leaves feed small trees, here,
twigs grow and crumble
squirrels leave husks
    from summer grass

in the winter birds will come
scattering seeds across the snow where you lie
and I will know

you are safe
    your molecules are migrating out
into the movements of the years, swirling
in sun, storm, bitter cold

you are singing the disintegrating cat song
a whisker song
a clawed paw song
a silent cat song that spreads out to the stars
hums through the universe
                    then falls back gently

teaching the old carbon and iron and calcium compounds
what it is to be a component of earth
                        dancing in the drifted leaves

and what it is to be
a part of all you loved)

if there is a Dog Star
there should be one for cats

# BASHŌ AFTER CINDERELLA (III)

## DEBORAH P KOLODJI

pumpkin vine

a mouse remembers

how to neigh

# INTO FLIGHT

## ANDREW ROBERT SUTTON

It was just one zero too many,
one gadget too far.
The books gave up and,
in a flurry, took flight.

How? Scientists couldn't say.
Where to? Only the mystic,
crystal-toting, tarot-reading,
lunatic fringe would even conjecture.

Hell, most kids didn't even notice,
cocooned in their networks, awash
in empty streams of bits and bytes.
That in itself might have accounted for the Why.

The little ones took to wing first—
the homilies and pocket Bibles.
They darted away quietly
between one glance and the next.

Then, the paperbacks,
Bradbury's stuff leading the way,
winging off to Mars, pulps in tow.
A few thought this a wonder.

Soon though, the Oxford dictionary,
Norton's anthology, and Shakespeare
(Riverside editions) were aloft.
Then came the law books. Lord! The law books.

That's when it became impossible
not to notice. Only then did anyone care—
when it was too much,
when it became inconvenient.

They interfered with things—
the beautiful, fluttering books.
They brought air traffic to a standstill,
and that was just for starters.

They frightened pets and startled drivers.
They smashed into windows
and had a predilection for power lines
that could very nearly be called vendetta.

Some of the volumes, in their vigor,
shed pages, showering the world
with poetry and cliffhangers
and little snippets of wonder.

Office districts were soon buried in white
like Narnia beneath its perpetual winter.
After a few damps nights, entire city blocks
were entombed in paper mâché.

Antique districts swirled into yellowed autumns,
while Washington was transformed into a Hitchcock-ian hell,
books of tax code circling slowly overhead
like buzzards awaiting their prey.


Some lonely readers thought to lure
their loved ones home. Other readers plotted
to recapture them by trickery—
their methods as varied as their genre.

Poetry lovers were seen sprinting
through meadows with butterfly nets,
or canary cages baited with binder's glue,
singing line and verse.

Mystery fans sleuthed while suspense
fans waited on tenterhooks. Horror
fans gathered to scribe ISBN numbers
into elaborate pentagrams of red ink.


Baristas advised wafting cappuccinos
out windows while lawyers filed injunctions
against authors, ordering them to cease
their trickery or face consequences.

Some readers even tried to signal them
with book lights from the rooftops,
and, for a single night, the world lit up
like a great ocean reflecting the night sky.

But, as difficult as they were to pen, the words
were ten times more elusive on the wing.
Try as readers might, the books wouldn't listen
to reason and they couldn't be caught.


Certain people had the temerity to shoot
at them, drunk and cocksure,
thinking the entire thing some grand sport.
That proved to be unwise.

Hemingway, Twain, and, surprisingly, Dickens
wouldn't stand for such impudence,
and the men with guns
suddenly couldn't run fast enough.

Once it was clear the books wouldn't come down,
citizens demanded solutions.
Officials the world over took steps—
convened in capitols, passed resolutions.


They evicted the molly-coddling librarians,
chained shut the library doors
boarded up the busted windows,
posted guards.

Briefly, it was poetic.
All the books fluttering
like exotic butterflies in gardens
or snowflakes in enormous globes.

The books didn't tire, though,
and soon the libraries, too, were aloft,
hovering like giant zeppelins, plunging
cities, then entire states, into twilight.

And then one night, just like that,
without any ceremony or fanfare,
they left the world, ascending,
never to return.

Yes, the text was still there:
digitized, sanitized, organized.
But it wasn't the same,
and it wasn't long before people knew it.

Like salt without savor,
like flowers without scent,
the text was without soul
and offered nothing to its readers.

There were no more sanctuaries of silence,
no temples of free thought.
There was only a gaping void
where no one had expected one.

The world had become a darker place.
Soon, men began fashioning themselves
paper wings scribed with wild tales,
their eyes fixed heavenward.

# PAST NEBULA AWARD WINNERS

## 1965

Novel: *Dune* by Frank Herbert
Novella: "He Who Shapes" by Roger Zelazny and "The Saliva Tree" by Brian
   Aldiss (tie)
Novelette: "The Doors of His Face, the Lamps of His Mouth" by Roger Zelazny
Short Story: "'Repent, Harlequin!' Said the Ticktockman" by Harlan Ellison

## 1966

Novel: *Babel-17* by Samuel R. Delany and *Flowers for Algernon* by Daniel Keyes
   (tie)
Novella: "The Last Castle" by Jack Vance
Novelette: "Call Him Lord" by Gordon R. Dickson
Short Story: "The Secret Place" by Richard McKenna

## 1967

Novel: *The Einstein Intersection* by Samuel R. Delany
Novella: "Behold the Man" by Michael Moorcock
Novelette: "Gonna Roll the Bones" by Fritz Leiber
Short Story: "Aye, and Gomorrah" by Samuel R. Delany

## 1968

Novel: *Rite of Passage* by Alexei Panshin

Novella: "Dragonrider" by Anne McCaffrey
Novelette: "Mother to the World" by Richard Wilson
Short Story: "The Planners" by Kate Wilhelm

# 1969

Novel: *The Left Hand of Darkness* by Ursula K. Le Guin
Novella: "A Boy and His Dog" by Harlan Ellison
Novelette: "Time Considered as a Helix of Semi-Precious Stones" by Samuel R. Delany
Short Story: "Passengers" by Robert Silverberg

# 1970

Novel: *Ringworld* by Larry Niven
Novella: "Ill Met in Lankhmar" by Fritz Leiber
Novelette: "Slow Sculpture" by Theodore Sturgeon
Short Story: No Award

# 1971

Novel: *A Time of Changes* by Robert Silverberg
Novella: "The Missing Man" by Katherine MacLean
Novelette: "The Queen of Air and Darkness" by Poul Anderson
Short Story: "Good News from the Vatican" by Robert Silverberg

# 1972

Novel: *The Gods Themselves* by Isaac Asimov
Novella: "A Meeting with Medusa" by Arthur C. Clarke

Novelette: "Goat Song" by Poul Anderson
Short Story: "When It Changed" by Joanna Russ

# 1973

Novel: *Rendezvous with Rama* by Arthur C. Clarke
Novella: "The Death of Doctor Island" by Gene Wolfe
Novelette: "Of Mist, and Grass, and Sand" by Vonda N. McIntyre
Short Story: "Love Is the Plan, the Plan Is Death" by James Tiptree Jr.
Dramatic Presentation: *Soylent Green*

# 1974

Novel: *The Dispossessed* by Ursula K. Le Guin
Novella: "Born with the Dead" by Robert Silverberg
Novelette: "If the Stars Are Gods" by Gordon Eklund and Gregory Benford
Short Story: "The Day before the Revolution" by Ursula K. Le Guin
Dramatic Presentation: *Sleeper* by Woody Allen
Grand Master: Robert Heinlein

# 1975

Novel: *The Forever War* by Joe Haldeman
Novella: "Home Is the Hangman" by Roger Zelazny
Novelette: "San Diego Lightfoot Sue" by Tom Reamy
Short Story: "Catch That Zeppelin" by Fritz Leiber
Dramatic Presentation: *Young Frankenstein* by Mel Brooks and Gene Wilder
Grand Master: Jack Williamson

# 1976

Novel: *Man Plus* by Frederik Pohl
Novella: "Houston, Houston, Do You Read?" by James Tiptree Jr.
Novelette: "The Bicentennial Man" by Isaac Asimov
Short Story: "A Crowd of Shadows" by C. L. Grant
Grand Master: Clifford D. Simak

# 1977

Novel: *Gateway* by Frederik Pohl
Novella: "Stardance" by Spider and Jeanne Robinson
Novelette: "The Screwfly Solution" by Raccoona Sheldon
Short Story: "Jeffty Is Five" by Harlan Ellison

# 1978

Novel: *Dreamsnake* by Vonda N. McIntyre
Novella: "The Persistence of Vision" by John Varley
Novelette: "A Glow of Candles, A Unicorn's Eye" by C. L. Grant
Short Story: "Stone" by Edward Bryant
Grand Master: L. Sprague de Camp

# 1979

Novel: *The Fountains of Paradise* by Arthur C. Clarke
Novella: "Enemy Mine" by Barry B. Longyear
Novelette: "Sandkings" by George R. R. Martin
Short Story: "GiANTS" by Edward Bryant

# 1980

Novel: *Timescape* by Gregory Benford
Novella: "Unicorn Tapestry" by Suzy McKee Charnas
Novelette: "The Ugly Chickens" by Howard Waldrop
Short Story: "Grotto of the Dancing Deer" by Clifford D. Simak
Grand Master: Fritz Leiber

# 1981

Novel: *The Claw of the Conciliator* by Gene Wolfe
Novella: "The Saturn Game" by Poul Anderson
Novelette: "The Quickening" by Michael Bishop
Short Story: "The Bone Flute" by Lisa Tuttle [declined by author]

# 1982

Novel: *No Enemy but Time* by Michael Bishop
Novella: "Another Orphan" by John Kessel
Novelette: "Fire Watch" by Connie Willis
Short Story: "A Letter from the Clearys" by Connie Willis

# 1983

Novel: *Startide Rising* by David Brin
Novella: "Hardfought" by Greg Bear
Novelette: "Blood Music" by Greg Bear
Short Story: "The Peacemaker" by Gardner Dozois
Grand Master: Andre Norton

# 1984

Novel: *Neuromancer* by William Gibson
Novella: "Press Enter []" by John Varley
Novelette: "Blood Child" by Octavia Butler
Short Story: "Morning Child" by Gardner Dozois

# 1985

Novel: *Ender's Game* by Orson Scott Card
Novella: "Sailing to Byzantium" by Robert Silverberg
Novelette: "Portraits of His Children" by George R. R. Martin
Short Story: "Out of All Them Bright Stars" by Nancy Kress
Grand Master: Arthur C. Clarke

# 1986

Novel: *Speaker for the Dead* by Orson Scott Card
Novella: "R&R" by Lucius Shepard
Novelette: "The Girl Who Fell into the Sky" by Kate Wilhelm
Short Story: "Tangents" by Greg Bear
Grand Master: Isaac Asimov

# 1987

Novel: *The Falling Woman* by Pat Murphy
Novella: "The Blind Geometer" by Kim Stanley Robinson
Novelette: "Rachel in Love" by Pat Murphy
Short Story: "Forever Yours, Anna" by Kate Wilhelm
Grand Master: Alfred Bester

# 1988

Novel: *Falling Free* by Lois McMaster Bujold
Novella: "The Last of the Winnebagos" by Connie Willis
Novelette: "Schrödinger's Kitten" by George Alec Effinger
Short Story: "Bible Stories for Adults, No. 17: The Deluge" by James Morrow
Grand Master: Ray Bradbury

# 1989

Novel: *The Healer's War* by Elizabeth Ann Scarborough
Novella: "The Mountains of Mourning" by Lois McMaster Bujold
Novelette: "At the Rialto" by Connie Willis
Short Story: "Ripples in the Dirac Sea" by Geoffrey A. Landis

# 1990

Novel: *Tehanu: The Last Book of Earthsea* by Ursula K. Le Guin
Novella: "The Hemingway Hoax" by Joe Haldeman
Novelette: "Tower of Babylon" by Ted Chiang
Short Story: "Bears Discover Fire" by Terry Bisson
Grand Master: Lester del Rey

# 1991

Novel: *Stations of the Tide* by Michael Swanwick
Novella: "Beggars in Spain" by Nancy Kress
Novelette: "Guide Dog" by Mike Conner
Short Story: "Ma Qui" by Alan Brennert

# 1992

Novel: *Doomsday Book* by Connie Willis
Novella: "City Of Truth" by James Morrow
Novelette: "Danny Goes to Mars" by Pamela Sargent
Short Story: "Even the Queen" by Connie Willis
Grand Master: Fred Pohl

# 1993

Novel: *Red Mars* by Kim Stanley Robinson
Novella: "The Night We Buried Road Dog" by Jack Cady
Novelette: "Georgia on My Mind" by Charles Sheffield
Short Story: "Graves" by Joe Haldeman

# 1994

Novel: *Moving Mars* by Greg Bear
Novella: "Seven Views of Olduvai Gorge" by Mike Resnick
Novelette: "The Martian Child" by David Gerrold
Short Story: "A Defense of the Social Contracts" by Martha Soukup
Grand Master: Damon Knight
Author Emeritus: Emil Petaja

# 1995

Novel: *The Terminal Experiment* by Robert J. Sawyer
Novella: "Last Summer at Mars Hill" by Elizabeth Hand
Novelette: "Solitude" by Ursula K. Le Guin
Short Story: "Death and the Librarian" by Esther M. Friesner
Grand Master: A. E. van Vogt
Author Emeritus: Wilson "Bob" Tucker

# 1996

Novel: *Slow River* by Nicola Griffith
Novella: "Da Vinci Rising" by Jack Dann
Novelette: "Lifeboat on a Burning Sea" by Bruce Holland Rogers
Short Story: "A Birthday" by Esther M. Friesner
Grand Master: Jack Vance
Author Emeritus: Judith Merril

# 1997

Novel: *The Moon and the Sun* by Vonda N. McIntyre
Novella: "Abandon in Place" by Jerry Oltion
Novelette: "Flowers of Aulit Prison" by Nancy Kress
Short Story: "Sister Emily's Lightship" by Jane Yolen
Grand Master: Poul Anderson
Author Emeritus: Nelson Slade Bond

# 1998

Novel: *Forever Peace* by Joe Haldeman
Novella: "Reading the Bones" by Sheila Finch
Novelette: "Lost Girls" by Jane Yolen
Short Story: "Thirteen Ways to Water" by Bruce Holland Rogers
Grand Master: Hal Clement (Harry Stubbs)
Author Emeritus: William Tenn (Philip Klass)

# 1999

Novel: *Parable of the Talents* by Octavia E. Butler
Novella: "Story of Your Life" by Ted Chiang

Novelette: "Mars Is No Place for Children" by Mary A. Turzillo
Short Story: "The Cost of Doing Business" by Leslie What
Script: *The Sixth Sense* by M. Night Shyamalan
Grand Master: Brian W. Aldiss
Author Emeritus: Daniel Keyes

## 2000

Novel: *Darwin's Radio* by Greg Bear
Novella: "Goddesses" by Linda Nagata
Novelette: "Daddy's World" by Walter Jon Williams
Short Story: "macs" by Terry Bisson
Script: *Galaxy Quest* by Robert Gordon and David Howard
Ray Bradbury Award: Yuri Rasovsky and Harlan Ellison
Grand Master: Philip José Farmer
Author Emeritus: Robert Sheckley

## 2001

Novel: *The Quantum Rose* by Catherine Asaro
Novella: "The Ultimate Earth" by Jack Williamson
Novelette: "Louise's Ghost" by Kelly Link
Short Story: "The Cure for Everything" by Severna Park
Script: *Crouching Tiger, Hidden Dragon* by James Schamus, Kuo Jung Tsai, and
    Hui-Ling Wang
President's Award: Betty Ballantine

## 2002

Novel: *American Gods* by Neil Gaiman
Novella: "Bronte's Egg" by Richard Chwedyk
Novelette: "Hell Is the Absence of God" by Ted Chiang

Short Story: "Creature" by Carol Emshwiller
Script: *Lord of the Rings: The Fellowship of the Ring* by Frances Walsh, Phillipa
    Boyens, and Peter Jackson
Grand Master: Ursula K. Le Guin
Author Emeritus: Katherine MacLean

## 2003

Novel: *Speed of Dark* by Elizabeth Moon
Novella: "Coraline" by Neil Gaiman
Novelette: "The Empire of Ice Cream" by Jeffrey Ford
Short Story: "What I Didn't See" by Karen Joy Fowler
Script: *Lord of the Rings: The Two Towers* by Frances Walsh, Phillipa Boyens,
    Stephen Sinclair, and Peter Jackson
Grand Master: Robert Silverberg
Author Emeritus: Charles L. Harness

## 2004

Novel: *Paladin of Souls* by Lois McMaster Bujold
Novella: "The Green Leopard Plague" by Walter Jon Williams
Novelette: "Basement Magic" by Ellen Klages
Short Story: "Coming to Terms" by Eileen Gunn
Script: *Lord of the Rings: Return of the King* by Frances Walsh, Phillipa Boyens,
    and Peter Jackson
Grand Master: Anne McCaffrey

## 2005

Novel: *Camouflage* by Joe Haldeman
Novella: "Magic for Beginners" by Kelly Link
Novelette: "The Faery Handbag" by Kelly Link

Short Story: "I Live with You" by Carol Emshwiller
Script: *Serenity* by Joss Whedon
Grand Master: Harlan Ellison
Author Emeritus: William F. Nolan

# 2006

Novel: *Seeker* by Jack McDevitt
Novella: "Burn" by James Patrick Kelly
Novelette: "Two Hearts" by Peter S. Beagle
Short Story: "Echo" by Elizabeth Hand
Script: *Howl's Moving Castle* by Hayao Miyazaki, Cindy Davis Hewitt, and
    Donald H. Hewitt
Andre Norton Award: *Magic or Madness* by Justine Larbalestier
Grand Master: James Gunn
Author Emeritus: D. G. Compton

# 2007

Novel: *The Yiddish Policemen's Union* by Michael Chabon
Novella: "Fountain of Age" by Nancy Kress
Novelette: "The Merchant and the Alchemist's Gate" by Ted Chiang
Short Story: "Always" by Karen Joy Fowler
Script: *Pan's Labyrinth* by Guillermo del Toro
Andre Norton Award for Young Adult Science Fiction and Fantasy: *Harry
    Potter and the Deathly Hallows* by J. K. Rowling
Grand Master: Michael Moorcock
Author Emeritus: Ardath Mayhar
SFWA Service Awards: Melisa Michaels and Graham P. Collins

# 2008

Novel: *Powers* by Ursula K. Le Guin
Novella: "The Spacetime Pool" by Catherine Asaro
Novelette: "Pride and Prometheus" by John Kessel
Short Story: "Trophy Wives" by Nina Kiriki Hoffman
Script: *WALL-E* by Andrew Stanton and Jim Reardon. Original story by Andrew Stanton and Pete Docter
Andre Norton Award: *Flora's Dare: How a Girl of Spirit Gambles All to Expand Her Vocabulary, Confront a Bouncing Boy Terror, and Try to Save Califa from a Shaky Doom (Despite Being Confined to Her Room)* by Ysabeau S. Wilce
Grand Master: Harry Harrison
Author Emeritus: M. J. Engh
Solstice Award: Kate Wilhelm, Martin H. Greenberg, and the late Algis Budrys
SFWA Service Award: Victoria Strauss

# 2009

Novel: *The Windup Girl* by Paolo Bacigalupi
Novella: "The Women of Nell Gwynne's" by Kage Baker
Novelette: "Sinner, Baker, Fabulist, Priest; Red Mask, Black Mask, Gentleman, Beast" by Eugie Foster
Short Story: "Spar" by Kij Johnson
Ray Bradbury Award: *District 9* by Neill Blomkamp and Terri Tatchell
Andre Norton Award: *The Girl Who Circumnavigated Fairyland in a Ship of Her Own Making* by Catherynne M. Valente
Grand Master: Joe Haldeman
Author Emeritus: Neal Barrett Jr.
Solstice Award: Tom Doherty, Terri Windling, and the late Donald A. Wollheim
SFWA Service Awards: Vonda N. McIntyre and Keith Stokes

# 2010

Novel: *Blackout/All Clear* by Connie Willis
Novella: "The Lady Who Plucked Red Flowers beneath the Queen's Window" by Rachel Swirsky
Novelette: "That Leviathan Whom Thou Hast Made" by Eric James Stone
Short Story: "Ponies" by Kij Johnson and "How Interesting: A Tiny Man" by Harlan Ellison (tie)
Ray Bradbury Award: *Inception* by Christopher Nolan
Andre Norton Award: *I Shall Wear Midnight*, by Terry Pratchett

# 2011

Novel: *Among Others*, Jo Walton
Novella: "The Man Who Bridged the Mist," Kij Johnson
Novelette: "What We Found," Geoff Ryman
Short Story: "The Paper Menagerie," Ken Liu
Ray Bradbury Award: *Doctor Who*: "The Doctor's Wife" by Neil Gaiman (writer), Richard Clark (director)
Andre Norton Award: *The Freedom Maze* by Delia Sherman
Damon Knight Grand Master Award: Connie Willis
Solstice Award: Octavia Butler (posthumous) and John Clute
SFWA Service Award: Bud Webster

# 2012

Novel: *2312* by Kim Stanley Robinson
Novella: *After the Fall, Before the Fall, During the Fall* by Nancy Kress
Novelette: "Close Encounters" by Andy Duncan
Short Story: "Immersion" by Aliette de Bodard
Ray Bradbury Award: *Beasts of the Southern Wild* by Benh Zeitlin (director); Benh Zeitlin and Lucy Abilar (writers)
Andre Norton Award: *Fair Coin* by E. C. Myers

# 2013

Novel: *Ancillary Justice* by Ann Leckie
Novella: "The Weight of the Sunrise" by Vylar Kaftan
Novelette: "The Waiting Stars" by Aliete de Bodard
Short Story: "If You Were a Dinosaur, My Love" by Rachel Swirsky
Ray Bradbury Award: *Gravity* by Alfonso Cuarón (director); Alfonso Cuarón
    and Jonás Cuarón (writers)
Andre Norton Award: *Sister Mine* by Nalo Hopkinson
Damon Knight Grand Master Award: Samuel R. Delany
Distinguished Guest: Frank M. Robinson
Kevin O'Donnell Jr. Service to SFWA Award: Michael Armstrong

# ACKNOWLEDGMENTS

Many thanks to:

Kij Johnson, editor of *Nebula Awards Showcase 2014*, who generously shared information about the nuts and bolts of putting together this anthology.

Eleanor Wood, literary agent extraordinaire, who handled contracts and payments with aplomb and style.

Lou Anders, who acquired the anthology for Pyr, and his capable successor as editor, Rene Sears, who brought it to completion.

Melissa Raé Shofner, assistant editor, who ferreted out all typos and copyediting issues. Any remaining problems are caused by a malign universe.

And Catherine Roberts-Abel and the rest of the production staff at Pyr, who produced the lovely volume you now hold in your hands.

# ABOUT THE EDITOR

Greg Bear is the author of *Blood Music*, *Forge of God*, *Eon*, *Darwin's Radio*, and *War Dogs*, as well as the forthcoming *Killing Titan*. He sold his first short story in 1967, helped found San Diego Comic-Con shortly thereafter, and has been invited to consult on numerous topics, including space, biotech, and national security. He is married to Astrid Anderson Bear, and they have two children, Erik and Alexandra.

*Photo by Astrid Anderson Bear*

# ABOUT THE COVER ARTIST

John Harris's art looms large over science fiction. Since the 1970s he has painted covers for some of the greats of the genre, including Isaac Asimov, Orson Scott Card, Jack McDevitt, Ben Bova, John Scalzi, and Ann Leckie, among many others. In 1984, NASA invited Harris to watch the launch of the space shuttle Endeavour and commissioned a painting of the launch, which now hangs as part of the Smithsonian Museum collection.

In addition to illustrating writers' works, Harris has created a series of over seventy pieces envisioning his own created world, a visual archaeology of imagined places and culture. A selection of his paintings was collected in 2014's *The Art of John Harris: Beyond the Horizon*. Also in 2014, Harris was nominated for a Hugo Award for Best Artist. In 2015, Harris won the Chesley Award for Lifetime Artistic Achievement.

Harris brings a sense of monumental scale to his future landscapes, but even the weightiest planet or most isolated spaceship invites the viewer in. The vibrant color and impressionistic brushwork of his paintings only emphasize the concrete realism of his imagined worlds.